FINDING
MR. WRITE

FINDING MR. WRITE

KELLEY ARMSTRONG

FOREVER

New York Boston

Forever
Hachette Book Group
1290 Avenue of the Americas, New York, NY 10104
read-forever.com
@readforeverpub

First Edition: June 2024

Forever is an imprint of Grand Central Publishing. The Forever name and logo are registered trademarks of Hachette Book Group, Inc.

The publisher is not responsible for websites (or their content) that are not owned by the publisher.

The Hachette Speakers Bureau provides a wide range of authors for speaking events. To find out more, go to hachettespeakersbureau.com or email HachetteSpeakers@hbgusa.com.

Forever books may be purchased in bulk for business, educational, or promotional use. For information, please contact your local bookseller or the Hachette Book Group Special Markets Department at special.markets@hbgusa.com.

Print book interior design by Taylor Navis

Library of Congress Cataloging-in-Publication Data

Names: Armstrong, Kelley, author.
Title: Finding Mr. Write / Kelley Armstrong.
Description: First edition. | New York : Forever, 2024.
Identifiers: LCCN 2023051336 | ISBN 9781538742747 (trade paperback) |
   ISBN 9781538742754 (ebook)
Subjects: LCGFT: Novels.
Classification: LCC PR9199.4.A8777 F56 2024 | DDC 813/.6—dc23
   /eng/20231103
LC record available at https://lccn.loc.gov/2023051336

ISBN: 9781538742747 (trade paperback), 9781538742754 (ebook)

Printed in the United States of America

LSC

Printing 1, 2024

CHAPTER ONE

DAPHNE

I need a penis," Daphne said.

On her laptop screen, she watched Nia's chopsticks clatter to the café table a thousand miles away. "Yes! I have been waiting for this day!" Nia snatched up her phone and jabbed the screen. "I've been thinking Plenty of Fish or—"

"I'm not talking about dating."

Nia stared, and then burst out laughing. "Well, okay then. Ms. I-don't-do-casual-sex has finally been in the wilderness too long."

"None of that," Daphne said. *Although, to be perfectly honest…No, none of that. Sadly.* She leaned back in her patio chair on the deck of her Yukon home. She was "having lunch" with Nia, who was in Vancouver. Daphne got Nia's autumn scenery—the busy city patio, with its bustling street and sidewalk—and Nia got hers, with its lake and forest and snow-capped mountains.

Daphne continued, "Remember that article about an author who submitted her book under a man's name?"

"And got five times the responses than she had under her own. You're thinking you could sell *Winter's Sleep* easier if you were a man. I know it can feel that way, but…"

"I did sell it."

Nia bolted upright. "What?"

"I'd gotten another rejection, and I drank some wine and remembered the article and said, 'Screw it. Let's try that.' So I tweaked a few things in my cover letter—more survivalism, more zombies, less romance."

"What? Tell me you didn't get rid of the romance."

"Not in the book. Just in the description. I pasted in the new cover letter, attached the manuscript, and hit Send."

"I thought you were only supposed to send the full manuscript if they asked for it."

"I figured if I was going to be a man, I didn't need to follow the rules."

"And it worked?" Nia snorted. "I'm not sure whether to laugh or dissolve into a puddle of weeping despair. So you got an agent who thought you were a guy. What'd they say when you told them the truth?"

Silence.

Nia's eyes bugged. "They still think you're a guy? You've talked, right?"

"I told him I live off the grid in the Canadian wilderness and don't have cell service. I expected he'd want me to get my ass into cell range so we can talk, but apparently, you don't tell guys like Zane Remington to do that. You accommodate the quirks of their literary genius."

"Zane Remington?"

"I was drunk."

"So your agent thinks you're a dude named *Zane Remington*?"

"Who lives in a house he built himself, from trees he felled himself. Zane hunts and fishes and is completely self-sufficient up here. Like Theo is, in the book. Except without the zombies. Oh, and Zane has an MFA degree."

"Of course he does. So you got an agent who sold *Winter's Sleep* to a publisher. What happens when that publisher goes to look up this Zane on social media? Have him sign a contract? Deposit a check with his totally fake name?"

"Er…" Daphne waved a hand. "Well, you see, I have this friend who is not only a lawyer but has an MBA, and she's rather brilliant. I'm certain she can suggest the perfect solution to my dilemma."

"Uh-huh. Do you know my hourly rate, McFadden? How much did you get for this book?"

"Five hundred."

"Yeah, no offense, but that'll get you an hour and a half of my time, even at the friends-and-family rate."

"Five hundred *thousand*. Three publishers wanted it, and there was a bidding war."

Nia blinked. She looked...Well, she looked exactly how Daphne probably did when *she* got the news. Daphne had never come near to fainting in her life, but for a moment the world had faded dangerously close to black.

"Hold on," Nia said. "I'm doing this wrong." She cleared her throat and raised her voice. "Oh my God, Daphne! You sold your book!"

Daphne smiled. "I did, thank you. As for hiring you to fix my mistake, I'm kidding, of course. I need to come clean. I was hoping my *brilliant* business lawyer BFF could advise me on how to do that without losing my deal...or getting my ass sued for fraud."

"Do you *want* to come clean?"

"Honestly? I would love to be Zane Remington, ridiculous name, outrageous backstory, and all. This is exactly what we've discussed—whether I could hide behind a pen name so I don't need to..." Daphne shrugged. "You know."

"Deal with the insta-fame that will land at your door when the world discovers your freaking amazing book?"

Daphne made a face. "More like avoid the utter humiliation of failure. I just..." She shifted. As much as she loved to write, she was terrified of putting herself out there as a writer. Better to cloak herself in the anonymity of a pseudonym than to mess up her book's chances with her own awkward shyness. "I never considered using a male pen name, but it's been...freeing, you know? It can't last, though. So I need a lawyer-approved escape hatch."

Nia pursed her lips and studied Daphne's face. "Would you stick to being Zane if I could come up with a plan that let you?"

"Hell, yeah."

"Then leave it with me."

Six Months Later

CHRIS

Chris Stanton had a job interview. To be a writer. Or, at least, to play one for author photos. That was what Nia had told him, though she'd also suggested the job might entail more, depending on what the client—the *actual* writer—required.

Whatever Daphne McFadden required, he would be it, because he desperately needed this gig.

Chris was in trouble. Business trouble. He'd made the mistake of trying to help a university buddy who'd lost his shirt in a divorce. His buddy convinced Chris to leave a good job so they could open their own accounting firm together. Chris soon discovered it wasn't the divorce that bankrupted his friend—it was the thousand-dollar-a-week coke habit.

When his new partner started dipping into the business's piggy bank, Chris caught him fast because, duh, *accountant*. Yet Chris's name was still on the door, meaning he got sued along with his buddy. That's when Nia Paramar—a lawyer who'd been his client for years—offered him an escape hatch: If he would portray author Zane Remington for her best friend, Nia would help Chris with his legal problems. That could be the difference between him needing to sell his car or live in it.

Chris had done his homework, and he knew Daphne McFadden's

book was a big deal. It had already gotten very enthusiastic early reviews and been moved forward to a spring release.

Then he'd read what Daphne said about her alter ego. Zane Remington was a man's man, one of those Hemingway-esque types who lived deep in the wilderness and stocked his freezer with moose while composing works of creative genius.

Who would best portray a guy like that? An actor who thought he *was* a guy like that. A Chris Hemsworth wannabe who cruised through life on a wink and a grin. *He* hadn't acted since high school drama club, but Nia had agreed he could...get creative with his credentials. And she'd warned Daphne he'd be using a stage name for privacy. Since "Chris" was already his name, he'd stick with that, though he'd tap into the Hemsworth association by using his mother's maiden name: Ainsworth.

To play the part, Chris had costumed himself in a designer flannel shirt, faux worn blue jeans, and unlaced work boots that hadn't seen a split second of actual work. He'd rented a pickup—an obnoxiously oversize one that looked completely out of place in gas-conscious Vancouver.

For years, his stylist had wept each time Chris said, "Just trim it up, please." So she'd practically exploded in excitement when he asked if she could do something fashionable with his hair.

At least he'd made someone happy. The problem was that the person he needed to make happy was Daphne McFadden.

As he drew close to the restaurant where they'd agreed to meet, he spotted the author at a patio table. Nia had described Daphne McFadden as a "hot curvy brunette who can swing an axe with one hand while penning a smart, kick-ass zombie novel with the other." In other words, Daphne *was* Zane Remington. So why the gender swap? He didn't quite understand it, but he trusted Daphne knew her business better than he did.

The woman he saw looked perfectly pleasant and sturdy. He eyed her as he slowed to find parking.

That was when she looked straight at his pickup...and also when he saw a little compact car preparing to reverse into the only parking spot left. Chris took a deep breath, sent up a silent apology to the car's driver, channeled, *I'm an MFA grad with a half-million-dollar book deal*, and stole the spot. From the patio, Daphne nodded her approval, and he exhaled.

Dick move, but it was what Zane would do.

Chris hopped out of his truck just as a spot across the road cleared and the compact car zipped into it. The door opened and out stepped the kind of woman whose heels made her taller than half the men around her. Wavy mahogany hair with red highlights that caught the midday sun, a generous figure in a hip-hugging dress, which revealed arms and legs and glutes that said someone knew her way around a gym.

Damn...

He suddenly realized the woman, who was wearing shades, was looking straight at him. His first impulse was to check his fly. Then he remembered that he'd just stolen her parking spot.

Damn...

Chris glanced around for an escape and noticed Daphne still watching him from her bistro table. This was his audition, and if he fled from this magnificently pissed-off Amazon, he could never be Zane Remington. Daphne's book required a salesman who was 100 percent confident in the masterpiece he'd penned. Chris really needed this job, which meant he needed to be that salesman.

"Hey," he said as the woman drew close enough to hear. "Sorry about that. If I'd known *you* wanted that spot?" He emphasized the *you* while giving her an appreciative once-over.

Distaste oozed from her every pore. Were those freckles across her aquiline nose? He was a sucker for freckles.

"You mean stealing a spot from an elderly woman with a cane would have been all right?" she said, not even pausing as she strode past him.

"Depends on how good she looked for her age," he said, falling in stride with her.

He had a grin and a wink ready for when she glanced his way. She only picked up speed. He cast an uncertain look at Daphne, but the author watched him with continued interest.

"Looks like we're going to the same place," he called to the Amazon.

The woman didn't respond, just strode onto the patio and took the table beside Daphne's before pushing her shades onto her forehead.

Chris leaned onto the woman's table, letting his shoulders square and muscles ripple beneath the plaid designer shirt. He lowered his voice. "I really do feel bad about stealing your spot. How about you let me buy you dessert later?" His gaze trailed down her form. "You do eat dessert, right?"

Her golden-brown eyes flashed in outrage, and he replayed what he said and inwardly winced. Paired with his once-over, she'd taken it as a pointed comment on her figure. Shit. This was why Chris didn't flirt.

He opened his mouth to backtrack. Backtracking, however, was Chris. It wasn't Zane. And Daphne was still watching from the next table.

"That's a yes, then?" He smiled. "Excellent. Dessert, on me." His smile sparked, wicked. "Take that any way you like."

"You're blocking my view." She flicked her fingers, shooing him off.

He resisted the urge to slink away and tossed her a smirk as he straightened. Then he sauntered over to Daphne, who looked *very* pleased with his audition so far.

Chris slid into the seat across from the author and extended his hand. "Chris Ainsworth." He grinned, hoping it extended to a twinkle in his eyes. "But you can call me Zane Remington."

Her gaze crawled over him as she shut her tablet. "I'll call you anything you like."

"And I can call you ... Daphne? If I'm not being too presumptuous."

"My name's actually Nora."

"Ah, a pen name within a pen name. Clever. So you prefer Nora?"

"No," said a husky voice behind him. "*I* prefer Daphne."

Chris turned, slowly, to see the woman whose parking spot he'd stolen.

"Daphne McFadden," she said. "And I believe"—she inhaled sharply, as if the next words pained her—"that you are at the wrong table."

DAPHNE

As Chris Ainsworth regaled her with stories of his acting career, Daphne's fingers itched to pick up her phone and text Nia.

What did I ever do to you?

What secret grudge had her best friend been nursing that compelled her to inflict Chris Ainsworth on Daphne? It was a prank. It had to be. She'd finish lunch with this boor, and when she texted the inevitable WTF to Nia, her friend would reply with instructions to a coffee shop for a latte with the real actor she'd selected to play Zane. Compared to Lumberjack-Hipster here, whoever Nia had really chosen would seem perfect.

Yet the more Daphne thought about it, the more she was convinced that—to Nia—Chris Ainsworth *was* perfect for this job.

Nia and Daphne both hated to complain about men getting the edge in business. The obvious comeback from others was "Maybe it's not them, maybe it's you." How did you insist that you knew, beyond a shadow of a doubt, that you were just as good? Women weren't conditioned for that kind of confidence.

Daphne remembered going to the signing of a very famous male author who wrote romances, despite his insistence otherwise. While waiting to hear him talk, she'd overheard him telling the store staff how he lifted weights in the hotel gym pre-signing because "the ladies" loved firm biceps.

Then there was the online forum where librarians had been complaining about how some of their colleagues fawned over a good-looking male author, and how they couldn't get a popular female writer in for a visit, because everyone wanted the guy, who charged twice as much.

Did Daphne really blame Nia for selecting Chris Ainsworth? This was a business decision, and if "arrogant and attractive white guy" would sell more books, then Nia would find her exactly that. Which she had.

Except Chris was more than merely attractive. He had a classically handsome face, with chiseled and perfectly proportioned features. Summer-green eyes and dark blond hair that curled slightly in the breeze. Even his body had that classic Y shape, with narrow hips, strong shoulders, and biceps that strained at his slim-fitting shirt as he leaned on his arms.

Daphne's catnip was fit guys with wholesome good looks, charming smiles, and a twinkle that said, *Don't be fooled by my wildcat exterior—I'm a kitten inside.* Chris fulfilled the first part just fine. But the last one? This guy was neither wildcat nor kitten. He was a feral tom, strutting around and pissing on everything in sight.

Still, in Nia's defense, filling this role had been such a Herculean task that Daphne had been two days from giving up the charade and coming clean. Nia had found a way for her to sign the contract with a bunch of legal cartwheels that Daphne still didn't quite understand. Basically, she was legally doing business as Zane Remington, whose name she'd registered as a corporation, with the copyright held by that. If everyone presumed the actual author was male, well, she'd never actually claimed that.

So she hadn't needed an actor for the legal part or even for the early publicity. Then the publisher decided to move her release forward—by five months—which made the situation desperate. Nia had taken charge of that, and Daphne's only stipulation was that she needed a professional actor—she couldn't take the chance of having an ordinary guy play the part. Then, at the last minute, Nia called to say she had "the guy."

This guy.

"After that," Chris said, "I did a series of ads for high-end vehicles. Nothing you'd be familiar with." He waved toward her car with a chuckle.

She bit back the urge to say it was a rental. *Do not feed the trolls.*

"Most recently," he continued, "I played a bit role in—"

"You've established your acting credentials, Mr. Ainsworth. I want to talk about this particular job. It might not be your thing."

Chris lounged in his chair, long legs so far into the aisle that the poor server had to go another way to get past. "I'm an actor. I play roles."

"This one is primarily modeling. You would be the face of Zane Remington."

He reached into his pocket, pulled out a pair of glasses and put them on. "Alakazam. I *am* Zane Remington."

He steepled his fingers, and maybe he was supposed to look intelligent, but his expression suggested he should order the prune smoothie.

Daphne continued, "There may also be situations where you are required to give very short, very simple interviews, which I would coach you to answer through an earpiece. In the event of technical issues, you'd have scripted answers. Most questions will be about the book, which Nia sent to you."

"She did."

"Will you be comfortable representing it?"

He leaned back again, forcing the man behind him to tug in his chair. "Oh, I didn't *read* it."

"Not the whole thing, but I'm presuming you skimmed a few chapters."

"Is that necessary?"

Daphne opened her mouth. Shut it.

Chris continued, "I'm an actor. I emote the lines I am given. You tell me what you want me to say about your book, and I say it. I'm sure it's wonderful, but"—he shrugged—"I'm not much of a reader."

There it was, dangling before her. The excuse to say no. Hell no. This whole idea was absurd. Better for her to come clean to the publisher and—

Her phone buzzed. A text from her newly assigned publicist.

Melody: Haven't gotten that pic I asked for.

Melody: Don't be shy. It's not your jacket photo. I know you don't want that, and we are honoring your wishes.

Melody: We just want to get to know you. Put a face to your incredible book.

It was dangerously close to pub time, and Melody had to know what they had to work with. Could they send Zane's official author pic out with release promo? Or was it best only displayed on the website after clicking through three links and watching an ad for a celebrity bio?

Daphne glanced at Chris, with his ridiculous good looks. She surreptitiously snapped a shot as he launched into a story about the time he'd been mistaken for Captain America while walking past Vancouver's Fan Expo.

She hit Send. No message. Just the photo. Then she waited for her excuse to end this lunch from hell. Waited for Melody to LOL and tell her to send a real photo, because no way in hell did this man pen a dark zombie thriller with a teen girl protagonist.

Melody: Holy shit.

Daphne smiled and prepared her "ha-ha" response. *Hey, you said you wanted a photo. Didn't say it had to be me.*

Melody: Please tell me that's you.

Melody: I just showed it to the publicity director, and I think she's hyperventilating.

Melody: Please, please, please, tell me that's you.

Daphne: You'd prefer someone a little more author-ly, right? Older?

Melody: Are you kidding???!!!

Melody: I need the professional shots ASAP. We'll recommend a photographer if you need it. I'll let you go. I can see you're having lunch. Thank you!!!

Daphne lowered the phone and looked at Chris, who was still talking, as if unaware she'd been on her phone.
Now what?
If Nia recommended him, he couldn't be as bad as he seemed, right?
She cut into his monologue. "When can you start?"

CHAPTER TWO

It's real," Daphne whispered, holding the padded envelope in her trembling hands. "Really, really real."

Tika—bless her canine soul—did not judge Daphne's temporary lack of vocabulary. The husky only danced at her feet, sensing her excitement. Then Tika raced to bring her favorite ball, and Daphne threw it toward the lake. As Tika tore off, Daphne pulled the book from the envelope.

Her book. In actual book form.

Yes, words were not her friend today, but could anyone blame her? She was holding a dream made real.

In less than a month, people were going to read her story. People who were in no way related to Daphne.

When Tika returned, Daphne threw the ball again. Then she lifted the book into the sunlight and grinned a silly smile that stretched her face until it hurt.

Her book. Okay, it read "Zane Remington" on the cover, but that didn't matter. She'd written every word in this book. It was hers.

At the Edge of the World.

The title still threw her. She'd called the book *Winter's Sleep*, but the publisher said they wanted to position her book as more of a literary thriller, which made her laugh. It was about a zombie apocalypse. Not exactly highbrow.

Taking a deep breath, Daphne flipped the book over to read the jacket copy. Instead, she found herself staring at Chris Ainsworth.

His face took up the entire back cover.

At that, she felt her first twinge of pricked ego. His picture on her book. That was the point, of course, but the *entire* cover? His photo was more important than anything about the actual book?

She opened it and found the synopsis printed inside the book jacket. She skimmed the words and tried not to squirm. Her editor had reworked her version into something that, well, vaguely resembled the actual story.

The main character, seventeen-year-old Theodora, had grown up in Vancouver, now Seattle. She'd been on her first camping trip in the Yukon—now Alaska—when the zombie outbreak erupted. The book began three years later. The zombies had made it to Alaska, and everyone Theo knew was dead or turned. The city girl had become a survivalist.

In Daphne's fictional world, zombies hibernated in winter—hence her original title. That meant Theo had six zombie-free months to hunt and build and prepare. Yet summer was the time when game was plentiful...and that was when the zombies woke.

The synopsis portrayed Theo as a kick-ass heroine, while in reality, Daphne aimed for her character to be clever and resourceful rather than a superhero. It also gave away a twist that wasn't revealed until halfway through the book. And, to her surprise, rather than glossing over the romance angle, the jacket copy made it seem *more* important than it was.

So, yep, the synopsis wasn't exactly accurate, but she trusted that the publisher knew what it was doing. The main thing? She was holding a copy of her book. And in less than a month, it would be released into the wild.

She could not wait.

CHRIS

Chris sat on the balcony of his micro-apartment with the package Daphne had sent: a copy of her book. It'd been waiting when he returned from a long day of legal meetings, as Nia worked her magic on his case. Now he'd poured himself a beer, collapsed into the one chair that fit on his balcony, and exhaled for what felt like the first time today.

Things were going to be okay. Oh, he'd still take a financial hit from his ex-partner's mess—one he couldn't really afford—and he might have to slink back to his former firm, but he'd survive with his professional reputation largely intact. He might even get to keep his car. And it was all thanks to this little package he held in his hands.

"Thank you, Daphne McFadden," he murmured.

He tore open the wrapper and gazed down at...his face.

It was surreal, seeing his face on a book cover, but it was also like looking at an amateur portrait of himself, where he could catch bits that looked familiar, but the overall impression was that of looking at a stranger.

He'd had the same reaction when he got the shots from the photo shoot. *Is that really me?*

In high school, Chris had been what girls had affectionately called "a cute math geek." In other words, attractive enough but gawky and acne-prone. After he took on his first job, he'd nearly collapsed from stress at tax time, and a friend took him to the gym. There, Chris discovered both a remedy and a passion; his body took to it and filled out.

Around the same time his face had started to change, not only losing the acne but the youthful softness, too. He'd seen photos of his father and grandfather, and they'd been the sort of men who looked better at forty than twenty. His mom always joked that she'd married a sleeper hottie.

So part of his disconnect with the jacket photo was the fact he still didn't picture himself as that guy, but it was more, too. When the publisher wanted to add a "small" photo of him to the book jacket, Nia had suggested ways to disguise Chris. He appreciated that, even if he knew Nia suggested it mostly for Daphne's sake. She couldn't have people recognize her book's author as Vancouver accountant Chris Stanton.

Chris also didn't want to be recognized as a book author when he wasn't one. For the jacket photo, moody lighting shadowed his face, and the angle added to those shadows. He wore his Zane glasses and his Zane hairstyle and his serious-author Zane expression. Add in the photo editing, and no one was going to recognize him, which was good because it was not a tiny author photo inside the jacket.

It was the entire freaking back cover.

He held it up again and felt a stab of guilt. A memory flashed, one of being in a bookstore with his older sister. Gemma had picked up a hardcover adult novel and flipped it around to the back cover, with its giant author photo.

"This is going to be me someday," she said.

"An old man?"

She flashed him the finger. "You know what I mean. My photo, on a book someday, when I'm an author."

His sister was the writer in the family, and now it was *his* photo on the back of a book. At least Gemma wouldn't see it—young-adult wasn't her genre—and even if she did, she might only think that it kinda looked like her brother. It couldn't be, of course. Chris might read nearly as much as she did, but he didn't write.

He fingered the book. It didn't feel right, seeing his photo on Daphne's book.

It had been her choice, though.

Why had she chosen a male pen name? He had a feeling it wasn't a random decision, and that bothered him.

April 18, twenty-five days to publication

Daphne: Did you get the copy I sent?

Chris: Copy of . . . ?

Daphne: The book?

Chris: Right! Yes, it arrived. Was going to text. Thought you said my photo would be a square on the back cover. It IS the back cover. The ENTIRE cover.

Daphne: Any chance you're going to read the book before it comes out?

Chris: I've started. It's a lot of words.

Daphne: 90,000 of them.

Chris: Wow. I did read the summary. Sounds like a good book.

Kinda dark, though, don't you think? With the zombies and the end of the world and all?

Chris: D? You still there?

APRIL 20, TWENTY-THREE DAYS TO PUBLICATION

```
From: Alicia Koval
Subject: Another Starred Review!!!

Zane,

Yep, Edge just got its third star, squeaking in
just under the wire. That's a star from all the
major industry reviewers so far. Well, except
Kirkus, but Kirkus doesn't like anything.
  Congrats!!!

  Your very happy editor,
  Alicia

P.S. Trish tells me you haven't sent the new
photos in yet. Can you do that ASAP, please?
Thanks!
```

APRIL 21, TWENTY-TWO DAYS TO PUBLICATION

Chris: So, about those "casual" photos the publisher wants. I'm thinking "man bun."

Daphne: I'm thinking "hell no."

Chris: Sumo ponytail?

Daphne: Not even answering that.

Chris: I've started growing my hair out, in case I need to do any in-person promo. I'm going for a sexy golden mane thing, Chris Hemsworth, circa 2015.

Daphne: Or Fabio, circa 1990.

Chris: I'll schedule a haircut.

Daphne: Thank you.

APRIL 24, NINETEEN DAYS TO PUBLICATION

Chris: Got the haircut. I feel like I need something different for the photos, though. Maybe a full beard. I think Z would grow one up there in the winter. Nicely trimmed but full and bushy.

Daphne: A hipster beard.

Chris: That sounds like a no. Maybe a goatee?

Daphne: Definitely no.

Chris: How about scruff? A little sexy too-busy-to-shave scruff.

Daphne: Stop. Just stop. You look fine.

Chris: Hold on. I haven't shaved in a few days. Let me send
   you a pic.

Daphne: That's not really necessary.

Chris: Too late! What do you think?

Chris: D? You still there?

Daphne: Leave it.

Chris: You sure? Ten minutes with a razor and it's
   gone.

Daphne: Leave it.

Chris: Awesome!

APRIL 25, EIGHTEEN DAYS TO PUBLICATION

Chris: The new photo shoot is tomorrow. I know we agreed on
   jeans, but I'm having trouble choosing. I've got old jeans,
   new jeans, new jeans that look old. I like the old ones best
   for Z. They're snug and worn—but I'm worried the lighter
   color doesn't do my ass any favors.

Daphne: Send pics.

Chris: Which ones?

Daphne: All of them.

APRIL 28, FIFTEEN DAYS TO PUBLICATION

Chris: Okay, so I got my new photos. Sending you my fave now. Did a little Photoshopping ;)

Daphne: The last time a guy sent me a Photoshopped pic, it wasn't his smile he enhanced.

Chris: LOL No, it's not that kind of pic. Though, if you wanted…

Daphne: No, I do not.

Daphne: Wait. You Photoshopped yourself in front of my lake. At my house. With my dog.

Chris: He's a real cutie.

Daphne: SHE'S a real cutie.

Chris: I think Z would have a male dog. He looks like a black wolf with blue eyes. Very Z. I'm thinking I'll call him Ernie. Ernie Hemingway. Get it?

Daphne: SHE already has a name. HER name is Tika. And she is MY dog.

Chris: What if I put a cat in the photo instead?

Daphne: House cats don't wander the wilderness up here.
They'd get eaten.

Chris: What if it was a large one? My friend has this big Maine
Coon. We could pretend it's a lynx.

Daphne: Cut the dog. No cat. Cell service is flickering.
Gotta run.

CHRIS

Chris laughed as he pulled up the badly Photoshopped photo of him with Tika in front of Daphne's lake. He'd had no intention of sending it to the publisher. The goal had been to amuse Daphne—and maybe poke at her a little. Give her something to distract her from the fact she had a book coming out in a few weeks, and the pressure to do well grew with each passing day.

Chris remembered his first major client—a business that had fired its accountant a week before taxes were due. Multiply that tenfold, and he had an inkling of what Daphne was going through.

She didn't have any reason to worry. The book was amazing. It'd be easier if he could admit that he'd read it, but he had to stay in character, at least until he'd proven his ability to play a role.

In the meantime, he could sneak a little bit of himself into the portrayal. Like the goofier side that had made this photo. Just a little gentle poking to distract and—he hoped—amuse her.

To that end...

He pulled up the number of his wildlife-rehab client and hit Call.

APRIL 29, FOURTEEN DAYS TO PUBLICATION

Chris: Remember how we talked about Z having a cat?

Daphne: I'm trying to forget.

Chris: LOL Okay, so I started thinking. I have this friend of a friend who owes me a favor and, well, one word. Cougar.

Daphne: What you do with your private time is your own business.

Chris: What? Oh. Cougar. Ha!

Chris: No, it isn't that kind of cougar. Not that I have any problem with that—older just means more experience, right?

Daphne: Cell service flickering.

Chris: So this friend-of-a-friend runs a wildlife-rehab center on Van Isle, and they just got in a cougar cub, so I got some pics.

Daphne: Of the cub? Okay. I'm a sucker for baby wildlife. Send.

Chris: Done!

Daphne: Uh, this is a picture of you cuddling a cougar cub.

Chris: Yes! See? It'll win the cat-lover demographic without tarnishing Z's masculine rep.

Chris: Second pic incoming!

Daphne: So...looks like the cub ate your shirt.

Chris: Funny how that happened, huh?

Daphne: You are now shirtless, cuddling a cougar cub. Wait, is that blood?

Chris: Shit! Forgot to 'shop that out. Kitty had claws. Weird, huh?

Daphne: I think there's someone at the door.

MAY 2, ELEVEN DAYS TO PUBLICATION

Daphne: WTF???!!!

Chris: Language, D. You're a kid's book writer, remember? Oh, sorry. I'm not supposed to say that. You're a literary speculative-fiction novelist, whose book features a teenaged protagonist in a brutal but inspiring coming-of-age story.

Chris: That's the line the publisher gave me.

Daphne: You asked for access to the Zane account so you could keep abreast of the publisher's plans for my book while I took a weekend off. You promised you would never EVER respond to an email directed to Zane.

Chris: I didn't respond to a new email. I noticed you left the cougar-cub pics out of the latest batch, so I passed them along. I was being helpful.

Daphne: You passed them photos I had decided against using, and then you responded to questions about those photos, which were used in a major online article about the book.

Chris: I was being helpful.

Daphne: Two days, Chris. I was gone for two days.

Daphne: Also, you said you rescued the cub from a grizzly.

Chris: They asked where it came from, and I said to myself WWZD?

Daphne: ???

Chris: What Would Zane Do? Rescue the cub from a grizzly, of course. I was about to say "charging grizzly" but I thought that oversold it.

Daphne: You Photoshopped yourself in front of my house again. There are no cougars in Whitehorse, Chris.

Chris: Huh. Are people questioning it online?

Daphne: No. Because they're too busy staring at the photo of a half-naked hot guy cuddling a cougar cub!!!

Chris: Well, that's good, right?

Chris: Are you mad because I wasn't holding your book in the picture? I thought of it, but that cub was a handful.

Chris: Maybe I could get the cub to hold the book in its teeth. What do you think?

Chris: D?

MAY 6, ONE WEEK TO PUBLICATION

From: Lyndsay Grant
Subject: Round-up

Hey Zane,

I'm your new publicist. Trish moved on last week. Also, your first publicist, Melody, sends her best from her new job.

I know it seems like a bit of a revolving door here in publicity, but I can assure you that I am ready to hit the ground running! In fact, given the interest that Edge is generating, I'm going to be working on your book exclusively for the next few months. So exciting!!!

In addition to the starred reviews (congrats!!!) we have confirmation that the following publications will be reviewing Edge:

New York Times Book Review (!!!)

Los Angeles Times (!)

USA Today

Globe & Mail (Canada, your home & native land)

Also, Edge has been featured as a "most anticipated book of spring" on the following lists:

Los Angeles Times

NPR

Amazon

Goodreads

Any questions, I'm here.

Yours,

Lyndsay

P.S. I love the mountain lion photo! I send it as an option when publications request your author photo, and for some reason, that's the one they keep picking ;)

CHAPTER THREE

DAPHNE

<u>Chris Ainsworth Pros/Cons</u>

Note to self: When he's getting on your nerves, read this.

Cons

1. OMG, this guy is such an asshole.
2. Fine, "asshole" goes a bit far. He's arrogant. Also intrusive, pretentious, dismissive, self-centered.

Pros

1. My publisher loves him.
2. His arrogance doesn't seem to negatively affect the marketing. In fact, it seems to help, as if everyone expects Zane to be a prick.
3. He makes me laugh, even if he isn't trying to.
4. Fine, he's a hot guy who takes hot photos. Yes, I'm shallow.

Semi-Con

1. He hasn't read the @$%! book. Okay, this is ego, isn't it? I'm hurt that he hasn't even skimmed it. He has nothing but praise for it in interviews. Considering he

supposedly wrote the book, the praise is kinda weird, but again, it seems to be what they expect.

2. So this isn't really a "con." It just kinda stings. When that happens, reread those starred reviews that Nia edited to include MY name. I wrote the book. Remember that.

MAY 10, THREE DAYS TO PUBLICATION

Daphne gripped the sides of the toilet bowl and focused on the feel of the cool porcelain as her stomach threatened to heave again.

Just three days, and it would be over.

No, three days and it would *begin*. Real people would read her book and post reviews and tell her she sucked. Or they wouldn't read her book, and the publisher would have a warehouse of unsold copies and her career would be over before it began.

Daphne leaned over the bowl as her stomach bucked.

"D? You still there?"

She opened one watery eye and struggled to focus on the cell phone perched on the back of her toilet, speaker icon lit.

She made a noise Chris could take as assent.

"Good," he said. "I really needed someone to talk to about this. I had no idea it would be so *stressful* playing Zane. I know you're excited. Everything is great for you. You wrote the book and your job is over, and now you can just sit back and reap the rewards."

She glared daggers at the phone. Beside her, Tika growled.

"Is that your stomach?" Chris asked.

Chris didn't wait for a response. He didn't need one. The man could carry on a conversation all by himself. Last week, she'd made the mistake of saying he could call to discuss his growing workload, so now he called. Also texted. And emailed. But mostly called.

He didn't need anything—this was the calm before the storm. But he was dealing with a lot of stress from the release of this book *that he did not write and had not even read.*

Daphne could feign cell-service issues, but she didn't actually mind these calls. She could listen to him fret and fuss and tell her how she must be so excited, and the overwhelming urge to strangle him long-distance gave her something to focus on besides her utter terror as her publication date approached.

"The phone interviews are getting kinda stressful," he said.

That made Daphne freeze, her head over the bowl.

"All right," she said slowly. "We can definitely cut back on your workload. Like I said last week, you absolutely don't need to do these by phone." *In fact, I'd rather you didn't, but you insist, and while some of your answers make me cringe, my publisher is thrilled.*

"No, the publicist said phone or video chat is preferred by journalists. The problem is that sometimes they ask questions I can't answer."

"Which is why we were supposed to use an earpiece," she said.

They'd done that when the phone interviews started last week, but Chris had an alarming habit of answering questions before she could formulate a response. When they'd had technical difficulties, he'd flown solo and aced it. For the last two, they'd skipped the earpiece.

She continued, "I would never want you doing anything you're uncomfortable with. I know there's been a lot of interest in interviews, far beyond what I ever imagined."

"Because of me," he said with a soft chuckle. "I mean, the book's good. It must be, if it got those circled reviews, right?"

A pinprick stabbed behind Daphne's eyes as she pushed to her feet. "*Starred* reviews. I know that interviewer thought you were adorable getting that wrong, but..."

"Adorable because I'm a baby author. I'm not expected to know all this. My point is that you've obviously written a good book, and I'm good at promoting it. We make an awesome team."

"If you're asking for a raise, don't hint, Chris. Just ask—"

"No raise. Not yet." Another chuckle, and despite her annoyance, she noted it was a very sexy chuckle indeed, one that rippled through her every time she heard it.

Oh, Chris. You could be so perfect.

Too perfect. That was the problem. A guy like Chris Ainsworth had to be a jerk. Otherwise, he'd be clearly hiding a secret past as an axe murderer.

"What do you need, Chris?"

"More face time. I need to be you, D, and I can't, because I don't know you well enough."

She thumped onto her writing recliner, and Tika took up residence at her feet. "But you aren't *supposed* to be me. You're Zane. That's the whole point."

"I'm Zane, but Zane is you. You wrote this book. You live that life. Well, except for the part about rescuing cougar cubs from charging grizzlies, but I'm sure you could, if you tried."

"Also if there were actual cougars here." She paused with her hand halfway to her water glass. "Wait, I thought you rescued it from a *non-charging* grizzly."

"Er, that was the first interview. The one I did yesterday…I might have gotten carried away. She loved it, though. Sent me her phone number in case I had anything more to add."

"That's not why she sent you her number."

He chuckled. "It might have had something to do with the photo I sent her, too."

Daphne thumped back in the recliner. "Oh God. Please don't tell me you're sending dick pics."

"Of course not." He paused. "Unless you want me to. Maybe I could accidentally send them. Like 'Here's a photo of me holding a bear cub, whoops, that's not a bear cub.'"

Daphne pressed her knuckles into her mouth to hold back a laugh. *Do not encourage him.*

"I'm kidding, D. I'd never do that. Do guys really think a woman is going to get an unsolicited dick pic and say, 'Mmm, gotta get me some of that'?"

Her next words evaporated. *Damn you, Chris. Don't say things like that.*

Every now and then, Chris would say something insightful. Something smart and funny and sweet, and it was an even bigger tease than the shirtless photos.

He continued, "The point is that to do these interviews, I need to get to know you better. Know where you live. How you live. There's a flight this afternoon. I can be in Whitehorse tonight."

She shot upright. "Whoa. Wait. You want to come *here?*"

"I need to immerse myself in you." A low chuckle. "Er, that didn't come out right. I think it would help to get to know you better, D. I wouldn't be a bother. I'd just follow you around for a couple of days, watch you work, live your life, immerse myself in your creative process."

"My creative process involves me parking my ass in a chair and typing. There aren't any helpful thought bubbles."

"I could read over your shoulder as you write—"

"No, no, no." Daphne shuddered. "Let's table this conversation, Chris. Any questions you have, just ask. I really need to go, though, before my cell service cuts out."

"Yeah, I know. Okay, bye, D. Talk later."

When he ended the call, she closed her eyes and exhaled.

Just a few more days. Get through the next few days, and the book would be launched into the world, and everything would be fine.

CHRIS

Chris hung up the phone and smiled to himself. That went well. Okay, it would have gone even better if Daphne had agreed to let him visit, but he'd work on that. For now, he had distracted her, and that was the main thing. Pretty sure he'd even made her laugh, if those choking sounds were any indication.

He knew she was more stressed than ever. So he'd been calling, feigning his own anxiety, while reassuring her that she had no reason to worry. And if he could also make her laugh, even better.

Chris chopped Belgian chocolate into chunks and threw them into the batter. He was baking brownies to send express for Daphne's release day, since he wouldn't be there to deliver them in person. He couldn't admit he'd made them himself, either. Definitely not a Chris Ainsworth thing. He'd bought cookies from a high-end bakery and saved the box to pack them in.

There were two tricks to baking. One: Follow the recipe. Two: *Follow the damned recipe.* He'd been baking since he was a kid, and while he'd grown up watching his mother and grandmother throw in a pinch of this and a handful of that, Chris was all about precision. Find the best possible recipe and test it out. Later, being an experienced baker, he could tweak, but once he'd achieved perfection, he followed his revised recipe exactly with the best possible ingredients.

How many times had extended family members joked that he'd make some woman very happy one day? It'd been true for a while. In high school and university, girls loved his baking. Then, after his Steve Rogers transformation, that skill seemed less appealing to the women he dated, and he'd started pretending he didn't know his way around a kitchen.

Maybe that has something to do with the type of women you date these days?

True. He attracted a very different type of woman now, and when he tried to go back to his old type—the quirky, geeky, brainy girls— they eyed him like he was a high school jock hitting on them while his friends laughed in the background.

The last woman he'd dated had seen a novel on his nightstand and said, "You read books?" in the same tone she might ask if he googled photos of underage girls. All his lines to Daphne about not reading—so many *words*—came verbatim from that short-lived relationship.

As Chris put the brownies into the oven, his gaze shifted to the box and ribbon. He'd need to put a note in it. As he thought, his memory tripped back to the day he met Daphne.

Oh yes, *that* was the answer.

Then he remembered another part of their first conversation, when he'd offered dessert on him, and a fresh idea pinged.

Hell no. He wouldn't dare do that.

True, but this wasn't him. It was Chris Ainsworth. And *he* would totally do that.

DAPHNE

She needed to buy Chris a release gift, as thanks for everything he'd done. He'd already sent hers. She smiled at the thought of the brownies...and the note that came with them. She'd woken up sick with stress, and that note had washed it away.

Dessert on me, as promised.

She'd been enough of an emotional wreck to tear up at that. It'd been incredibly thoughtful of Chris to send her a gift on release day and even more thoughtful to ask Nia what she'd want.

Then she'd realized the note was on the back of a photo. She'd flipped it over and...

It was Chris. Naked, with the open box of brownies very strategically placed. She'd laughed so hard she'd given herself a stomach cramp. Then she'd fixed a coffee and cut a brownie and texted him a thank you.

Chris: I get brownie points for not sending a dick pic, right?

Chris: Brownie points. Get it?

That made her laugh anew.

Chris: However, if you want the missing part...

Another laugh, because the string of emojis that followed said the offer was tongue-in-cheek. She'd replied that the view was lovely even without the rest. Then taken another look at the photo.

Even now, in her car, Daphne sighed at the memory of that photo. It was definitely going in her nightstand drawer. Such a gorgeous man. Pure fantasy fodder, which was where he needed to remain. It'd be easy to jump on the signs he wasn't quite the asshole he seemed...and use the excuse to jump on *him*. But she needed to keep this professional.

Even if he wasn't her employee—which he was—and even if he was interested—which he wasn't—Daphne wasn't emotionally built for flings. She'd always had boyfriends, and past high school, each boyfriend could have been the one. That was how she chose them. She knew she'd get emotionally invested, and she wouldn't do that with anyone she couldn't envision beside her in twenty years.

Those post–high school relationships had eventually come to amicable ends as she realized they *weren't* "the one."

Then came Anthony. She wouldn't say he was perfect. Any guy who seemed perfect was scamming you. But he'd been perfect for her. A fellow architect who shared her love of the outdoors and who read her writing and encouraged her to continue.

Anthony saw through her chilly exterior and understood how deeply she cared. In return, she'd let him in more than she'd ever let any of those previous boyfriends. She'd finally accepted his invitation to move in and hadn't renewed the lease on her apartment.

Then came her mom's cancer diagnosis, and Daphne was no longer the baggage-free woman Anthony had fallen for. She had responsibilities and, worse, she embraced those responsibilities because it was her mom, damn it.

Daphne didn't have siblings. Her dad left when she was young. It had always been just her and her mom. Now the most important person in Daphne's life was dying, and Anthony was complaining because she had to cancel lunch to accompany her mother to chemo. Daphne and Anthony would have decades of lunches, but he didn't understand this was all she had with her mom. When the chemo was no longer working, Daphne had to reschedule a weekend getaway to discuss her mother's final stages, and that proved to be the last straw for Anthony.

The experience taught her a valuable lesson about relationships. Mom had raised her to be self-sufficient and independent and to find someone who accepted that about her, embraced it even. Daphne had thought Anthony was that person. In reality, he'd only embraced her independence when it meant she wasn't relying on him for help. Once that independence *inconvenienced* him, it was another story.

Having been through that, she knew there wasn't room for anyone in her life right now. That life had changed so much in the past few years. Mom's death, moving to the Yukon, getting her book published. If she brought anyone into that, she risked them turning out to be another Anthony, happy to accommodate her "eccentric" life until they realized it wasn't a whim, that she didn't intend to move south again, didn't intend to go back to a stable career as an architect.

All of that had nothing to do with Chris Ainsworth, who would be horrified if she was thinking the word "boyfriend" and him in the same headspace.

What mattered now was that she would repay his brownies with a nice gift. He'd said he liked single-malt scotch during an interview.

Daphne pulled out her phone and began searching for a Vancouver delivery service.

CHRIS

Chris sat at the kitchen island in his condo, perched on a high stool, chin resting on his hands as he stared at the very expensive bottle and wished he liked scotch.

A card lay beside it with a typed message, printed by the delivery service.

Chris,

The brownies were delicious! The perfect remedy for release-day stress. Thank you. And thank you for everything you've done. You have made everything about this process better and easier. I'm not sure I could have done it without you, and I wouldn't have wanted to try.

Daphne

That message was the mirror image of the note he wished he could have sent Daphne with the brownies. She'd always been quick with her gratitude for his work, but that was polite praise, careful not to rocket Chris Ainsworth's mile-high ego into the stratosphere. Here, she'd let her guard down.

Except it wasn't Chris Stanton she was thanking. It was Chris Ainsworth, and the scotch drove that point home with the force of a baseball bat.

When he first opened the gift, he'd deflated. It seemed the kind of generic present you might pick for a guy you didn't know well. Then he'd realized it wasn't generic at all—he'd mentioned liking scotch in an interview. Daphne had taken the time to choose a thoughtful gift. The problem was, it was thoughtful for the Chris she knew.

Part of him said to stop, just stop. This was a professional relationship, and his crush on Daphne violated her trust in him. But, see, there was the loophole. Chris *Ainsworth* was her employee, and Chris *Stanton* had the crush. That made it okay, right?

Yeah, probably not.

He fingered the scotch label. Then he straightened and went to find a tumbler so he could send Daphne a photo of her gift being properly appreciated.

As for the rest, he'd figure that out later.

CHAPTER FOUR

Daphne: Edge is going to debut number two on the New York
Times list!

Chris: That's good, right?

Daphne: It's AMAZING!!!

Chris: Cool. Maybe you'll hit number one next week.

Daphne: LOL. Nah, there's a Stephen King book in
number one.

Chris: Who?

Chris: Wait! I know that guy. He does movies, right? I liked "It."
Does he also write books?

Daphne: Yes. Yes, he does.

MAY 29

Daphne: OMG! Edge hit #1!!!!!

Chris: Huh. Guess that Steve guy isn't so good after all.

Daphne: His book came out months ago, and I probably
outsold him by two copies. My publisher is THRILLED,
though. They want more books!

Chris: You need to write more?

Daphne: I WANT to write more.

Chris: Huh. But I guess if they pay you well, that's good, right?
You can afford to move someplace warmer.

Chris: D? You still there?

MAY 30

Chris: Hey, D! Did you see the email? Your publisher wants me
to go on tour. Cool, huh?

Daphne: No.

Chris: Not cool?

Daphne: No touring. It's in the contract.

Chris: I don't mind. I'd like signing books. I'll wear my glasses.

Daphne: I mean Lawrence, my agent, put a clause in my contract. I don't have to do touring or in-person events unless I hit a certain sales level, which I will never—

Daphne: Lawrence just texted. Can I get back to you?

MAY 31

Daphne: You got the information for the tour, right?

Chris: I did!

Daphne: Four stops. We're going to need to prepare. A lot.

Chris: But you'll be with me, right?

Daphne: They'll assign you an escort.

Chris: Uh, that's an interesting perk, but I think I'm good.

Daphne: What?

Daphne: Not THAT kind of escort. A media escort.

Chris: That doesn't sound nearly as interesting. Why don't you come along?

Daphne: It's complicated.

Chris: I don't think it is. You're the writer, and you should be there.

Daphne: I...I can't.

Chris: Cell phone troubles incoming, right?

Daphne: No. I just...I'm really busy. And you'll do great. I know you will.

Chris: Okay. We'll talk later. I gotta go.

JUNE 2

Daphne: What the #$%@ hell, Chris?

Chris: You actually typed #$%@. That's so cute.

Daphne: You agreed to an in-person interview? At MY HOME???

Chris: It's New Gotham magazine. You saw the email from Lyndsay. Wait, is it still Lyndsay? I can't keep track.

Daphne: Chris...

Chris: You saw the email. This is HUGE. They want to fly all the way to Whitehorse to interview Zane. New Gotham Magazine! Even I know what that is. I don't think we could say no.

Daphne: How about letting me try?

Chris: Honestly, D, it didn't seem like your publisher was actually asking. They were just letting you know it was happening. If you want to tell them you've changed your mind, go ahead. I'll stay out of it.

Chris: D? You still there?

Daphne: Yes. You're right. They didn't seem to be asking. Sorry I snapped.

Chris: I've got this. Don't worry. It's not until next Friday. I'll drive up.

Daphne: Do you even know where Whitehorse is?

Chris: Couple hours north.

Daphne: By PLANE.

Chris: Then I'll fly. I still have that bonus you paid me for hitting the New Yorker list.

Daphne: New York Times.

Chris: I'll call once I'm there.

Daphne: You are not coming here.

Daphne: Chris?

DAPHNE

Chris was on his way to Whitehorse. To her house. And she still didn't know how this happened. As she frantically cleaned, Nia kept texting.

Nia: Stop cleaning.

Daphne: I'm just tidying up.

Nia: I've seen your house. It's freakishly clean. Always.

Nia: Some people stress-eat. You stress-clean.

Nia: It's just Chris.

Daphne: It's not 'just Chris.' It's a New Gotham film crew. A FILM CREW. Coming to my house.

Nia: You mean a photographer. They're a magazine, Daphne.

Daphne: They have a new TV show, and they're filming a segment on Zane.

Nia: !!!!!

Daphne: They told us YESTERDAY. They'll be here for two days. TWO DAYS.

Nia: That is amazing promo!!!

Daphne couldn't argue with that. She could, however, totally freak out over it.

Her phone rang. It was Nia.

"Yes?" Daphne said as she answered.

"Put me on speaker. That way I won't interrupt your crazy-ass cleaning."

"You are now on speaker."

A long pause.

"Nia?"

"Are you okay, Daf? I mean, besides the current freaking out. Are you okay with all this?"

"With the book doing so well? I'm torn between being thrilled and full-on hyperventilating panic, but we've discussed this, and I'm not currently in need of soothing. Check back tomorrow."

"I mean the Zane stuff. Chris is great. He really is, and I'm thrilled you two are getting along so well."

Daphne's stomach clenched at that. This was the problem with Nia knowing Chris and being the one who set them up. She wasn't comfortable telling her friend when Chris did something like agree to an interview without consulting her. As far as Nia knew, Daphne was delighted with Chris. Not entirely untrue, but it still pricked her conscience when Nia gushed over how well they were getting on.

Daphne said nothing as she inspected the sofa for dog hair.

Nia continued, "This is different, though. It's one thing to have his photo on your book or have him giving interviews. You never cared about those things. But him going on tour instead of you? Being interviewed in *your* house?"

Oh yes. That was very different, and Daphne was struggling not to feel something dangerously close to resentment. Admitting that, though, would be admitting that there were flaws with the plan she and Nia had brainstormed together.

"I'm fine with it," Daphne said.

"He's going to be in your house, pretending he wrote your book and—"

The beep of an incoming call cut Nia short.

"It's Chris," Daphne said. "I need to take this. Call you back?"

Nia said sure, and Daphne took a moment to switch calls. Why would Chris be phoning two hours before his flight departed? To cancel. That seemed the only explanation. He'd cancel, and a film crew would show up tomorrow afternoon to find the house occupied by a woman who was definitely *not* Zane Remington.

Daphne answered with a tentative "Hello?"

"Hey!" Chris said. "It's me."

The knot in her stomach tightened. That breezy tone warned of bad news.

He was going to say he wouldn't make it. Something had come up, maybe an audition for a real job.

"Daphne? Did I lose you?"

"No, I'm here."

A soft chuckle. "Good. I know your cell service is wonky, but I've got four solid bars here. Maybe you should get another provider?"

"It's been good lately." She paused. "Wait? Where are you?"

Another chuckle, this one a bit forced. "Close to you, I hope. That's kinda the problem. I'm lost."

"What? You're in Whitehorse?"

"Outside it. On your road. At least, that's what the signpost said, but it's a dirt road and I haven't seen anything in miles. There aren't even any houses."

"You—" Daphne put him on speaker and scrambled to open her email. "You're supposed to be on the midnight flight. I'm picking you up."

"Surprise!" Another chuckle, this one still a bit forced. "I caught an earlier flight and rented a car to surprise you. Except all I have is your street address, and the GPS swears it doesn't exist. I got to the right road, and, man, what are they thinking, renting out little cars at the airport? These are mountains! Dirt roads and mountains! I nearly went into the ditch, and then there was a moose just standing in the road. Did you know there are moose here?"

Daphne squeezed her eyes shut. "Yes. Yes, there are."

"Well, someone needs to train them to stay off the road."

"Tell me where you are, and I'll come get you."

"Uh…"

"Look around. What do you see?"

"Trees."

She shook her head. "What's the last thing you passed."

"Trees. And a moose. Maybe if I just keep going?"

"It's a long road, and it's only going to get worse. Can you add me as a friend so I can track your location?"

"Oh! Right! Hold on." A few seconds passed. "There. Do you see me?"

"I do. Stay where you are. Don't get out of the car. There are grizzlies."

"What?"

"I'm kidding. Well, not about there being grizzlies. I have one that visits the yard every now and then. Mostly it's just black bears, lynx, coyotes, foxes, and porcupines. Oh, and I saw a wolf last week."

"I'll…stay in my car."

CHRIS

Chris did not stay in his car. He couldn't, not with this spectacular view. He'd pulled over halfway down a *mountainside*. Perched on the hood of his rental car, he could see the valley stretched out for miles. Endless green in so many shades that his mind boggled.

He took a deep breath. Crisp clean air flooded his lungs. It *smelled* different here. *Tasted* different, if that made any sense. He'd noticed it as soon as he'd left the tiny Whitehorse airport.

Also, he'd seen a moose. An actual not-in-a-zoo moose. He'd come around the corner, the tiny car skating in the dirt, and the moose had been ambling across the road. Seeing him, it'd galloped into the forest on impossibly long legs, and he'd sat there, catching his breath, torn between "I just saw a moose!" and "I almost hit a moose!"

He might be a city boy, but he knew that car-moose encounters rarely went well for the car . . . or the people inside. He'd been channeling Chris Ainsworth with that "train them to stay off the road" comment, but he'd been serious about the rental agency having cars this tiny. They'd sold out of SUVs before he arrived, and he ended up with a subcompact that slid on these hills like a skateboard and would provide as much protection in a wildlife encounter.

"You look like you're lost, city slicker."

He jumped up as Daphne rounded the corner on foot. Seeing her, his heart did a double slam. God, she was gorgeous. Today, she looked like a sporting goods ad, the sort he might see in a magazine and think, *Maybe I should get out of the city more often.* She wore boots and athletic shorts that just covered her ass and showed off her curves and muscles to full advantage. A T-shirt hugged her generous chest, and she wore her hair up in a messy ponytail, tendrils curling down around her sunglasses.

She also had that most necessary of accessories: a dog. This one was as gorgeous as her owner, looking like a fluffy black wolf with blue eyes. He focused his attention there so Daphne wouldn't catch him ogling her. Then he hopped off the car hood and crouched, calling, "Tika!"

The dog stopped dead and growled.

"That's not her name?" he said.

"It is. But she's half wolf. Last person who made a sudden move around her...?" Daphne shook her head. "So much blood."

She caught his look and smiled. "I'm kidding, Chris. She's a quarter wolf, tops. You just startled her, that's all."

She patted the dog, who leaned into her leg, sucking up the attention. When Chris stepped forward to pet her, though, Tika growled, ears flattening.

"Weird," Daphne said. "She never does that."

Great. He'd been in the Yukon less than an hour, and he'd already made Daphne come fetch him and pissed off her dog.

A truck whipped around the corner, dust flying. Seeing them, the driver hit the brakes and leaned out the driver's window with his gaze fixed on Daphne. He was about their age with rugged good looks, dark wavy hair, and the tanned skin of an outdoorsman.

A gray wolf leapt from the back of the guy's pickup. Chris jumped. He might even have yelped.

Daphne smiled. "It's just a husky."

The dog ran over and greeted Tika with kisses and whines, while the guy in the pickup looked at Daphne as if he'd like to do the same to her.

"Robbie," Daphne said. "This is...Zane. A...a friend of mine."

Chris stuck out a hand. The guy's gaze swung down and stopped at Chris's feet. Chris looked at his dress shoes, once polished brown, now gray with dust.

"Better get your friend some proper footwear." Robbie's gaze slid to the rental car. "And a proper vehicle. Did he get stuck going *down*hill?"

"I was admiring the scenery," Chris said.

Robbie looked from Chris to Daphne and back again. "Yeah, I bet you were. Next time, don't do it from the middle of the road. That's a surefire way to get yourself killed." He shook his head. "Tourists."

Robbie turned to Daphne. "You coming to the neighborhood BBQ tomorrow? Pam said you haven't answered yet. I volunteered to pop by and deliver the invitation in person."

Daphne smiled up at him. "That's sweet, but I can't make it. Work."

He leaned on the window ledge. "You need any wood chopped? I can do that for you."

As Robbie's gaze devoured Daphne, Chris bristled. Oh, he wanted to do a lot more than chop her wood.

Daphne only smiled and shook her head. "I've got plenty, and I like chopping it myself. Good exercise. Thank you for offering, though."

"You need anything—anything at all—you just give me a shout. I know you're out there by yourself. Some things require a man's touch."

Robbie's gaze bounced off Chris dismissively. Then he called his dog into the truck and rolled off down the hill.

DAPHNE

How embarrassing had *that* been, dealing with Robbie's crap in front of Chris? Only a handful of people lived on the lake—six houses, to be precise, two of them summer-only. Daphne adored all her neighbors...except Robbie. After he'd moved into a rented shack last year, he'd taken one look at her house and decided he knew how to get an upgrade. After all, she was a woman on her own. She needed a man. To chop wood.

She knew exactly where Robbie wanted to stuff his wood.

Worse, it wasn't even because he liked her. She was just the chick he'd need to bang to get into her house.

Living so isolated, she didn't dare tell him to screw off. He knew where to find her. He also knew she lived alone. She couldn't even rely on her dog to scare him off—Tika was too fond of his dog.

The month after Robbie moved into the neighborhood, Daphne installed a security system. She hated that. It was bad enough that she felt unsafe in her own home. So much worse that she knew who made her feel unsafe and could do nothing except refuse his advances politely for fear of setting him off.

It rankled so much. And now Chris had witnessed her humiliation, watching her be all sugar-sweet to such an asshole.

"Do you want to drive?" Chris asked, holding up the keys.

Yep, compared to Robbie, Chris was a sweetheart.

Daphne took the keys and whistled for Tika. The dog eyed Chris, and for a moment, Daphne thought she wasn't going to get into the car. But after giving him a careful once-over, the dog hopped in, as if maybe the guy wasn't so bad after all.

You and me both, pup. You and me both.

As Chris walked to the passenger door, her brain pulled up a snapshot from five minutes ago, when she'd rounded the corner to see him lounging on the hood of the car, in his expensive loafers and pressed jeans and button-down shirt rolled up to his elbows. He'd looked like one of those intentionally incongruous advertisements that strode the line between quirky and stylish. An ad for that scotch she'd bought him.

Why, yes, my clothing and my vehicle are completely unsuited to this environment, but a man who looks like me is at home wherever he goes.

And this was the guy who'd be lounging around *her* home for three days.

CHAPTER FIVE

CHRIS

Holy shit, this place was amazing.

The line stuck on repeat in his mind as Daphne drove down the wooded drive. Then the drive opened to the house and the lake and...

Holy *shit*.

This was Daphne's *house*. She woke up to a view straight out of a wilderness resort brochure.

He had to stop gawking like an idiot. Chris Ainsworth would not gawk. Ainsworth was "something of an outdoorsman," he'd told Daphne in that tone that said he was being modest. Like Zane, Ainsworth fancied himself a man of the natural world, as at home chopping wood as mixing dirty martinis for two. He was not going to get out of his vehicle gushing and gaping like a city mouse who rarely set foot outside Vancouver.

So Chris swung open his door and—keeping his gaze away from the vista—he got his luggage and followed Daphne inside.

As she explained, the second floor was actually the main level, to take full advantage of the view. Perhaps, but the view that knocked the mountains from his mind was the one provided while she led him up the stairs, Chris's gaze on level with her ass.

"I didn't show you the door code," she said, stopping abruptly. "Do you want to do that now?"

He tried to get his brain to catch up with her words, but he could only make some incoherent noise she obviously took as no. She continued up the steps. He let her get two above him, just to give her space, not at all because he was a lech who wanted that view of her ass again.

"That'll be your room," she said, pointing once they reached the top of the stairs. "You can put your stuff in there."

He walked into the room, and his gaze immediately fell on a king-size bed, the covers pulled so tight he couldn't help imagining pulling her onto them, bouncing down onto the cool sheets as the midday sun shone in—

"This is your room," he said.

"I'm taking the guest room downstairs."

"What? No. *I'm* the guest. Just show me where—"

"You're the homeowner, remember? This is the main bedroom."

His mouth worked for a moment. "The film crew isn't going to come in here."

"I can't take that chance. *Nothing* can suggest this isn't your house, including the bedrooms."

She walked out. Still carrying his duffel, he followed.

"This isn't right," he said. "It's your home."

"For the next two days, it's yours. I'm the maid."

"What?" He stepped into her path. "No, Daphne. Absolutely not. If you want to stick around, you can be my girlfriend."

"Can I?" Definite sarcasm there, and he heard his tone and inwardly winced. As Chris Ainsworth, though, he couldn't let that show. He rolled his shoulders and leaned against the wall. "Sure. They'd buy it. Guy like Zane's bound to have a girlfriend. Or three." His lips twitched when he said it, but her look only darkened.

"No, Chris, I'm not playing part of Zane's harem."

"I was kidding. You and Zane would be exclusive. You're a fellow writer he met online, both working on your novels, and you helped him with *Edge*."

"I *helped* him?"

Chris adjusted his lean, warming to his subject. "Helped a lot. He couldn't have done it without you. You're like..."

"His muse?"

"Exactly. You're smart and gorgeous and a great writer, and you inspire him—"

"I inspired him to write *my* book?" She stepped toward Chris. "Do you know how many men in history have taken credit for books written by their wives and girlfriends? I realize that I'm perpetuating that already, and I don't feel good about it, but there is no way in *hell* I'm going to play your girlfriend, your muse, the wannabe writer gazing up at you adoringly, drinking in your every word, dreaming of someday being half as good as you."

Daphne's eyes blazed as she moved closer, and he swore he could feel the heat radiating off her. She looked magnificent, strumming with life, fiery and furious.

Furious with you, idiot. Stop mooning. Reverse course or you are going to be sleeping in that lake, possibly at the bottom of it.

"I—I see your point. I'm sor—" *That's not Ainsworth.* He lifted one shoulder in a shrug while offering that most nonapologetic of apologies. "I'm sorry if you were offended. I just wanted to be sure you had a role."

"I do have a role. Caretaker. I clean your house and cook your meals so you can write, and I will do so off camera, because we need to tread very carefully and pray no one I know watches the show and recognizes my house."

Shit. He hadn't thought of that. "Good point."

"An excellent point, which is why I didn't want..." She shook her head. "I'm playing caretaker because it makes sense. I'm not doing it to be pissy. Let's just get through this interview, and then we'll discuss long term how we want to handle the in-person obligations, so we're on the same page. For now, settle in, maybe go for a walk. I'll make dinner."

CHRIS

A walk sounded like a fine plan. Get out of Daphne's hair and explore her property. That would work so much better if he could get off the porch.

He looked down at Tika, standing in front of him, her fur bristling as she growled.

"I was given permission to leave," he said. "In fact, right now, I think she'd rather I left."

Tika just kept growling. Not forcing him back inside, he suspected, but warning him off the property entirely.

Dogs usually liked him. He'd spent the last decade dreaming of a house with a yard so he could get one again. The problem was that in Vancouver, unless you had a few million to spare, you weren't getting a yard. He'd been looking at the suburbs, weighing his need for a yard and dog against the convenience of a commute he could bike in ten minutes.

Then came the thieving partner and the lawsuits. Now the lawsuit was being settled and his firm looked poised to survive the reversion to single-partner. All thanks to Nia. Well, Nia and Daphne, because without this job he might have been filing for bankruptcy. Now he was recovering his equilibrium and his business, plus he had the income from playing Zane Remington.

The income from playing Zane. Earned as Daphne's *employee*. Not a partner in her business. Which meant he damned well shouldn't be making business decisions for her, like accepting a film interview. Especially when that meant kicking her out of her bedroom for two nights and forcing her to play hostess. Worse? He hadn't accepted because he truly thought her publisher wouldn't take no for an answer. He accepted so he could spend time with her and prove himself.

Prove himself? Yeah, as the kind of guy who'd accept an interview on her behalf and then make her sleep in the guest room while playing caretaker to his cut-rate Ernest Hemingway.

"I screwed up," he told Tika. "But I'm going to make it up to her. I'm giving the best damned interview ever, and then, afterward, I'm going to tell her the truth."

And upon hearing that heartfelt confession, Tika curled her lip, clearly unimpressed.

"I'm going to start by being helpful," Chris continued. "Right this second. I'll do something to pay her back for having me here. I'll cut the lawn."

He looked around. There was no lawn. It was forest, with a meadow that wasn't meant to be trimmed. Then his gaze lit on something halfway between the side porch at the lake. An axe wedged in a piece of cut wood.

That's what neighbor-dude offered to do, wasn't it? Chop wood for Daphne. She'd refused because she was capable of cutting her own wood. But she was busy dealing with an unexpected guest, so he could do this for her.

Chris had never actually chopped wood. The requirements, though, as he understood them, were threefold. An axe, which was right there. Wood, which was strewn throughout the forest. And a bit of muscle.

He flexed, his biceps popping. "I do believe I have everything I need."

He swore the dog rolled her blue eyes. Yet she made no move to stop Chris, and he strode past her to find suitable lengths of fallen wood in the forest.

DAPHNE

Daphne breathed deeply as she chopped vegetables, struggling to recover her equilibrium, which would have gone better if she weren't chopping onions. Tears were streaming down her face, and she wiped her eyes on her shoulder and sniffled.

No tears allowed. No misplaced anger. No awkward annoyance. She'd told Chris that giving him the main bedroom wasn't about her being pissy, and while that was true, she'd felt pissy at that moment, especially when he'd suggested she play his muse. It made sense to be the caretaker, but part of her had been mulishly digging in to make a point.

She knew the interview was a prime opportunity. *New Gotham* magazine *plus* a segment on their show? Just this morning, her editor had emailed her the review that would accompany the article, and it was the equivalent of a full-spread color ad. From a business standpoint, there was zero reason to be pissy. From a writer standpoint, though…

It stung. She hadn't realized how much until Chris suggested she play his girlfriend. With that came the realization that she'd pandered to the very system she'd railed against.

Editors and agents might take a man's book more seriously? I'll submit my book as a man and hire a man to play me while I sleep in the guest room and make his meals. Ha! That'll show them!

The fact that she'd sold the book as Zane didn't necessarily prove that playing a man helped. It might have been the different cover letter. It might have been the different attitude she adopted as Zane—the confidence and the ego and sense that she didn't need to soften her communications with exclamation marks and smiley faces.

None of that was Chris's fault. She needed to treat him like a guest, not growl at him like an intruder.

Speaking of growling, she should make sure Tika wasn't bothering Chris. She had no idea what was up with the dog. A little voice whispered that she should heed Tika's caution. Didn't people always say that dogs could see through whatever persona a stranger adopted? If a dog didn't like you, it was a bad sign. Except that Tika's "bad dude" sense was clearly defective if she tolerated Robbie.

Daphne finished chopping vegetables and went to the front window, knife still in hand. She looked out and—

—the knife dropped, almost skewering her foot. She yanked open the patio door and raced outside.

"Stop!"

Chris froze in place, axe lifted like a baseball bat.

"What the hell are you doing?" she shouted, which was a mistake, clearly prompting him to demonstrate, the axe swinging down—

"Stop!" The word came as a shriek now while Daphne clambered down the steps.

Chris froze.

She lifted her hands. "Do not move. Please."

She jogged past Tika, who was watching Chris, her tail wagging in anticipation of the bloodshed to come.

"Lower the axe carefully," she said. "Do not swing it."

"I'm just cutting up this limb."

"If you continue on that trajectory, the only limb you will cut is your own."

She took hold of the axe shaft and placed her hands over his. Then she carefully followed through with the swing, the blade missing the tree piece and stopping an inch from his lower leg.

"Oh," Chris said. "Huh."

She took the axe from him. "When's the last time you chopped wood?"

"It's...been a while."

"Let me rephrase. Have you ever chopped wood?"

"Uh..." He shifted his weight. "I think the axe I used before was different. It's all about the tools, right?" He held out his hands. "Let me try that again."

Daphne tightened her grip on the axe and made a mental note to lock it in the utility shed. "I don't need wood, Chris. I have tons." She motioned to the piles stacked tight between pairs of trees. "That's just part of it. I have two cords of seasoned wood, and I'll add more in the fall."

"Huh. So why was that guy offering to chop wood for you?"

"Because he's..." *An asshole looking for a better place to live.* "Because he's a good neighbor. I'll take this and finish making dinner. Why don't you go for a walk with Tika? I'll bring down the bear spray."

"Bear spray? What for?"

"The squirrels. They're very dangerous this time of year."

He paused for a beat and then chuckled. "That's a joke, right? The bear spray is for bears."

"It is."

"So I should spray myself with it. Bear repellant." When she hesitated, he smiled. "*That* was a joke, D. I spray *them* in the eyes."

"Only if they show signs of aggression. Otherwise, you retreat slowly while making yourself as big as possible. Don't turn your back. Don't run."

"You, uh, seem like an expert. Get attacked by bears a lot?"

"I've only encountered two black bears on trails. Both walked away. It's safe. The spray is an extra precaution. Let me go inside and grab it."

DAPHNE

After dinner, Daphne didn't know what to do with Chris. They'd talked for an hour as they'd prepped for the filming. Then he'd gone out onto the deck with a beer. Being early June in the north, the sun was still blazing down, even as the clock struck nine. The deck faced south, which meant it got hot, and he'd stripped off his shirt. Now he was lounging, shirtless, against the railing, gazing out over the lake as he chugged his beer.

At the risk of objectifying the guy, it was like coming home to find that a friend had snuck a cool new piece of tech into her home. A moment's pause of *Where did this come from?* followed by a heartfelt *I don't care, but I know exactly what I want to do with it.*

Her gaze sliding down his perfect abs to the button on his jeans.

Didn't Nia insist there was something to be said for spontaneity?

Daphne shook her head sharply. There would be none of that. Even if she somehow declared herself ready for a fling, this was her employee. Thinking about him that way was wrong.

Right?

It was wrong, wasn't it?

Forget about finding something to do with Chris. He was busy soaking up the evening sun and enjoying his beer.

She eyed him again and sighed. First stop: a cold-water splash. Then she'd pull out her laptop and get some work done. She had a few new scenes to write for the sequel, and none of them involved anything even mildly sexy, thank God.

Daphne settled in. It always took a few minutes for her muse to get going—like starting her pickup midwinter after forgetting to plug in the heating block. A few cranks of the engine, and it was primed, the scene roaring—

The hairs on her neck prickled, and she lifted her gaze to see Chris, still shirtless, now poised on the other arm of the sectional sofa, watching her.

She started to close her laptop.

"No no, keep going," he said.

She shook her head. "I thought you were busy, so I was just finishing a scene."

"Continue, please. I've never seen you write."

"It's not much of a spectator sport. How about we—?"

"I'd like to watch, if that's okay with you." He leaned forward with a quick grin. "That didn't sound right, did it? Watch you write, I mean."

Her mind hadn't even peeked down that other possible path until he mentioned it. Damn him.

Was there any excuse that might convince him to put on his shirt?

We get a lot of mosquitos in the house. You may want to cover up.

He continued, "If I'm going to play a writer, I should know how it's done. I won't bother you. I promise."

She opened her mouth to tell him, more firmly, that she could not write while being watched. Then she remembered her resolve not to snap at him.

"Okay," she said. "But be warned, it isn't very exciting."

She twisted just enough that he was out of her line of sight. Then she resumed the scene, slowly at first, the motor cold again. After a few lines, the engine caught and—

"Why that word?"

Daphne jumped and twisted to find Chris leaning over her shoulder.

"I was noticing your word choices," he said. "Like that one there. You used 'ensnared' instead of 'caught.'"

"Uh-huh."

He eased back. "I've often wondered that about authors. How do they decide when to use five-dollar words instead of five-cent ones? Is it to help readers build their vocabulary?"

Or to show off their own vocabulary?

He didn't say that, but she heard it, and swallowed the snarky comeback.

Be nice.

Deep breath. "Sometimes a fancier word has a nuance the plain one doesn't. Other times you've used the plain one twice already on that page, and you need a synonym to avoid echoes. In this case, it's dialogue from a pompous ass. He'd use 'ensnared.'"

"Makes sense." Chris eased back. "Keep writing. I'll just ask questions as you go."

Daphne closed the laptop. "If you want to watch me work, how about I do this instead?" She walked to a drawer, opened it, and took out a sheaf of papers.

"Editing?" he asked. "I was actually pretty good at that in middle school. I loved commas. You can put them in wherever it looks good. Like art. Here, let me help—"

She hugged the papers to her chest and pulled a chair up to the kitchen island. "It's not editing. It's business work. You want to know more about being an author? This is one of the profession's dirty little secrets." She lowered her voice to a whisper. "It's not all sitting around making up stories. You're running a small business."

She laid out the pages.

Chris picked up one. "You paid five grand for website design? I've got a buddy whose nephew does them for a case of beer."

She plucked the invoice from his hand. "We can discuss marketing later. Right now, I need to enter these expenses into my online ledger."

He stepped up behind her and peered at the screen. "You know you can hire people for that, right? They do it, like, professionally."

"You mean bookkeepers?"

"That's the word. You're making enough money that you should be offloading all the tasks that don't require your personal attention so you can focus on the things only *you* can do, like writing. An accountant who also does bookkeeping could not only take this part off your hands but help with tax-saving opportunities."

He cleared his throat. "Or so I've heard. From my accountant. I don't do my own. There's so many numbers. All that math."

"I don't mind math," Daphne said.

"Really?" Another throat clearing. "I mean, sure, if that's your thing. Unless you really love bookkeeping, though, you should consider hiring someone."

She sighed. "I know. It's just that all the details are up here." She tapped her forehead. "What this receipt was for. Why I needed to buy that. I worry that I'd spend as much time explaining it as just doing it myself."

"Not with a good bookkeeper. Once they have a handle on your cash flow and regular expenses, you don't need to tell them specifics." He pulled a receipt from the pile. "Two recent young adult novels. Someone might think these were just for reading, and not a legitimate expense, but a bookkeeper would understand that you're conducting market research."

He was actually dead-on, and here was the conundrum of Chris, the reason Daphne couldn't dismiss him, the reason she'd found herself getting an emergency haircut and manicure yesterday.

She could say she was attracted to him only because he was, well, hot. She could even joke about this being her new prerogative as a successful single author. Guys in her position routinely showed up for events with a starry-eyed young thing who could barely spell "bestseller." Therefore, she was entitled to lust after Chris.

Yet that had never been her thing. Never would be. If that was all Chris was, she could easily dismiss him as eye candy. Every now and then, though, she caught glimpses of something more. Of a guy who could carry on a deep conversation. Of a guy who was sweet and thoughtful and a little bit goofy.

Like now, when he'd picked up that receipt and known exactly why she bought the books. An insight that shouldn't come from a guy who thought commas went wherever they looked good.

Show me more of that, she thought, and as soon as she did, another part of her whispered, *And then what?*

Oh, she had some answers for that. So many answers, most involving positions, and a few involving toys. But there were other answers, too, the meaningful ones that would slide in after the fun. Intense conversation, sharing ideas, comparing interests.

She wouldn't be the superior bitch who declared there weren't any intellectual depths to Chris. Even if there weren't, it didn't mean they couldn't find common ground.

There *was* common ground. She thought he was hot…and he agreed.

Daphne choked back a laugh. For some people, that'd be enough, at least short term. But she'd never been that person.

She closed her laptop. "We should probably get to bed."

The words came out before she could process them, proving it was definitely past talking time.

"Yeah, big day tomorrow," Chris said.

And that was it. She'd accidentally lobbed a ball straight at him, and he hadn't even lifted a hand to catch it. Guess that answered any questions. Not that she should be entertaining any.

"What time does the crew get in again?" he asked. "One?"

"The flight lands at one. They should be here by two."

He nodded. "Okay, well, let me know what needs doing in the morning. Chores or whatever. I'm here to help."

There was no bravado to those words. They weren't *Let me know if I can carry anything heavy for you, little missy*. They didn't sound like an empty and offhand suggestion, either. A genuine and very sweet offer of help, and it was like those glimpses of a smart and insightful guy. What the hell was she supposed to do with that?

Nothing. That's what she was supposed to do with it. Be glad he seemed willing to help out, and just hope that interest didn't fade once the vacuum cleaner came out.

"Good night, Chris," she said.

He lifted a finger. "Zane. For the next two days, I only answer to Zane."

She smiled. "Fair point. Good night, Zane."

"Good night, D."

Daphne couldn't sleep. She tried to tell herself it was because she was in her damned guest room, but that was just grumbling. Everything in her environment was fine. Comfy bed. Perfect temperature. Complete darkness courtesy of the blackout blinds. Complete silence from living in the middle of nowhere. Tika lay beside her, radiating comfort and security.

The problem was her writer's brain. She'd been halfway through a new scene when Chris decided he wanted to watch her write. Now, every time her brain started drifting, it replayed that unfinished scene, and with each iteration, it blossomed a little more. At first, it was only a mental outline—Theo on patrol when she spotted what turned out to be a fox…which started lurching her way, and she realized it wasn't rabies, but something much worse: the first infected animal.

While Daphne had finished the first draft of the sequel to *Edge*, it needed something more, and this was her main revision. Was it weird to be excited about your own ideas? Maybe, but she'd been jonesing to write this since she had the epiphany a few days ago.

Daphne tossed and turned enough that ever-patient Tika started to grumble. When the poor dog finally decided she'd rather sleep on the floor, Daphne gave up, pulled on track shorts and an oversize tee, and tiptoed upstairs, wincing as Tika's nails clicked behind her.

At the top of the stairs, Daphne glanced around the corner toward the main bedroom. The door was closed. With an exhale of relief, she ducked into the kitchen and warmed milk in the microwave, being careful to hit Stop before it dinged. Then she made hot cocoa and took it to her writing spot.

She'd left the scene with Theo heading into the woods, accompanied only by her dog, Mochi. But as Daphne sat there, facing the huge window, she saw the deck beyond, and Chris's image from earlier materialized, conjured by her treacherous imagination.

You said you wanted to write the Theo scene, and instead you're giving me this? Really?

It was like when Tika pretended she needed to go potty and really just wanted to con Daphne into an extra walk.

Focus.

Theo was stepping into the forest…

A door opens behind me, the slow creak of it barely audible even in the silence. I freeze, breath held, as I peer over my shoulder into the settlement. The sound comes from the cabin where Atticus is staying. If he sees me, he'll give me hell for going out alone after dark.

I slide into the shadows and lower my hand to Mochi's head, asking her to be quiet. Atticus steps out. He's shirtless, his muscled—

Ack! That was *not* the story. Reverse!
Daphne cut that and tried again.

I slide into the forest. Branches sigh in the breeze, and I inhale the sharp tang of pine. I take another step. The lake stretches out before me, shimmering in the moonlight. Something ripples twenty feet from shore. Then a familiar head of dark-blond hair breaks the surface. Atticus. As I duck behind a tree, he walks from the lake, water running off his muscled shoulders and his chest, glistening—

Daphne slapped shut her laptop. She sat there, her head back, eyes shut. At a click, she glanced left and, for a moment, she thought she was writing again, this time penning a scene of Chris coming out of her bedroom, his dark-blond hair sleep-tousled, his chiseled face cast in half shadow, his muscled shoulders appearing over the back of the sofa and then his chest, nothing but bare skin all the way down to…Okay, he was wearing sweatpants, but they rode low, down on his hips, the muscles there riveting her gaze as she stared.

Now *that* was a sexy gluteus medius.

And *that* was also a phrase she never expected to use in her life.

Daphne realized she wasn't conjuring Chris in her literary mind. He was actually out of the bedroom. She started opening her mouth, and then realized something else—if she was seeing his hip—and that very sexy stretch of muscle—he was angled to the side, which meant he wasn't coming her way.

Chris tiptoed to the stairwell and peered down. Making sure he wouldn't be disturbing her, just as she'd checked to be sure his door was closed. He paused there, head tilting as if straining to listen.

God, the guy was gorgeous, cast in shadowy moonlight, half naked, his cheeks dark with beard shadow. The sexiest thing, though, wasn't that stubbled jawline or those perfect biceps or even that oh-so-tempting strip of bare hip. It was the way he paused, listening, considerate of the fact that he might wake her. Once he was sure he hadn't, he tiptoed with such care that she had to smile. To withstand northern winters, the house was solidly built, and that included floors so thick she wouldn't hear him from below unless he tap-danced.

He tiptoed to the door leading to the deck. For a moment, he stood there, hand on the knob. Then, with another glance back toward the stairs, he eased open the door. He was halfway out when he gave a start and looked down.

"Hey, Tika," he whispered, and Daphne realized the dog had slipped from her side. "Couldn't sleep either? Or keeping an eye on the dude stealing your person's bed?"

His voice was different. Not the timbre, but the tone, wry and soft. From sleeping, she presumed. He wasn't fully awake yet, not fully himself yet.

"I'm just stepping out," he whispered to the dog. "Please don't eat me. Also, please don't bar the door and leave me out there. It's kinda chilly."

Daphne bit her cheek to keep from laughing. He eased the patio door open a little more, his gaze on Tika. Daphne tensed, ready to interfere if Tika objected to Chris going out, but soon he was on the deck.

"Coming with me, are you?" he whispered as he reached a tentative hand down. A skritching, as if he was petting Tika's coarse ruff. "Now I'm allowed to pet you? Whew. Unless it's a trick. Getting me to step *all* the way out so you can slam the door shut behind me." A soft laugh. "I'm onto your plot, pup. You go out first."

He waved a hand, and Tika went outside. Then he followed, leaving the door cracked open before he moved into the full-length window in front of her. He was barefoot and shirtless, his sweatpants baggy until he leaned his forearms onto the railing and gave her the perfect view of a perfect ass.

Seriously, Daphne? You're going to sit in the dark and drool over your unsuspecting guest?

She should say something. She really should. And she would… soon.

Chris lowered his hand to Tika's head, and the dog didn't just accept the petting, she leaned into him. Chris grinned in such unabashed delight that Daphne's heart skipped.

Who are you, Chris Ainsworth? Who are you really?

She sat there, watching him as he gazed out at the lake and petted Tika. When the dog glanced Daphne's way, her heart stopped. Chris was going to turn around and catch her creeping on him.

He didn't, but the thought was enough for her to rise from the sofa. She set down her laptop, walked to the door, and pushed it farther open.

"Hey," she said softly.

He looked over and winced. "Oh geez, sorry, I didn't want to wake you."

Did he say "Oh geez"? His expression was so unguarded and genuinely contrite that her heart fluttered.

"No," she began. She was about to say she'd come up for a glass of water and spotted him outside, but that might still imply the noise had woken her. "I, uh, I was…" She stepped out and pointed through the window to her laptop on the reclining end of the sofa. "I was there."

He smiled. "And I was blocking your view."

Not exactly.

"No, no. I just didn't want you to turn around and see me sitting in the dark, like some kind of creeper."

He laughed, and it wasn't the laugh she'd heard before from him, always somewhere between forced and self-aware, as if he were, well, an actor playing a role. This was a real one, as he relaxed against the railing and patted Tika.

"Stealing my dog, huh?" she said.

He tensed. "Your dog, your author's role, your bedroom."

"No, no." She fluttered a hand. "I'm kidding about Tika, and the rest was my choice."

"Still…" He glanced inside. "There's no reason I should kick you out of your bed. The film crew isn't staying here. We can stage it before they arrive. You'll sleep better in your own bed."

In her own bed…where he'd been sleeping. A bed that would still be warm from him, still smell of him.

She swallowed hard and tried for a breezy tone. "No, Chris. Seriously. It wasn't the guest room that drove me up here. I was obsessing over a scene, and it's done now." *Liar.* "I'll just finish my cocoa and head back down."

"Hot chocolate?" He perked up, and it was so adorable she had to smile.

"Would you like some?"

He hesitated, and then said, "No, it's late. I'm fine."

She opened the deck door. "I'm getting you a cocoa. Whether you drink it or not is up to you."

While she heated the milk, he grabbed a shirt from his room.

"Little chilly out there?" she asked as he put it on.

A self-deprecating laugh. "Yeah. It's warmer than I expected, though. Being the north and all." His face screwed up. "That sounded like I thought there'd be snow in June."

"Oh, people expect snow year-round. They arrive at the airport with winter coats in July. While it's never hot enough to need air-conditioning, I *will* be hauling out the fans soon."

She handed him his cocoa. He went back onto the deck and held the door for her, which she took as an invitation to join him.

She stepped out. He moved to the railing and gazed up at the sky.

"I was hoping for the northern lights," he said.

"Uh…"

He glanced over, his smile wry. "Wrong weather, I'm guessing."

"Wrong season. It's not *impossible* to get them in early summer. They're actually there when the solar wind activity is strong, but it rarely gets dark enough to see them at this time of year."

"Solar wind activity?"

She smiled. "I'll spare you the science."

"No, I should know it, in case I'm asked, as Zane."

As she explained, she could see his brain whirring.

"That's…a lot," he said when she finished. "I think I'll stick with 'solar wind activity.'"

"Good call." She leaned on the railing. "I like the legends better. Not surprising, being a writer. The local indigenous are—"

"—the Kwanlin Dün First Nation tribe," he cut in. "I memorized that. It's important."

She smiled. "It is. This is their land. Now, I don't know the Kwanlin Dün tradition regarding the northern lights, but the Tlingit one warns against looking up at the lights because they're spirits trying to lure people away. Then there's lore that says the lights are the spirits of stillborn children."

"Oh," he said, inhaling sharply. "That's ... Wow."

He leaned on the railing beside her and sipped his cocoa. She did the same, gazing out at the moonlit lake as they enjoyed the night in silence.

CHAPTER SIX

Pros/Cons to Sleeping with Chris Ainsworth

Pros

1. He's sorta sweet, when he wants to be. No, not "sorta"—he *is* sweet. Also funny and kind with bursts of…something.[3]
2. He's hot.
3. So hot.
4. I haven't had sex in…let's not calculate, shall we?
5. Have you seen him? No, really. Have you seen him?

Cons

1. This is a professional relationship.
2. I don't do casual sex.[1]
3. It takes two to tango, and he's not exactly jumping me.[2]
4. This is a *professional relationship*. Employer-employee. Remember that.

FOOTNOTES

[1] But I could, right? Maybe? First time for everything and all that?

[2] Would I want him jumping me? No. In fact, the not-jumping-me part is a mark in

his favor. He's respectful. Unless he's actually not interested. Uh, yeah, it's entirely possible he's just not interested, so maybe all this is a moot point?

[3] And here's the real issue, well, besides the fact I'm not sure he's actually interested. Those bursts of "something." Glimpses of a guy I could really fall for, and that would be bad. Bad, bad, bad.[4]

[4] Why bad? I'm…not sure.

Conclusion: There will be no hooking up with the hired help. Geez, Daphne. Stop, just stop.

CHRIS

Chris lay in bed. Sun peeked out from the bottom of the blackout blind, where he hadn't pulled it down far enough. His watch said it was 8:25. He'd originally set his alarm for eight, not wanting to laze in bed while Daphne made breakfast, but after their late night, he'd reset it for nine so he wouldn't wake her by thumping around.

Last night…

When he'd first gone to bed, he hadn't been able to sleep. The house was so quiet. Like, completely and eerily quiet. He'd spent the last eight years living in downtown Vancouver, where he slept with white noise to cover the traffic. Here, he'd almost been tempted to play the white noise to fill the silence. That had seemed sacrilegious, though, so he'd gotten up instead.

After that hour talking to Daphne and enjoying the night scenery, he'd zonked out and slept harder than he had in months. It was only when light blazed that he'd bolted up, the bright strip of sunshine screaming that he'd slept until noon. He hadn't. The sun rose earlier here than at home.

Now he was awake and thinking of last night. Of their time on the deck. Of how he'd forgotten to be Chris Ainsworth. He'd been sleepy, not thinking straight, and just forgot. He should be in full-on panic mode right now, desperate to repair the damage. He wasn't because...well, because there didn't seem to have been any damage.

He'd been himself, and Daphne hadn't reacted at all.

No, that wasn't quite right. She hadn't reacted *negatively*. She'd been more relaxed and comfortable than he'd ever seen her.

The early evening had started fine, with them on the couch talking about writing and accounting, but there'd still been an awkwardness because he had to play Chris Ainsworth. Later, when he'd forgotten the act, it'd been magic. He hadn't felt that comfortable with anyone in years. He'd wanted to stay out there all night, talking and laughing and just being with her.

This could be something. He'd suspected that for a while, but now he was sure of it. He had something with Daphne. Something he'd been looking for, even if he hadn't realized it. The possibility of a committed relationship. Not a fling. Not a brief affair. Something real.

And how would that work? She lives two hours away—by plane. Do you expect her to upend her life and move to Vancouver with you? Or are you going to leave your own life behind, leave all your family and friends, to come up here?

He pushed that aside. Just because he wanted more than a fling didn't mean he had to work through living arrangements before the first kiss. Put the cart back behind the horse.

The point was that he wanted to start something with Daphne, and wherever it ended up, it had to *start* with intention.

That meant he had to take this slow. Let her get to know him.

Get to know Chris Stanton.

He needed to tell her the truth before the film crew arrived. Give her time to assimilate it before they got here.

I'm not actually an actor, Daphne. I'm an accountant.

It's more than that. I'm not the guy I've been playing, either. I created

Chris Ainsworth to be what I figured you'd expect. A little dense. A little self-absorbed. A little bit of a dick. Not too much, but yeah, Chris Ainsworth was a struggling actor who'd throw himself into the role of Zane Remington and be whatever you needed.

Yet he'd proven that he—Chris Stanton, chartered accountant—*could* be Zane Remington.

Or had he? This film segment would be his first live performance. Maybe he should wait until afterward.

No. He had to tell her so they could resolve this before the crew arrived. Give her all the time she needed to regain her equilibrium before those cameras turned on, because this segment was a huge deal.

So maybe he should get past the filming first? Not do anything to give her cause for concern?

Chris's fingers itched for his laptop. This required a balance sheet—in favor and against coming clean pre-TV-segment. But he'd left his laptop at home because it wasn't a Chris Ainsworth accessory. Maybe if he could find some paper? Daphne was a writer. She'd have paper, right?

He'd draw up a balance sheet to help him weigh—

Downstairs, Tika erupted in a canine *Invasion! Invasion!* alert. Chris strode into the bathroom and looked out the window to see a truck rolling down the long drive.

The vehicle stopped, and a woman got out of the passenger seat. A woman who looked like she shopped at the same place he had when assembling his outdoorsy Zane wardrobe. She wore an orange puffer vest over a long-sleeved shirt, trail shorts, thick hiking socks, and boots.

The film crew.

He was almost out of the bedroom before an odd chill stopped him. He looked down to remember he was still naked and snatched clothing from the chair as he raced past.

When he reached the hallway, he realized he'd grabbed his sweats, which was far too "Chris" for a first impression.

What would Zane Remington do, surprised by an early film crew first thing in the morning? He spotted his Zane glasses, and put them on along with his boxers. Glasses and underwear. Fully dressed. At least for Zane.

Chris galloped down the stairs to find Daphne trying to corral Tika. The dog barked ferociously at the door, as if the knocking signaled a battering ram.

"It's the film crew," Chris whispered, as if the crew might hear him through a solid steel door, with a dog barking.

Daphne's eyes widened, and her watch-bearing arm shot up.

"They're early," he said. "Really early."

She looked down at herself, dressed as she'd been last night, in track shorts and an oversize tee that didn't disguise the fact she wasn't wearing a bra. Not that he'd noticed.

Hell, yeah, he'd totally noticed. And was noticing again…and feeling the reaction of noticing.

"Tika!" He reached for the dog, his hand going to her collar. "Let's greet our guests while Daphne changes."

I am totally not using your dog as cover for a very inconvenient morning hard-on. Nope, nope, nope.

He led Tika to the door while mentally reciting bond-amortization-method formulas.

"Chris?" Daphne said.

He glanced over. She waved at his lower half, and his cheeks heated, certain she'd noticed—

"You're, uh, only wearing boxers," she said.

"And glasses."

She sputtered a laugh. "Yes, and glasses."

"Think they'll object?"

She paused. "'Object' is not the word I'd use."

"Then I'm good to go. Tika and I will distract them while you dress."

He waited until she'd gone back into the room, and not at all because he was watching her track shorts ride up—

This dog isn't going to shield you forever, buddy.

Chris turned away from the view and called "Just a moment" to the crew banging on the door. Did his voice drop an octave when he did? Possibly.

He got behind the door, his hand still on Tika's collar. She'd quieted, and if he wanted, he could take pride in that. Her person was safely in her room, and Tika trusted that together, the two of them could protect Daphne from whatever lay beyond that door.

In truth, Tika probably only cared about the first part. Daphne was safe, and Chris... *Well, whatever, dude. You'd make fine cannon fodder.*

Chris unlocked the door and yanked it open. Something beeped. A camera? Already? He fixed on his best Zane smile, a little smug, a little *Why yes, I am Zane Remington, newly minted #1 New York Times bestselling author.* Tika twisted in his grip, and he glanced down to see the dog giving him serious side-eye.

He lifted his gaze to the newly arrived crew and let his smile grow a fraction. "Why hello. Welcome to my humble abode."

The woman in the orange puffer vest stared for a second. Then her gaze slipped down him and back up.

"Well, hello, Mr. Remington," she said.

"Please excuse my terribly inappropriate attire," he said. "I didn't expect you this morning, and I was up late writing."

Tika wrenched from his grip, backing away and growling at the very moment an alarm wailed. A car alarm? His gaze shot to the truck outside, only to realize the wail came from the house.

That beeping, you idiot. It was the security system, warning you to disarm it after you opened the door.

Shit! He locked his knees before scrambling back into the house. He was Zane Remington, who would not panic, despite the siren wailing over their heads.

"My apologies!" he shouted to be heard over the alarm. "Let me fix that!"

He backed up, and Tika nearly knocked him over to get inside ahead of him. He thought she was running from the sound. Instead, she blocked his entry, her legs planted.

You are not the guy I let pet me last night. You are that jerk from yesterday, and you are not coming back into my house.

No, it was more like *You are not getting near my person again.*

"It's okay, Tika!" he called, voice rising so everyone could hear. "I know you hate the alarm!"

He sidestepped, prepared for Tika to lunge, but she wasn't that kind of dog. She just fixed him with a look that said she was not happy at this reversion of character. Not happy at all.

Chris strode to the alarm panel, its red light flashing. And then he remembered that Daphne had offered to show him the code…and he'd said no.

He didn't know the security code for *his own house.*

Chris lifted his chin. Calm. Imperious. He lived in the wilderness. He was a bestselling author. He had an *MFA.*

He tapped random numbers on the keypad. Then he frowned, his most thoughtful, authorial frown. "How odd," he said. He tapped the same numbers.

"Mr. Remington?" the woman said.

One bead of sweat formed at his temple. "How very odd," he said, and prayed his voice sounded steady.

Uh, don't worry about that, buddy. She can't hear it over the screaming security alarm *that you cannot turn off despite it allegedly being* your house.

A blur appeared to his right. It was Daphne, running for the alarm.

"Excuse me, sir," she said, wedging between him and the panel. Her fingers flew over the keypad, and the alarm stopped.

She shook her head at Chris. "You forgot the new code, didn't you?" Without waiting for an answer, she turned to the woman. "I changed it yesterday when we had a security concern. I told Mr. Remington the new code but…" She rolled her eyes. "You know writers. He was so caught up in work that he obviously wasn't listening. Again." She passed Chris an affectionately exasperated smile.

"And that is why I have you, my dear," he said, finding his Zane voice and ignoring Tika's warning growl. "You keep me on track even when the muse steals me away." He turned to the woman. "May I introduce my incomparable and indispensable housekeeper—"

"—Dana," Daphne said. "But the person you're here to see is Mr. Remington. I'll just trot upstairs and make coffee while he dresses." She stage-whispered with a smile, "Clothing, sir. I know that brain of yours is busy plotting the next book, but you should probably put on some clothing."

She headed for the stairs. "Coffee, tea, and freshly baked muffins will be ready in twenty minutes."

DAPHNE

I'm not ready. I'm not ready at all.

As Daphne baked the prepared muffin batter, that was the refrain that kept running through her head, only to be countered with another.

You don't need to be ready.

This isn't about you.

It's Zane. It's all Zane.

And how did she feel about that? Such a good question. It was what she wanted, wasn't it? Let a professional be the center of attention while she melted into the background, freed to focus on her work. That was what she did as an architect, and it was the way she liked to work.

Write the books. Stay in the background. Let Chris do his thing.

Yet she really was putting her career in his hands, wasn't she? How much did she trust him to play Zane Remington?

Such a good question.

She'd come to trust him to do short interviews. They got the same questions on repeat, and he riffed on her database of answers.

But this was live. It was up close and personal…and he hadn't even read the damn book.

The timer went off. As Daphne grabbed the oven mitts, voices drifted in from outside.

Chris took them outside?

She should have shown him around yesterday. A fifteen-minute tour of the property so he could give the same to the crew when they arrived.

When they arrived *this afternoon.* She thought she had time.

"A target?" the interviewer—Sofia—said down below. "Ooh, looks like someone knows how to hit a bull's-eye. What kind of gun do you use, Zane?"

Daphne tripped over her feet running for the patio door. Even if Chris knew guns, he'd have no idea what kind *she* had.

"Whatever tool serves the purpose," Chris said below. "That's what guns are up here, whether it's hunting or defending. They're a tool. Never a toy."

Okay, that was a good answer. Daphne held the patio door open a crack as she eavesdropped.

"Of course," Sofia murmured. "But I'm sure our viewers would like a little insight into the tools *you* use. What's your favorite gun?"

Daphne yanked open the door, ready to call…something. Anything.

"Actually," Chris said. "This may come as a surprise, but I prefer the smaller weapons. I know, some men like them big, and I'm not going to say anything about that"—he fake-coughed into his hand while saying "overcompensation," making everyone laugh—"but I prefer the smallest weapon that will do the job. Now, if you come over here, you'll get the best view of the lake."

"In a minute," Sofia said. "Leaving guns aside for a moment, let's talk about archery. Your bio says—"

Daphne lunged out the door just as an acrid smell tickled her nose.

The muffins! Shit!

She shouted, "Coffee break!" a little too loudly and then dashed to rescue the burning muffins.

CHRIS

Was there anything better than this? Sitting on a deck, overlooking a wilderness paradise of lakes and mountains, with a mug of freshly ground coffee in one hand and a freshly baked muffin in the other? There was even a dog. Tika was stretched on the deck, panting softly as the crew tried to coax her over with muffin bits. She was having none of it, having firmly planted herself at the feet of her person. Even that only added to the perfection of the scene, a gorgeous woman with her loyal canine standing guard.

The only thing that would make this moment better?

If he could choke down a bite of the muffin or a sip of the coffee. Oh, there was nothing wrong with either. The coffee smelled incredible, and he knew from yesterday that the taste lived up to the advertising. The muffin was a little brown at the edges, but that was how he liked them.

The problem was his stomach, which had twisted into a hard knot that refused to accept even a nibble.

He'd led Daphne to believe he could pull off the macho Zane stuff, and he couldn't, and that was...

...humiliating.

Oh, he knew it shouldn't be. Knowing how to chop wood or shoot a gun wasn't a requirement for being male, but it kinda felt like it.

How did he admit he was nothing like Zane? That he hadn't even camped since he was a kid?

He'd thought he'd dodged the gun question, but it was only a matter of time before Sofia returned to it. He had to tell Daphne the truth. Now. She had to know he didn't have the experience he claimed and wasn't an actor who could even be relied upon to act the part.

He only had so many chances before Sofia realized Zane's bio was fake. That could ruin Daphne's career. If Daphne knew the truth, they could come up with a plan, one she would be—he hoped—confident that her partner was competent and self-aware enough to follow.

Let's just hope she agreed, and she didn't kick his ass out for lying.

Oh, I'm sorry, Sofia, but Zane came down with a sudden illness and won't be able to finish the interview. I hope you got enough footage.

"Zane?"

Hearing Daphne's voice, he snapped out of it, only to see everyone looking at him expectantly, which suggested someone had been saying "his" name for a while now.

"Lost in plotting again, huh?" Daphne said, rolling her eyes for Sofia. "He is such a writer."

"Occupational hazard," he said with a smile.

Sofia leaned his way. "I was just saying that I'd love to get some footage of you holding a rifle. Can we do that? Show us your guns?"

He stretched his arm out and popped his biceps, but it only got polite laughs before Sofia lasered in on him again.

"I'd like to see you handling the rifles," she said. "Talk about them, load them, maybe fire a few rounds at a target?"

Okay, he wasn't overreacting. This line of questioning wasn't going to end, and he needed Daphne's collaboration to pull it off. For the sake of her book.

Chris hid his panic with a thoughtful frown. "Is that really such a good idea?" Before Sofia could speak, he continued, lowering his voice. "*Edge* is intended for young adults. Teenagers. Yes, in the book, Theo uses firearms for survival, and at some point, we could discuss that and I could show the sort of gun she might use. But, given the intended audience, I would hate to do anything that might seem like I'm glorifying firearms."

"He has a point," Daphne said quickly. "Readers might like to see what sort of rifle Theo uses, but it really should be framed as educational. Like showing the landscape she inhabits." Daphne waved at the wilderness.

"What type of gun does she use?" Sofia said.

"A Browning composite rifle," Daphne blurted. "Which Zane has in his locker— Oh, you were asking Zane. Sorry. I'm the keeper of his series bible, and I got excited by the chance to show off."

"Yes," Chris said. "I'll show you Theo's rifle. First, though, might I suggest you get some more footage of this lovely, pristine wilderness? I'm going to help Dana tidy up."

"You don't need—" Daphne began.

He bowed. "I insist." He picked up the coffee tray and motioned for her to get the door.

DAPHNE

When they were in the kitchen, Daphne whispered, "I'm not sure we should let them wander around unsupervised. I wasn't kidding about the grizzly—"

"I need to talk to you."

She stopped as he set the coffee tray on the counter. A quick glance toward the windows showed the three-person film crew descending the steps. They wouldn't go far, would they? It'd been a few months since she'd last seen the grizzly, and it'd taken off when it heard her.

"Is it about the guns?" she said. "I'll open the safe for you and—"

"I'm an accountant."

Daphne cocked her head, certain she'd heard wrong. "You're counting on…?"

"I'm an accountant. Not an actor."

She waited for the punch line. Because there had to be one. Seeing she was stressed over this interview, he was trying to lighten the mood.

"You're…?" she began.

"A chartered accountant. Chris Stanton. I'm Nia's accountant, actually."

She was about to laugh when a memory flashed. Nia and Daphne meeting for lunch when Daphne came to town for the Surrey International Writers Conference.

"Oh, I have a new accountant," Nia had said. *"If you need one, I'd totally recommend him. Super smart. Super sweet. And hot."*

"Hot?"

"Weirdly hot. For an accountant." Nia paused, fork halfway to her lips. *"I shouldn't say that. Bad stereotyping, Nia. I'm sure there are tons of hot accountants out there."*

"*You're crushing on your new accountant?*"

"*What? No. Totally not my type. However, if you should need a new accountant . . .*" She waggled her brows. "*I could hook you up.*"

Oh God. No. Nia wouldn't.

"Daphne?" Chris said.

She clutched the counter edge, her knees wobbling as her stomach lurched.

"Nia knew . . ." she began, unable to get the rest out.

"No. I mean, she knows I'm her accountant, obviously. And she offered me a chance at the Zane job, because I kinda needed legal help. A lot of legal help."

Daphne stared at him.

"*No,*" he said emphatically. "I didn't do anything wrong. Nia wouldn't have set us up if I was some kind of criminal."

"Just if you were an accountant . . . when I needed an actor."

"I have some acting experience," he said. "Which I, uh, may have exaggerated to Nia . . . and exaggerated more to you. But Nia didn't know I was putting on a whole other persona as Chris Ainsworth. That was all me. I played the guy I thought you'd expect, because I *really* needed the job. Daphne?"

She was running for the bathroom. She made it to the toilet just in time.

"Daphne?" he said behind her.

She frantically waved for him to leave. "Stress," she mumbled, still looking at the toilet. "I stress-puke."

Yep, definitely her sexiest trait. And now she was doing it right in front of . . .

Who was she doing it in front of? She wasn't sure anymore.

Not an actor.

That was all she could think about right now. Chris wasn't an actor, and there was a film crew outside.

This was why he'd come clean. He was telling her he couldn't do this. He'd tried playing Zane—he really had been doing an amazing job—but now he was finished. Somewhere between the security-alarm drama and the firearm questions, he'd realized this was not what he'd signed up for, and he was out.

Quitting the role of Zane Remington.

While a film crew was outside, waiting to interview Zane Remington.

She leaned over the toilet again. Chris wisely retreated and shut the bathroom door.

Why couldn't he have told her yesterday, when there would have been time to cancel the interview? Or this morning, when the crew showed up early, and she could have claimed he was sick and she'd been about to call them?

This wasn't Chris's fault. Okay, it was a little, for lying to her. But also a little her fault for insisting on an actor and shutting Nia down when she suggested anything else. Nia had been working under an impossible timeline, and she knew Chris could handle it—which he had. Daphne should have trusted her.

Daphne had been so desperate to be published. She kept thinking she'd have a chance to come clean. When? Each step—getting an agent, getting a publisher, getting a huge marketing push—had been such a dream come true that she barely dared to breathe for fear of shattering it.

This was her fault for being scared and desperate, for wanting more than the universe deemed her worthy of, and now she was in so deep she couldn't get out without ruining everything, and that was exactly what she needed to do because she would not pressure Chris to stay—

The door creaked open. She turned and, as she did, she caught a glimpse of herself in the mirror, face blotchy, hair wild, eyes watering, and Chris was standing there, seeing her like this.

Which was the last thing that mattered, wasn't it?

"I'll be out in—" she started mumbling when he thrust something into her lowered field of vision. Thrust *two* things: a bottle of mouthwash and a glass of water.

Daphne's eyes teared up, which might look adorable on some women, but it just set her nose running.

"I'm sorry," she said.

He gave a laugh that sounded startled. "I think that's my line, D."

Hearing him call her by Chris Ainsworth's presumptuously assigned diminutive set her eyes burning with fresh tears. She'd hated when he called her that…until she realized she didn't really hate it at all.

"I'm sorry," he said as he pushed the water into her hand, the glass cool against her sweaty palms.

She shook her head as she took it—and the mouthwash—and turned to the sink. She used the mouthwash and drank the water and then raked her hair back, as if that would help.

"You have no reason to be sorry," she said.

"Uh, yeah, I do. I wanted to say something before the crew arrived, and then they showed up early, and I should have waited, but with all the questions I couldn't answer, I panicked. I was terrified of blowing this for you."

"I understand."

She stood facing the mirror, trying not to look at him, but still catching his face over her shoulder.

"You don't need to be so nice, D. I should have realized how stressed you were and held off on the confessional."

"This is more than you expected, and I understand why you need to quit. I'm grateful for everything you've done, and I'll handle it from here."

He blinked at her in the mirror. "Quit?"

"This is too much. You're not an actor, and this has escalated out of control. That's why you told me, right?"

"No." He laid a hand on her arm and turned her around. "No, Daphne. Not at all. I told you because I realized I need help to pull this off. You deserved to know that you didn't hire an actual actor. I got caught up in the role, but goofing around on text messages and phone calls is one thing. Being here and pretending to be someone else? Realizing I could get caught out and ruin your career? I couldn't do that."

"If you did want to quit, you're under no obligation—"

"I don't. Let's get through this interview and then discuss next steps. My priority right now is not screwing this up for you."

Her eyes filled with tears again.

"Oh, and by the way . . ." He leaned into her ear. "I totally read your book. Twice. And I cannot wait for the next one."

She burst into tears. Not just tears, but jagged sobs that came from nowhere, as if she'd been stuffing all her stress behind a wall, and it finally broke.

"Oh God, I'm sorry," she said, putting her hands over her face. "Here you are, trying to be nice, and I start ugly-crying."

"Doesn't look like ugly-crying to me. And I'm not being nice. I really did love—"

"Stop." She wagged a finger at him in mock reproval, sniffing back tears. "Keep that up, and I'll never stop crying. Apparently, I've been wound even tighter than I realized."

He pulled her into a half hug and patted her back. "You've been under a lot of strain, and this didn't help. But I *will* help. I'm not Chris Ainsworth, who might blithely say asinine things and mess this up for you. I know I'm in over my head, and I need help. But, if it's any consolation, I also know your book backward and forward. You said Theo uses a composite rifle. She has a compound bow, too, right?"

Daphne sniffled and nodded.

"See? I might barely know my rifles from my shotguns, but I know the book. We can do this. Okay?"

"Okay." She looked up at him. "Thank you."

"For being a city boy who might not know which end of a gun to hold?"

She smiled. "For being a guy who'll *admit* he doesn't know which end of a gun to hold. And who'll lie and tell me I'm not ugly-crying when…" She looked in the mirror and made a face. "Well, between that and stress-puking, it can't get any worse, right?"

He gave her another quick hug. "It'll be fine. Now, since the crew is still taking pictures of the pretty scenery, let's discuss—"

A scream reverberated through the house.

"Was that—?" Chris said.

"From outside."

Oh no. The grizzly.

CHAPTER SEVEN

CHRIS

Daphne ran for the patio door as Tika fell in beside her. At this moment, there was one—and only one—thing that Chris should be thinking about.

Holy shit, the film crew is being attacked by a grizzly!

This was not what he was thinking about. At least, not more than tangentially, as he was quite certain they were only being menaced by a grizzly, which was bad, but not the same as an active mauling.

Instead, he was thinking about Daphne, who had gone from stress-puking and stress-sobbing to charging out the door to stave off a grizzly. If he'd been the type, he might have swooned.

He was also thinking of the last time he'd made a girl cry. Seventh grade. She'd asked him to dance, and he'd said no—not because he didn't want to dance with her but because he had no idea *how* to dance. He'd found her crying in the cloakroom, which could have been the start of a very sweet middle school romance, if her friends hadn't threatened to kick the shit out of him.

Now he'd not only made Daphne cry but vomit—the latter definitely being a first, and not a proud one. He'd handled his confession all wrong. He wanted to tell her before he screwed up, and in his panic he hadn't stopped to realize he could have muddled through a little longer and found a better time.

And now there was a bear. Well, probably a bear. Was it wrong if he was thinking this might actually be a good thing? Not if the film crew got hurt, obviously, but maybe they'd decide they had enough footage and leave. Then he'd be alone with Daphne to talk about where they'd go from here. And...well, he'd be alone with Daphne.

A small grizzly scare. Was that too much to ask for?

Daphne was down the porch steps and running toward the babble of raised voices. As they raced across the open yard, Chris had the thought that he really should get in the lead. He was Zane Remington. He ate bears for breakfast.

Except...and here was where sometimes being a smart guy got in the way of masculine heroics. His brain quite reasonably told him that Daphne was the bear expert, and if he raced into the lead, he'd be the one needing rescue. Better to stay at her heels, ready to offer help and support...and screaming, if required.

Speaking of screaming...

They rounded a cluster of trees to see Sofia pressed up against a tree, babbling in terror while her two camera operators filmed. That was all Chris could see. Sofia and the crew. Not a bear—or beast—in sight.

Daphne and Chris both stopped, and Chris frowned. Were they faking an animal attack for the segment?

"Oh God." Sofia's eyes rounded as she saw Chris. "Wh-what is that thing?"

Chris followed her gaze. There, in the tree, was a lump of brown that he'd initially mistaken for a squirrel nest. When he peered at it, beady eyes peered back. A short snout opened to reveal yellowing rodent fangs.

"The porcupine?" He said the word slowly, as if she might actually be looking at a grizzly he couldn't see.

"That is *not* a porcupine. It's as big as that dog!"

Not quite, but he got her point. Including its tail, the beast was nearly three feet long.

"That's a normal-size porcupine," he said. "Maybe you're thinking of hedgehogs? They don't live in this part—"

"J-just do something. Quick. Before it shoots quills at me."

"That's a misconception. You need to get close enough for them to hit you with their tail, which can embed and release quills. If you recall that scene in *Edge*, where Theo—"

He caught Daphne's head shake. The media-training package instructed them to connect all interviewer questions to the book, but yes, this probably wasn't the time.

Chris cleared his throat. "You're far enough away—"

"N-no, it's going to attack."

He looked at the camera duo, still filming, and he briefly wondered whether this was a setup. *Novelist saves interviewer from deadly quilled rodent.* But the terror on Sofia's face seemed genuine. In that case...

"All right," he said, deepening his voice an octave and taking on his authoritative Zane tone. "I'm going to step between you and the beast, while staying out of quill range. Once I'm between you, get out of the way. If it attacks, it'll come for me."

He glanced at Daphne, who nodded her approval. As for the porcupine, he swore the critter rolled its eyes. It was just sitting in the tree, shooting them nothing except baleful looks.

"I'm coming over," he said, and then did exactly that, sidestepping with exaggerated care. "Now, while I said they need to hit you with their tail, it is possible for quills to come dislodged if they lash their tails in anger, which may give rise to the quill-shooting myth. You'll recall that's what happened in *Edge*, which was actually based on an encounter I had myself, deep in the forest. I was confronted by an entire family of porcupines intent on—" He stopped short, mostly because he had no idea where to take that story. "And now I am between you and the beast. Take two steps backward, and Dana will whisk you to safety, while I monitor for signs of attack."

Daphne sidled over as cautiously as he had. The porcupine watched her, unconcerned.

"No," Chris said for the cameras as he glared at the porcupine. "Do not look their way. Your attention is on me. I am the threat. Eyes on me."

Yep, he was pretty sure the critter was rolling its eyes. It gave one half-hearted chatter, and Chris tensed his jaw, his glower intensifying.

"None of that," he growled.

"We're clear, sir," Daphne said.

"All right. Then everyone head back to the house. I'll follow once you're all safe."

"Shouldn't you shoot it or something?" Sofia said.

The porcupine looked her way, as if affronted.

"No," Chris said firmly. "We do not shoot animals out of fear. The fear is *our* problem. This beast is on its own territory, and we are the intruders. It is leaving us in peace, and so we should do the same. Mutual respect between neighbors in our shared forest home."

Okay, that was a little over the top, but both camera operators made noises of agreement. Daphne steered them toward the house. Then she came back with Tika, who had been keeping her distance from the porcupine.

"Everyone safe?" he said.

Daphne glanced over, caught the amused twitch of his lips, and laughed softly. "Crisis averted, thanks to the fearless Zane Remington," she said.

"It was nothing, dear lady. Nothing at all." He tipped an imaginary hat to the porcupine. "You did a fine job in your supporting role. See the front desk for your SAG check."

Daphne shook her head, and they went to join the others.

DAPHNE

Okay, so the porcupine encounter was…Daphne wanted to say "ridiculous" but then, two hours later, she saw the footage and had to tip her own imaginary hat to Chris. While the raw footage would be fully edited, the magazine execs were anxiously awaiting scenes from this interview—being part of their first foray into TV—so the crew took a break to speed-edit the porcupine encounter while Daphne went inside to clean and prep lunch. When she came out, they had sample footage and it was…well, anything but ridiculous, really.

As an unpublished writer, she'd heard horror stories about the book-editing process. They're going to do terrible things to your manuscript! They'll change characters! Rewrite dialogue! Cut scenes! Alicia hadn't changed a single word—she'd only made suggestions, mostly about higher-level aspects like plot elements—and if Daphne agreed, then Daphne made the changes in her own words. Editing, she'd discovered, was a blessing, helping mold her ramblings into clean and cohesive storytelling.

That's what the camera crew had done with that raw footage. In their case, it was all cutting. Splice, splice, and resplice to turn an absurd animal encounter into a heroic rescue. In the new version, Sofia and the camera duo had been walking through the woods admiring the scenery when her male camera operator yelped "Look out!" and Sofia saw the porcupine and screamed. A split second later, Chris was there.

Skip the bits where he talked about hedgehogs and downplayed the danger. That would have ruined the tension. Instead, cut straight to him sidestepping into danger's path, while instructing and reassuring Sofia in his Zane voice. They even left in one part where he referenced the book—her publicist would be thrilled.

From there, cut to a closeup of him glaring at the chattering porcupine. Daphne'd had to bite her cheek to keep from laughing at that, but on film, it actually looked like a tense standoff. Then one final segment of Daphne's back as she herded Sofia to safety while Chris stood guard against the killer rodent.

The execs loved it. "More of this!!!" they messaged Sofia. More of what? Wander the forest looking for wildlife Zane could stare into submission?

Luckily, Sofia didn't suggest that. Sure, she'd panicked over a porcupine, but Daphne wasn't holding that against her, having seen plenty of tourists do the same.

Daphne kept hoping Chris might find time to get away from the crew so they could plot their new Zane strategy, now that she understood he was someone she *could* plot with. Which was a huge relief.

He wasn't an actor. Wasn't an asshole. Wasn't someone who never read anything longer than a fortune-cookie message.

Chris was an accountant. A sweet and smart guy who wasn't afraid to get a little silly.

He was someone she could work with. As for getting time alone, when Chris suggested helping Daphne clear up after lunch, Sofia put her foot down. Look what happened the last time he left her alone. No more of that. If she was braving the wilderness, she needed her protector.

In the afternoon, there was a book-talk interview by the lake. After the porcupine incident—when he'd proven he'd read the book—Daphne had no problem leaving that in Chris's hands. She took some downtime, prepping muffin batter for tomorrow and, yes, doing a bit of stress-cleaning.

Soon it was time for an afternoon break. Then there'd be another film segment before the crew left for the evening, and she could grill up some bison burgers while she and Chris talked.

She loaded up the coffee tray and added a plate of freshly baked cookies. Then she headed outside to the patio table where Sofia was telling the story of her first celebrity interview.

"I get home, so proud of myself for getting him to answer tough questions, and the recording was gone."

"Did you have a backup?" Chris asked.

"I was so nervous I couldn't even be sure I'd hit Record. So here I am, this amazing interview with zero proof it happened— Oh my God, do I smell cookies?"

Daphne thrust out the tray.

"You're the best, Dana," Sofia said as she snatched a cookie.

Daphne smiled. While she suspected Sofia was overdoing her enthusiasm, it was in a genuine way that didn't make Daphne feel like she was being patted on the head. Daphne might be uncomfortable playing cookies-and-coffee-bearing assistant, but the truth was that she would personally love a "Dana" of her own.

Daphne was playing a legitimate role, and Sofia's happy coffee slurping reminded her of that. It was just awkward because, well, she should be the one with a Dana. But the role reversal was her choice, and she honestly preferred hiding in the kitchen and baking cookies and mentally working through revisions. That was the weird irony of being a published author. She didn't want to entertain and charm a film crew. But she *did* want the recognition that came with having written the book.

Can't have it both ways, kiddo.

Or, maybe you could, if you'd found a way to do it that didn't involve hiring an actor-who-is-actually-an-accountant to play you.

"Sugar and caffeine to tide us all over until dinner," Chris was saying as she roused from her thoughts. "And on the topic of dinner, as your host, I should recommend a restaurant. I was thinking of…"

He trailed off, brow furrowing as he turned to Daphne. "What's that place I like, Dana?"

Ooh, nicely done. "Which one, sir? The Mexican or the Caribbean?"

"They're both excellent." He turned back to the others. "I heartily recommend either, depending on your food preferences. I think one requires reservations." Another glance Daphne's way.

"I'd recommend reservations for either, and I can do that, having the numbers—and the restaurant names—on my phone."

He smiled. It wasn't a Chris smile, she thought, with a pinprick of surprise that she could tell them apart. There was the Chris Ainsworth smile and the Chris Stanton one, and this one was pure Zane Remington. For a guy who insisted he wasn't an actor, he had his parts down pat.

Zane's smile was perfect for the role, with just the right touch of self-aware self-deprecation. The guy who pretended to be a little abashed that he couldn't remember a restaurant name, when really, he was proud of the fact he didn't have room in his brain for such trivial data.

"What would I do without you?" he said.

"Accidentally wander into that burger joint because you remember it, when the only reason you do is because you got food poisoning there the last time?"

The others laughed, and Chris added the perfect *I am such a hopeless genius* heavenward eye lift.

"So true," he said with a sigh. "Now if you could make reservations for three for, say…" He checked his watch. "Six?"

"Actually, no," Sofia said. "We are getting such good footage. I thought we'd stay and catch the sunset."

"That would be past my bedtime," Chris said. "It is the Land of the Midnight Sun, after all."

"Also the sunsets aren't great here," Daphne said. "With the mountains and all."

"Then we'll skip the sunset but use the extra hours of daylight for more filming. Let's get dinner delivered." Sofia pulled out her phone. "What app service do you use here?"

"Uh, Dana Express," Daphne said.

"Unfortunately for Dana, yes," Chris said with a smile. "We're outside the city limits. So Dana will need to order and pick up. I'll ride along with..."

He trailed off and didn't finish that sentence. Which was good. Yes, she'd love to have him along to talk, but it made no sense for him to join her. Also, she wasn't keen to leave the house with a film crew in it. While she'd hope they wouldn't snoop, she'd only done the most superficial rearranging. Her bathroom drawers still held most of her toiletries and her closet still held most of her clothing.

"Let me pull up a menu, and you can tell me what you'd like," she said. "I'll arrange pickup for six."

CHRIS

It was now eight. Dinner was eaten, and the film crew were playing the guests from hell, lingering on the flimsiest of pretenses. Sofia had said they wanted to film more, but they were still at the table, with poor Daphne inside washing dishes.

Time to be more proactive. Give them one last video opportunity, and then they could be on their way. And he knew just the thing. Oh, it wouldn't make for great television, but that was the point. Not only would it be so boring they might decide to leave, but it would give him Daphne time *without* excusing himself from the shoot.

"See those ripples on the water?" Chris said, pointing at the lake. "Fish are jumping. Perfect for a little fishing. I often do that after dinner. Dana and I row out, and we fish for tomorrow's dinner while

I contemplate nature and imagine my next scenes. We could get footage of that."

"That sounds..." Sofia began tentatively, as if hating to tell a best-selling novelist that his idea sucked.

"Sounds like a riveting segment?" Chris rose. "Agreed. You can get footage of me out on the empty lake, with the mountains reflected in the water. It's a beautiful sight, isn't it?"

"It is lovely," Sofia admitted.

"Once you have that, you can head off to your hotel without needing to wait for us to row back. Get your footage and then relax in your rooms and come tomorrow for lunch—"

"We're actually coming before breakfast. I want the morning light on the lake, and the forecast calls for mist. I thought we'd get some footage of you hunting."

He thought fast. "That's an excellent visual. However, this isn't the place for shooting more than snowshoe hares and grouse, and they're both out of season."

"There's a season for rabbit hunting?" the female half of the camera crew said, sounding rightfully dubious.

"Not officially, but people in the Yukon are very conservation minded, and this *is* breeding season." Did rabbits have a breeding season? "Now, I could take you caribou hunting, which we see Theo doing in the book, or even go after a Dall sheep." He pointed at the mountain, squinting into the sun. "Keep an eye up there for white dots. Those are the sheep."

"Sheep hunting in the mountains?" Sofia said. "That sounds incredible."

"It is, but it's also highly illegal at this time of year. Same as caribou or moose hunting. Which is why we can't do, well, any hunting, really. Now, if you really want pictures of me hunting in the morning mist, we can do the visuals. But I can't actually shoot anything. That would be wrong. Conservation is key, whether it's me or Theo in the book. Imagine what would have happened if people had hunted all the game before the zombies came. There'd be no bountiful refuge for Theo and the others. It's all about resource management. Which means we can stage a hunt, but I'm not actually going to fire a gun and risk my neighbors thinking danger's afoot."

"Fire a gun?" Daphne said, sounding alarmed as she hurried out the patio doors.

"I was saying I will *not* fire a gun," he said. "I will only pose as if I'm firing one. Tomorrow."

"Tonight he's fishing," Sofia said.

Daphne slowly turned to him.

"*We're* fishing," Chris said. "The two of us."

Panic touched her eyes, and he tried to indicate that it was okay, he knew how to fish, but that apparently wasn't a message easily transmitted in looks and gestures, because she motioned that she needed to talk to him.

"Don't worry about the dishes," he said. "The crew will be leaving as soon as they get some footage. I'll meet you at the dock after I grab life vests."

"They're in—"

"—the shed," he said with a smile. "My memory may be scattered, but I do remember that." Mostly because he'd seen them there earlier, when he'd done a frantic survey of the shed's contents. "Meet you on the dock in five."

She still hesitated, but he made little shooing motions that would be incredibly condescending coming from anyone but Zane Remington. He tried to add a reassuring smile from himself.

She was obviously worried that he was getting into something he couldn't pull off. He'd explain once they were out. He'd been on hundreds of fishing trips with his family, the last being just this past weekend. They had unlimited access to his grandparents' prized boat, and someone went out at least every other weekend in the summer, with Chris joining when he could.

After one last anxious glance, Daphne retreated into the house.

"All right," Chris said in his Zane voice. "Two life vests coming up."

He started down the stairs.

"Is that really necessary?" Sofia asked as they descended.

"Hmm?" Did she mean was it necessary to take Daphne with him? He opened his mouth to claim the boat required two people.

"Life vests," she said. "I know, safety first, but they're not exactly photogenic. I hate to be shallow but…"

"A bulky life vest will not do me any favors, especially if you're shooting from a distance. I'll look like I've been eating too many of Dana's cookies." He laughed at his own joke, even while secretly wincing. That veered dangerously close to fat-shaming, but Zane would make the joke.

"Exactly," Sofia said. "Unless you can't swim."

"I helped bring home the gold for my team in high school."

That wasn't a Zane boast. Chris had been on the gold medal–winning high school team. Okay, he'd barely made the cut, but he *was* a strong swimmer. Credit all those years of jumping off his grandparents' boat to paddle around when the fish weren't biting.

While the Chris part of him wanted to argue that they shouldn't show Zane boating without a life vest—he *was* writing for teens, after all—Zane wouldn't say that. Chris didn't need a life vest, and the lake was so small and calm that Daphne would only have them for guests. This was something he could agree to, suppressing only a small pang of discomfort.

"All right then," he said. "We will forgo the vests tonight." He peered out at the lake. "She's a sheet of glass, and there isn't another soul on her. Perfect."

He still needed to go into the shed for the fishing rods and tackle. He might not understand the differences between different guns, knives, and axes, but here he could point out that "Zane" had equipment for fly-fishing, regular angling, and deep-sea fishing. He took the correct gear box and felt rather Zane-smug for not needing to hesitate.

With the box and rods in hand, Chris strode toward the dock. The path took him to a small beach-like area, with a tiny bit of sand and a gradual walkout. The dock was off to the right, and he hadn't been that way yet, but he'd seen it, along with a kayak moored on this side and another small boat on the opposite side. It wouldn't exactly be his grandparents' cabin cruiser, but on a lake this small, you wouldn't even get up to speed with that.

Chris reached the dock and saw the second boat...which was... a canoe.

He turned to see Daphne walking over, carrying two paddles.

"You forgot these, sir," she said.

"I thought we'd take the motor boat tonight."

She laughed, the slightly-too-loud laugh that he'd come to know was her "on-screen" laugh for the crew. "Oh, you're very funny, sir." She turned to the others. "It's an in-joke. The lake is for nonmotorized vehicles only. Every now and then someone tries to get that changed to allow motorized fishing boats, but Mr. Remington leads the charge to oppose it. He's *such* a conservationist."

"Yes," he said quickly, puffing up with self-importance as he launched into Zane-pontificating mode. "No one likes the sound of motors on a quiet lake, but they also disturb the local ecosystem, particularly nesting waterfowl. The best way to enjoy streams and lakes is"—he waved at the kayak and canoe—"silently gliding along and truly enjoying nature, in all her glory."

Which presumes you have some vague idea how to operate either of those vessels.

He thought he was keeping his expression Zane-confident, but a little of his panic must have leaked out, because when she passed over the oar—paddle?—she lightly squeezed his hand.

"Now, sir," she said. "Tell me you're going to let me take the back tonight." She glanced at the crew. "The person in front just has to paddle. The one in back steers. It's the driver's seat, so to speak, and Mr. Remington really likes being in the driver's seat."

"I do," Chris said with a blazing smile that was relief. "However, having written a book with a very capable female protagonist, I would be the last person to suggest that I should drive by sheer dint of being male. Dana is, dare I admit it, an even better paddler than I am."

"You're too kind, sir." Daphne looked around. "Seems like the paddles weren't the only thing you forgot. Weren't you getting the life vests?"

"We decided against them," Sofia cut in. "Now, if everyone is ready…"

Chris moved past Daphne, who was holding the canoe steady. As she'd pointed out—allegedly for Sofia—the front person got in first.

As Chris moved past Daphne toward the bow, he whispered, "I really can fish, D. And swim. It'll be okay."

She still looked worried. Maybe she hadn't heard him? They'd talk more once they were out of the crew's earshot.

He sat on the front seat and glanced back. Daphne gave a tight nod, which he hoped meant he was sitting correctly. Had he ever been in a canoe before? He wasn't sure. If he had, it was so long ago he didn't remember anything about it.

As Daphne arranged herself, the crew switched on the cameras. Chris had requested they film Dana only from the back or a great distance "for her privacy."

Chris looked at the nearest camera and said, "Like many lakes in the Yukon, this is a glacial one. That means a glacier eroded the land and then melted. You may have noticed in *Edge* that Theo usually camps along a lake like this, for fishing and fresh water and, if it's not winter, a quick swim for bathing." He reached over the side to touch the water. "And I do mean quick." An exaggerated shiver. "Glacial lake, glacial temperatures."

It actually wasn't that bad. He wouldn't exactly be leaping off the dock for a morning dip, but he wouldn't die of hypothermia if he fell in. And on that note, the entire purpose of his little speech had been to avoid falling in...because talking to the camera gave him the chance to watch how Daphne sat and how she used her paddle.

"I suppose I should help," he said, loud enough for the cameras to hear.

"Heaven forbid," Daphne said. "You just sit there and talk, sir. You're better at that anyway."

He rolled his eyes dramatically, took one last look at how she operated her paddle before he twisted around in his seat.

Hold it like this, one hand above the other, with a gap between them. Move from the shoulders and waist, dipping the paddle in and out.

Soon they were flying through the still water, and he'd love to think that was him, but he wasn't the only one in this canoe with some serious muscles.

They were about a hundred feet from shore when Sofia shouted, "We forgot to mic you!"

Her voice carried easily in the silence of the lake, but Chris pretended he couldn't hear and only waved, as if she were wishing them bon voyage.

They kept paddling until they were finally far enough, and Daphne slowed her strokes.

"Time for a little demonstrative fishing?" he said, reaching back for the rod. "If you keep her steady, I'll handle this part. I really *can* fish."

"That's great," she said. "However, you're missing a key component of the required equation, *sir*."

He glanced down quickly. No, he had the rod and the tackle box, and he'd confirmed the box contained hooks and lures.

"Fish," she said.

"Hmm?"

"You need fish. That's what I was trying to tell you. There aren't any game fish here."

As if on cue, a fish jumped from the water to catch a flying insect.

"Leaping lake lizard?" he said.

"Oh, it's a fish. A little grayling. There are some out here, but not many of the proper size."

"But I saw people out this afternoon. With fishing rods."

"And beer," she said, stretching her legs. "People *do* fish in this lake. They just don't expect to catch anything. Putter around. Have a beer. Chat with your buddy. Enjoy a gorgeous afternoon while pretending you're doing something productive."

"Uh…"

"Yep. That's why I wanted to discuss it."

He winced. "I thought you were concerned that I didn't know how to fish. Okay. So…" He looked around. "Even if I did manage to snag one of those little guys, they won't see it from the shore."

"Yep."

"Would lures even work on them?"

"Nope."

"So I'm screwed?"

"Yep."

"Great." He slumped onto his seat. "Footage of the mighty Zane Remington getting skunked." He glanced over. "Hey, maybe I can use that. I'll say I got skunked, make a joke of it, and then use the opportunity to point out that there are no actual skunks around here. Self-deprecation plus a pompous Zane lecture moment."

"You *are* good at those."

"Notice how I slip in references to the book? Media Training 101."
She smiled at him. "I noticed. Thank you."

"See? We can pull this off." He looked around. "Except when I fail to check whether there are actual fish in the lake before I suggest fishing. Or when I fail to ask whether you have a motorboat."

Another warm smile. "You're doing fine. Here's my suggestion. We paddle around a bit to give them scenic shots. Then we go back, and you say you surveyed the situation and realized the fish aren't as active tonight as it appeared."

"The water is so clear I can see the lack of fish. Notice how clean the water is? That's what a nonpolluted lake looks like, blah, blah. Drawing on my vast experience of wilderness living—which I used in my book, *At the Edge of the World*—I can tell that fish are not forthcoming, blah, blah. Got skunked. No actual skunks in the Yukon, however, that reminds me of the time I encountered one out east."

"You really are good at this. Let me get us turned around, and we'll hug the western shoreline for the best shots. You play human fish-finder while I navigate."

He saluted. "Aye-aye, Captain."

Chris settled into his front seat and peered over one side and then the other, shading his eyes for added effect. The water really was clear enough to see all the way down, including the odd fish that was, as Daphne said, barely bigger than a minnow.

He was leaning over when a gun fired on shore. He nearly fell into his seat and then rocked forward, hands going behind his neck.

"Is that the crash position for planes?" Daphne said.

He glared at her.

"Sorry," she said, smiling. "It was really cute, though. You have excellent reflexes...even if it's slightly less than situationally appropriate."

"Hey, you never know. I might have ducked just enough to save me from being hit in the head by stray rifle fire."

"That was a beaver."

"Someone's shooting *beavers?*"

The corners of her mouth twitched. When she saw he was serious, she coughed, as if to erase the smile. "No, the sound you heard was a beaver tail hitting the water."

"Someone dropped a beaver from a plane? See, I wasn't wrong, assuming the crash position."

She hesitated, until he smiled to tell her he *was* joking this time.

"Beavers slap the water to warn of danger," he said. "You know where I read that? In my book, *At the Edge of the World*. I'm such a genius."

"Not if you need to read the book *you* wrote in order to learn things."

"Don't mock my memory issues. That's mean."

She shook her head.

"So that was a beaver," he said, peering around. "Warning its family about us, I presume?"

"Possibly. See the dam over there?" She pointed to what he sheepishly realized he'd mistaken for a random pile of branches. "There's another over by my place."

"That is so cool. I've never seen a beaver in the wild."

Silence. Then she choked on a laugh.

He replayed what he'd said. "Hey." He jabbed the paddle her way. "No beaver jokes."

"You started it. Never seen one in the wild, huh? Only on your computer screen?"

"Are you judging my love of nature movies, woman? They're very informative. Did you know that, in its natural environment, the beaver displays an unusual affinity for bikers and pizza-delivery boys?"

The laugh started at a sputter and then became a snorting wheeze, as Daphne covered her mouth with one hand.

"It also—" he began.

"Stop."

"You started it. Now—" He twisted fast as he caught sight of something moving in the water. "Holy shit, is that a beaver?"

"Ha-ha."

"No, seriously."

The large shape swam right under the boat, and Chris lunged to watch it come out the other side. He didn't think. He just moved—fast. The canoe started to tip.

"Chris!"

He did the logical thing. Or what his brain screamed was the logical thing. If the canoe was tipping, the obvious way to fix that was simple physics. Redistribute weight.

He instinctively reacted, and he had 0.5 seconds to be very proud of that before the bottom slid under his feet as the canoe tipped the other way. He didn't have time to recover. He'd jumped backward, and so when his feet slid, he also *tumbled* backward, flipping the entire canoe with him.

CHAPTER EIGHT

DAPHNE

Daphne hit the water. Her first thought was no thought at all. The shock of the cold slammed everything from her brain. That lasted only a moment. Then water closed over her head, and she was five again, shoved into the deep end, the water closing over her head.

I can't swim!

That was what she'd screamed then, water filling her mouth and lungs. It was what her brain screamed now.

I can't swim.

No, it was okay. She was wearing a life vest. She always wore one, even in this calm lake, because she *couldn't* swim.

Then a memory flashed. Climbing onto the canoe without a vest, too embarrassed to say anything. It was just the lake. She'd be fine.

She was not fine.

She told Chris that she'd steer near the shore for a better view. That was a lie. She'd wanted to stick to the edge because it was shallow. Yet she hadn't reached that yet, and her kicking feet touched nothing below.

Go up.

That was what the swim instructor taught her, the private one her mom hired trying to at least teach her water safety, but Daphne had been so terrified she hadn't made it past the second lesson. Still she remembered this much: get her head up and tread water. She *could* tread water.

Chris was there, somewhere, and the film crew was watching. She wasn't going to drown. Just get her head up—

Her head struck something hard. Panic flared. She must have gotten turned around, gone down instead of up—

No, she *had* gone up. She knew that. Something was over her head, pinning her down. She reached up and her hands whacked into something smooth and curved.

The canoe. She was *under* the canoe.

She smacked her fists up. The canoe was fiberglass. It wouldn't sink. She should be able to breathe under it. But if there was a gap of air, she couldn't find it and her lungs burned, her brain screaming that she needed oxygen, needed it *now*.

She punched again, as if she could propel the canoe up, but her hands only smacked against the fiberglass. If she couldn't touch down, then she couldn't get the leverage to push the canoe up.

Swim out from under it.

How?

She tried to corral her thoughts, but they ran wild, her lungs ready to explode. She was five again, under the water, screaming, the world going black—

Something grabbed her. The current, weeds, *something* pulled her under. She screamed then for real, water filling her mouth and then—

Light. It was suddenly light, and she could breathe, gasping in mouthfuls of air.

"I've got you," a voice said.

Warm arms tightened around her.

"I've got you."

Chris.

I've got you. Her eyes filled, tears scorching hot against her freezing skin.

"You're okay," he said. "We're almost there."

Something brushed under her kicking feet. She could barely feel her feet, numbed from the cold, but she knew she was touching sand and rock as her body lifted from the water. Then wet moss and more sand against her back as Chris set her on the shore.

She was lying on her back, looking up, and when Chris leaned over her, the setting sun haloed his head, turning his dark blond hair to the bright gold of an angel. Her gaze settled on his wide lips.

Couldn't she have drowned just a little more? Enough to require mouth-to-mouth resuscitation?

Really? That was what she was thinking after nearly dying?

She blamed oxygen deprivation.

"I . . . I can't swim," she said. "In case . . . case you didn't . . . figure that out."

Those wide lips curved, the smile not reaching his worried eyes. "I'm so sorry, D."

"I should—should have mentioned it."

"And I should have asked."

He reached down to hug her, the heat of him coming through his drenched shirt, like a blazing fire after a long night of snowshoeing, and she fell into his arms, shivering.

"That was great," came Sofia's voice from the distance. "At first, I was like, mmm, a bit much, staging the canoe capsizing, dramatic rescue, but that end part? You coming out, soaking wet, with Dana over your arms? That was . . ."

Sofia trailed off, as if she'd drawn close enough for a better look.

Daphne choked and sputtered, turning her head to one side as she retched up lake water. Then she started shivering again, this time convulsively.

"Oh my God!" Sofia said. "You didn't stage—"

Chris scooped Daphne up. "We need to get her in the house. *Now*."

CHRIS

"Alone at last," Chris said.

Daphne looked over at him from the deck chair—where she was completely cocooned in blankets, propane heater blazing at her feet, mug of cocoa in one hand, towel wrapped around her wet hair—and she laughed. At first, it was a choked half laugh. Then it got louder and she started snorting. Her hand flew over her mouth in that adorable way it did when she thought—incorrectly—that her snorting laughs were *less* than adorable.

Daphne was fine. Thank God. He didn't even want to think about what could have happened. When he'd dumped a shot of Irish whiskey into her cocoa, he might have added some to his as well, to banish the memory of that moment when he'd surfaced, looked for her, and seen an empty lake. That moment when he realized he'd turned down life vests for *both* of them.

"Chris?" she said.

He took a burning gulp of booze-laced chocolate. "Never thought we'd get rid of them. Sure, staging a drowning might have gone too far, but they just weren't leaving. Film crews."

This time, she didn't laugh. Didn't even smile.

"You saved my life," she said.

He started to make a joke about her saving *his* life, this job having rescued his professional career, but it'd be as poor a joke as the film crew one.

He *wanted* to joke. Make light. Make her laugh. Especially make her laugh.

Instead, he said, "I wouldn't have needed to if I hadn't agreed to skip the life vests."

"And, being an adult, I should have insisted on one for myself."

He understood why she didn't. For the same reason he'd pretended he knew how to chop wood. No one wants to admit to what they perceive—or worry others might perceive—as a failing. A guy not knowing how to chop firewood. An outdoor enthusiast who can't swim.

"We need a signal," he said.

"For . . . ?"

"'Ack! I need to talk to you! Now!' Which you did try to give me. So a signal plus a pact that we'll listen and not presume we know what the other person means, like me thinking you were just concerned I couldn't fish, when you were trying to tell me there *were* no fish."

"And a pact that we will signal, even if it means admitting to something embarrassing, like not knowing how to swim."

"I—" he began, and then made a face. "I was going to say I could teach you, but then I realized that if you live on a lake and don't swim, there's probably a reason."

She shrugged. "No huge trauma. Just something when I was a kid. First day of swimming lessons I got pushed in, and no one noticed until I passed out."

"Oh, is that all?" he said. "Nearly dying? Not traumatic at all."

"It wasn't like that. Not really." She pulled up her knees, hugging them with one arm. "Okay, a little, but mostly because it happened a few days after my dad walked out."

His breath caught, and when she glanced over, she was scrunching her nose in an expression that could seem like distaste, but he'd come to know was self-consciousness. She'd cracked open her door more than she intended to, revealing a vulnerability she'd rather keep hidden.

"It was fine," she said. "He was an ass, and we were better off without him."

Chris clamped back a reply. He wasn't a therapist, but even he was sure having a shitty father walk out still left a lasting dent in your psyche. Pairing that with a near drowning would explain why she didn't swim. In her place, he might not have even been able to live on a lake.

He sipped his hot chocolate, looked into the flames, and considered his next move. She'd opened up a little, and he really wanted to know more. Did he dare nudge that door? Zane would shove it open. Chris Ainsworth would just casually stroll in, as if he hadn't noticed it'd been closed. Chris Stanton would hover on the other side, frozen in uncertainty.

Maybe it was time to borrow from Zane and Ainsworth. Just a smidgen.

"I think you said you grew up in BC, right?" he said as offhandedly as he could. This wasn't exactly top secret data, he reminded himself. Just normal conversation between two people sitting on a deck, sharing cocoa and a fire and a setting sun. "Is your mom still there?"

A pause. Such a long pause. Okay, maybe it wasn't top secret data for most people, but Daphne wasn't most people. He'd overstepped.

He caught her expression, and his heart dropped.

"Oh," he said. "She's…" He struggled for a word. "Gone."

"Four years ago. Cancer." Daphne's fingers kneaded the blanket. "We had some warning. Time to do everything she wanted. Not enough time, but…"

She shrugged. Then she abruptly stopped kneading the blanket, and he was ready for a quick change of subject, but she smiled and said, "She's the one who convinced me to move up here after she was gone. I'd been in the Yukon on a project. I won the contract to design a government building. A small one. But still, I got to spend two seasons here and fell in love."

"You're an architect?"

She frowned at him. Then she made a face. "I never even mentioned that, did I? Sorry. I don't mean to be all secretive. If it's not something I have in common with Zane, it just wasn't important for you to know it. Yes, I'm an architect by trade. I run my own business, and I haven't taken on new projects since selling *Edge*, but I haven't quit, either. Writing isn't usually a forever job. Anyway, Mom knew I loved it here and encouraged me to buy property. I got lucky and found this."

"Did you..." He looked at the house. "Did you design *this* house?"

That shrug, pushing off anything that might lead to a compliment.

"Wow," he said. "That is—"

"Mom also encouraged me to write Theo's story."

Chris bit his cheek to keep from laughing at the way she dove into the topic change, like swerving to avoid an out-of-control eighteen-wheeler. If starting a compliment got her to switch tracks to other personal things, he was going to need to do that more often.

Still, the little she had revealed about the house told him something—that living up here was no temporary whim. The Yukon was her dream place, and she'd moved up here and built her dream home. That wasn't temporary.

Shit. He didn't want to think about what it meant for the hope of a committed relationship, and committed was the only way he was doing this. That wasn't selfishness, either. It was the dawning acknowledgment that a fling with Daphne would leave a bigger hole than if he'd never scratched that itch, because it was an itch that went a whole lot higher than his boxers.

He shook off that thought. She'd given him a chance to pursue a personal conversation, and he wasn't going to miss out on it.

"Your mom knew about *Edge?*" he said.

Daphne nodded. "It was a little different back then. The main character wasn't named Theo. And I wasn't writing it down. It was just a story I was telling Mom to get her through chemo. She made me promise to write it, which is why..."

Daphne turned away, looking over the lake.

"Why it's so important to you," he said softly.

"It is. Theodora was Mom's middle name. I've written other things, stories I thought were more likely to get published. Young adult postapocalyptic zombie novel? No one buys those these days. But I kept coming back to Theo. Not just for Mom, but because this was the story that spoke to me." Daphne lifted her mug. "How much booze did you put in this?"

"Why? You want more?"

She laughed and then said, "Actually, I might."

She started to rise, and then he lifted a thermos from under his blanket and passed it over.

"You're one step ahead of me," she said. "Thank you."

As she poured more spiked cocoa, he said, "So you moved up here after your mom passed. Any siblings back home?"

She shook her head. "It was just me and Mom. I have grandparents, all still living, all great, including my father's parents. He's in Asia or something. I haven't seen him in years. But his parents are wonderful to me, and they were wonderful to Mom. It's not their fault their son grew up to be an asshole." She passed back the thermos. "And you? Your family?"

Now he was the one shrugging. "Mom, Dad, older sister, two grandparents."

She peered at him. "I won't prod if you don't want to talk about them, but I hope you aren't holding back because *I'm* a little lacking in the immediate family department."

"Maybe. Sorry. They're great. Well, all except my sister. Gemma's a pain in the ass." He smiled over. "Kidding. Mostly. We're close. In fact, I just saw everyone last weekend, when we went fishing. Which I do know how to do, though admittedly it's a little different in the Pacific Ocean."

She smiled. "Just a little." She curled up, hands cupping her mug. "Tell me about it."

DAPHNE

She had made up her mind. She was going to have a fling with Chris. Well, if he wanted one, obviously, and she suspected she was being optimistic even thinking she had a chance at that.

Yes, she'd told herself—repeatedly—that she wasn't emotionally capable of hookups, but maybe she was overreacting. Maybe it was a matter of finding the right guy, one she could trust. Chris seemed like he could be that guy.

As for more than a fling, she absolutely was not ready for that. She'd finally gotten her life on track after her mom's death, and it was more than "on track." She was living out her dreams, and she needed to get herself steady in that before she even thought of adding another dream. Especially when *that* dream—the one of someone to share her life—could destroy the rest. Finding someone willing to move up here and endure the strange lifestyle of an off-the-grid-living novelist? That was too tall an order. Maybe someday. Not now.

"More than a fling" wasn't an option anyway. Chris was out of her league.

Nia would give her shit for thinking that, but Daphne wasn't being modest. It was an objective fact, like when a prospective client offered her an architecture job and she had to acknowledge that she didn't have the skills—yet—to manage something that complex. There was reaching for the stars . . . and then there was telling someone you can get that star for them.

Chris was the whole package. Gorgeous, sweet, smart, and funny. Maybe someday he'd meet his perfect match—a neurosurgeon who'd modeled her way through med school—but until then, he was building his career and enjoying all the benefits that came with being a hot single guy in a big city. Couldn't blame him for that.

But while she knew she wasn't long-term partner material for him, her self-confidence was strong enough to know she was "weekend fling" material.

She'd been celibate far too long, and the more time she spent with Chris, the more she realized how badly she needed some fun. Safe, no-strings-attached fun.

If he made a move, she'd let him know that door was open. Wide open.

CHRIS

After staying on the deck until dark, Chris slept like the dead, not rising until sun blazed through the window, and he realized he'd forgotten to draw the blinds. He leapt up, certain he'd overslept and the crew would be there any moment.

It was six thirty.

Wide awake, he lay in bed, debating whether he could slip out and start coffee quietly enough when he caught the click of Tika's nails on the stairs and peeked out to see Daphne creeping silently toward the coffeemaker.

An hour later, they were deep into a walk with Tika, slurping coffee from travel mugs as they wandered along a lakeside trail. The water was absolutely still and veiled in lacy fog. Chris was resisting the urge to send photos to his parents and Gemma. He would, eventually. They knew he was "up north" for a few days "with friends." Nothing wrong with photos.

He hadn't been concerned that his family might accidentally see a picture of him as Zane Remington and recognize him. But now…well, now it was getting a little more complicated, with this TV segment and the media attention the book was getting. He still wasn't *too* worried. Zane didn't act or sound like Chris Stanton, and his clothing and hairstyles were totally different.

He should discuss all this with Daphne. For now, he was too busy enjoying walking and talking with her, surrounded by landscape where every turn looked like a postcard.

What would it be like to live here? He remembered what Daphne said about coming up and falling in love. He got it, he really did. The problem was that his life was in Vancouver, both personal and professional, and he wasn't ready to give that up, no more than Daphne would be willing to give up her dream home.

What about living here part-time? Could he telecommute? Contrary to Daphne's claims, she had both good satellite internet and good cell service.

What are you doing, buddy?

Thinking.

Maybe you should, I don't know, ask her out before you make plans to move in.

But he was an accountant after all. He considered all the factors. He knew what he wanted, and he had to be sure it worked before he chased it. What he *wouldn't* do was rush. No woman wanted a guy positioning himself as a friend, only to make the leap to more two seconds later.

Anything worth doing was worth doing right. And Daphne McFadden was definitely worth doing right.

Er, no, that didn't come out correctly either.

Still, not untrue.

Chris took a quick sip of his coffee and then cleared his throat. "So, what's it like up here in the winter?" he asked. *Seriously? Why not just ask if she has an extra closet and a spare set of keys?*

"Cold," she said with a smile. "But I like it better than the lower mainland, actually. I'm not good with the Pacific Northwest's idea of winter."

"Rain, rain, and more rain? Gray skies and icy drizzle?" He actually didn't mind the gray and mild winter.

"Yep. I prefer snow and sunshine. Once you have the snow, it doesn't feel that cold if you bundle up. Short days, but I kind of like that, too. It's like part-time hibernation—spend my mornings and evenings writing and reading by a roaring fire and my afternoons getting out and enjoying the snow."

"Winter sports?"

She nodded. "Up here, minus twenty doesn't keep people indoors." She waved at the lake. "I can hike or ski or snowshoe across it and visit areas I can't reach by foot in the summer. I'm thinking of biking across this winter, so I can go further."

"Biking?"

"With fat tires, of course. Winter doesn't keep Yukoners from their bikes. And then there are the sled-dog teams. They cross a few times a day."

"Sled dogs? That'd be cool." He looked at Tika, quietly wandering along the lake edge. "Do you pull sleds, girl?"

"She does. For me, at least. Sometimes for practicality—hauling wood. Sometimes just for fun. You should see her pulling me on a toboggan across the lake, running as fast as she can, loving it as much as I do. It's…" Daphne blushed, as if she'd shown undue enthusiasm. "It's fun."

"It sounds awesome. Can you clear the ice and skate?"

"Sure, there are always patches cleared for hockey—"

Tires crunched gravel. It sounded less than twenty feet away, but after nearly two days at Daphne's house, he'd learned that sound meant someone was driving down the mountain, hundreds of feet away.

When the crunching gravel got louder, he checked his watch.

"They're early again," Daphne said.

"Damn."

"Yep."

She straightened, relaxed-Daphne sliding away as she shifted into efficient-Dana mode.

Chris sighed, gulped his coffee, and pulled the glasses from his pocket. The crew's rental truck engine died, its doors squeaked, and he squared his shoulders and headed through the last hundred feet of forest to meet them.

Daphne didn't hurry to catch up. Enjoying the last moments of peace. He couldn't blame her. It had been such a nice morning…until they showed up.

Ahead he made out the distant shape of a figure. The male camera operator was a beefy, middle-aged guy with sandy brown hair. He must have gotten out of the truck early to snap a few shots of the lake through the trees.

"Morning," Chris called, just as Tika's low growl wafted from the lakeside.

Yep, don't blame you for that either, pup. Such a nice morning, interrupted.

"Chr-Zane!" Daphne called, and the alarm in her voice made him wheel. She seemed to be jogging toward him, but he couldn't see more than her shoulder and hip behind a tree. That's when he heard a low huff behind him and turned around as the bulky figure stepped from the shadows.

Chris looked up, way up, and realized this was absolutely not the cameraman. Even then, his brain didn't fully process what he was seeing. Brown hair. Huge shoulders, thick with fat and muscle as the figure moved with rolling steps, massive arms hanging down.

Massive *paws* with massive curved claws.

Chris lifted his gaze past six feet, past seven feet, at least eight feet in the air to look into the broad face of a...

"Grizzly," he whispered.

CHAPTER NINE

DAPHNE

She'd reacted too slowly. When it came to wildlife that could kill you, any reaction was always too slow.

Now the grizzly stood right in front of Chris, close enough that he could reach out and touch it, and he was frozen there, staring up at a thousand-pound brown bear.

For its part, the grizzly just stood there. Stood and considered, nostrils twitching as it processed the data its nearsighted eyes didn't provide.

Daphne kept her gaze fixed on the grizzly's face. Chris was too close to turn and run—and was making no move to do that, thankfully, because unless you were Usain Bolt, you were not outrunning a grizzly.

What mattered now was the bear's reaction. So far, it had none.

Daphne was watching but also listening. Alert for signs of agitation. A curled lip, a huff, a licking of the lips, a popping of the jaw.

The grizzly just stood there, towering over Chris.

I don't have my bear spray.

Her mouth opened to say exactly that, but she shut it fast. Do not tell Chris what she *didn't* have.

Everything. I damn well lack everything. It was a walk around the property.

Tika didn't even have her bell on. Daphne had removed it so it wouldn't clang in the background while filming, and she hadn't bothered putting it back on this morning.

Daphne wasn't sure that would have mattered. They'd been talking. The bear should have heard them. It must have been focused on its scratching post and maybe on the sound of the crew's truck.

As for the crew, thankfully, they must not have heard Chris and headed for the house.

"Don't do anything." That was what she said, when she finally found her voice.

Chris gave a shaky laugh. "Not planning to."

"You're okay. It isn't showing any signs of aggression."

"And if it does?"

She swallowed. What did she say to that?

You're three feet from a grizzly, Chris. Unarmed. Even if you had a gun, you're too close.

"The eyes," she said. "Go for the eyes."

Which was bullshit, but she had to say something.

She cleared her throat. "I'm going to come closer."

"What? No. Take Tika and get somewhere safe."

If she could have laughed at that, she would have. Very noble, but yeah, that wasn't happening.

"I want it to see you aren't alone," she said. "It's considering the situation, and it doesn't feel threatened so far, which is good. It's the wrong season for it to be hungry—plenty of food around and too early to be preparing for hibernation. We just need to politely show it that you aren't alone, in case it gets any ideas."

Chris didn't answer. He kept looking up at the grizzly, but his stance was firm and solid, and that helped.

"Think tough," she said. "Think Zane."

Still no response. He was busy focusing instead of talking. Good. She tapped her leg, telling Tika to follow, though the dog was already glued to her side. Tika was growling steadily, which was good. Growling was a calm warning, meaning she didn't see immediate danger, either.

As they moved forward, the bear's nostrils widened. Daphne tensed, but the bear didn't huff or lick its lips. It smelled Daphne and Tika getting closer and assimilated the data. Its gaze shifted, just enough to take them in as Daphne drew within a few feet of Chris. She stopped. The bear swung its attention back to Chris, and she tensed again.

"Step back," she murmured. "Ease in our direction and give it room to leave."

He started to move, and the bear began twisting away. Good. It just needed a clear exit route—

"Oh my God!" a voice squeaked.

Everything in Daphne clenched. The film crew. They must have been coming through the forest, not realizing what was happening, and now they were going to spook the bear into attack.

Except the bear did no such thing. It thumped down onto all fours and began walking in the other direction. Not exactly running off in terror, but ambling purposefully, like Daphne spotting a threatening figure in a dark parking lot.

Fleeing? No, I'm just making my way in this direction, which is where I was headed anyway.

She exhaled in relief and turned to Chris, who stood frozen in shock. Then, seeing her, he put out his arms, and she didn't think twice. She fell into them, exhaling as she whispered, "You did great."

He gave another shaky laugh and patted her back. "No, that was all you."

"Oh my God!" Sofia said again, closer now, and Daphne jumped out of Chris's arms.

Sofia gaped at him. "Did you just stare down a grizzly bear?"

"What? No—"

Daphne shot him a quick look and mouthed *Take it.*

Chris still hesitated, but when she firmed that look, he gathered his Zane cloak around him and straightened.

"Are you all right?" he said to the crew. "That must have been quite a shock for you."

Daphne bit the inside of her cheek, but Sofia only gazed up at him, doe-eyed.

"You saved our lives," she said. "All of us. You *stared down* a grizzly."

A hearty laugh with just enough false self-deprecation. "Oh, I wouldn't say—"

"You did. We saw it. You were between Dana and the bear, and you scared it off by just staring at it."

Chris hesitated, and Daphne realized how it must have looked from Sofia's angle, coming up behind them. Daphne nodded for Chris to take the credit.

"We frightened the poor creature," he said. "It was curious, and it only needed to be told—with a firm and unflinching look—that we were not easy targets, should it be a bit peckish. It is breakfast time after all." He laughed at his own joke. "And on that note, what do we all say to breakfast? I, for one, am starving. Early-morning bear encounters will do that."

"You feel like you could eat a bear?" the female camera operator said with a smile.

"Exactly. But I would settle for coffee and Dana's fresh-baked muffins."

CHRIS

Chris was in the bedroom dressing for the first video segment. Earlier he'd been wearing comfortable lightweight pants—suitable for outdoor rambles—and a form-fitting T-shirt, suitable for showing off his assets to Daphne. If she was interested in seeing them, that is. He still wasn't sure on that part.

For the shoot, he'd wear expensive cargo shorts and an even more expensive flannel shirt. Who knew flannel could *be* expensive? He wasn't even sure anyone watching would know the difference, but the clerk at the trendy "gorpcore" store assured him it made a difference. Of course, given that the store catered to young Vancouverites who only wore their gorpcore fashion to the office, he suspected it wasn't actually suitable for climbing mountains. In other words, Daphne wouldn't wear this shirt. Even Zane probably wouldn't. But it was what people would *expect* a guy like Zane to wear, so he'd bought it.

He was shaking out the shirt, wondering if he should iron it—do you iron flannel?—when a knock came at the door. The crew was outside eating their morning meal, with Daphne having added egg sandwiches to the menu.

She must be clearing plates and checking on him while she was inside. They hadn't had time to talk since the bear encounter, and he really wanted to. His heart stuttered every time he thought of it.

A grizzly bear. Right in front of him.

"Come in," he called.

The door opened as he gave the flannel shirt another shake, assessing.

"Good timing," a voice said...and that voice was not Daphne's.

He wheeled to see Sofia.

He started to apologize for welcoming her in when he wasn't dressed. Then he realized Zane would not apologize...and she really didn't seem to mind.

"Hello there," he said, taking his voice down an octave as he offered a lazy smile. "I'm trying to decide whether this shirt will work on camera." He lifted it in front of him.

"Is there an option for leaving it off?" she said.

He laughed his hearty Zane laugh. "Sadly, I fear I have little excuse for walking around bare-chested for this morning's shoot."

She moved closer. "On a more serious note, Zane, I wanted to thank you for saving my life."

"Er…" He coughed and gave a solemn nod. "It was nothing. Really."

"No, it was. I keep trying to focus, but all I can think about is that bear. It was"—she shuddered—"huge. And those claws."

"The danger, truly, was minimal. I surprised it."

"So you aren't still freaked out *at all*? Your adrenaline isn't still pumping?"

He hesitated and went for some honesty. "It was nerve-rattling."

She stopped right in front of Chris, and he had to cement his feet in place. Stepping away was definitely not a Zane move.

Maybe she was just getting close to say something she didn't want the others hearing.

Her hand touched his hip, and she moved up against him, face lifting to his.

Oh shit.

Chris Stanton would gently remove her hand, step back, and make an awkward joke. Zane…well, Zane would go for it, but that was out of the question. He needed to refuse without any risk of insulting or embarrassing Sofia. Make the wrong move, and she could retaliate by ruining the segment. Which was *Daphne's* segment. Her book. Her career.

A laugh sounded beyond the door. The male camera operator's booming laugh.

Chris straightened fast, eyes going wide. "Did you hear that?" he said.

Sofia's hands slid up his bare sides.

"Bear!" he said, stumbling out of her reach. "The bear is back."

He didn't hear what she said. Didn't see her expression. He was already running.

He yanked open the door.

And Daphne was standing right there. In the dining room area. Walking to the kitchen with a stack of dishes. She turned and saw him coming out of her bedroom. *Running* out, half naked, with Sofia following.

"Bear!" he said, because it was all he could think to say. "I heard the bear. We need to get the shotgun. Now!"

He grabbed the plates from her, clattered them onto the table, took her arm, and ran for the patio doors.

DAPHNE

Daphne didn't remember going onto the deck or down the stairs. All she saw was that moment when her bedroom door flew open, Chris standing there, shirtless, with Sofia reaching for him.

Chris must have heard her come into the house. He'd been in the bedroom with Sofia, heard the dishes rattle as she carried them, and he'd panicked and ran out.

Ran out yelling something about... a bear?

It was so absurd that she wanted to laugh. Instead, she felt as if she was going to be sick. Chris had been in her bedroom with Sofia.

Her stomach lurched.

Sofia was a beautiful woman who was obviously attracted to Chris, and what they did was none of Daphne's business. She wasn't thirteen, seeing the boy she liked kissing another girl and wanting to let the air out of their bike tires. In the adult world, "liking" someone is a million miles from a relationship.

Grow up.

Except she *was* grown up, and part of being grown up was that you didn't fool around in your host's bedroom. You didn't fool around with the woman who was interviewing you for a segment *about your host*. A segment that was a huge deal to that host, which you could destroy because you wanted to get in a little—

Oh God, she was going to puke.

Well, at least you didn't walk in on them while they were—

Definitely puking.

The world went dark, and for a second, she thought she'd actually doubled over. Then she realized they were in the shed. Chris turned her around, lightly holding her wrists.

"Nothing happened," he blurted. "I know what it looked like, but nothing happened."

Because you heard someone coming and realized you hadn't locked the door.

"It's fine," she said coolly. "I wouldn't have walked in."

"What? No. Nothing was *going* to happen." His words spilled out almost too fast for her to keep up. "I was putting on my shirt, and I thought it was you knocking, only it was Sofia and she..." He took a deep breath, and even in the dim light, she could see him going red. "She came on to me. I said I heard the bear and ran."

"Bear?"

He threw up his hands. "It was the only thing I could think of."

She looked up into his face and burst out laughing.

He mock-glared at her. "I blanked, okay."

"And then dragged me out here to get the shotgun?"

Another wild toss of his hands. "I don't always think well under pressure."

"You could have turned her down gently. No need to drag in the poor grizzly."

"Yeah, I turn her down, and she gets embarrassed—or pissed

off—and suddenly the show doesn't have any usable footage, because the film somehow fell in the lake."

"It's digital." She lifted her hands. "But yes, I get what you're saying. I believe she's too professional to retaliate through the interview. But we don't know her well enough to be sure."

"And it's *your* promo. *Your* book."

"Thank you. I'm sorry you were put in that position."

"It's fine, but now I don't know whether she'll realize the bear was an excuse and be offended or accept the temporary excuse and make another pass at me. I need a real reason—something she can't take personally."

"*It's not you, it's me.*"

"Exactly. I know you didn't want to pretend we were a couple, but maybe, if we could just hint at it?"

"Are you asking me to be your fake girlfriend, Chris?"

He blushed. "If that's okay. Or we can come up with something—"

Footsteps sounded outside the shop. *Running* for the shop.

"Zane?" Sofia called. "Dana? Is there really a bear? Do you need help?"

"We need to—" Chris began.

"I've got this." Daphne reached up to stroke his cheek, let Sofia see her touching Chris in a way that said they were more than author and assistant.

"Good idea," he said . . . and kissed her.

The first second was shock. The next second was panic.

Did he think she'd been going to kiss him? He must have.

And then she forgot shock and panic and pretty much everything else in existence because Chris was kissing her and . . . Oh, wow.

His mouth was firm and somehow also teasing, his lips barely opening. A confident kiss that said he knew what he was doing, but also that he wasn't doing all he could, respectful of the fact that this was a charade, while making it such a damn good charade that she wished it wasn't a charade.

And you call yourself a writer? What kind of nonsensical blather is that?

The nonsensical blather of a brain too untethered to form rational thought beyond *Oh God, Chris Stanton is kissing me, and he is such a good kisser.*

Yep, obviously she really was thirteen again.

She didn't notice where his hands were. Didn't even notice where his body was in relation to hers. She was entirely caught up in—

"Oh!"

The voice came from behind her. Who the hell was that? Whoever it was needed to leave and let Chris keep kissing—

Shit! Sofia!

The whole point of this kiss was standing behind them.

Daphne whirled in shock that was only half feigned. "Oh my God." Her hands flew to her lips. "I'm so sorry. I thought we closed the door."

"It's okay, babe," Chris said, putting his arm around her.

"Babe"? Really? That better be Zane speaking.

Chris pulled her to him as if she might scamper off like a spooked fawn. "I'm sorry, Sofia. I needed to talk to Dana." He cleared his throat. "I reacted poorly earlier, and I made a silly excuse. Then I realized how it looked to Dana—me shirtless in my room with you—so I had to get her out here and explain. You both deserved better, and I apologize."

Far from looking angry, Sofia stared as if she'd seen a unicorn. "Oh! Yes, of course. I had no idea you two…"

Chris's arm tightened around Daphne. "We're very private people. No subterfuge was intended."

"I understand." She looked at Daphne. "Now *I'll* apologize. To both of you. If I'd known he was in a relationship, I'd have stayed away."

Chris nodded and then cleared his throat. "You know, I just realized that I missed my morning dip."

"Morning…?" Daphne murmured, too low for him to hear.

"A swim. In the lake."

"It's kind of…"

"Cold?" He smiled. "Exactly how I like it. Refreshing and ice-cold. The perfect way to start my day."

Chris strode past them. "Let me get my bathing suit, and I'll meet you at the beach."

Daphne tried not to stare after him. He did know how cold it was, right? He'd been in the water last night when they capsized.

"I'll tell the crew," Sofia said with a smile. "We wouldn't want to miss this."

CHRIS

So freaking cold.

He focused on his strokes, taking him out across the lake, the speed warming him as he went while the cold water cleared his head.

Clearing your head is the reason you decided to go swimming in a glacial lake, buddy.

True, but it wasn't the *entire* reason.

Daphne kissed him.

Okay, he kissed her, but it'd been her idea. Fine, she'd been doing him a favor, fending off Sofia's attention, but it *had* been a kiss. A real kiss. Daphne in his arms, pressed against him, her lips parting under his. That little noise she hadn't seemed to know she was making, a noise that slid into his mind and hit Replay on the bedroom scene, except instead of Sofia, it was Daphne.

Daphne coming into the bedroom. Daphne telling him how frightened she'd been, how magnificently he'd scared off the bear, how her heart was still thumping, primal urges awakened, desperate for an outlet. Daphne whispering what she wanted to do to him—

Keep swimming, buddy.

Just to the island and back. That'd be enough.

He touched the shallow waters of the island and turned around. In the distance, he could see Daphne waiting on the shore, and when he blinked, his brain slid in the image from last night, the one he'd been too worried to process at the time.

Daphne in his arms, drenched, clothing clinging to her as she looked up into his eyes.

Her lips parted. "You saved my life."

She reached for him, arms going around his neck, mouth going to his, warm and pliant and hungry—

Need another lap, buddy?

Maybe just one more.

DAPHNE

Chris was on his third lap from the island, which was damned impressive, and Daphne would be in awe if she wasn't too busy staring at him, arms rising from the water in powerful strokes that rippled down his muscular shoulders and back. She swore even from this distance she could see the sun glinting off his tanned arms, turning him a Greek-god shade of bronze.

There were worse ways to spend a morning.

"You're a lucky lady," Sofia said beside her.

Daphne made a noise Sofia could take as agreement.

"I really am sorry for hitting on him," Sofia said. "I had no idea he was in a relationship."

"We were keeping it quiet. You couldn't have known." Daphne paused. There was something else she could say. Did she dare? If it were her, would she want it said? Yes.

Daphne cleared her throat. "He just…he found it awkward because you're in charge of this interview. I know his response wouldn't have affected that, but…"

"Shit," Sofia said. "I never saw it that way. Okay, good to know. Thank you."

"I know you didn't mean it like that."

"I didn't, but having been on the other side of that equation, I never want to be on this side of it. On the topic of workplace romance and power dynamics…"

Sofia pointedly looked out at Chris.

"Oh, he's not really my boss," Daphne said. "I'm just playing his assistant to help with the shoot. Like he said, we're private people. We weren't comfortable having our relationship on-screen." She realized how that could sound and added, "That's my choice, not his."

"Good. I've interviewed a couple of authors who had, shall we say, mentees? Young writers drawn into their circle, expecting mentorship and getting something entirely different. This didn't seem like that."

"It's not. At all."

"Good. He's not what I expected. Debut author with a number one bestseller. He has good reason to be pleased with himself, and he obviously doesn't have any ego deficiencies, but he's more than that."

"He is."

They both watched as Chris emerged from the lake, the sun lighting him just right. His hair glinted, and water ran rivulets down his body, grabbing the eye and leading it over perfect pecs, down his stomach toward drenched bathing trunks that left remarkably little to the imagination.

Sofia leaned in to whisper, "I might hop in that glacial lake myself for a little cooldown."

And I'll be right behind you.

While Sofia conducted the second part of Zane's interview, Daphne sat on the porch with a coffee and the video footage.

At her feet, Tika let out a low grumble. After the bear incident, the dog wanted to be out there, patrolling the property.

"None of that," Daphne said. "I'm working."

Another grumble.

"It *is* work. Sofia asked me to check it over."

All right, maybe Sofia had winked when she suggested Daphne look at the footage. And maybe she'd queued up two particular clips. One showed Chris coming out of the water with Daphne in his arms after they'd capsized. He was soaking wet, shirt and trousers clinging to every line of his body. He had her in his arms, and his face was shadowed with concern.

Now *that* was book-cover worthy. Oh, sure, a little voice might *tsk* at her for the knight-in-shining-armor trope, but screw that. There was a time and a place for every fantasy, including this one.

The second clip was Chris coming out of the water after his swim, and sure, Daphne had seen that live, but there was nothing wrong with replaying it…and replaying it…and replaying it. Just making sure the lighting was right. That's all.

When footsteps slapped up the steps, she ALT-Tabbed so fast he might think she'd been watching porn.

Well, PG-rated porn, at least. Fodder for late nights and—

"Good footage?" Chris asked.

She jumped again as he slid in beside her on the bench.

"All good," she said, slapping the laptop closed.

"Great. I came to tell you they'll be leaving after lunch."

Daphne made a show of exhaling and collapsing on the tabletop.

Chris chuckled. "Right? And I'm sure you're in a hurry to get rid of me, too."

"No, not at all."

Did that come out too quick? A little too eager? If so, he didn't seem to notice, but only continued with "I wanted to talk about flights. I shouldn't be seen getting on the same one they do."

"Good point."

He *could* pretend he was jetting off to another interview, but she wasn't giving him any excuse to leave earlier than necessary. Yes, even with that kiss, she had no idea whether she stood any chance of a fling with Chris, but she realized it didn't matter. Okay, it mattered in the sense that she wanted it—really wanted it—but even if she knew it wasn't going to happen, she still wanted to spend more time with him.

"I know the crew is flying out tonight," he said. "I'll go in the morning. I could get a hotel room tonight..."

"Don't be silly. Tomorrow is fine."

Or the next day. Maybe the next after that? Or "never" seems good. Does "never" work for you?

Where did that come from? If he wanted anything, it would be short and sweet, which was perfect.

"Tomorrow would be good," she said firmly. "The morning flights are super early, but if you need to get back to Vancouver..."

"I don't."

"Then there's a midafternoon departure..."

"Perfect."

"Zane!" Sofia called.

Chris straightened and lifted a hand, as if she might not see him there.

Sofia came jogging up the steps, the two camera operators following.

"You need to see this," Sofia said. Then she spun on the operators. "Show him."

The female operator set her phone down between Chris and Daphne. On the screen was a still photo of Chris. That was all Daphne saw at first. Then she noticed the hulking brown bear.

The shot was taken from an angle where all she could see of Chris was his profile, jaw tense, gaze lifted to the bear's. The grizzly stood there, looking down at him.

Holy shit, had he *really* been that close? Daphne had kept telling herself she'd underestimated the distance.

Chris and the bear were close enough that they could have been slow-dancing in middle school, barely a ruler's length between them.

"That was..." Daphne breathed, feeling stunned. "Wow. You were close."

"It's the angle," Chris said.

The camera operator flapped her hand, as if telling them that part wasn't important. Then she hit Play, and Daphne realized it was a video. The sound had been scrubbed. You couldn't hear Daphne giving instructions. Nor Tika growling. Nor Sofia freaking out. None of them were in the shot, either. It was just Chris and the grizzly, locked in a stare-down.

Then the bear backed up, dropped to the side, and loped off.

As the bear left, words scrolled across the screen: #1 NYT BEST-SELLING AUTHOR ZANE REMINGTON ("AT THE EDGE OF THE WORLD") FACES DOWN GRIZZLY AND WINS.

"I made sure to include the book title," the operator said. "And the number one bestseller part. They're also in the post, along with the hashtags and the show name and Sofia's name. All the metadata for the bots."

"Nice." Daphne patted Chris's back. "Impressive."

"Uh, no, you're the one who—"

She patted his back harder. "Damn impressive."

He got the message. It didn't do her any good to take credit.

Daphne looked at the camera operator. "The clip looks great. Thank you."

"Oh, that's not why we're showing you," Sofia said.

Sofia pointed at the stats—the likes and shares and comments. Daphne glanced at them, blinked, and looked again. The numbers weren't just climbing—they were zooming up so fast she felt dizzy watching.

"A hundred *thousand* likes?" she said, not sure she was seeing right.

"And that's only one website," Sofia said.

"I know a few influencers," the operator said. "I gave one of them an exclusive."

"Your bear stare-down is going viral, Zane," Sofia said. "Welcome to your fifteen minutes of fame."

CHAPTER TEN

CHRIS

After lunch, the mist rolled back in, and Sofia decided that was the perfect time to bring out the guns. Even Chris knew fog meant it was the worst possible time for any shooting, but he had to admit they did get good footage. Also, the mist meant no one expected him to actually fire the gun.

Daphne showed him how to hold it, and the crew got a few moody shots of him aiming at something in the fog. It was pure kitsch, but if it sold books for Daphne, he'd wade knee-deep in the icy water and pretend to take shots at nonexistent waterfowl.

Then the filming was done, and it was time for the crew to leave, right?

Ha! Don't be silly. Why would you leave this gorgeous piece of Canadian scenery for a tiny motel room, when that piece of scenery came with a roaring propane fire to ward off the chill, free Wi-Fi to monitor stats on your viral video, and a selection of ice-cold beers and coolers.

Personally, Chris wouldn't have brought out the beer and coolers. Or the charcuterie board with artisanal cheese and wild-game salami. But, in Daphne's defense, it wasn't as if she offered that while the crew was making moves to leave. They were clearly planning to hang out here until their flight, and so she had to play good hostess. He *did* enjoy his beer and plate of goodies; he'd just have enjoyed them more without three-quarters of the company.

It was Daphne who finally did the *Oh, would you look at the time?* bit. As the crew was packing away their equipment, something caught Daphne's ear, her attention yanked toward the driveway.

"Everything okay?" he murmured.

She hesitated. Then she said, "Can you help them pack?"

He grinned. "Happily."

"I'll be right back."

DAPHNE

It'd been Tika who'd heard someone arriving. There was no crunch of gravel, which meant the visitor came on foot. The lack of a growl or warning bark—just a curious lift of Tika's head—meant it was someone she knew.

Daphne hurried down the steps and around the side of the house in time to see Robbie strolling along the driveway. Tika spotted his canine companion and took off.

Daphne broke into a jog, running up the driveway to cut Robbie off before he got any closer to the house.

"Well, someone's happy to see me." He waggled his brows. "Getting tired of your little friend already?"

Did he mean Tika?

He waved toward the crew's truck. "Least he got himself a proper rental."

Chris was her *little friend*? She could have laughed. He outsized Robbie by about two inches in height and twenty pounds in muscle.

She settled for shaking her head. "We took his rental back." She nodded at the truck. "That's business clients."

His brows rose. It seemed to take a while for the wheels to turn. "Oh, right, you draw houses."

"I'm an architect," she said.

Play nice. Don't give him any reason to be suspicious. Politely send him on his way because if the crew comes out here, you're screwed.

At the thought, her heartbeat picked up, and she took two calming breaths while she pretended to watch the dogs play.

"Can I talk to you later?" she said. "I just need to finish up—"

"Are they hiring you to draw them a house?" He peered at the truck. "Where did they find land? Is it a teardown?" He looked at her. "You'd tell me if there was land for sale around here, right?"

"It's not for my job, Robbie. It's for my friend's."

"Your friend is helping someone build a house?"

"No. He's up here on business, and since he's staying with me, I offered to host his meeting—"

"Bye, Dana!" a voice called, and Daphne looked to see Sofia and the crew walking toward their truck with Chris right behind them.

CHRIS

The neighbor. That was who Daphne had heard and run out to meet. What's-his-name, who very clearly wanted to get more neighborly. Asshole.

Okay, that didn't make him an asshole, but Chris still got those asshole vibes, and not because he'd insulted Chris on their first meeting.

Okay, not *entirely* because of that.

Was there something going on between Daphne and neighbor-dude? Did she like assholes?

He almost laughed at the thought. Uh, no, by the time he'd left their first meeting he'd known that Daphne McFadden definitely did not go for assholes. But presumably neighbor-dude wouldn't be an asshole to her.

Chris watched them as he escorted the crew to their truck. Daphne and neighbor-dude huddle-talked while their dogs played together.

The guy was decent looking. Okay, he was good-looking. And living out here meant he was outdoorsy. Was this Daphne's inspiration for Zane? Neighbor-dude was a lot less polished than Zane, but that sophistication had been Chris's take on the role. He got the feeling "polished" wasn't Daphne's type, any more than "asshole."

Hey, Chris could be a little rough around the edges if he wanted. He could be so damned unpolished, he'd walk through the house with his shoes on and not even ask whether it was okay.

Take that, neighbor-dude.

His inner voice sighed. Deeply.

Fine. That was more rude than "rough around the edges." Daphne wouldn't like rude. Just a little more real. Like her. Daphne wasn't Zane. She wasn't fake. She didn't shop for designer flannel and probably laughed at guys who did.

He looked down at his two-hundred-dollar flannel shirt.

Sofia called to Daphne, saying goodbye. When she used the Dana name, Chris tensed, but he could see Daphne saying something, no doubt laughing it off as a mistake.

"Should I go say goodbye?" Sofia said. "She was such a great hostess."

"Mmm, better not. That's a neighbor, and he's a bit of an ass. You might want to flee while you still can."

Before he comes over here and realizes what's going on.

Chris hadn't even thought of that.

Because you were too busy being jealous to realize Daphne is holding him off before he blows her cover?

And now the neighbor was heading their way while Daphne jogged along, trying to intercept him.

Shit!

Chris put out his hand to help Sofia into the truck, which was the gentlemanly thing to do and not at all to hurry along her departure.

"Hey!" neighbor-dude called. "You guys have a lead on some land for sale here?"

Sofia's face scrunched as she twisted in her seat. "What did he say?"

"He's looking for a building lot," Chris said. "They're hard to come by out here. I swear he asks everybody." He tapped his temple. "Too long in the woods."

Sofia nodded knowingly, and he shut her door before turning to block neighbor-dude.

"Hey, Reggie," he said.

The man's mouth tightened. "It's Robbie."

Chris tried to steer him away from the truck, but Robbie dug in his heels. Then the window rolled down.

"If you're looking for a building lot," Sofia called, "I saw a notice at our hotel for a land lottery."

"Yeah, I'm not made of millions," Robbie grumbled. "'Lottery' doesn't mean 'free.'"

Daphne grabbed Robbie's arm, saying, "Whoa! Don't get run over." The truck hadn't moved yet, but she used the excuse to direct him off to the side as she waved goodbye to the departing crew.

"It's nice of you to stop by, Robbie," she said as the truck rolled down the drive. "I'm sure I'll see you around—"

"I need to borrow your hatchet. Handle broke on mine."

She hesitated, and something like panic crossed her face before she said, "Uh, sure. It's in the shed. Hanging on the left."

As Robbie sauntered off, Chris inched closer to Daphne.

"Well, there goes *that* hatchet," she muttered.

Chris frowned.

"Once he has it, I'll never see it again," she said.

"Then tell him no."

She gave him a look. "I live alone in the middle of nowhere. I'm not saying no to a guy like that."

Chris's whole body tensed. "He's threatened you?"

"No, no. It's just..." She shrugged. "He wants a permanent place to live, and guys like that think the world owes it to them. If the world won't deliver, well, there's a lonely spinster down the road with a sweet setup."

Chris rocked forward, fists clenching, gaze locked on the shed door.

Daphne put a hand on his arm. "I'm fine."

"If he's harassing you—"

"It's not like that. I'm sure he doesn't realize I feel harassed."

"Then he needs to pull his head out of his ass and put himself in your shoes."

She smiled at him. "Thank you. But people like that are functionally incapable of putting themselves in anyone's shoes."

"Then they should read a damn book to get some practice."

The way she looked at him then, her eyes on his, her lips slightly parted, reminding him of that moment in the shed, when she'd leaned toward him, just before they kissed.

Which gave him an excellent idea.

He moved closer and lowered his voice. "Earlier, you helped me with Sofia. If you want help with Robbie..."

She looked at Chris. Then her lips curved in the most amazing smile. "Are you offering to be my fake boyfriend again, Chris Stanton?"

"I am."

"Would it involve kissing?"

He hesitated. His brain warned that maybe he'd misinterpreted last time, and she *hadn't* meant to kiss him, and now she was making sure that wouldn't happen again.

But that smile said something else, so he shut off his brain, followed his gut, and smiled. "It could."

"Good, because there's no fake dating without kissing." She took hold of the front of his shirt and pulled him to her, and before he fully registered what was happening, Daphne was kissing him.

With the first kiss, he'd been restrained. Putting his best effort forward to showcase his talent while being hyperaware that it was supposed to be for show, so he couldn't get carried away.

This time…?

Well, this time, there was no doubt she'd started it, and he could just follow her lead.

It was a valid plan. Very logical. Very chartered-accountant Chris. Except chartered-accountant Chris was now kissing a woman who set his brain—and every other body part—on fire.

Kicking aside restraint, he kissed Daphne, his mouth opening to hers, his body pressed to hers, until he could feel her thighs against his, her breasts against his chest, her arms around his neck, his hands on her ass.

How did his hands get there? He wasn't quite sure. He only knew that she was pressing into him, letting out a soft little moan of pleasure as he cupped her ass and pulled her against him.

He hefted her legs around his hips, his hands wedged between her ass and the tree.

Tree? Where did that come from?

He shifted position, one eye peeking to be absolutely certain she was okay with this. That was when he saw someone standing there.

Who the hell—?

Oh, right, Robbie. The actual reason Chris was making out with Daphne.

Robbie stood there, arms crossed, glaring. Then he turned on his heel and stomped off…and Chris went back to kissing Daphne.

Just kissing. Nothing more.

Umm, her legs are around your hips, and you're grinding—

Shut up.

There's a word for that. You're a writer now, buddy. You should know it.

Shut. Up.

Maybe it was more than a kiss, but he still held back from going further because this was not an opportunity he should exploit. Unless she wanted it exploited.

"Oh!" She snapped from the kiss so fast her head hit the tree.

He jumped back…and dropped her. Literally dropped her two feet onto the ground. "Shit!"

He scrambled to help her up, but she was already twisting to rise, her elbow catching him in the nose. She jerked back, blurting apologies, and his leg got caught around hers, both of them tumbling to the ground. Then his nose started to bleed, because of course it did.

Daphne stared in horror before yanking off her sweater and pressing it to his nose even as he protested. They sat there on the ground, catching their breath.

"I'm *so* sorry," she said.

"My fault," he said through the sweater. "I dropped you."

"I mean—yes, I'm sorry about your nose—but I'm sorry about…" She ducked his gaze. "I got carried away with the kiss."

"Mmm, pretty sure that was me."

She shook her head. "I backed into the tree and then put my legs around…" She trailed off, cheeks going bright red.

"Uh, no. The tree was me. The legs were me. Or if not completely me, then sixty percent me. I got carried away."

She seemed ready to argue. Then she stopped. "Where's Robbie?"

Chris frowned and looked around, hoping he was selling the look of confusion.

"Did he leave?" Daphne asked.

"I guess so. Huh. Never noticed."

She laughed and shook her head. "I didn't notice, either. Definitely carried away. I'll blame nerves from the shoot. Hey, it's better than stress-puking, huh?" She made a face. "Did I actually say that? So smooth."

"Making out *is* better than stress-puking. So anytime I'm around and you need to work off a little stress…" Chris waggled his brows, making her laugh. Then he said, "I'm teasing. If you're stressed, I'll distract you with bad jokes and questions about bear safety."

She looked at him and then said, "You're really sweet, you know that?" She made a face. "Is that okay? Calling you sweet? I'd say 'nice,' but that can be a loaded word."

Chris faked a whine. "'Nice guys finish last. Women say they want nice guys, so why can't I get a date?' Yeah, not being an asshole doesn't make you nice. It's a scale, not a Boolean dichotomy."

She smiled over at him. "Well, you actually *are* nice, and to me, that is definitely a compliment."

"Then I'll take it as one. Thank you."

Daphne nodded, and the nod just kept going, as if she wasn't sure what to do. She glanced to the side, where Tika lay patiently.

Say something, buddy.

Like what?

Something. Anything. Yeah, that kiss didn't end quite as smoothly as you'd have liked, but there's still an opening. She just complimented you.

She also admitted she was as into that kiss as you were. Nudge that door. See where it leads.

"I, uh…" he began.

Come on. Say something, damn it.

"My nose seems to have stopped bleeding."

Seriously? That's what you're going with?

"I'm so sorry," she said.

He smiled. "It does that. Sneeze too hard, and I'm spraying blood everywhere."

You're beyond help, you know that?

Daphne laughed. "It's still better than stress-puking."

"Oh, I don't know. For prom, I finally got up the nerve to ask a girl I really liked. She said yes. I showed up at her door, and she opened it too fast, and it clipped me in the nose. I got blood all over her dress."

I give up.

Daphne winced. "Ouch."

"Right. So I guess, what I'm trying to say is…"

I cannot wait to hear where this is going.

He wasn't sure where he was going.

Shocker.

But he could see an opening there, something about girls—women—he liked and bloody noses.

No, stop.

A segue. Something sweet and funny and—

"Tell me she just changed her dress," Daphne said. "Or used a corsage to cover up the stain. Or that she went with it, blood and all, a funny story to tell."

He shook his head. "She freaked out. She said she'd only agreed to go out with me because the guy she really liked asked someone else, and she wanted to make him jealous, and how could she do that with blood on her dress."

"I hate her."

There! The door is open. Jump. Fast. Jump now.

Chris did jump...because the moment he went to say something, his phone buzzed.

He would have ignored the interruption. But after their fall, the phone was halfway out of his pocket, and the vibration sent it tumbling out.

He still intended to ignore it. But Daphne reached to pick his phone up for him, and as she did, she froze.

"Is that our Lawrence?"

Our Lawrence?

Shit. Daphne's agent.

Nia had set up a fake number for Zane, which forwarded texts to Daphne and calls to Chris. First, though, calls diverted through a voicemail service that asked the caller to leave a message and press 1 only if it was urgent.

Lawrence knew Zane hated talking by phone, so he emailed. Now Lawrence was calling...after pressing 1 for urgent. Daphne stared down at his phone, panic on her face.

"Do I...?" Chris began.

"Yes!"

She shoved the phone at him, and he hit Talk.

"Zane Remington speaking," he said.

"Hey, Zane, it's Lawrence. I hate to call but you haven't answered my email, and it really is urgent."

Email? That would go to Daphne. He glanced at her, but she couldn't hear Lawrence, and he wasn't sure about putting him on speaker.

"Ah," Chris said. "No, I haven't been checking my mail. The film crew kept me very busy."

Daphne's wince told him she *hadn't* been checking it.

"Let me go read it," Chris said. "I'll get back to you—"

"It's about the tour."

"All right. I'll read—"

"It starts next week."

"What?" Now Chris was the one wincing because that was not a Zane exclamation. He cleared his throat. "Next week, you say? I was told it would be fall. August, at the absolute earliest. I know it takes time to set these up with the bookstores."

"Well, they're making it happen. Strike while the iron's hot, and it's scorching right now. I just got a text about a video? Something about a grizzly bear?"

"Ah, yes. That."

"*That* is going viral, and *after* the tour was arranged."

Chris glanced over to see Daphne's total panic. She'd parsed out enough from his side of the conversation to understand what was happening.

Chris said, "Let me have a look at your email and—"

"I can give you the details. We really need to get moving on this."

"I understand. However, this isn't a good time to talk. I have"—his gaze touched on Daphne's sweater, balled up on his lap—"a nosebleed." A Zane chuckle. "Yes, terribly embarrassing, but I bopped my nose, and there is blood. I really do need to call you back."

"Ten minutes?"

"Fifteen."

"Fine."

DAPHNE

Daphne forwarded Lawrence's email to Chris. Then they set up a timer on the kitchen table and read it over.

Eight minutes remaining.

There was a tour. Not this fall, but starting next week in Los Angeles. Launching at the LA Times Festival of Books. Wasn't that usually in April? May? Not this year, apparently. This was why they were scrambling to arrange a last-minute tour. Because they'd scored a vacated seat on a panel at one of the world's most prestigious book festivals.

She couldn't say no to that. Yes, being last minute, excuses were possible. That's why Lawrence was so eager to talk. He was making sure Zane was free.

She could come up with an excuse, and that would be just fine...if she wanted to piss off the LAT Book Fest and the stores that had been ready to host Zane. Not to mention upsetting her publicist and publisher.

Zane wouldn't care. If a last-minute tour was inconvenient, he'd cancel. But Zane wasn't actually the author of *At the Edge of the World*. If he were, he wouldn't give a damn how well it sold because he was the kind of author who only cared about reviews and awards. Not gross material concerns like sales. If his publisher was upset about him refusing a tour? *Well, that's what happens to real artists, isn't it? They get steamrolled by the man and his petty concerns.*

In that regard, Daphne was the polar opposite of Zane, and the sort of writer he'd turn his nose up at. Such a hack, always thinking about money. Except regular writers—who did not have trust funds or successful spouses—*needed* to think about money, and authors like Daphne worried about damaging their careers because they wanted to *have* a career.

Maybe it'd be different as Zane. Maybe the creative-genius schtick would work. Maybe no one really expected a man to make himself available at the last minute, scrambling to accommodate everyone else's plans.

And maybe no one expected her to make herself available at the last minute, either. She could be completely overreacting, letting herself fall prey to the horror stories about publishing, which she now knew to be grossly exaggerated, if not altogether false.

Would she take that chance, though? No. Turning down the tour wasn't an option.

Unless she had to. Because there was a very important part of the equation she'd forgotten.

"Could you do it?" she said to Chris. "I didn't even ask—"

"I can, but I'd like to ask you to do something, too."

Her gaze slid to the timer. He turned it around so they weren't watching the countdown.

"Come with me," he said.

She blinked.

"Come on the tour. Please." He leaned across the table. "I know it's not your thing. I know this is why you hired me, and if you need me to do this alone, I will." He met her gaze. "But I'd rather do it with you."

She stopped, a refusal halfway to her lips. He could pull this off by himself. He wasn't actually Chris Ainsworth, wannabe actor who'd never read the book. She trusted him to handle this.

But he wasn't saying he *needed* her there.

He was *asking* her to be there.

I'd rather do it with you.

A tour with Chris. Just the two of them, and if he had any interest in a fling, that was when it would happen.

He smiled at her. "It'll be fun. You know it will."

She bit her lip.

"And you kinda want to." He leaned in and lowered his voice conspiratorially. "You don't want the limelight, but you'd like to meet your readers. See them. Listen to what they have to say about your book."

"I..."

"You've given up something, D, by having me play the author of your book. You deserve to get the best parts of it back. Hearing—firsthand—how actual readers react to your story. Not interviewers. Not reporters. Not a thirty-year-old accountant. Actual teenagers who love your book." He met her gaze. "Will you come with me?"

She nodded mutely, not daring to speak. Deep inside, there was still a girl who wasn't sure he was serious, a girl who'd learned that when a popular boy asked her to go someplace—join him for lunch or a ball game—he probably wanted help with his homework.

Was that what Chris was doing? Pretending he wanted her company when he really just wanted her help?

But when she nodded, he smiled, and it was such a genuinely delighted smile that her doubts melted.

"Excellent," he said. "Now let's call Lawrence."

"I can email—"

He lifted a hand. "Please allow the accountant to handle this."

"Accountant?"

"Fifty percent accountant, fifty percent number one *NYT* best-selling author who definitely knows his own worth. First, can we stick with Daphne?"

"What?"

"Calling you Daphne instead of Dana. That got confusing, and I think you'll be more comfortable with Daphne. You definitely can't fly as Dana. As for hiding my own name, they know Zane is a pseudonym, so I'll insist on buying my tickets for anything requiring identification. The hotel rooms can be in the publisher's name."

"They can do that?"

"I have clients give me receipts booked that way. If we need to show ID, I'll ask you to do it." His lips quirked. "As my assistant." He looked more serious. "That's what we'll need to do. The assistant thing. The publisher could write off your expenses if you're my assistant but not if you're my partner."

Did he mean otherwise they'd pretend to be a couple?

"We'll go with that," she said. "But they don't need to pay my expenses. I can—"

"Let me handle it."

He called Lawrence.

"I have read the email," he said when Lawrence answered. "I am prepared to discuss details."

"So you can do the tour?" Lawrence asked.

"Of course," Chris said loftily. "People have gone to a great deal of trouble to arrange this. In the future, though, I must ask that I be on the ground floor of any such discussions. Clearing next week will not be easy. Yet I will do it in recognition of the efforts others have made."

Which was exactly Daphne's reasoning, but somehow Chris made it sound as if he were making a huge sacrifice for others, and Lawrence rewarded him accordingly, thanking him for being so accommodating and promising to speak to the publisher, who never should have gone this far without confirming Zane's availability.

"Now, details," Chris said. "First, I will be accompanied by my assistant, whose expenses will be covered."

"You have an assistant?"

"Of course. This book is turning out to require the sort of administrative oversight I'm hardly in a position to provide. I'm a writer, not a secretary." He shot Daphne an apologetic look, but she only smiled. She knew the difference between his Zane opinions and his Chris ones, and he didn't need to clarify.

Chris continued, "Her expenses will be covered, and she will accompany me to all events and signings, where she will provide all necessary assistance."

"Your publicist will be accompanying you."

"Excellent. However, I still require Daphne. Now, I know I'm putting you on the spot with these requests, Lawrence, but I am quite willing to speak directly to the publisher about them. If that is the case, I would like someone from their accounting department on the call, so that we might discuss the profitability of this tour, which I presume they have not arranged to treat me to a mini-tour of the States."

Lawrence chuckled. "Not exactly. Yes, it's about selling books. The tour should keep you on the bestsellers lists, which will further prod sales. I suspect the store events will require a purchase to attend."

"Then the publisher's profit will allow Daphne to accompany me. I also require business-class seats on all flights of more than an hour. I'm over six feet tall. I cannot sit in economy."

Daphne stared at him. That was never going to—

"I can't guarantee it," Lawrence said. "But I'll definitely try."

"Daphne also requires business class, being nearly six feet herself."

Lawrence hesitated.

"If they wish to argue, remember that I want an accountant present. Two business-class seats for all flights over an hour. For flights under an hour, business-class seats on trains are preferred for ecological reasons. As for hotels, four stars only. Two rooms. Adjoining. High-speed internet. King-size beds."

"That should be fine."

"Good. I would also like a per diem. I don't wish to fuss with saving and submitting receipts. If they say they cannot do that for tax purposes, I will—again—speak to someone in their accounting department. We will discuss the per diem, but they must remember that I am a very active man. I have a high metabolism."

"Understood."

"Excellent. Send me their responses—"

"Hold on."

Daphne tensed. Lawrence was going to suggest Zane rein in his demands. Lawrence would do what he could but, really, Zane was overstepping.

Lawrence continued, "I'll need you to be in LA a day early to meet with some people. We have film interest."

"Film interest?"

"Film and television. We've had it for a while. But Lucy has been fending it off."

"Lucy?" Chris looked at Daphne, who shrugged.

"Your film agent."

She had a film agent?

Lawrence continued, "We were gambling on strong opening sales to bolster interest and maximize the playing field. I've whittled the list down to seven, and as long as you're in LA…" He chuckled. "It *is* home to Hollywood, after all. The players are there, and if they're serious about acquiring this property, they'll agree to meet with you Friday before the festival."

"'That is…" Chris looked at Daphne, who was too thunderstruck to answer. "Acceptable," he said. "Yes, I believe that will be acceptable."

CHAPTER ELEVEN

CHRIS

"Film interest," Daphne breathed, her eyes glassy with shock. "He did say that, right? That people are interested in making a show out of my book."

"Nah." Chris handed her a beer from the fridge and thumped onto the sofa. "He said the producers are interested in a novel by another of his authors, and he was wondering if you could meet with them while you're passing through LA."

She stared, as if processing that.

He stretched his foot to knock it against hers. "I'm kidding, D. Pretty sure agents don't sub in other authors for talks like that. That'd be wild, though."

"Like hiring someone to play an author?"

He grinned. "Something like that. Are you really surprised that Hollywood has come calling? I figured you just weren't interested."

"No, I'm...I mean, I should be interested, right? Or shouldn't I? Can they make things worse? What if I pick the wrong company, and they butcher my book?"

"They can't actually butcher your book. They can butcher their adaptation, but that doesn't change one word of your book. And whether you sell rights or not is up to you. I know zilch about it. My suggestion would be that we meet with them so you can hear their pitches. That's all they're doing. Pitching."

"Right. Yes. Wow. I...I need to think about this. Can I ask them questions? About what they'd do? How they envision the adaptation? Or would that be too forward?"

His brows shot up. "They're coming to *you*, D, and your book is making *bank*. Unless you have a coke habit I don't know about, you don't need their money." He paused. "Please tell me you don't have a coke habit." He pressed his hands together as if in prayer. "Please, please, please."

She smiled. "Been there, done that?"

He rolled his eyes. Last night, he'd told her the whole story of why he'd needed Nia's legal help.

"No, I don't need the money," she said. "I think an adaptation would be cool, but you're right that I shouldn't shy from asking questions. I'm afraid I might get starstruck and just sit there, nodding and grinning."

"Oh, I will definitely ask questions for you. I take my position as quasi-conservator of your literary genius very seriously. And we'll have plenty of time to talk on the flight."

He held his breath there and watched her expression. He kept waiting for her to change her mind about joining him, which was partly why he'd insisted on business-class seats and four-star hotels. Yes, she deserved it, but it was also, possibly, a bribe.

"Come on tour with me, babe, and I'll show you a good time."

Yeah, at the rate you're moving, the only good time you'll be showing her is those fancy seats and hotels. You planning to do anything with those king-size beds?

Yep, he was going to sleep. So much sleep.

Kidding. Kind of. No, he was not expecting to get Daphne in bed, because that would be wrong.

You sure? I'm thinking it'd be right. Oh so right.

He said "expecting" would be wrong. "Hoping" was a whole other word, but only if it meant the start of a longer relationship. Eyes on the prize, with no rush to get there.

That inner voice sighed deeply, but it knew he was right.

In response to his last remark, Daphne brightened and said, "We will have time to talk. And it'll be easier to talk if we're in business class. Fingers crossed for that."

"Oh, you're getting that." Even if he needed to quietly upgrade them himself.

She sipped her beer. "So I guess it's prepping and packing time."

"It is."

"Three days to get ready."

"Yep."

Silence.

He cleared his throat. "I'm sure you'll be glad to have some time to yourself. A quiet house and a chance to write before we fall into the chaos again."

"And you'll need to tie up work. Is this going to be okay? You weren't planning on a week off."

"Three days will let me get caught up, and I'll be connected for urgent business. I did request high-speed internet."

"And I thought that was for chilling in your room with Netflix."

"Netflix and chill," he said, waggling his brows.

Daphne laughed. "Oh my God. I was doing research for *Edge*, following teen blogs to be sure I had the voice down, and I saw what that means for actual teens. The next time Nia used it, I had great fun poking at her."

"Yeah, in my case it was a teenage cousin who told me. Way to make me feel old." He considered riffing on "Netflix and chill" and seeing how she responded. But no, he would do nothing to suggest he might be down for a mere hookup. Slow and steady.

He settled in, sipping his beer and smiling as she did the same, an easy silence falling over them. He hated leaving. He had to, of course, and he'd see her again in a few days, but he'd love to find some excuse to invite her back to Vancouver with him.

Hey, maybe you could hang out with Nia. Get a little big-city shopping time in before our trip.

Yeah, the former presumed that Nia wasn't busy, and the latter suggested that Daphne needed a new wardrobe for the trip. He'd seen how she dressed at their first meeting. She had the wardrobe for this.

He just wanted to bring her home with him. Unfortunately, his apartment was a tiny one-bedroom, which meant no. Not yet.

"So..." He scratched his stubbled chin, which reminded him that he could shave, being between the shoot and the tour. "Since you're stuck with me tonight, and you've done quite enough cooking, and I'd rather not rummage through your cupboards to make dinner for us. Want to go out?"

She smiled. "I'd love to."

DAPHNE

For the first twenty-four hours after Chris left, Daphne did nothing but clean and catch up—on everything from correspondence to sleep. Sleep most of all.

The problem with sleeping so long and so hard was that by the second night, she wasn't tired enough, and that unsettled sleep dragged nightmares in its wake.

First came the ones of being on tour. She'd drifted off smiling at the thought of meeting readers. She'd craved that in a way she hadn't expected. Of course, she *wanted* them to read it. That was the point of writing it. Entertaining herself, yes, and in this case, her dying mother, but also sharing her story with the world. Entertaining readers the way other writers had entertained her.

Once the advance copies had been out for exactly two weeks—yes, she'd marked it on her calendar—she'd begun haunting Goodreads. Oh, every writer in every writing community cautioned against it. But Daphne was an architect, she was accustomed to criticism, ready to learn and grow where possible, and chalk it up to a personal taste difference where applicable.

The first four reviews had set her heart floating. Three loved it, and one liked it with a few justified quibbles. The week those reviews came in, she'd written ten thousand words on the sequel.

Then came the fifth. She'd only read it once, but could recite it by heart.

> Loved Atticus and Finn. Kept hoping Theo would get bitten by a zombie and die. She never stopped whining.

Daphne knew this kind of response was not uncommon. Some readers who fell in love with the guys decided the girl wasn't worthy of them, as if the protagonist was their romantic rival. That lucky girl had two guys competing for her, and she was such a stuck-up bitch that she didn't give either of them a chance because she was too busy doing silly things like trying to stay alive. *Zombies want to eat me. My family is all dead. I don't know if I have enough food to get through the winter.* Waa-waa. So much whining.

Rationally, Daphne could ignore the review. Instead, she found herself hunched over her manuscript searching for introspection that could be interpreted as whining. She started fretting that she'd made Theo unlikable—too independent, too chilly, too closed off...too much like herself.

She'd stopped reading reviews because as much as she loved the pure joy of seeing a reader connect to her story, the negative ones cut too deeply into her confidence and impeded her ability to write. But now she'd go on tour and meet readers face-to-face, where—she hoped—they'd be less likely to say that they wanted her main character to die.

She fell asleep on that high. Soon she dreamed she was at a signing, happily watching Chris sign while she opened the books and took down name spellings. Then a young woman passed Chris and walked up to her.

"You lied to us," she said.

Daphne hesitated, sticky note in one hand, marker in the other. "Lied?"

"You said he wrote it." The girl jabbed a finger at Chris. "You lied. To us. To your readers."

"It wasn't like that. It's just a name."

"A man's name. What kind of message does that send to girls like me? Girls who want to write books like this?"

"I didn't mean—"

"It doesn't matter what you meant." The girl slammed the book down on the signing table. "What matters is that you did it." She turned on her heel and walked away.

Daphne bolted from the dream and ran for the bathroom. When she came back, she sat on her bed.

The girl in her dream was right. Because the girl in her dream had been her. Thirteen-year-old Daphne watching a female author speak and thinking *That could be me* for the first time ever. Thirteen-year-old Daphne standing in front of endless shelves of young adult books, most written by women, giddy at the possibility.

That was what she wanted. Then she'd gotten frustrated and sent that email under a man's name, and now *Edge* wasn't even on the young adult shelf because they hadn't marketed her book to teenage girls. Her book was "better" than that. It sat on the mainstream shelf. Was that because it had a man's name on it?

She'd lied to readers. Misled them. She hadn't meant to. She hadn't considered them—this was about seeing a dream come true and then being terrified of doing anything that could destroy it.

The other day, she'd thought Zane would refuse the tour because he wouldn't care about a career in writing. She did.

How much *did* she care? How tightly would she hold on to this lie?

How much of her book's success was the book itself? And how much was Chris? Chris as Zane, handsome and polished and confident. And just Chris as Chris, clever and quick-witted and charming.

It *was* a good book. Pushing past imposter syndrome, she knew it was good. She also knew that Zane helped get eyes on it and that made a difference. You can tell the best story in the world, but no one's reading a book they haven't heard of.

Did she trust that she could write? Yes. Did she trust that she could find a readership? Yes. It might not be as big as Zane's, but she didn't need all this. She just needed enough to keep writing.

She checked the clock. Five a.m. Of course it was. Because *OMG, I need to do something* moments always came when nothing *could* be done.

She popped off an email to Nia. Just a simple "Call me" with an added big fat lie of "Nothing urgent! No rush!"

Less than twenty minutes later, her phone rang.

"You're up early," Daphne said.

"Not as early as you," Nia said. "Did something happen? Feedback from the shoot?"

"No, no. It's just…"

Daphne told Nia what she'd dreamed.

"I need out," Daphne said. "What I'm doing is wrong. I'm deceiving people, and I need to stop."

"Hit pause on the doom-spiraling," Nia said. "Time for a two-minute reality break. Ready?"

Daphne inhaled. "Ready."

"Your publisher knows Zane is a pen name, and thousands of authors use them. Most keep their real name hidden. Some women use male pen names. Some men use female ones. Some authors refuse to have photos taken. Some adopt a disguise for photos, and some even adopt an entire fake persona for signings and events. Then there are the ones who use twenty-year-old photos. And don't even get me started on the fake bios—they're as fictional as anything in the actual books. Then there are the celebrity novels. You know most of those are ghostwritten. Do the people reading them know it? Does the celeb admit it? Oh, I'm sure there are exceptions, but it's a standard practice."

"For marketing. I didn't do it for that, yet Chris *has* helped sales."

"Which makes you feel guilty. Do you think those celebrities feel guilty? Fine. Skip the celebs. Regular authors who use pen names are not trying to deceive readers. It's about privacy. Which is exactly what you wanted. To get your book published and stay out of the limelight. Are there readers who feel deceived when they discover an author uses a fake name or a fake persona or a fake photo? Sure, but that wasn't the author's intention, and that persona is not what they're selling. The *book* is what they're selling. I don't owe my clients one whit of personal information. I owe them what they're paying me for—damn fine legal expertise. Readers are paying for your book. Not for Zane Remington. Sure, some *would* pay for Zane Remington, but that isn't a service he's offering."

Daphne smiled and shifted. "But I still want to come out."

"I agree. It's the rationale that I'm arguing with. You did not set out to deceive readers. However, this has gone way beyond a fake name, bio, and cover photo."

"I know, and I feel terrible. This isn't what you had in mind when we came up with the plan, and if it could get you in any trouble—"

"Stop. It can't, and I'm the one who pushed this solution on you, so if anyone should feel bad, it's me."

"You didn't—"

"Did. But the point is that neither of us foresaw TV segments and tours. No matter how careful you are, the risk is growing exponentially. It's not a question of *if* you'll be outed. It's a question of *when*. Someone *will* recognize you. Someone *will* recognize Chris. We need to get ahead of that."

Daphne swallowed. "Okay. I'll notify my agent before the tour—"

"Not before the tour. It's too soon, and it'd throw everyone into a tizzy. For now, don't say anything to anyone except Chris. I need to deep-dive into this and find you an exit strategy."

"One that doesn't torpedo my career."

"That's baseline," Nia said. "As a lawyer, I want a solution that doesn't hurt my client's career. As a friend, I want one that makes you look *good*. We want to focus on why you did this without throwing your publisher under the bus by implying they wouldn't have bought your book under your name."

"They might have."

"Yeah, not for that much and not with this positioning. But what do I know? I'm just the best friend of a writer who tried damned hard to get anyone to look at her amazing book, and then as soon as she put a guy's name on it, she got a half-million-dollar deal. Sheer coincidence, I'm sure."

"But since we don't know what *would* have happened, no one else is to blame. I got frustrated. I sent it out using a male name. Then I panicked when it sold."

"Which we'll make clear," Nia said. "We will fix this. Just give me time to come up with a strategy. And whatever we decide, Chris has to be part of the conversation."

"Of course. I'll talk to him. And thank you for finding him. He's been amazing."

"He's a pretty amazing guy, huh?"

Daphne blushed. "He is."

"And you like him?"

Her instinct was to deflect and dodge. To be clear she liked him *as a person*. Instead, she took a deep breath and said, "I like him."

"Good." Nia switched to her *Pinky and the Brain* voice. "Everything is going according to plan."

Daphne sighed. But for once, she didn't argue.

"Thank you," she said.

"That's what best friends are for. Now get up, do some writing, pack for tour, and call me from LA. I am *dying* to hear how those Hollywood meetings go."

CHRIS

It was the last night before the tour, and Chris was soundly asleep after one final phone call with Daphne. They'd discussed ideas for Zane's exit, which he was fine with—he couldn't wait for everyone to know she was the real author. They'd also excitedly made plans for tomorrow. Well, he'd certainly been excited, and she'd seemed happy, so yep, they were both excited. He was going with that.

When the phone rang, he bolted up, certain he'd overslept and Daphne was calling from the airport wondering where he was.

Then he saw his sister's name on his phone. He glanced at the clock—1:10.

With a groan, he answered. "Tell me it's urgent," he said. "Tell me something is on fire and that you are not calling at one in the morning to be a brat."

"Me?" Gemma said. "I'm the older sibling. You're the brat. And I'm calling because, if I'm right, you've done the brattiest of all bratty possible things."

"Uh…"

"Worse than when you changed my alarm clock so you could find all the Easter eggs first. Worse than when you used my training bra as a slingshot. Even worse than when you threatened to tell Mom about my party if I wouldn't give you a joint."

"*Beer*. I said *beer*."

"Whatever. Tell me this isn't you."

His phone buzzed with an incoming text. It was a still shot from the grizzly stare-down video.

His first thought: *Oh shit.*

Second thought: *How'd she recognize me from a sliver of my profile?*

Third thought: *She's your sister, dumbass.*

"You sold a book?" she said. "Seriously, Chris? It's not enough that I've spent the last few years having friends—*friends*, ew—asking for my little brother's contact deets. Not enough that you're running your own company. Not enough that all that hasn't gone to your head. Now you're an author? *I'm* the writer in the family. *Me*."

"When's the last time you wrote something, Gem?"

"Shut up."

"Just saying," he murmured. "I've been pestering you to get back into writing for years."

"So this is like when you stole my bike, thinking I was done with it because I hadn't ridden in a year?"

"I didn't write a book."

"But you're the guy in this video."

He considered lying. Considered it for less than one second, because this was Gemma and he'd never do that to her. So he told her the truth.

When he finished the story, Gemma said, "This woman couldn't get her book published, so she stuck a male name on it and it sold? Figures. Okay, I forgive you. You got stuck in a bad place with your business partner—I told you he was a creep—and you fixed it by helping this woman get out of *her* bad place. Which is such a Chris thing to do. On second thought, no, I still hate you. You're too good. Tell me she's hot, and that's the real reason you did it."

When he hesitated, she sputtered, "Oh my God, it is? She's hot, and that's why—"

"I needed her friend's help, and she seemed like a nice person stuck in a bad situation."

"Who is also hot." Gemma burst out laughing. "Okay, I hate you a little less now. You're still human. She does know you're not this cool Zane dude, right?"

"Yes, she knows my Clark Kent side, the accountant who is secretly a dork."

"Oh, it's no secret, bro. Not to anyone who knows you. Okay, so you're playing author for this woman, and yes, I will keep quiet about that. But if I figured it out, someone else will."

"We're working on an exit strategy."

"Good. In the meantime, I'm downloading the book. It'll give me something to read tonight."

"It's one in the morning, Gem." He paused. "You okay?"

"Fine, fine. Just not sleeping great."

He sat up. "Oh shit. The divorce. The negotiations started, didn't they?"

"Yep, the fun has begun, including Alan showing up and parking his twenty-three-year-old girlfriend and eleven-month-old baby in the waiting room. You know, I might not be the math whiz in the family, but if that kid is eleven months old, and Alan walked out sixteen months ago…"

"I'm so sorry, Gem."

"Eh, don't worry. I'm totally using it for the divorce. What an idiot, huh? Couldn't even hide the kid for a little longer."

Chris's heart ached for his sister. He knew her marriage had been worse than she'd ever let on, and he felt incredibly guilty about that—his whole family did—but Gemma was Gemma. If she'd made a mistake marrying Alan, she'd soldier through and handle it herself. Even now Chris couldn't get her to talk about it.

"Do you need anything?" he said. "I could—"

"According to my insomniac digging on Zane Remington, you are headed for Los Angeles tomorrow. Even if you weren't, I'm fine."

"I'm sorry I forgot about the divorce proceedings, and I'll call you every day to see how you're doing."

"Ugh, you're such an annoyingly perfect little brother. Fine. Call. But only if you share author-tour dish."

"Only if you consider writing again."

"Fine. Maybe. Whatever. So about this woman you like. Have you baked for her yet?"

"Baked for her?"

"That's your secret weapon, Chris. Bake her something."

"I made her a batch of brownies for the book release."

"Good man."

"And then I pretended I bought them at a bakery."

"Oof," she said. "You are such a guy sometimes. Bake her more brownies. Admit you made them."

"Yes, ma'am."

"Bake me a batch, too."

"I'll make brownies and send them before I leave."

"*Such* an annoyingly perfect little brother." Her voice softened. "Good night, Chris."

"Good night, Gem."

CHAPTER TWELVE

DAPHNE

Daphne was sitting in business class. With the "rich people," as her mother always said when they'd boarded a flight. On the last vacation they'd planned together, when they knew the end was coming fast, Daphne had bought business-class seats for a trip to France, nearly emptying her savings to pay for them. Then the doctors decided her mother shouldn't be flying, and they'd settled for a train to Banff, still business class, which had delighted her mother.

"Someday," her mother used to say, "you'll sell your books and fly business class around the world."

Daphne had laughed. "You have no idea how much books actually make, do you, Mom?"

"You'll be different."

And now, here she was, flying business class on her very first book tour, and her fingers kept itching to take a photo for her mom. Maybe that should hurt, but instead it made her smile.

She could say her mom would be proud, but her mom had already been proud of her, and that was what mattered.

She'd dropped Tika off with the neighbor, Pam. Then she'd caught an Air North flight—that was the Yukon airline, which she preferred to use, even if it didn't have a business class.

Chris had met her at the Vancouver airport. Now they were on the flight to LA.

"I have leg room," Daphne crowed. "And elbow room."

"Pretty sweet, huh?"

"No, *these* are pretty sweet."

She lifted the box of brownies Chris had brought. They were the same kind he'd sent her at release. Last week, she'd considered contacting the bakery and trying to get a box shipped to the Yukon. Good thing she hadn't, because the brownies hadn't actually been from there. Chris had baked them.

He'd *baked* the most delicious brownies she'd ever had.

"Still looking for the photo, though," she said as she waggled the box.

He grinned and shrugged. "I figured you already had one. The view doesn't change."

She wanted to follow up on that. Joke about ways the view could change…maybe if there wasn't a strategically placed brownie box. She'd punted a ball that he hadn't ignored but hadn't exactly knocked back, either.

She hadn't forgotten their kiss the other day. On a scale of fake-dating kisses, from polite to "totally designed to convince someone you were in a relationship," that kiss was a twelve. Maybe thirteen.

It hadn't felt fake. It'd felt as if they were five minutes from ripping off clothing, and with him pressed against her, there was no way she'd mistaken how much he'd been into it. But he hadn't mentioned it since Lawrence's call had interrupted them.

At least he'd brought brownies.

"You know what you could have tucked inside instead?" she said as she set the box down. "The recipe."

"Ah, but if I give you that, then you won't need me to bake them for you. I know what I'm doing. As long as I hold the recipe hostage, you have to keep me around for the brownies."

"Fair point," she said. "I can't see any other reason why I'd keep you around."

"Then I guess I *should* have included the photo."

She laughed. That felt like flirting.

The flight attendant came by with a tray of orange juice, water, and something else.

"Sparkling water?" Daphne said, pointing at the bubbly clear liquid.

The attendant smiled. "Sparkling wine."

Daphne took one of those glasses. So did Chris.

When the attendant moved on, Daphne leaned over and whispered, "It's still morning, and we aren't even off the ground yet, and we're getting booze."

"Now you know why I pushed for business class." He held out his glass. "To an amazing tour for an amazing book."

Her cheeks warmed, but she clinked glasses, saying, "And to an amazing fake author."

He laughed and sipped his wine.

"Would you like a brownie with that?" she said, lifting the box.

"If you're willing to share."

"I am."

CHRIS

In LA, a car picked them up at the airport. Not a taxi, either. A black town car, complete with chauffeur who met them at the luggage carousel and insisted on taking their luggage. The car also held a full snack service of food and beverages. Chris was trying very hard not to gawk and giggle like a kid whose parents rented him a limo for graduation. Daphne was doing plenty of grinning, as she had on the plane, and he was just going to play it cool and enjoy her excitement.

The snacks came in handy once they hit the city and the car moved so slowly he could have walked alongside it...backward. He'd heard of LA traffic. A client had lamented it during a recent meeting, and Chris had commiserated as if he'd suffered through it a hundred times. Truth was, he'd never actually been to LA.

Being in traffic gave them time to come up with a list of questions to ask the film people, since they'd now need to go directly to the meetings. They were supposed to have two hours at their hotel to freshen up, but this traffic meant they'd be changing in a restroom. Daphne seemed a little panicked by that, but he assured her that no one cared if they weren't looking their best. They weren't actors—just a novelist and his assistant.

That reasoning worked until they reached the meeting hotel with only five minutes to spare. They dashed to their respective restrooms for a quick freshen-up. For Chris, that meant changing his shirt and shoes and splashing water on his face. He expected Daphne to take longer, but she was out before he was. She'd put on a dress, restyled her hair, *and* applied makeup.

"That was fast," he said.

"Being a wee bit stressed, I figured it was better not to linger in the immediate vicinity of toilets."

He laughed at that. He considered offering himself up as a tribute for make-out stress relief instead. Nope. Play it cool. Give her no concerns that he expected this trip to include a hookup. It was all about getting to know each other.

They hurried down the hall toward the room indicated on Lawrence's email.

"Did your bathroom have linen hand towels?" he whispered to Daphne as they walked.

"And three kinds of designer-label hand soap," she whispered back. "I was tempted to slide one into my luggage. It's a hotel. They're freebies, right?"

"Tell me which one you wanted, and I'll make sure it falls into my pocket."

She laughed and also relaxed. He took hold of the smoked-glass meeting-room door, opened it, and ushered her in. He stepped through with an apology on his lips only to find...

"No one's here," Daphne whispered, as if someone might step from behind the giant potted plants. "Did we get the right room?"

He backed out the doors to where he'd seen a discreet schedule on the wall.

3 PM–6 PM: Edge meetings

He checked his watch. 3:07. Daphne read the schedule, checked her own watch, and then they went back inside.

"Is that *more* food?" she said. "I'm still stuffed from the spread in the car."

It was indeed more food. A small buffet stretched along the wall.

"Isn't this LA?" she whispered. "I thought no one here ate."

He walked over to look down at the spread. "It's a little-known LA secret that charcuterie boards have no calories. At least not if they're made up of meats and cheeses people like us don't even recognize."

"Good to know. Better hope the studio folks are hungry."

They grazed a bit at the table, mostly picking and talking as they waited. When ten minutes passed—and it was now 3:17—Daphne declared their three o'clock meeting canceled.

"It was a last-minute thing," she said. "That's fine."

"It is. Remember that two more couldn't make it on such short notice, but they're still interested. It's not this or nothing, even if you do decide you want to option it. What time's the second meeting?"

She checked Zane's email. "3:45."

"Let's get comfy then."

DAPHNE

At 3:30, the door swung open and a middle-aged man strode in, followed by a quartet of sleekly dressed twentysomethings.

Chris rose and extended a hand. "Mr.—"

"Zimmerman," he said.

Chris shot her a quizzical look, and she discreetly shook her head. This was not their second appointment. It was their first.

"Damn traffic," Zimmerman said as he shook Chris's hand. "Typical LA, huh?"

Chris gave his Zane laugh. "Indeed."

One would think a resident would know that and prepare for it.

"Can I just say how much I love your book." Zimmerman kept pumping Chris's hand. "Absolutely riveting. My assistant"—a vague nod that incorporated all four young people—"gave it to me the other day, and I could not put it down."

"That's very kind."

"Not kind at all. *Truth.* Genius, my boy. Absolute genius. The plotting, the characters. Especially the characters. Theo? She's wonderful. Just wonderful. So clever and resourceful." He turned to the quartet. "Isn't she great?"

Agreement all around.

"We loved the book. Absolutely loved it. Everyone said, 'We *must* have this book.'"

More noises of agreement. Zimmerman took a seat at the table, and his assistants flanked him in pairs. Chris sat with Daphne beside him.

"And this is my—" Chris began, gesturing at Daphne.

"Lovely to meet you, dear. Now"—his gaze locked on Chris's—"let's talk adaptation. I like to rip the bandage off right away with the question every writer wants answered. What would we change?"

Chris nodded. "I understand changes *will* be required. Screen is a new medium, which naturally requires alterations."

"So glad to hear you say that." Zimmerman leaned in conspiratorially. "You would not believe how many authors expect to see their book directly translated to screen."

Chris smiled. "Personally, I can't imagine anything more dull."

He'd argued about saying that, but Daphne had insisted. It was true. A direct translation of any book would be boring. There were long passages of Theo alone, working and planning and worrying. That worked for a book; it would not work on-screen.

Chris continued, "We've all seen adaptations where the translation stuck too close to the source material. It doesn't do either of us any favors. I want a good film because that's how I'll bring in new readers."

Zimmerman beamed. "That's the spirit, my boy. All right then. Let's dive in. We'll start small. I see Jennifer Lawrence playing Theo."

Chris hesitated, but quickly recovered with a small laugh. "I would love to see a Jennifer Lawrence type in this. She was amazing in *The Hunger Games*."

"No, I mean *the* Jennifer Lawrence."

"I…" Chris cleared his throat and managed another laugh. "She's a little older than Theo, but makeup can do wonders."

"We're aging up the character. I'm thinking thirty." He jabbed a finger at his assistants. "We want *them* in those seats. Young people who grew up on *Hunger Games*."

One of the two young women cleared her throat. "I was only nine when—"

At Zimmerman's glare, she squeaked, "And I loved it."

"That's what we want," Zimmerman said. "Kids who grew up with the *Hunger Games*, only they aren't kids anymore. They're adults, and they're looking for something a little sexier, a little more..." He snapped his fingers. "What's that movie?"

Blank looks from all four.

"With the bondage. Based on books."

"*Fifty Shades?*" one of the young men said tentatively. "But that came out in—"

"That's what we want. Sexy *Hunger Games*."

"With zombies," one of the other assistants said, grinning like she'd guessed a *Jeopardy!* question.

"Zombies?" Zimmerman snapped. "No one's had a zombie hit in three years. Go stand in the hall."

Daphne started to force a smile, presuming he was joking, but the young woman slid from the table and slunk into the hall.

When the door closed behind her, Zimmerman leaned over and said, "I'm thinking vampires."

CHRIS

"We loved the book," said the woman who'd just entered the room with her quartet of assistants. Meeting number four. By this point, Chris no longer bothered with names.

"I loved the book," the woman repeated. There'd been no long handshake this time. Just a fist bump. As they sat, she enthused over *Edge*. Wonderful. Amazing. *So good.* Could not put it down. Pure genius. The plot, the characters, the setting. Absolutely wonderful.

That was what they all said. So wonderful, and all it needed was, well, a complete overhaul of that wonderful plot, characters, and setting, depending on what was currently hot. Or what the boss *thought* was currently hot.

"So good," the woman said. She turned to her four underlings. "Right?"

They agreed, as always.

"I just…" The woman fluttered her hands. "I don't think I can convey how excited we are about this project. We cannot wait to put your wonderful book on-screen and share it with the world. That would be exciting, wouldn't it?"

"It would," Chris said.

The woman shifted, as if this wasn't quite the level of enthusiasm she expected.

"Your book," she said. "On a screen. If I were a writer, it'd be a dream come true. Your words come to life. The chance to *see* the story you wrote."

Chris wasn't even a writer, and he knew this was bullshit. Writers like Daphne and Gemma saw the story in their heads. It *was* real to them. It *had* come alive for them. They didn't need someone to put it up on a screen.

Yep, after three of these meetings, he'd gone from excited puppy to curmudgeonly cynic. More important, it wasn't just him. Daphne had a faraway look that told him she was present in body only.

"That's great," Chris said. "We really appreciate your enthusiasm, and we appreciate you speaking with us today. We're very excited about the possibility of seeing *Edge* on screen."

Did she notice the use of "we"? Nope. He'd figured that out during the last meeting. The execs tended to use it themselves, and he presumed it meant "the team" rather than the royal we, but at this point,

he no longer gave a shit. If it meant he could include Daphne, then he
was rolling with it.

"We want to see it on-screen, too," the producer said. "That's why
we're here." An obligatory laugh from the assistants. "We are *so*
excited."

"That's great," Chris repeated, trying to sound as if he meant it.
"While we're on the topic of adaptations, tell me a few scenes you'd
remove." He held up his hands. "That's not a loaded question. I've
asked it of the last couple of folks, too, and this isn't a competition to
see who'd change the least. We respect changes. We just want a sense
of how your changes would align with our vision."

"I am so glad you're open to changes."

"I've heard that," Chris murmured. "Now, admittedly, we do have
limits. If you wanted to make the main character thirty, that's a problem. If you wanted to make her male"—*producer two*—"that is also a
problem. If you want to relocate it to space with aliens instead of zombies"—*producer three*—"that's a problem. In those cases, I'm going to
be blunt, you should just have someone write an original screenplay
rather than optioning our book."

"Agreed," the woman said. "I have no intention of making changes
like that."

"Good. So, let's try something else to get a sense of your vision. Take
a scene from the novel and tell us how you'd envision it on screen."

The woman stopped, her mouth open.

One of her assistants leaned forward. "If I might be so bold, we discussed this earlier and I'd like to talk about the scene where Theo
meets Atticus."

"Yes!" the producer said. "I loved that scene. So dramatic. The first
meeting between potential love interests. I wouldn't call it a meet-cute,
but…"

Her assistants laughed.

"So tell me about that scene," he said. "Frame it for me."

"Why don't I let Tricia here—"

"No, I want to hear it in your words." Chris met the exec's gaze. "You *did* read more than the synopsis, right?"

She bristled. "Of course."

"More than a skim of the first chapter?"

"I read the entire book, as I said."

"Great." He leaned back in his chair. "So block out Theo and Atticus's first meeting for me. In your own words."

DAPHNE

Four execs, and none had read the book. She told herself that was okay—they were very busy people—and it *would* be okay...if they just admitted to it. If they hadn't gushed over the book and her writing and how they were "so excited" only for her to realize they'd just read the paragraph-long description on the cover flap.

Someone in their office—an underling in charge of finding new projects—had stumbled on *Edge*. That person read the flap copy and thought it sounded viable. That person or someone else in the office actually read or skimmed the book to prepare for the meeting.

It wasn't about *Edge*. It was about getting in on the ground floor of a hot new property that might come with a built-in audience and proven appeal. Daphne understood that. She really did. Personally, she didn't care how or why *Edge* got on the screen. It would be the next stage—once the writers got hold of it—that people would actually read and adapt it.

She just wanted honesty.

From Hollywood?

Yes, that wasn't usually the place one went for honesty, but it was more than that. She wanted the respect of being treated like a business partner and not a flaky creative who needed her ego pumped.

Tell me you haven't read it yet, but you love the concept and would like to work with me on it. Don't treat me like a teenager squeeing over the chance to see her story on-screen. Talk to me as if I'm an adult who understands how this can be mutually beneficial.

That was why she'd had Chris say he understood those benefits as well as understanding the need for changes.

And by "need for changes," she'd meant scenes would likely need to be removed or added, secondary characters removed or added, backstories tweaked, whatever worked better on-screen. If they walked in and said they wanted to discuss another setting or changing Theo's ethnicity or making Finn or Atticus a girl, she'd have been fine with that. Instead, what they'd suggested told her they didn't want her story—just the barest trappings of her concept plus the growing audience.

As number four left, Daphne leaned over to whisper, "Would you kill me if I wanted to sit this last one out?"

"I would completely understand."

"Thank you."

Daphne slid into the hall to find a man and a woman talking in hushed voices as the woman checked her watch.

"Ms. Begum?" Daphne said.

The woman turned, and her annoyance smoothed out. "Yes?"

"I work with Mr. Remington. So sorry to keep you waiting."

"Oh, I know why we were waiting."

The man rolled his eyes and mimicked, "Oh my God, you wouldn't *believe* the traffic." He shook his head. "You'd think they flew in from Kansas. No disrespect to Kansas. That's my home turf." He extended a hand. "Colin McKay."

"My partner," Ms. Begum said. "I wasn't sure Colin could make it or I'd have let your agent know."

"Daphne McFadden," she said, extending a hand.

"We are looking forward to meeting with your boss. I enjoyed his book very much."

Daphne tried not to sag and plastered on a smile. "That's good."

"I have a question before we go in. I know Mr. Remington lives in Canada's Yukon. Any reason why he set the book in Alaska?"

"That...might not have been his idea."

Ms. Begum laughed. "Ah, appealing to the wider market. I wondered, especially when the book didn't seem to be set near the coast."

"Mmm, yeah. Consider it inland Alaska."

"Do you think he'd object to a more coastal Alaska setting? I know the perfect place—we've filmed there before. When I was reading the scene where Theo and Finn get stranded on a raft during a storm, I kept imagining it in the ocean instead of a lake. Rocky coasts, crashing waves..."

"I think Mr. Remington would be quite open to changes like that." Daphne reached for the doorknob. "Let me take you in."

She ushered Ms. Begum and Mr. McKay inside and introduced them.

As Ms. Begum shook Chris's hand, she said, "I very much enjoyed your book, and I'm happy you had the time to see us today."

Mr. McKay extended his hand. "And I haven't had a chance to read it, but I'm looking forward to doing that. Today, I'm just here to listen."

Chris looked over at Daphne, his brows raising in unspoken question.

"I think I'll stay," she murmured, and took her seat beside him.

CHAPTER THIRTEEN

CHRIS

They were finally in the hotel. The meeting with Begum and McKay had run until nearly seven, and by then, they were both wiped out. It felt like a week's worth of frustration and disappointment and hope all crammed into a few hours.

They hadn't discussed the film meetings yet. Chris could tell from Daphne's expression that she was, once again, a million miles away. This time, though, it wasn't disengaging to protect herself; it was sinking into a whirling mass of thoughts, sorting through them all. Happy thoughts...or so he hoped.

As for him, he'd felt all that frustration and disappointment and hope along with her. Once in the car—another hired town car—he texted Gemma to see how her day had gone.

> **Gemma:** I love the book! Still reading, but it's exactly the break I needed.

> **Chris:** I'm glad. How was today's negotiation meeting?

> **Gemma:** Can we talk about the book instead?

> **Chris:** We sure can. What part are you at?

They'd continued like that until Chris and Daphne reached the hotel, which was so close they could have walked. Chris had wondered why they didn't just stay at the meeting hotel, but after seeing that one, he'd presumed it was because *that* hotel—while suitable for Hollywood meetings—was not meant for mere writers, even if they were bestsellers.

He was wrong. Their hotel was equally nice, but tiny, the sort he knew from client accounting would be considered "boutique." Which meant small and fancy rather than grand and fancy. Definitely no meeting space room here.

As they checked in, Daphne stayed quiet, giving only murmured answers to his questions, until they were upstairs.

"You want me to leave you alone for a while?" he said.

She turned and blinked, and he swore he could see her mentally rising to the surface.

Her eyes widened. "No. I'm so sorry. I've barely said five words—"

"It's been an exhausting day. If you want a quiet night in with room service, that's fine. If you want dinner out together, that's fine, too. Totally your call."

"I'm not ready to call it a night, but I'm not sure I want to go out and people."

He smiled. "No peopling then. How about room service in your room? We can talk about the meetings, and you can kick me out whenever you've had enough."

Or . . . not kick me out.

Nope, he wasn't going there, however much he might want it.

Here's the thing about hope, buddy. It only gets you so far. After that, you need to take matters into your own hands.

He'd wait and see how the evening went. Maybe a little flirting and, if that worked, a kiss.

Yep, definitely going to be taking things into your own hands tonight. Alone. In your shower.

"That sounds great," Daphne said. "If you're up for company."

His brain was still stuck on what that inner voice had been saying, which put an entirely different spin on Daphne's response.

Yeah, at this point, I think she could tell you her shower was broken and joke about sharing yours, and you'd only end up sitting on the bed while she used your shower.

"Chris?"

He shook it off. "Yes. I mean, that sounds good. Room service for two."

Sigh…

"You okay?" she said. "You seem a little out of it. Tired?"

"No, no. Now let's see your room. Make sure the shower's working."

She frowned, and he remembered that part of the conversation had been entirely in his head.

He shook his head and laughed. "Just kidding. The last time I was at a hotel, the shower was broken."

"Ah."

"If it is, you can always use mine."

What the hell is that? It isn't flirty. It doesn't even make sense.

He quickly added, "That's why we have adjoining rooms."

He swore he heard that inner voice do an inner face-palm.

Daphne smiled and shook her head. "Long afternoon, wasn't it?"

"The longest."

"Think our rooms have a minibar?"

"If not, I'm telling them to bring the drinks up *before* dinner."

"Excellent plan." She opened her door and stepped in. "Oh my God."

"What's wrong?"

She wheeled, eyes widening. "The shower is broken."

Run with it. Come on, you can do it. Take the ball and run—

"Couldn't resist," she said, squeezing his arm ever so gently. "Either this room is gorgeous or I'm so tired that anything with a bed looks like the Ritz."

The ball is right there. Grab it and—

Daphne walked over to the bed and collapsed face-first on it with a little moan of pleasure.

If you fumble this, that's it. I really and truly give up on you.

He walked over to stand at the foot of the bed, gave a dramatic pause, and then collapsed backward onto it.

Fine. This is acceptable. The ball is in play.

Daphne turned her face sideways, and he did the same.

"Fancy meeting you here," he said.

She laughed softly. "Not a bad place to meet."

"Not bad at all. I could joke about finally getting you in bed, but that seems a little…" He scrunched his nose. "Obvious?"

"And not really your style."

"True. My style is more…" He reached one hand up to gently touch her face, as he met her eyes. "Hey."

She blushed. Then she leaned into his hand—

His cell phone blared. It didn't just ring. It *blared*. He snatched it up to hit Ignore, but as he did, Daphne leaned over and saw the caller.

"Lawrence," she groaned as she sat up. "He's waiting for an update."

Chris realized that it was possible he'd never hated anyone quite as much as he hated Lawrence.

"It can wait," he tried, but Daphne was already rubbing her eyes and rolling her shoulders, as if roused from sleep.

"I really should email him," she said.

He tapped in a quick text to Lawrence and showed it to her. She nodded, and he hit Send. The message said that he was exhausted and wanted to collect his thoughts but would call soon.

That took care of Lawrence, but it didn't rewind the clock. Daphne was up and adjusting her hair and looking everywhere except at him.

"Hey," he said.

She glanced back at him, still stretched on the bed. Something flickered in her eyes. A flash of regret for a lost moment? Maybe they could recapture it.

No, recovering a moment was always awkward, and he was too good at awkward already. Also, didn't he keep telling himself he wasn't jumping into bed with her? Doing that—even semi-innocently— seemed guaranteed to derail his plan. Slow and steady.

He pushed up on one arm, propped on the bed. "Do you want to talk about the film stuff? Or shelve it for a while?"

"Both?"

She sat on the end of the bed. Close enough for him to reach over and tug her down into a kiss. He didn't because, yeah, he might fumble the ball—a lot—but he also understood when he'd be grabbing for one she hadn't thrown.

The moment had passed. She needed something else right now.

"Is that a bottle of bubbly?" he said.

She started to smile, as if he were joking, but then she followed his gaze to a basket on the desk. She bounced up and grabbed it, then returned to the end of the bed again and set the basket between them.

"Ooh, goodies," she crowed. "From the film people. I guess this was supposed to be *your* room."

"No, it's supposed to be the author's room. Which means the basket is yours. Let's see what you have."

The card on the basket said it'd been sent by Begum and McKay. Then the hotel had added in gifts from two others.

"Apparently, Zane Remington likes..." He lifted a bottle.

"Single-malt scotch." She peered at him. "You don't actually like scotch, do you?"

"Pfft. Of course I like—"

"Liar. I saw your face when you spotted that bottle."

"It's the brand."

"But the one *I* gave you was a brand you like," she says.

"Exactly."

She leaned back on the bed, propped on her elbow facing his way. "Name it."

"Glen...something? From Scotland?" He leaned back, too, and faced her. "I think it had a deer on the label. Or a thistle. I only know labels. That's how I remember which one to buy."

"Good. I mean, if you'd only said you liked scotch because you thought Zane would, I'd appreciate your honesty. But since you really do like it, when I get my first royalty check, I'm buying you a whole case of it." She lifted a hand. "No, I insist."

"I..."

"Hate scotch?"

"No, no, it's just..."

She reached over, took the scotch bottle, and opened it.

"Screw glasses," she said. "I'm going to be a cretin and drink single-malt straight from the bottle." She took a slug, eyes watering as she gasped. "Wow. That's good." She held it out. "Your turn."

He took the bottle.

"Bottoms up," she said.

He braced himself, took a long drink, and—

He nearly dropped the bottle as he sputtered and coughed.

"Poor baby," she said, patting him between the shoulder blades. "That just went down the wrong tube, didn't it? Here, take another drink. That'll help."

He lifted his hands. "I surrender."

"So you lied?"

He hesitated. She lifted the bottle.

"I lied," he blurted.

"Totally lied." She moved her face closer to his. Then both of them were lying on the bed. "Such a liar. A very sweet liar, who didn't want to hurt the feelings of someone who got him a gift, but still…"

"Sweet?"

She sputtered a laugh. "I was going to say still a liar. But yes, also very…" Her gaze met his face less than a foot away. "…Very sweet."

He inched forward, testing his welcome. She leaned toward him and—

His phone buzzed.

Lawrence: NP. Get back to me when you're ready to talk.

Chris had never been the phone-throwing sort, but he finally understood the appeal.

He shoved the phone into his back pocket, looked over toward Daphne, and found himself staring at an empty space on the bed.

Daphne was sitting up, rifling through the basket.

I hate you, Lawrence. Oh, I'm sure you're a very nice guy, and you did sell Daphne's book for a crapload of money, which I appreciate, but I am still blocking your number.

"How about the bubbly?" Daphne said, waving the bottle.

He hesitated, but once again the moment had passed, and he had to trust it would return on its own.

It would. He'd make sure of that.

"Sure, break out the bubbly."

"Can we talk about the meetings?" she said as she retrieved the glasses. "We really should get back to Lawrence. It's after ten p.m. in New York, and he's obviously waiting."

And the longer he waits, the more he'll call. "Let's get this over with," he said.

They talked about the meetings. Daphne didn't care that the first four people had connections to the biggest studios. There was little point in having a TV adaptation if it didn't at least fundamentally resemble your book. All she'd get from that was one-star reviews on the book because it wasn't exactly like the show, plus emails from readers angry that she'd let them "ruin" her book.

She liked Begum and McKay, but just because they seemed like a good fit didn't mean they would be. It also didn't mean they'd commit to an option. Her agent wanted a paid option, and Chris wholeheartedly agreed.

An option meant they paid for the exclusive right to shop the project to studios for a set period. A shopping agreement was the same, except usually no money would change hands until a studio accepted the project.

Daphne deserved to be paid for taking her book off the film market. That was just common sense, but the market had apparently been slowly shifting toward freebies. Chris was glad Daphne's film agent was holding out for better.

Chris ordered room service dinner while Daphne jotted notes for Lawrence. They'd decided to email him Zane's thoughts instead of calling. If he—or Lucy the film agent—wanted to talk, that could wait until morning.

By the time dinner arrived, the email had been sent. Lawrence had replied with a thumbs-up and a promise to forward it to Lucy, which seemed to mean they could set that aside and await the next step.

They ate dinner in the sitting area, Daphne on the love seat, Chris in the armchair. Afterward, Chris answered a couple of business emails while Daphne did the same.

"Okay," he said as he finished up the last one. "Work done, and it's barely nine. Do you want to kick me out yet? Or chill and watch a show together?" He lifted his gaze from the phone, a grin sparking. "I think they have Netflix."

He waited for her response. Was she going to snatch the bait, make some "Netflix and chill" joke that he could riff off of? That might be a way to get them back where they'd been earlier. Start a little double-entendre'ing that could lead to flirting that could lead to...

"D?" he said. She was sitting sideways on the love seat, facing the other way, laptop in place. One hand lolled on the floor. Chris scrambled to his feet.

"Daphne?"

Her lips parted in the softest snore.

Chris laughed under his breath. Seems she'd already made her plans for the evening, and he couldn't blame her. She must be exhausted—early flight plus the roller coaster of the meetings this afternoon.

The question was: What to do with her? She was very soundly asleep and not in the most comfortable spot, with her feet dangling over the end.

Did he leave her and slip out? Did he carry her to bed? What if she woke up while he was putting her to bed and thought he had something else in mind?

Do *you have something else in mind?*

Of course not.

Then don't worry about it. She knows you better than that.

True.

Yep, so maybe you should listen to me more often.

He ignored the voice and walked to the bed, where he pulled back the covers. Then he gently carried her over. She barely stirred. He set her down, pulled up the covers, and stood there, looking down at her.

Don't make this creepy.

He wasn't trying to make it creepy. He was taking a moment to look at her, so deeply asleep and peaceful, her dark hair spread over the pillow.

He bent over and very softly kissed her temple. "Sweet dreams, D," he murmured. Then he slipped back to his own room.

DAPHNE

Daphne had dreamed of Chris. Floating in that semi-lucid state before waking, she wasn't quite certain of the specifics of the dream, only that she wanted to slide back there and stay awhile. There'd been a bottle of scotch and a very sturdy tree and brownie batter, and she had no idea how all that had fit together—or if she wanted to know—but it didn't matter because there'd also been Chris. Which was all any dream needed to make perfect sense.

When she couldn't quite find the dream again, her brain surfaced but lingered there, writing its own version, because that was what she did. She told herself stories, and this one was still ephemeral, woven of sight and sound and smell and feeling. Mostly feeling. The feeling of his body against hers, his mouth against hers, the crushing need to get closer to him. The rest was a delicious jumble—a sliver of stubbled jawline, a whiff of peaty scotch, a soft laugh, a flash of his green eyes, the smell of evergreen trees, a low groan at her ear. She groaned back, pressing into the pillow, imagining it was him, his hands running down her back—

The buzz of her phone sent her flailing. One moment of confusion, followed by one very sharp surge of annoyance.

Goddamn it, Lawrence. If that's you again—

Except Lawrence's calls forwarded to Chris's phone. She looked to see a name she didn't recognize.

Sakura Mori.

Who was…?

Her new publicist.

Daphne fumbled to answer, only for her foggy brain to realize it was actually a text.

> **Sakura:** Hey, so I can't get hold of Zane, and I have both your numbers. Are we still on for breakfast?

With a groan, Daphne started to type back and say yes, they were still on and they'd see Sakura at nine. Then she saw the bedside clock.

9:15

She scrambled up and looked around. Her brain was still reorienting after that dream. She'd fallen asleep on the sofa, hadn't she? Then why was she in bed? For one brief moment, she expected to look across the sheets and see Chris there.

The other side of the bed was empty, with the covers still turned up. Okay, so that hadn't happened.

Was that a pang of disappointment?

Not exactly. Yes, she would hate to forget having sex with Chris, the memory reduced to a few sexy flashes of scotch, trees, and brownie batter. Still, if they *did* have sex, that would imply more sex was coming, and given the choice between forgetting the first time and never having a first, second, and third time…

Your publicist is waiting downstairs. For breakfast. While you stand here regretting the lack of amnesiac sex with Chris.

She reached to grab clothing…only to realize she was wearing it. Because he'd put her to bed fully dressed rather than take liberties, even innocently.

Was *that* disappointing?

Nope, it was sexy. Even sexier than erotic dreams of scotch and trees and—

Publicist. Late. Move!

She flew to the adjoining door, banged her fist against it…and the door opened, as if having not been properly shut. She caught one glimpse of Chris on his stomach, tangled in the covers, naked. Like totally naked, one twisted sheet covering his hip but riding up high enough to give a full cheek view—

He opened one eye and looked straight at her.

"Oh my God." She stumbled back, smacked into the nightstand—*that* was going to bruise—and slammed the door. "I'm so sorry," she called through it. "I knocked, and the door must not have been pulled shut."

A lazy, sexy chuckle. "It's fine. You can come in. I'm decent."

She hesitated. Did he think he was wearing underwear? Or did he just figure the sheet covered enough? Either way, he'd given permission, right?

She pushed open the door to see him untangling the sheet, and the polite part of her wanted to back out before he realized he had nothing under it—but he *had* given permission, right?

He kicked aside the sheet, and then tugged down the leg of his boxers, which had ridden up with the sheets.

"Everything okay?" he asked, as he pushed the sheets aside with his foot.

She tried to answer. A little corner of her brain screamed, *Publicist! Late!* but the rest shushed it because Chris was lying there in his boxers, looking tousled and sexy and ripped and *damn*.

"D?" He stretched, muscles rippling.

Are you giving me a show, Chris? Please tell me you're giving me a show, and not just sleepy and disoriented. Tell me you're flirting.

He'd seemed to be flirting last night, when he'd joined her in flopping on the bed, and later, when she'd teased him about the scotch. Then Lawrence had called, damn him.

Had Chris been flirting? Was he flirting *now*?

Damn it, she couldn't tell. No, the truth was that she was afraid to guess. She'd made that mistake before. Okay, fine, it'd been high school, but it'd happened twice. Cute guy being friendly, seeming to let his gaze linger extra long, finding excuses for slinging a casual arm around her shoulder or laying his fingers on her arm, her friends all saying, "Obviously he's into you"…only to find out he was *not* into her. He was just being friendly, and she'd made a move and…oof. Even now, that old humiliation burned.

Was this different?

Maybe if she took another step into the room? See what happened?

His lips curved in a smile that was definitely flirty. Then he scooched over and patted the bed.

"Come sit, and we'll order coffee." He yawned. "Too early to get up just yet."

Early.

Late.

Shit.

"I…I knocked because Sakura texted."

There. She'd told him. No need to explain that they were late for breakfast. Later, she'd text her apologies to Sakura and pretend she'd just gotten the message.

"Right," he said, running a hand through his hair and only tousling it more. "New publicist. Breakfast at nine. We have plenty of time. It's only…"

He saw the clock and bolted upright.

"I know," she said. "That's what I came to say. She texted me."

He swung his legs out of bed. "How are we late? I set the alarm." He peered at the clock and swore.

She saw the problem. The clock showed a little dot beside the PM indicator.

"Never trust hotel clocks," she said.

"No kidding."

She quickly texted Sakura.

> **Daphne:** Ack! Just got this! Set the hotel clock alarm, and it was on PM. Give us 10 minutes.

She showed the text to Chris. When he nodded, she hit Send.

"She'll be in the hotel restaurant," Daphne said. "First one ready heads straight down."

"Race?"

She smiled, trying not to regret what could have been. Coffee in bed with near-naked Chris.

God*damn* it.

Her phone buzzed.

> **Sakura:** I'll order coffee. See you in 10!

Daphne pushed off her regrets and ran to get ready.

CHRIS

Daphne was already in the restaurant when he arrived. Because of course she was. How the hell had she managed that? Chris hadn't showered, hadn't shaved, just pulled on clothing, washed his face, brushed his teeth, and ran his hands through his hair when he couldn't immediately find his brush. She'd still beat him, and she looked as fresh and polished as if she'd spent an hour getting ready.

When he stepped into the restaurant, she saw him, her lips curving in a smile that had his feet stutter-stepping. She lifted a hand, as if he somehow might miss seeing her. He tugged his shirt and slowed to switch into Zane mode, which meant focusing on this breakfast meeting and not wishing like hell he was back in bed.

He'd woken the second Daphne knocked on his bedroom door. He'd only been half asleep anyway. He'd heard the knock and the creak of the door swinging open and done nothing. Just lay in bed, letting her come in, seeing what she'd do.

What she'd done was exactly what he'd hoped she'd do. Stopped for a look. He'd given it just long enough, before she might realize she was ogling him and retreat. Then he'd opened one eye, pairing it with a lazy smile, hoping to entice her in... and instead she'd beat a hasty retreat, which he really should have expected.

Still, he'd tried again, inviting her in and posing, just a little. Okay, fine. Posing a lot. And she'd watched. She'd made no secret of watching, which was exactly what he wanted... until she mentioned the text and he realized they were late for their breakfast meeting.

Even if he'd followed his determination to keep it slow and flirty, did he want her distracted? Thinking about the fact she was missing a meeting, making someone sit in the restaurant while she flirted with him?

Mmm, I think there might have been more than flirting coming. But we'll never know because you—

He silenced the voice. This trip was *not* about getting Daphne in bed. It was about getting positive publicity for her book. Anything else was a bonus. Okay, a very good bonus, but still, he had to prioritize, at least until the tour was done.

"Good morning, sir," Daphne said, smiling up from the table.

He should tell her to stop calling him that. Except...was it wrong that it was kinda hot? Especially the way she said it, with a slight teasing smile, a private joke between them.

Nope, he was not telling her to stop.

He turned to the publicist, who couldn't be more than a few months out of college. She was dressed impeccably, with oversize glasses that made her look even younger.

"My deepest apologies," he said to Sakura as he took his seat.

"I already explained," Daphne said. "I was the one who set the alarm, and I was supposed to wake you up. I didn't see the time was set wrong."

Chris didn't like her taking the blame for what was his fault. But she was the assistant here, and he couldn't argue without it looking odd.

"Tonight we'll both set alarms," he said.

"Actually, tonight you're going to want to set multiple alarms," Sakura placed two sheets down, one in front of each of them. "You have a full day tomorrow, starting with a morning flight."

"Ah," Chris said. "The elusive itinerary."

He hadn't meant it to sound critical, but in his Zane voice everything sounded critical, and Sakura flinched.

"I'm sorry," she said. "I was working on it up until this morning. There are still a few things to be added."

"Last-minute tour means last-minute arrangements," Daphne said. "I'm amazed at how fast this came together. I thought it took weeks to arrange a tour like this."

"We got lucky with the LA slot," she said. "They had a cancellation on the panel and reached out, and we'd already been trying to whip something together. Publishing is not the fastest-moving beast."

Chris lifted the itinerary. "It's very full."

This time, her flinch was more of a tense, complete with a flash in her eyes that said Zane was already turning out to be exactly what she expected. An asshole.

Which was kinda Zane's brand, but here was the thing about acting the part of an asshole. Sometimes, it was great. He could demand first-class treatment and refuse unreasonable requests and set boundaries, and it'd be chalked up to *He's an asshole.*

But he didn't want to be that to someone like Sakura. Once branded that way, though, he had to do backflips of niceness to counter it.

"Full is good," Daphne chirped, a little too brightly.

"It is," Chris said. "I meant that I'm happy to see it so full. Thank you. I know that was a lot of work."

Mmm, still not quite right. Chris's voice would make that sound like genuine appreciation. Zane's made it sound like praise delivered from on high.

He continued before Sakura felt obligated to respond. "All right. So let's look at today. The panel is at two, so we need to leave at..."

Was that time right? They had to leave in ninety minutes?

"Traffic," Sakura said. "Plus they like you to be on-site two hours early so they can be sure you're there. There's a green room where we can hang out and wait."

Chris caught Daphne's expression. "Do we need to stay in the green room? Or can we look around the festival?"

"Absolutely. We'll take a wander."

The server came, and they ordered breakfast, Sakura adding that they were "in a bit of a hurry." Then it was back to the schedule.

"Panel from two until three, followed by the signing. That ends at five. After that, if you need a bite to eat, we'll have to grab it from the green room because we're hitting a few stores for stock signings."

He frowned. "I thought it was only the festival signing today." He heard how that sounded and added, "Which is fine. I'm just trying to get it all straight."

"Stock signings mean you're only signing store stock," Daphne said.

He laughed, a real one. "Hence the name?" He lifted his mug. "More coffee required."

Sakura gave him a smile for that. "It's all new to you. I know. Please feel free to ask questions."

"Or ask Daphne, who is much smarter about these things than I am."

"Maybe if you read those emails I sent you, sir."

Their eyes met, and her lips twitched. She knew he read everything she sent. But Zane would not, and her obviously gentle teasing had Sakura relaxing because it painted him as not a complete asshole.

Sakura said, "At stock signings, you sign whatever books they have in store. Then they put on the 'Signed by Author' sticker and, if we're lucky, move them to a more prominent location. But yours is already in a prominent location, so we don't need to worry about that."

"Because it's such an awesome book," he said.

When Sakura hesitated, he smiled. "I'm kidding. I know it's in a prominent location because it's a newly minted bestseller." He glanced at Daphne. "See, I read some of your emails."

"Gold star, sir."

Sakura relaxed. "You'll sign, and you'll meet the booksellers, if that's all right."

"Now that's the part I'll be good at. Chatting up booksellers. The signing? I'm still working on that."

"You have been practicing, right?" Daphne said.

"Of course."

It was a reminder to Sakura that "Zane Remington" wasn't his real name. He'd suggested that—since Daphne planned to "out" herself as Zane post-tour—they should use every opportunity to remind people Zane Remington was a pseudonym. It helped set the stage for the reveal and ensure the signed books wouldn't be worthless.

"After the signing, we're done for the day," Daphne said, reading the schedule. "There's a dinner reservation at eight, if you want it, sir."

Sakura cleared her throat. "Actually, dinner is part of the itinerary. It's with a few select buyers for the regional stores."

"Then a car brings us back to the hotel by ten," Daphne said.

Damn. Chris had expected to be done after the festival, take Daphne to a nice dinner—screw the per diem—maybe walk around LA, make sure they both had enough coffee so they didn't fall asleep on the sofa.

That'd be great for him, but not so great for Daphne's book, which was *the point* of this tour. Ten wasn't unreasonably late. Maybe the restaurant would be close enough for them to walk back, relax, go to his room, relax some more...

"Is this right?" Daphne said, pointing at the itinerary. "Meet in the lobby for car service at four? In the *morning?*"

"Uh, yes, sorry," Sakura said. "The flight's at six. It's just a hop up to Seattle, I know, and there are plenty of flights, but we have a plum spot on a morning show. I hope that's okay? We did get business class for you both, despite the short trip."

"Guess you can sleep on the flight, sir," Daphne said.

And he could forget any other plans for the evening.

Well, shit.

CHAPTER FOURTEEN

DAPHNE

She was at the LA Times Book Fest. With *her* book. Oh, sure, she could pout and say it didn't count when Chris wore the "author" badge, but screw that. She was here, and her book put her here. Better yet, she wasn't the one who had to get up onstage in front of…

She looked around and shivered. It was a gorgeous June day, and maybe that added to the crowd, but people weren't just milling about—they were packing the seats.

Or, at least, they were packing the seats for the main panels and the huge names. Presumably Zane would be on a smaller one. Which reminded Daphne that she'd forgotten to see who else was on the panel. Her cheeks flushed. Her first event, and she'd already committed a major faux pas.

She turned to ask Sakura, but the publicist was checking something on her phone.

Daphne looked around and wondered, not for the first time, whether she could make some excuse and go off exploring on her own. Sakura was lovely company, but Daphne felt like a kid at an amusement park with an elderly relative. They were sedately strolling, not taking in panels or checking out signings. Chris had to be Zane, who would be content to stroll while awaiting his own moment in the spotlight. But maybe his assistant could slip off.

"Sorry, guys," Sakura said. "I need to make a call."

The moment Sakura stepped out of earshot, Chris spun on Daphne. "I think I just saw Stephen King."

"Oh, so you actually do know who that is?"

"Sure, he wrote the *It* movie, right?" Chris grinned, and it was a blaze of a grin that set her pulse racing. "Yes, I know who Stephen King is, and I'm fifty percent sure I just saw him. Would it be wrong to sneak off? Stalk him, just to be sure? Maybe get a stealth selfie?"

She waggled her finger. "Stealth selfies are always wrong, sir."

"Is it also wrong that I kinda like it when you call me sir?"

He waggled his brows, and she had to stifle a laugh.

He stepped closer. "It is very crowded. Maybe we can *accidentally* get separated from Sakura and stalk possible Stephen King?"

"And then have Sakura panicking thinking you're lost and won't make it to your panel?"

He sighed. "Killjoy."

"It's my job, sir."

He grinned again and seemed about to speak when Sakura hurried back, looking flustered.

"Everything okay?" Daphne asked.

"A bunch of our authors are here today, and it's just me and another publicist. I'm assigned fully to you, because of the tour and because it's your first-ever event. But there's another author, a really big name—" She stopped short, flushing. "Not that *you* aren't a big name."

"I'm a debut author," Chris said. "However well *Edge* is selling, I'm still new. I presume this other author has been around longer."

"Yes. She's…a bit… That is to say, she's understandably aware of her standing and…"

"She has certain expectations," Daphne supplied.

Sakura exhaled. "Exactly. She was supposed to come with two assistants, so she didn't need a publicist, only they apparently both demanded a raise this morning, and she fired them."

"Ah," Chris said. "Strategic negotiation timing, which failed because it neglected to take into account the fact that their boss is an ass."

Sakura coughed to cover a laugh. "Something like that. But now she doesn't have anyone, and she's demanding a publicist, and my colleague is there now, but the author doesn't know him and she knows me."

"And she's insisting on you," Chris said. "Go on. We've got this."

Panic sparked in Sakura's eyes. "I can't. It's your first time. If anything goes wrong…"

"Tell me where to go and what to do," Daphne said. "We have this. Really."

Sakura still hesitated.

Chris lowered his voice to a stage whisper. "Between us, I'm not *quite* as helpless as I seem. I've even been known to find a restroom and return to Daphne all on my own."

"Mmm, there was that one time, sir."

He mock-glared at her. "And you will *never* stop bringing that up."

Daphne said to Sakura, "He's right. He doesn't need my help half as much as he pretends to."

"I'm just lazy," Chris drawled. "And Daphne is very good at taking care of me. Seems rude not to let her."

"We have this," Daphne said when Sakura hesitated again. "Give us the rundown and go."

CHRIS

They still weren't sure whether they'd spotted Stephen King. Daphne had even grabbed a program, and he wasn't on it, but when you were that big of a name, maybe you stayed incognito until your event.

Speaking of events…They found where Zane's would be held before they went hunting for Mr. King, and they both set alarms to get him there fifteen minutes early. The whole time Daphne kept Sakura in the loop via text:

Found the panel tent!

Heading to the tent now!

Dropped off Zane and confirmed he's in the right place!

Made sure he's wearing his name tag right-side-up and carrying a copy of his book!

Chris was now waiting backstage, after being directed there by staff. It was just him and a young woman clutching a book. He considered introducing himself, but she seemed to be studiously avoiding his gaze, so he decided approaching her would be unwelcome and possibly creepy. He settled for a friendly Chris nod and smile.

He was reading the program when an older woman walked in, headed straight over, and pointedly looked at his book.

"Mr. Remington, I presume," she said.

While her tone seemed sharp, she smiled when he looked over. He tried to read her name tag, but it was facing backward, intentionally or otherwise. Daphne had meant to find out who else he was on the panel with, but they'd both forgotten. Now he realized that was an inexcusable oversight.

"I started your book on the flight," the woman said.

Yep, definitely inexcusable. He should not only have checked out his co-panelists but at least tried their books.

He opened his mouth and then shut it.

She smiled. "Not going to ask me how I like it?"

"I was, and then realized that's awkward. If someone likes it, they'll say so. Otherwise, I should just smile and say thank you." He smiled. "Thank you."

"Good call. Never ask someone how they liked your book. Yours is good so far. I like the dog. And the girl, obviously. I'm reserving judgment on the boys. I'm not sure if they deserve her, and I'm quite sure she doesn't need them." She paused. "That is to say, she doesn't need their help. Their companionship is another thing. Everyone needs that."

"They do."

"Be prepared to hear all about the boys from readers, though."

"I am."

He glanced at her name tag again, as if it might have miraculously flipped over.

She noticed it and flapped a hand. "Damn thing."

He saw the name. Blinked. Read it again. "You're…you're Tara Palmer?"

"Let me guess. You have a sister who read my books when she was young?"

"No, I mean, yes, she did. But I did, too. Well, one of your series. When I was sick and ran out of books." He made a face. "That sounds bad. I mean I started the series when I raided her room for books, and then I swiped the rest, until she caught me and accused me of bending the spines. So Mom had to buy me my own set. It was the one about the girl who wanted to be a blacksmith and could sing to animals and had a wolf…" He stopped, inhaling sharply. "I'll stop gushing now. Sorry about that."

"Ah, right. You're the Canadian. Always apologizing about things that don't require apologies."

"Which definitely includes gushing to an author about their

books," said a voice. Another man walked in. A little older than Chris. Bald. Black.

As the newcomer embraced Tara, Chris snuck a glance at his name tag. Dwayne Foster. He recognized the name from Christmas gifts he'd bought a preteen cousin. Dwayne wrote middle grade, mostly sports themed.

Okay, two fellow authors down. Two to go.

He was glancing around for the young woman, hoping to entice her over now that it wasn't just one creepy dude paying too much attention to her. Then the curtains parted, and a man walked in. White. Maybe late fifties. Dwayne murmured, "And that is my cue to go. Have fun."

As the older man looked around, the staff member appeared and told them all to head onto the stage and take a chair. They filed out. The young woman whose name Chris hadn't gotten zeroed in on the farthest chair. Dwayne took the next one. Chris realized that put him in the middle, and he stepped back, motioning for Tara to take it.

"No," she said, "that one's clearly reserved for the guy sitting on top of the *New York Times* list."

Chris still hesitated, but Dwayne gestured for him to sit there, so he awkwardly lowered himself into the seat. Then he turned for his first look at the audience, which was...

Full. Every seat was full, and people stood along the back.

Yeah, that's what you get when you're on a panel with Tara Palmer and Dwayne Foster.

He was *so* not prepared for this.

"I believe you are in my seat," a voice said.

Chris almost scrambled up. Then he saw who it was—the older author who'd come in last.

Tara tapped Chris's leg as if to keep him from rising. "No, Bruce. He's in *his* seat."

Chris checked the man's name tag. Bruce Buck. He didn't recognize the name.

"That is my seat," Bruce said. "As the—"

"—oldest guy here?" Dwayne said.

Bruce scowled at him. "Author with the longest career."

Tara cleared her throat.

"The most prestigious career," Bruce added.

Dwayne choked on a laugh, and Chris decided he really liked Dwayne. And he did not like Bruce Buck.

The woman on the end spoke up, her voice almost too soft to be heard. "Mr. Remington's book is number one on the *Times* list right now. He should sit there."

When Chris looked over, she smiled shyly and fluttered her fingers in a wave.

"Did he tell you that?" Bruce snapped. "He's lying. I read the lists every week. Jeff Kinney is camped out on middle grade, and on the Young Adult it's some girl whose name I can't pronounce."

Tara pronounced it perfectly, but Bruce ignored her.

Someone from the staff whispered, "Five minutes. Take your seats please," but the authors ignored him.

"Mr. Remington's book is on the adult list," said the young woman on the end.

Bruce scowled. "This is a panel for *children's* books."

Tara took the book from Chris's hand and passed it over. Bruce examined the cover. Frowned.

"The protagonist is a teenager," Chris said. "It's definitely YA. I'm not sure why the publisher insisted on marketing it as an adult book."

"Because the adult market is bigger and more prestigious," Tara said. "And as a man, you can get away with it."

"As a white man," Dwayne added.

Bruce rolled his eyes. "Oh, don't start that nonsense."

"Dwayne's right," Chris said. "It makes a difference." He glanced at Dwayne. "Sorry."

"Because your publisher gave your book a better shot at success?" Dwayne said. "Not your fault. I'd take it, too."

"He's Canadian," Tara said. "Ignore the unnecessary apologies."

Bruce looked up from reading *Edge*'s front flap. He snapped the book shut and sniffed. "Zombies? Of course. Anyone could hit the list with that nonsense."

"Then why don't *you* write it?" Tara said. "Been a while since you hit a list, hasn't it, Bruce?"

"My books win awards." He looked at Chris. "A word of advice, young man. If you want to be taken seriously, you need to write seriously. Take my latest novel." He held up a book. "The subject matter is both serious and timely. It's the story of a young woman from the projects, who becomes pregnant after a rape."

"*The projects?*" Dwayne said. "Please tell me you don't actually call it that."

Chris looked at the book, which showed a teenage Black girl on the cover. Bruce's hand partly obscured the author's name.

"Oh," Chris said. "You have a cowriter? I've always thought that seemed interesting. How did you do it?"

Bruce only stared at him.

"Ask it louder," Dwayne said. "He's hard of hearing." He raised his voice. "Zane wants to know who cowrote this with you. Or is it written from personal experience?"

Tara laughed. The young woman at the end had her fist in her mouth stifling her own laughter.

It was then that Chris realized there was no cowriter.

Before he could think of anything to say, Bruce glared at them all. "If you are referencing that nonsense about writing outside your own experience, I am a novelist. Writing outside my experience is what I do, and you cannot censor my right to express myself creatively." He jabbed a finger at *Edge*. "He also wrote about a teenage girl."

"Not the same thing, though maybe it should be." Dwayne cast an apologetic look at Chris. "No offense."

"None taken." *Since I didn't write it.* "It's a valid point. Maybe we can discuss that on the—"

"You will *not* discuss that on the panel." Bruce jabbed a finger perilously close to Chris's face.

"You okay if we bring it up?" Dwayne murmured to Zane. "Not to put you on the spot."

"No, go ahead. Like I said, it's a valid point, and I'm happy to hear opinions on it. I am new at this, after all."

"All right," the staff member said from the mic at the end of the row. "If Mr. Buck will please take his seat, I think we're about to start."

"Let's get ready to rumble." Dwayne grinned, and every author—except Bruce—grinned back.

CHAPTER FIFTEEN

DAPHNE

"That was a *bloodbath*." Chris looked dazed as Daphne led him toward the signing. "Here I was, expecting a nice sedate panel. I mean, it's authors, right? And then...that."

"A little intense?"

"I thought Bruce was going to challenge me to a duel. And I was barely even talking. It's like I was the only one he saw up there."

"The only direct competition."

"As the only other white guy? Wow." He shook his head. Then he gave her a sidelong smile. "It was kinda fun, though. Did I do okay?"

"You did great. You fielded the questions about writing from a female point of view perfectly. I know that was awkward."

"Only because the actual author *is* female. But that will be out soon. And then *you'll* have to deal with Bruce."

"Oh, I suspect Bruce and I won't travel in the same circles very often. Also..." She cleared her throat. "I may have missed the first bit of the panel, being in a fangirl daze when I realized who was sitting beside you. You probably don't know who Tara Palmer is, but—"

He swung to face her. "Author of *A Smith's Song?* With the most amazing canine companion ever?"

"Tika the wolf?"

His eyes rounded. "Of course! That's where you got Tika's name from."

"I think I've read every book she ever wrote. Three times. Maybe four."

"You and Gemma both. So, help me with some protocol. If an author is on a panel with another author they admire, is it considered bad form to ask them to sign a book?"

"Not if you buy it and line up with everyone else."

"I'm definitely buying it. One for me and one for Gemma. And Dwayne's latest for my cousin, who loves his stuff. And Amy's book, too, which sounded great."

"I read it last winter. *So good.*"

"Then we need two of those, three of Tara's, one of Dwayne's—"

"Three of Dwayne's. Nia has a niece and nephew that age."

"Two of Amy's, three of Tara's, three of Dwayne's, and none of Bruce's."

"Screw Bruce."

Chris laughed, and Daphne's phone buzzed. It was Sakura reminding her about the signing.

Daphne: Zane in tow. On our way there now.

Sakura: I'll be done in twenty minutes. I'll come over to help.

Daphne: We'll be fine. Catch your breath. We can meet up
after.

In twenty minutes, Daphne expected to be done and lined up for the other signings. Zane was a new author after all. Amy's book had been out longer and had been on the *NYT* list plus won awards.

Bruce was a known entity, and she and Chris might not want his books, but he'd be busy enough. Tara and Dwayne would definitely be busy.

And Zane Remington...Well, hopefully, they wouldn't make him sit at an empty table after his short line was gone. Daphne had seen that when she haunted bookstores. Authors—sometimes even names she knew—valiantly manning an empty signing table while people asked directions to the restrooms. She always bought a book.

A young woman in a staff T-shirt met them. "Mr. Remington? I'll be your line attendant. Oh, and I see you brought your..."

The woman trailed off, letting Chris fill in the blank, and Daphne was vaguely flattered that she didn't jump to the conclusion Daphne was clearly only his assistant.

"Daphne," he said in his Zane voice. "My Daphne, my indispensable D, my right hand, my partner in crime. This afternoon, she will be playing the role of my assistant."

The woman's look said she was kinda hoping for a bit more clarification on their relationship, and Daphne bit her cheek at that. But it was a good answer, one that didn't pin her into any role.

"I'll be flapping books for him," Daphne said. "And making sure his Sharpies stay fresh."

"Flapping books?" Chris said. "Do I even want to know what that means?"

The woman smiled. "She means opening them to the signing page for you. Did I hear that this is your first signing?"

"It is. Please tell me I have at least a couple of people waiting."

"Uh..."

Chris surreptitiously squeezed Daphne's forearm. "That's quite all right. It's a new book by a new author. We will dream of the day when the lineups are so long that ice is required for writer's cramp."

He smiled down at her, and her knees wobbled. He hadn't said the day "he'd" have a lineup. He hadn't said "he'd" need ice. That was for her. A wish for her.

Damn it, Chris, could you be less sweet? Please? So if I do realize you haven't been flirting with me, I can at least say you weren't "all that" anyway?

Except he *was* all that.

Damn him.

The woman cleared her throat, and Daphne realized she was probably staring up at Chris like a lovelorn teenager.

"Your table, Mr. Remington."

Daphne reached for a chair. Then she looked up and...

"A couple of people" did indeed stand in front of Zane's table. Behind them, the queue stretched until it was lost in the tangle of the crowds.

"This must be someone else's spot," Daphne said.

At the woman's frown, she realized that sounded insulting to Chris.

"I mean, is this his?" she quickly said, and added a lie: "I'd asked for sparkling water for Zane."

"Still water is fine," Chris said. "I don't think I'm going to get time to drink it anyway. If this is my book..." He tapped a copy of *Edge* propped on the table. "Then it's definitely our spot."

She stared at the lineup. "I..."

"Let me see about getting you that ice for your hand. I think you're going to need it," the woman said, smiling at Chris. Then she hurried off.

"D?" Chris whispered in Daphne's ear as she stood there, still convinced people were in the wrong place. He took her hand and squeezed it. Then he whispered, "Congratulations."

Tears filled her eyes. She squeezed his hand back and pulled out the chairs for them to get started.

CHRIS

Chris leaned against a tree, cradling his wrists. "Now I know the real reason you hired me. You write an amazing book that everyone wants signed, and someone else has to sign it." He shook his wrist. "Oww…"

"Hey, you aren't the only walking wounded." She lifted her fingers. "Two paper cuts from flapping books."

"Ouch." He took her hand, lifted it, and kissed her cut fingertip. "Better?"

Her cheeks reddened, and he realized how much he loved that about Daphne. She was tough and capable, but her emotions were easy to read, from her embarrassment to her worry to her delight.

After Sakura showed up, Daphne had slipped away to join Tara's line. He'd been lucky enough to spot her when she reached the front, blushing but glowing, too. She'd hurried back and held out the signed books with the biggest grin.

Now, when she blushed, he kept hold of her hand, running his thumb up her palm as their eyes locked—

"Well, that's done," Sakura said as she walked over. "Oh! Whoops."

Sakura started to retreat, but Daphne backed up fast, breaking Chris's hold.

"We were just comparing war wounds," Daphne said, waving her hand. "Paper cuts."

"Yep, those hardcover jackets can be sharp. Okay, then, so we have about thirty minutes. Do you want to relax while I find something for you to eat? There are usually some decent food trucks. I'll bring it to the green room."

"There's food in the green room, right?" Daphne said.

"Nibbles."

"We're fine with that. You can wander if you like or join us and get off your feet for—"

Sakura's phone buzzed. She looked down and her lips moved in a curse. She tapped back a text. A pause. More furious tapping as exhaustion and frustration settled over her features.

"One of our authors needs me," she said. "He's on in an hour, and he forgot his proof of admission, and the staff can't find him on the list, so he's threatening to turn around and go back to his hotel." A text dinged in. "Oh, look, another author needs me. She just finished her panel and can't find her signing spot. Cat herding. I swear this job is nothing but—"

Sakura looked up quickly. "Sorry. That should have been in my inner voice."

"No worries," Chris said. "They don't pay you guys enough for this."

"Don't pay you enough, period," Daphne said. "Which is why we've had four publicists already."

Sakura gave a tired smile. "You mean we aren't just feckless Gen Zs who don't want to work and don't understand the concept of company loyalty?"

"Loyalty is earned . . . after the bills are paid," Chris said. "Daphne and I were wondering why we kept getting new publicists, and she found the explanation online in some blog interviews. Between the cost of New York and current rates of inflation—" He stopped, realizing he was channeling Accountant Chris. He cleared his throat. "And we're delaying you from putting out fires that need putting out."

"Go," Daphne said. "I'll make sure Zane is fed for his stock signings, and I'll sneak a doggie bag into my purse for you."

Sakura thanked them and hurried off.

Daphne set her watch timer. "Thirty minutes to find the green room, eat, and ice your wrist."

"My wrist will be fine."

"Okay, then I guess we should find..."

She trailed off. Was she thinking what he was? That they didn't really need food that badly? If they could sneak a little private time before the agenda kicked in?

Chris opened his mouth at the same time Daphne did.

"Ladies first," he said with a slight bow.

"I was just wondering, maybe, if..." She glanced down and saw the book bag she'd set on the ground. "Oh! The book we got signed for your sister. We should send her a photo." She rummaged in the bag and held it out.

That was *not* what she'd been about to say. He'd lay solid money on it. But now she held out the book with a quiet air of desperation.

He considered his options only to realize, sadly, that finding an intimate spot in this very crowded festival wasn't happening.

"Sure," he said with the best smile he could manage. "Get out our copies, too, and we'll pose with all three. Unless you'd rather not show your face."

"It's your sister. I'm not going to hide."

She handed him his book, and took her own and Gemma's. They opened them to the signed pages and held them up while Chris snapped the selfie.

He leaned against Daphne for the photo, and she leaned back. They took a straight-smiling shot and then a few goofier ones. He picked two favorites and sent them.

"Okay, green room and food," he said as he tucked the books into the bag and hefted it. "Lead on, Indispensable D."

They'd just reached the building when Gemma texted back an all-emoji response. Then she added a text.

Gemma: Tara Palmer!?! I really do hate you

Chris: I got to sit on a panel with her, too. And talked to her.
She's great

Gemma: Hate you so much

He replied with a row of grins.

Gemma: On a more serious note, little bro…

Gemma: You look so happy

Gemma: Not sure when I've seen you that happy

Gemma: Tell me you're going to make a move

Chris: I'm making them. Slowly but surely

Gemma: Slow is acceptable. Just don't screw this up, okay?

Chris: Thanks???

Gemma: You know what I mean. Don't wait for every damn
star to align. You're a catch. Remember that

Chris: Aww.

Chris: Also, you might be biased

Gemma: Yeah? You want me to poll the friends who asked for
your contact info? Take it slow if that's what's needed, but
go for it

Chris: I plan to

DAPHNE

Chris collapsed against the hotel corridor wall as she got out her key card.

"Longest day ever," he said.

He was slouched, head lolled, tongue hanging out the corner of his mouth, eyes rolled up. His hair was sticking up on one side, and faint lines of exhaustion etched the corners of his mouth. She was pretty sure that was a salad dressing stain on his rumpled shirt. It didn't matter. He was still the hottest guy she'd ever seen. Maybe even hotter than when she'd first spotted him, perfectly groomed, getting out of his pickup at that Vancouver restaurant.

Nope, he was definitely hotter now. He was real now. Worn out from the long day, goofing around, not caring how he looked, just being himself.

"I definitely owe you overtime," she said.

His nose wrinkled. "I hope that's a joke, D, because I was *not* angling for overtime. Or seriously complaining about a long day."

"I know. But it was long. And exhausting. When the schedule said dinner would last until ten, I figured that was worst-case. We shut down the restaurant."

"Uh-huh. Is there even any point in going to bed if we just have to leave for the airport in four hours?"

Daphne hesitated. There was a hook dangling there. She should snatch it.

Ha-ha, yes, we should just stay up. Together. In my room. I have the keys to the minibar.

Word it right, and he could laugh it off if he didn't want to, but if he did?

We should totally do that. Who needs sleep?

He needed sleep. He had an early-morning interview—live on TV—followed by a radio interview, also live, and two print media interviews. Then stock signings all afternoon, leading up to the evening event.

"Tempting," she said.

"Right?"

That hook is definitely dangling. Take it. Screw the interviews. Screw the flight even. He's Zane Remington. He's allowed to be a dick.

She wanted this. She wanted it so badly, and they were already on the second night, with her chance of a fling evaporating.

He sighed. "But I suppose we should behave."

"If we don't, we put Sakura in a bad spot."

"And she doesn't deserve it."

"She really doesn't," Daphne said.

"So when do we get a break tomorrow? We're free before the signing, right? Can I take you to dinner?"

"I'll ask Sakura to leave it open for us, but I think I should be taking *you* to dinner."

"Nope." He raised his hands against argument. "Dinner on me."

She paused, and it took him a moment before he grinned, remembering the brownie photo.

"Hey, you want dinner on me, you can have dinner on me," he said. "Just not pasta, please. That gets messy."

"He says from experience."

Chris laughed. "I just have a good imagination, being a writer and all."

She smiled up at him, and then realized she was standing there, staring and smiling as if waiting for more. As if waiting for an excuse to forget their long-suffering publicist and do whatever they wanted.

Which was wrong. Damn it.

She lowered her gaze to her key card, and when she looked up, he was right there, his face over hers. He touched the bottom of her chin and lifted it. There was the briefest pause, as if giving her the chance to back away. Then his mouth met hers in a gentle kiss, his lips on hers, and his hands on her hips, but no other part of their bodies touching. Every nerve zinged, every muscle relaxed. She wanted to melt against him, but his hands kept her there, less than six inches away. The kiss was slow and sweet and left every part of her aching.

Too soon, he pulled back, whispering, "I've been wanting to do that all day."

Then he was gone. She wasn't even sure how it happened. Her brain was still fogged by the kiss, and the next thing she knew, his door was closing, leaving her standing in the hall, gripping her key card, her lips tingling from his kiss.

And what the hell was she supposed to do with that?

Nothing, she realized. That was the point. He'd kissed her and then slipped away before anything else could happen.

He was teasing her. First, this morning with the bedroom show, and now with that good night kiss that left her aching for more.

Which was the point, wasn't it?

She could be furious. Instead, she felt herself grinning.

Well played, Chris.

All right then, no more wondering whether he was interested. He was. Which meant Daphne was getting her fling.

"Good night, Chris," she whispered, and opened the door to her room.

CHAPTER SIXTEEN

CHRIS

Chris had spent the previous day dreading the 3:45 wake-up call, but when it came, he bounced out of bed, and he swore he could still taste that kiss.

He'd kissed Daphne, and she hadn't objected.

Low bar there, buddy.

He only smiled more as he yanked on his clothing. He knew what he was doing. Everything was under control. The next step, since she hadn't rejected his kiss—

Really low bar...

—was to let her know how he felt before things went further. Confirm that they were heading in the same direction. Yes, the long-distance aspect was a problem, but was she willing to acknowledge that it was something they'd need to eventually work out, and she still wanted to try?

Kind of rushing things, aren't you?

Rushing would be setting a date for the wedding. What he was doing was establishing a clear course of intention, as he always did. Whether he reached the destination depended on many factors, but it was where he was heading. A serious relationship. That was all. She had to know his intentions before they went any further.

He was still zipping his suitcase when Daphne texted.

Daphne: Checking us out. Meet you at the door.

He smiled. Ready before he was, as always. He still hurried, in hopes of sharing an elevator down … and maybe a good-morning kiss, but she must have texted as she was leaving. He reached the lobby just as she finished up at the desk.

As she walked over, he took a moment to admire her. She was dressed casually today, in slim-fitting jeans and a light jersey with the sleeves rolled up. Her hair fell in loose waves and her lips were bright coral. Ankle boots added an extra inch or two, and two businessmen waiting to check out turned as she passed. They continued to watch, brows furrowed slightly as if trying to figure out who she was. Because she seemed like some*one*. A model or an actor dressing down for a flight.

She looked amazing, and she was walking straight to him. When she leaned in to kiss him, he almost jumped in surprise. It was a quick graze of the lips, no more than a peck, but he didn't fail to notice the two businessmen exchange an eye roll, as if to say, *Of course, she's with him.*

Yes, gentlemen, she is.

He took her suitcase and rolled it outside, where it was still night. The car wasn't there yet, so he tucked them into a corner. Then he pulled her to him in a kiss, letting it stretch as long as he dared before he'd forget they were supposed to be waiting for a car.

He pulled back, just enough to speak, their lips almost touching.

"Good morning," he said.

"Good morning indeed." She sounded a little breathless, and he tried not to grin at that.

He started to ask how she slept, maybe flirt a little about that, when she reached up to lay a hand on his chest.

"We're going to have another long day," she said, "and before that takes over, I wanted to say something."

He struggled to focus on her words. That wasn't easy when all he could see right now were her lips moving, tempting him to kiss her again.

"I don't expect anything to come of this," she said.

That woke him up. "What?"

She ran her hand up his chest, her gaze slightly lowered. "Whatever we're starting. I know what it is, and I'm fine with that. Good with it, actually."

"What it is?" he said slowly.

"A fling. A bit of fun. Nothing serious." She moved closer to him. "That's fine. Good actually. I'm not . . ." She made a face, her gaze still slightly averted. "I'm not in a place for anything more." She looked at him then and smiled. "This is good. Whatever this is."

As his stomach plummeted, he wanted to ignore it. He just needed to change her mind.

Ignore her wishes and steer her in the direction *he* wanted to go.

That was not the way to start something. Not the way to start anything.

Before this went any further, he needed to speak up. No misunderstandings that would start digging a hole they might never get out of. She'd been clear, and he owed it to her to be the same.

"And if that's not what I want?"

He said the words in hope, a hope that her face would light up. That she'd only said she wanted a fling, because she thought it was what he wanted, and now he'd set her straight and—

"Oh."

That's all she said. *Oh.*

Then she stepped back.

"Well, that's . . ." she said, her voice shaky. "That's . . ."

"A problem?"

"I don't...I don't know."

Okay, at least she didn't say yes, it was definitely a problem.

"I'm not looking for a fling, Daphne. Not with you. That way lies disappointment. For both of us, but mostly for me." He tried to smile, but it felt painful and twisted.

Her eyes met his. "I..." she began. "That's not what I expected and—"

"Hey, lovebirds." Sakura's voice cut through the darkness, and Chris turned to see her in a town car, the window rolled down. "Time to go. We're running late already."

Daphne looked at him, panic lighting those gorgeous golden-brown eyes.

He leaned in with a quick kiss. "Let's put a pin in this. Either way, it doesn't change the rest." He squeezed her hand. "I'm still your Zane. Still right here beside you."

Her eyes glistened as if with tears.

"Guys?" Sakura said.

Chris took Daphne's bag and wheeled it to the trunk as the driver opened it.

DAPHNE

Daphne had been in a daze since climbing into that town car. She kept replaying what Chris had said, certain she'd misunderstood. She'd been sure he wouldn't want more than a fling, which made everything easy. But now he said he did...and that a mere fling wasn't an option.

Did she want more? Her inner girl screamed, *Yes! Yes! Yes!* But the mature part, the experienced part, the damaged part, they all folded up at the thought and whispered, *No.*

The last time she'd been on this route, she'd been hurt. Hurt worse than she liked to admit. Yes, she could share a drink with friends and throw Anthony on the table as they congratulated themselves on the losers they'd lost, the bullets they'd dodged. But that didn't keep it from hurting. She'd given her heart to someone who'd tossed it aside at the first sign of trouble.

If she said yes to Chris and it didn't work out, she'd never be tossing his name on that table as a bullet dodged. No, with Chris it'd be something worse. A chance-of-a-lifetime lost. He'd given her a shot, and she'd blown it.

At the core, that was what she was afraid of. Not of winning and losing him, but of winning him and being so afraid of losing him that she'd give up the things she'd worked so hard for.

If they eventually had to choose where to live, Vancouver would be the obvious choice. It was his home, and she'd grown up in the area. She'd convince herself that she didn't love the Yukon that much. She'd lie to herself to keep him. She'd surrender her own dream to be with him.

Then there was her writing career. What if it faltered—or crashed—when she came out as the author? She'd heard so many stories about seemingly supportive partners who didn't get what writing meant to their loved one, no more than someone might get what living off the grid in the north meant. Writing was just a job, right? If it got difficult or stressful, go back to her old one.

After Anthony left and her mother died, Daphne's world collapsed, but she'd built it back, better than ever. Did she dare risk that on a new love? How did she make sure she wouldn't gain him and lose herself along the way?

Chris had said they'd put this aside and give her time to think, and Daphne needed exactly that. On the car ride, he talked to Sakura, but he rested his hand next to hers, his pinkie hooking hers, reminding her that he was still there, whatever she decided.

At the airport, they grabbed coffee and settled in for the flight, both of them talking with Sakura. Then it was on to the short flight, where they sat side by side, but the noise made it impossible to talk about anything. Which was good. She needed time, and he was giving it.

They made it to the interview with five minutes to spare. Now Daphne was in the green room with Sakura, where they'd be able to watch the interview.

"How would you feel about skipping this?" Sakura said.

The publicist had been quiet since the flight landed. Tired, Daphne presumed, but when she looked over, Sakura was watching the viewing screen, her expression unreadable.

"Skip the...?" Daphne began.

"Live interview. I have it cued to record. We can watch it later."

"Shouldn't we stay? In case Zane needs anything?"

"He'll be fine. Even if he let loose an F-bomb on air, there's nothing we can do. How about we grab a coffee?" She lifted her paper cup of brown sludge. "Something better than this."

"I...really should stay."

Sakura nodded. "Okay, it's just that I was thinking about what Zane said yesterday. About wages and New York. I realized I need an accountant." She looked Daphne in the eye. "Would you know where I could find one?"

Daphne's stomach dropped, her mouth going dry. She told herself it was just coincidence, but Sakura's cool silence said it wasn't.

"Can we take that walk now, Daphne?"

Daphne nodded mutely and followed Sakura to the door.

She kept calm during the seemingly endless ride down in the

elevator. She breathed and ignored the twisting in her gut that screamed to find a bathroom. She was going to hold it together. For Chris's sake. Yes, her career was in more danger than Chris's was, but Sakura's comment targeted him, and that was all Daphne could think about.

They'd barely stepped outside into the cool Seattle morning when Sakura murmured, as if to herself, "Chris Stanton."

When Daphne said nothing, Sakura looked over. "That's his name, isn't it?"

Daphne stifled panic and mentally scrolled to her conversations with Nia, who'd led her through every imaginable exposure scenario, coming up with solutions until Daphne's nerves had settled.

"Zane Remington is a pen name," Daphne said. "That has been clear from the start, and he is entitled to his privacy."

Sakura held up her phone. On it was a digital-archive page for an accounting firm, with a photo of Chris that looked a few years old. Underneath, it read "Chris Stanton, BSC, CA."

Daphne pressed her lips together in annoyance she didn't need to feign and repeated, "He is entitled to his privacy."

"Well, he's not going to get it."

Daphne looked over sharply, bristling. She liked Sakura, who'd been nothing but helpful, but if she was threatening—

Sakura continued, "I've known lots of authors with pen names, and usually, the only time it's a problem is if they pick up a stalker or get a huge following. The huge following probably won't happen after one book. But stalkers?"

She glanced at Daphne as they walked. "You have seen Chris, right? You two are obviously more than author and assistant, so you know exactly what I mean. He's not my type—*at all*—but I can still objectively see that he is a *very* good-looking guy. If he were an actor, he'd be a dime a dozen, but as an author, he stands out. A lot. I was going to discuss it with you guys because, hot single author under forty? He's going to have problems."

"Okay," Daphne said carefully.

"But he's not just young and hot. He's not just an instant bestseller. He's also gone viral for facing down a grizzly bear."

"Minor-league viral," Daphne said, and at Sakura's look, added, "I know. Not the point."

"*This* is the point, Daphne." Sakura held up her phone again.

"Is that—is that a website?" Daphne said.

"Yep. Someone put this up yesterday."

Daphne read the URL again.

WhoIsZaneRemington.com

She asked if she could see Sakura's phone and took it with trembling hands. The website was just one page, done through free web design software. It was a horrible design, covered in photos of Zane overlaid with hard-to-read text.

Who is Zane Remington?

Calling all Zane fans. And if you're not a Zane fan, have you seen this guy??? Get out your fire extinguishers, ladies . . . and gents, if that's your thing :)

Check out that face. Those arms. Those abs (anyone with a shot of his ass please send it in because I'm sure it's just as hot!!!) And he's smart, too. He wrote a book! I haven't read it—books are for English class, amirite?—but it's supposed to be good.

So who is Zane Remington?

That isn't his real name. I know because I've looked everywhere, and my friend—who does read books—

says it's called a pseudonym. A fake author name so we can't track him down and offer to have his babies. Is that fair? No, it is not.

You know what to do.

Find Zane Remington.

"That's..." Daphne began.

"Concerning?"

"I was going to say creepy. Really creepy. But yes, also..." Daphne took a deep breath. "So people are trying to find out who Zane is, and that's a concern for the publisher. They've added managing it to the million tasks stacked on your plate."

"Oh no. The publisher won't care. It's added publicity. Doesn't matter if this person is a reader or not—it gets Zane's name and his book out there. If they find out about this website, they might weigh the ethics of leveraging it. Discreetly, of course. Ultimately, for them, it comes down to whatever sells books."

"So this is you...preparing us? Warning us?"

It wasn't. Daphne could tell by Sakura's tone. She was pissed off, and so far had shown no signs of being the sort of person who gets angry at her boss and takes it out on everyone around her.

"These people will find Chris Stanton," Sakura said. "It wasn't easy. I did an image search, and it took hours to track down that photo. That's buying you a bit of time. Even after I had that, I couldn't dig up much on Chris, and believe me, I am an expert. There's nothing worse than being assigned to a new author and discovering blackface costume photos on Facebook. I don't just search. I scour. With Zane, there was nothing, obviously. Chris is nearly as invisible. If he has a social media presence, it's locked down under a username, and 'Chris Stanton' is common enough that it took me two hours just to dig up a smattering of information."

"Okay."

"But that was enough to find out a bit about Chris's hobbies and such. You know what I *didn't* find listed there? Writing. Even when I dug back as far as his high-school yearbook. Not a single mention of him taking any interest in writing."

Now Daphne had to force out the word. "Okay."

"Then there's you. Daphne McFadden."

Daphne twitched.

Sakura continued, "You're an architect."

"Yes, I never said this was my career—"

"And you're nearly as elusive online. For millennials, you two either spend very little time online or you're very private people, with usernames and whatnot. But I *did* find you. Including this."

Sakura passed over her phone. Daphne was holding herself so tight she could barely stretch out a hand to take it. She braced herself, looked at the screen, and softly exhaled.

It was something she'd written under her own name. A published piece of writing.

So why the surge of relief? Because it wasn't even remotely connected to her fiction. It was an article in a regional architectural magazine edited by a friend who'd asked her to contribute.

"Yes, I wrote this article," Daphne said. "I'm surprised you found it, but I'm not sure why it's—"

Sakura reached over and scrolled up to the brief bio line at the bottom.

Daphne McFadden lives in the Yukon wilderness, where she spends her days dreaming up new ways to build ecofriendly northern homes . . . and her nights dreaming up new scenes for her northern zombie novel.

Her heart stopped.

When Daphne "became" Zane Remington, she and Nia had combed the internet for anything linking Daphne to *Edge* or even linking Daphne to writing. There was nothing.

Oh, Daphne was online. More than Chris, who'd admitted he didn't have any social media profiles. It just wasn't his thing. He kept in touch with his friends on group chats and such, and if he needed a profile, he had a username.

Chris was an accountant. He didn't want potential clients googling his name and finding him playing beer pong with college buddies. He had to be the kind of guy they could entrust with their money. Serious, even staid.

Daphne did the same—her social media presence was mostly restricted to friend groups. Yet there was one exception. Writing.

Daphne was a member of at least a dozen online writing communities. And every one of those profiles was completely locked down, with usernames that linked back to email accounts that used those same names.

If she had to put in a "real" name, she used a fake one. The online smokescreen gave her the freedom to speak openly about writing, but she'd always planned to use a pen name, so she'd left nothing connecting her writing life to Daphne McFadden.

Except this.

One line below an article in a very small, very specialized journal.

Daphne hadn't written that line. Her editor friend had. This friend had known Daphne was writing a zombie novel and added it to the bio line. Daphne had been annoyed. Her friend had teased her about being so secretive and saying it added human interest. So Daphne had let it go and forgotten about it.

Until now.

"Chris Stanton didn't write *Edge*, did he?" Sakura said.

Her tone said that wasn't a question, so Daphne didn't answer.

"Please tell me you wrote it, and your boyfriend agreed to play the role of your pseudonym."

Daphne glanced over.

Sakura shrugged. "If that's the case, I hope you had an iron-clad contract drawn up, one that confirms you wrote it and all rights remain yours, but if that's the situation, it's better than the alternative."

"Which is?"

"That you guys 'wrote' it together." Sakura air-quoted "wrote." "Meaning *you* actually wrote it and he helped brainstorm ideas, and for that he wanted author credit, and you didn't say no, either because you're blinded by love or you honestly think he's entitled to call himself an author for doing what a lot of writers' partners just naturally do."

"That's—"

"Then there's scenario three, where he's a guy you met at a writing conference, and he convinced you to 'cowrite' this book with him, meaning you did all the writing and he plays the role of author."

"No," Daphne said. "It's not that. One person wrote this book."

"That person being you."

Daphne said nothing.

"You *do* realize the position you're putting me in?" Sakura said as they walked past their third coffee shop without pausing.

"Yes, which is why I'm not confirming anything that might get you into trouble with your employer. Unless you're asking for confirmation to take to your employer, in which case, I'm also not giving it. If there is an arrangement, and if Chris didn't actually write the book, then everything has been handled legally. However, we are aware it could be an ethical issue and are already making plans to fix it."

"When?"

"After the tour."

"Good. That would be my suggestion," Sakura said. "It'd be a shit-show if it came out now. There are only three stops left. Once you're done, I would strongly suggest you fix this immediately."

"We plan to."

Sakura exhaled. "Okay."

"I'm honestly sorry this puts you in a bad position," Daphne said. "Can you dump Zane as a client? Say he did something and you no longer want to work with him?"

"Only if that 'something' is an unwanted sexual advance or an overtly racist comment."

"Oh."

"Yep. I'm sure there's a morality clause in your contract. They all have them these days. I wouldn't make a false accusation even to save my own career. I can't refuse to work with him midtour for a minor annoyance, and everything except harassment would be considered a minor annoyance. I could say he expects me to deliver his food and feed it to him, and as long as he wasn't being kinky about it, they'd tell me to just get through this tour and then they'll handle it."

"What can we do to make this better?"

"Well, what you could have done is warned me. I know why you couldn't, but I reserve the right to be pissy. I started suspecting something was up yesterday. In person, there's no trace of the guy I was dreading having to work with. He's a little *too* prepped with his writing answers, which made me nervous. And he checks in with you a lot. Talking to readers, booksellers, sales reps…He checks to be sure you're okay with his answers. It's discreet enough that they don't notice. But I did."

"Okay," Daphne said. "So be more careful about that."

"A little, yes. Mostly, though, I just need to know so I can be prepared in case the shit hits the fan."

"Okay."

Daphne must have sounded nervous, because Sakura's expression now held the first hints of sympathy.

"It won't," she said. "We just have a few days to go, and this website is the only concern I've found. Even then, if they realize Zane is actually Chris Stanton, they'll presume Chris Stanton is the guy behind the pen name. You have time."

"Okay."

"But we need to be vigilant. I have Google alerts set up."

"So does a friend of mine."

"Good. Can I give her more parameters? So there are two of us monitoring?"

"Please."

"Then let's get that coffee. And let's get through these interviews before you talk to Chris. You have a few hours off today. I'll make sure you get that."

"Thank you."

CHAPTER SEVENTEEN

CHRIS

After the interviews, Sakura had decided Chris and Daphne could go to lunch on their own. Which would have been great, if Chris hadn't been very aware that something was wrong. Daphne was upset, and she'd been trying hard to hide it, and he'd been trying equally hard not to fret about it during the interviews. Thankfully, they'd been mostly softballs, and he'd smiled and charmed his way through them.

He was surprised at how easy it was to be charismatic when playing a role. All his awkwardness and overthinking fell away, and he could be Zane Remington, smooth and charming in a way Chris himself never was. Of course, part of that meant not worrying whether what you say might be misinterpreted or sound blatantly insincere. So, in the end, he'd sacrifice being charming Zane for being genuine Chris.

As it turned out during their lunch conversation, Zane was the source of Daphne's worries, specifically a website dedicated to unmasking him. And really, if there was going to be a website devoted to uncovering your secret identity, one would hope for more than the crappy site she showed him.

He could make light because by the time they uncovered his secret identity, the point would be moot. In a few days, Daphne would come out to her publisher, and if they needed to keep "Zane" as the author, it'd be an open pseudonym, purely for branding, with everyone knowing a woman wrote the books.

So, lunch hadn't been the private time together they might have hoped for, but the conversation had been an important one, not only quelling Daphne's fears but helping them plan her authorial "outing" a little more.

Their personal-alert-team system was working, too. While he'd been in interviews, Nia had found the "Who Is Zane" website on her own and notified Daphne. Over lunch, he got a text from Gemma directing him to it. Everything was covered.

After lunch came stock signings, with all necessary appearances by charming Zane. Once that was done, Sakura made good on her promise to give them some real time off. It was only three thirty, and they had nothing on the schedule until the car would pick them up at six for the signing.

Plenty of time for a nice—albeit early—dinner for two. He'd suggest a cocktail in one of their rooms. Time to relax and talk about the good stuff that had happened so far. He had a few stories to tell her from the interviews, and he started one as they walked into the hotel.

"So the first thing she asks is whether I've ever seen *The Walking Dead*. That was a new one, and it gave me pause because I know you have, and I suspect Zane would have, but he'd never admit it. Since Zane won't be alive much longer, though, I decided to lean in your direction and said I'd seen the first few seasons and enjoyed them."

"Uh-oh. That was a trap," she said as the doorman held the doors.

He poked her arm. "Oh ye of little faith. I have been doing this for weeks, my dear. *Weeks.* I am an expert at trap spotting. Once I imply that I didn't watch the entire series, I set myself up for her asking why I stopped, which leads to me insulting the most influential zombie media of our time. When I said I'd only seen a few seasons, I said I was late to the show, not wanting to be unduly influenced."

"Nice."

They got in line at the front desk, where he continued, "Next she asked which was my favorite season."

"Uh-huh."

"I answered, choosing season three namely so I could link it to the scenes in *Edge* when Theo meets Finn and his community. Then she asked how *Edge*'s zombies differed from the ones in *The Walking Dead*."

"I'm sensing a theme."

"Pure coincidence, I'm sure. I answered that with an emphasis on *your* zombies. Next question: Which *Walking Dead* character was most like Theo? Then which character was most like Finn...and Atticus...and Mochi."

"Mochi?"

"She didn't seem to realize Mochi was a dog."

Daphne sputtered a laugh. "Just read the back cover, right?"

"Pfft, no. *I'm* the back cover, remember. You can't read that." He paused, head tilting. "Although, when you were away from the signing table yesterday, one woman did say she'd like to read *me*. I pretended to think she was a fortune teller."

Now Daphne was biting her lip to keep from laughing. He opened his mouth to continue, but the line cleared, and it was their turn at the front desk.

"We have two rooms reserved under Daphne McFadden," Daphne said, and then added their publisher's name.

"Oh!" The young woman's eyes rounded, and she fished under the desk, pulling up a copy of *Edge*. She laid it in front of Chris. "Could you sign this, please?"

Apparently, the booking had also included Zane's name. He smiled and took her pen with a flourish. Then he glanced at her name tag.

"Make it out to Millie?" he said.

"What?" She frowned. Then her eyes widened again. "Oh. No, it's not for *me*." Her nose wrinkled. "Not my thing, really."

He smiled. "Zombies aren't for everyone."

"It's about zombies? No, I mean reading."

He kept the smile on. "'Books are for English class, amirite?'"

Daphne gave a soft laugh at his quoting that website.

Millie laughed louder. "Exactly. I haven't cracked open a book since they made me read *Moby-Dick*."

"Ouch. Never finished that myself. By page twenty, I was rooting for the whale." He lowered his voice and said, "Most books aren't what you read in school. Find the right one, and it's even better than TV. Books have more time to dive into character and emotion."

He'd thought it was a game try, but he could tell he was losing her, so he trailed off and left it at that. Too bad, really. He might have rolled his eyes at that website line, but English class had turned more people off reading than time-table memorization had turned them off math. Which was a damn shame, on both counts.

"So make the book out to . . . ?" he prodded, pen over the title page.

"Oh, just sign it. Lots of authors stay here, and the manager says it makes them feel good if we ask them to sign a copy of their book."

"I see."

"Between us, I think he sells them on eBay."

"Ah."

Chris wrote: *To the manager of the Rosemont Hotel. Thank you for the lovely stay.* Then he added a scribble that was nothing like his Zane signature.

"Done." He closed the book and slid it over. "Now, if we could have our room keys."

"Your rooms aren't ready. Check-in is at four."

"Our company arranged early check-in for after two."

Millie checked her watch. "It's three."

"*After two*. Three comes *after* two."

Hmm, it seemed that asshole Zane wasn't completely gone, after all. Just lying low until required. In this case, though, it didn't matter. Millie had given their rooms to people who'd been there at two, because they weren't.

"Fine," he said. "We'll wait in the bar. Where would I find that?" He looked around the tiny lobby.

"Find what?" Millie said.

"The bar? Or restaurant?"

She shrugged. "We don't have one."

"Is there one nearby?"

Another shrug. "I don't know. I'm not old enough to drink."

"All right. May I speak to the concierge, please?"

"That's me today. We're short-staffed. I usually work in the back. Today, I'm everything."

Except helpful. "What does the hotel have in terms of facilities?"

Blank look.

"Where in the hotel could we wait?" Chris said. "Is there a coffee shop? Lounge?"

Blank.

He shook his head. He could argue this wasn't the four-star hotel he requested, but it *was* very fancy. Just also very small and, apparently, short-staffed. Looked like they were going for a walk—with their luggage, since he didn't trust Millie to hold it. Then Daphne tapped his shoulder and pointed at a sign.

Gym.

"You bring anything?" she asked.

He actually had packed workout clothing, thinking he'd need something to do while Daphne worked...in all their copious downtime. When he nodded, she said, "I have sweatpants and a T-shirt." She leaned in and whispered, "At worst, we can sit on the weight bench and wait until four. Does that work?"

It did.

DAPHNE

The gym was tiny, and also empty. Empty was good, as far as gyms went. She'd given up going to public ones when she built her house, instead using one of her spare rooms as a combination library and home gym.

There had to be good gyms where a self-conscious woman could exercise in comfort, but she'd never found one. She always felt the eyes critically assessing her physique. She'd also suffered through the endless string of guys wanting to "help." Sometimes that just meant telling her she was doing it wrong, because her lack of a Y chromosome made that inevitable. Other times, it was an excuse for them to demonstrate proper form and show off. And then there were the guys who wanted to help her achieve that proper form with hands-on assistance.

Okay, now breathe like this. Feel my hand on your sternum? Whoops, that's not your sternum, he-he.

She was long past the beginner stage, but somehow, the offers never stopped.

"Think we can lock the door?" he said as he wheeled in their luggage.

She smiled, mostly because she'd been thinking the same thing. "I don't think we need to worry. There's dust on everything except the treadmill."

"Ah, yes, the ubiquitous hotel treadmill. But there's supposed to be a window in front of it, overlooking the pool or lobby. What's the point of working out on vacation if everyone can't *see* you're working out on vacation?"

She laughed. "So *are* we working out? I'd like to, if that's okay. I could use the stress relief."

"I was thinking the same thing. Let's get changed then."

Daphne walked over to the changing room and opened the door. It was a single-size booth.

Huh, only one changing room. We can share, right? I'll just change over here, in front of the mirror, which I absolutely will not use to watch you at all. Because that would be wrong. Wouldn't it? I mean, your call.

Oh, he would be okay with it. He'd made that clear. But he'd also set his terms, and she had to respect that. No more sexy flirting. No more hopes of a hot fling.

So where did that leave her?

Terrified, that was where it left her.

"You can go first," she said.

He shook his head and waved. "After you."

And then she was in the tiny dressing room, all alone, with the door shut as she pawed through her bag looking for the sweats and T-shirt she'd brought for writing, because clearly on tour there would be lots of downtime, where Chris would want to work or go to the gym, and she'd curl up in her sweats and write.

She pulled out the pants and tee and winced. They were built for comfort, not style, and certainly not sex appeal.

Well, they *were* working out. If she'd pulled out a cute little pair of yoga pants and sexy sports bra, he'd wonder what she had in mind.

Oh, let me tell you what I have in mind, Chris. See that weight bench and squat rack? I want to—

She yanked on her sweats and didn't look in the mirror as she tugged open the door. He smiled at her and held the door as she walked out.

"Just leave your bag in there," he said. "This room is small enough as it is. Reminds me of my first apartment in Vancouver." He looked around. "Nope, my apartment was definitely smaller." He rolled his luggage into the room and propped it against the door, holding it open. "Did you ever live in Vancouver?"

She shook her head. "I took one look at what I'd be able to afford and decided I liked commuting."

"I don't blame you. That first micro-apartment I had was a sublet. The owner went overseas and left her cats behind. Cats. Plural."

He opened his bag and rummaged through it as he talked. Then he pulled out clothing and started undoing his shirt. Still talking. Still with the door open.

Should she turn away?

If he didn't want her to look, he'd close the door, right?

Maybe it was just open so she could hear him, and she was supposed to turn away.

Or maybe he knew exactly what he was doing and stripping right in front of her, using the excuse of telling a story.

Reminding her of what was on offer, should she accept his terms and conditions.

He flipped open the buttons on his shirt, one at a time, each revealing an extra sliver, and sure, it was just his chest, and sure, she'd seen it before—multiple times—but that didn't matter. She watched like he was opening a fully stocked fridge and she hadn't eaten in weeks.

Was he still telling the same story? He was still talking, and she should listen. There might be a quiz later. He'd ask a question, and she'd start randomly blurting muscle groups. Pecs. Delts. Abs.

Speaking of abs...

His shirt was now unbuttoned and pushed aside, and he reached to absently scratch that stretch of skin just below his belly button, drawing her gaze there. That perfect stretch of light hair arrowing down.

Chris undid the button on his fly.

Now Daphne was openly and obviously staring, and dimly aware that he was still telling his story, but it might have been in Latin for all she noticed.

The button on his jeans was now open and she held her breath, waiting for that fly to zip down. Instead his hands rose to his unbuttoned shirt. He took hold of each side and slid it off his shoulders, and her gaze went there.

Traps. Delts. Pecs. Biceps. Oh my.

Was she drooling? *Please tell me I'm not drooling.*

He let the shirt fall. Then his fingers returned to his fly, and her attention returned there, too. She should look away. Really, she should. But it was as if she no longer controlled the movements of her neck and eyes. They trained on his fingertips and stayed there.

He slid down his zipper, one tooth at a time. Then his fingers hooked in his waistband and he pushed his jeans down to his hips.

She'd seen Chris wearing boxers. He wasn't wearing boxers now. Today it was briefs. Black briefs, the waistband visible as he pushed down—

He stopped. The movement was so sudden that it broke the trance, and her gaze zoomed up to his.

"Water," he said. "I forgot to grab water. Is there any out there?"

She turned. "There's a fountain with paper cups."

"Could you grab me one?"

Uh...Sure?

She did as he asked, and when she came back, he was yanking up a pair of baggy workout shorts, one sliver of black briefs visible before it disappeared.

So that part of the show wasn't included without the full cost of admission. It was a sneak peek designed to leave her wanting more. As if she needed the incentive.

She looked at him as he pulled on a tank top. Loose fitting, like the shorts, but both still showed off plenty of skin and plenty of muscle.

"All right then," he said, downing the offered water and then swinging into the gym. "Where do you want to…" He trailed off as he looked around. "Huh. Slim pickings."

Daphne glanced around the gym and saw what he meant. They'd noticed it was small, but they hadn't looked closer. The treadmill took up half the space. That left a squat rack and single weight bench, which was shoved under the squat rack, there being no other place for it.

"Take turns, I guess?" Chris said. "Looks like it's all free weights. Is that okay?"

Daphne almost lied. *Free weights? Damn, I only know how to use machines.*

That's fine. Here, let me show you.

That was…oddly tempting, now that she thought of it. Not a stranger putting his hands on her to "correct" her hold or posture, but Chris "teaching" her to use free weights.

Breathe like this? I can't quite get it. Here, let me put your hand on my sternum? Whoops, that's not my sternum, he-he.

Daphne sighed inwardly. He'd set his parameters, and if she tempted him to break them, she'd feel guilty, and guilt didn't make anything sexy.

She did *use* free weights—exclusively these days, being all she had in her home gym. What caused a panic bubble was the realization that Chris expected her to lift in front of him. While he watched. That also wasn't sexy.

Why not?

Because it wasn't.

So watching him lift wouldn't be sexy?

Her pulse picked up speed at the image.

So that's sexy, but not a guy watching you?

She'd tell him to go first. There. Let him start and then, whoop, out of time.

Chris had turned away, though, and before she could speak, he was bending in front of the weight rack.

"How much?" he asked.

Sweat beaded along her hairline. "Why don't you go first?"

"I'm good. You warm up while I get this ready. It's one of those variable weight barbells. Might take some fussing."

"If it's too much trouble—"

"It's not. How much do you want for a flat bench press?"

She swallowed.

He turned and caught her expression. "And that's a loaded question, isn't it? I've seen guys do that in the gym to women." He lowered his voice to a gym-rat rumble. "That's all? I can lift four times that." His voice went back to normal. "I know that the chest press is one exercise where women lift a lot less. You won't get any judgment from me." He met her gaze. "On anything."

When she still didn't answer, he reached over and lifted a five-pound dumbbell. "This?"

That made her laugh and relax. The problem wasn't that she thought he'd question her not being about to press *enough*.

She flashed back to the last time a guy offered to set up the barbell for her, after he'd finished with it.

"That's a lot for a lady. You sure?"

"I am. Thank you."

"Okay, then." He'd winked. "Maybe time to get your testosterone levels checked, huh?"

She'd wanted to snap back something. Instead, she'd almost sunk into the floor as everyone in the gym turned to look.

"You want me to guess?" Chris's eyes twinkled. When she didn't answer, he eyed her upper body. "Ninety pounds? Maybe one hundred?"

"I just moved up to one hundred, but I haven't worked out in a couple of weeks, so ninety would be good."

"Done. Now how's that warm-up coming?"

She stretched, and he brought the barbell over, carrying it as if it was still the five-pounder. She got into position on the bench, and he placed the bar on her hands. Then he leaned against the treadmill.

"First time I did a bench press it was fifty pounds," he said. "And I almost dropped it on my head."

She hefted the weight. "Thirty for me. Which was just the bar. I asked the guy at the store for a smaller one—I know they have them—but he didn't carry them, because they're not for serious lifters."

"In other words, he only served men. Asshole."

She kept lifting, and he kept talking, taking over the conversation as she focused on her breathing. He was looking at her, but there was nothing critical in it. Just watching her as he talked. *Avidly* watching her, as if appreciating her form...which made her elbow give out on the last rep.

He caught and held the barbell. She'd been in no danger of dropping it, but she appreciated the gesture.

"Switch out between sets?" he said. "Or do you just want to rest and go again?"

"If it's not too hard to change weights, then we'll switch."

"Easy enough." He took the barbell and returned it to the rack.

"Does that even go high enough for you?" she asked.

"Pfft. No. I usually press two cows and a small goat."

That made her laugh. Then he looked down at the dial.

"It actually doesn't go high enough, does it?" she said, smiling as she sat up.

"It does not, and I should make that sound impressive, but this thing is made for casual workouts. It maxes out at one fifty."

She walked over to him. "Is that all?"

"I think you're going to need to lie across the bar for me. Sorry."

She sputtered a laugh. "Hey, if I could think of a sexy way to do it, I would, but I'd end up clutching the bar like a spider monkey."

"Don't sell yourself short, D. Spider monkeys can be very sexy."

She wanted to run with that. He'd teased her back, which meant flirting was still on the table. Now it was her turn, which would have been easier if she hadn't introduced spider monkeys to the conversation.

Damn it, she wasn't very good at this.

Of course, she wasn't the one who'd said spider monkeys could be sexy, so . . . Maybe they *both* weren't very good at this?

Chris lifted the bar and brought it to the bench. To accommodate the lighter weight, he put the bench on an incline.

"What do you normally press?" she asked as she settled in to his former spot, leaning against the treadmill.

"Little over two hundred."

She whistled.

He shrugged as he adjusted the barbell into position. "It's not that impressive . . . as I'm told repeatedly in public gyms. If I wanted to be bigger, I'd need to press more, but that isn't my goal. For me, it's what you said earlier. Stress relief."

He started to lift, and she let her gaze settle on his chest muscles, visible under the white tank.

He continued, "I hated gym as a kid. I suck at sports. Even in swimming, I barely made the team. The only person I want to compete with is myself. Mostly what I want from sports is fun. I can get that now that I'm older, and there are leagues where people are genuinely just there to enjoy themselves. But this"—he nodded at the barbell—"pure stress relief." He grinned over at her. "Can't argue with the results, though."

Her gaze swept over him. *Nope, can't argue with the results.*

"You?" he said, grunting a little as he kept going.

"Mostly training," she said. "Not for any competitive sports. That isn't my thing, either. But where I live, there are endless opportunities for outdoor activities, most of them hard, all of them challenging. A 'moderate' trail in the Yukon usually involves a mountain."

"So you work out for that."

She nodded. "I want to be able to climb mountains and paddle rapids. Mostly I can, but there are days when Tika and I are struggling up a trail and some seventy-year-old practically sprints past us, and I think 'That's what I want.' Being able to climb those trails now is good, but I want to be sprinting past youngsters when I'm seventy."

"Nice."

After that, they lost themselves in the workout and the conversation—switching off, changing exercises, and talking. So much talking, some serious, some light, all of it wonderful.

The scenery wasn't bad, either.

Yes, Daphne was being shallow. Too bad. If she acknowledged that a guy was a great conversationalist, it was perfectly fine to also acknowledge he looked incredible pumping iron, getting hot and sweaty, tank drenched, muscles glistening.

When Chris's phone buzzed, he barely glanced at it, still intent on their conversation. Then he cursed.

"Hmm?" she said.

"Our rooms are ready."

"Finally."

"And it's past four thirty, which means our chances of getting dinner in time are nonexistent."

"Room service?"

"I guess so. I did promise you a nice dinner out, though. Rain check?"

"Of course."

She wanted to say more, needed to say more, but as soon as she thought it, her heart started pounding like a jackhammer.

She didn't care where they ate, as long as she was with him.

So tell him that.

I'm scared.

Then tell him that.

Nothing ventured, nothing gained. And there was so much to gain. Also, so much to lose.

"Ready to go?" he said. "We'll order dinner at the desk when we get our keys."

She nodded and followed him from the gym.

CHAPTER EIGHTEEN

CHRIS

So, apparently, ordering room service required the hotel to have a restaurant. Or a kitchen.

Online delivery apps to the rescue. He'd found a nearby Thai place while Daphne was getting their keys.

Now they were on the elevator, and he'd wondered whether he should have rethought the "leave the gym without showering" strategy. Of course, *that* required the hotel gym to have a shower. Which it did not.

Did he stink? Or, maybe, the question should be, how bad did he stink?

Well, buddy, she's standing on the opposite side of the elevator, if that's any indication.

Should he joke about the smell?

If he did, would she feel obliged to deny it?

He snuck a glance over as he pushed the button. Wait. She didn't seem to be across the otherwise empty elevator to stay out of sniffing range. She was checking him out, which was much easier to do with a bit of distance.

Was he sure? He peeked at the reflection in the polished silver of the wall. Yep, she was checking him out. He bit his lip to keep from smiling and lifted his elbow to rest against the wall.

You are such a poseur.

Hey, if it worked, he was going for it. And it was working, just like the striptease in the changing room.

Oh, right, the striptease. Which you had to abort midshow when you realized you were about to pull down your trousers and show her just how much you were enjoying watching her watch the performance.

Er, right. Yeah. That'd been awkward.

Still, if she was enjoying this show, that boded well for his question, didn't it?

He leaned into the wall, flexing as the elevator doors—

"Hold that!" a woman said.

Chris did not "hold that." He did that really shitty thing where you pretend to be reaching for the button to hold the doors but, damn, you didn't get to it in time.

Except the man *with* the woman *did* get to it in time, sticking his hand between the doors, which bounced back open.

As the man stepped in, he looked at Chris. Looked away fast. Mumbled something and ushered his wife to the far side, as Daphne stepped toward Chris. There was a moment of shuffling, where Daphne sidestepped right up against Chris and the guy sidestepped right into his wife's view of Chris. Which would have been more amusing if the guy hadn't checked out Daphne at the same time.

Chris let his hand slip behind Daphne. Not quite putting his arm around her, but if the guy interpreted it that way . . .

Daphne leaned into his arm.

He stifled a grin and slung his arm loosely around her waist.

As the elevator began a slow chug upward, the man said, "Is the hotel gym any good?"

Chris waggled his hand and looked at Daphne, who said, "It exists. That's about the best you can say. Treadmill. A few free weights."

The guy rolled his shoulders. "Maybe I'll go."

His wife made a noise that suggested this would not actually be happening.

Chris watched the numbers roll up. The elevator hit the couple's floor first, and they stepped off. Once the doors closed, Daphne let out a choked laugh and leaned against him. He tightened his arm around her, pulling her into his side, and she laid her head against his shoulder.

Was it possible to mentally will the elevator to break down right now? What if his hand snuck out and hit the Stop button?

Huh, the elevator seems to be broken. Whatever can we do?

The signing tonight. Shit! Right!

The elevator stopped, and for a second, his heart did, too, as his brain flooded with images—not of sexy elevator time but of them frantically calling for rescue before the event.

Then the doors opened, and he realized they'd reached their floor.

Daphne stepped off, and his hand slipped from her waist. He reached to...to what? Pull her back onto the elevator? Awkwardly get his hand around her waist again while she strode off, luggage in tow?

She glanced back, frowning at him. "Are you on a different floor?"

"Just wiping off a sweat streak."

Sweat streak? Mmm, sexy.

Still, having made the really bad excuse, he had to take a moment to look as if he was wiping the elevator wall. Then he followed her to their rooms. She stopped outside one and held up both cards.

"Randomized room choice. Pick a card. We'll see whose works."

His did.

"Meet you at the adjoining door?" she said, and then headed to her own room before he could reply. A moment later, they were both unlatching the adjoining door from their respective sides. He pulled it open first, making her laugh as he nearly yanked her off her feet. She stuck her luggage in front of the door, propping it open, and ducked her head into his room.

"Nice."

"Identical to yours?"

"Yep." She leaned against the doorjamb. "So I guess we should shower first."

"Nah. I thought I'd go to the signing like this." He plucked at his tank top. "Think anyone will mind?"

"Oddly, I doubt they would."

"The smell might be a turnoff, though."

"I don't smell anything."

He turned toward her, a smile tugging at his lips as he leaned in— then his phone buzzed with a text.

Seriously?

He took out his phone without looking at the screen and went to set it aside. It buzzed again. His jaw set.

Not looking at it.

"You'd better check that," Daphne said. "In case it's Sakura, and there's a problem."

He picked up the phone.

Gemma: Rough day.

Gemma: Can we talk?

His shoulders slumped. "It's my sister. She had a rough day in the divorce proceedings."

"Ouch." Daphne backed up, straightening. "You should call her."

When he hesitated, she reached out, hand touching his. "Call her." Her gaze rose to his. "Then we'll talk."

DAPHNE

Daphne had pulled her luggage from the adjoining door to give Chris privacy. Bad timing on the call, but she'd forced herself to say those final words—"Then we'll talk"—so she couldn't squirm out of the conversation they needed to have.

She glanced toward the adjoining door. On the other side, she could hear Chris talking to his sister. She didn't know the details, only that Gemma was going through a shitty divorce from a shitty husband, and Chris had grumbled that getting her to admit how shitty it made her feel was an exercise in frustration. Gemma wanted to pretend she was fine, that she didn't need help much less pity. Daphne got that. She *really* got that. So if Gemma was opening up, then she'd get all the sibling time she needed.

Daphne sat on the end of the bed to check phone messages. She'd been doing that routinely all day. With Nia, Gemma, and Sakura all scouring the web for trouble, she couldn't afford to ignore messages.

There was nothing new. Nia had found some online threads earlier where people were trying to track down "Zane," but while it was intrusive and crept into stalker territory, it hadn't crossed that border.

> Hey, let's see if we can find out who this guy really is. For shits and giggles and possibly offers of marriage.

Nia said they had time. Things weren't escalating. The grizzly video had, as Daphne said, gone only mildly viral, and that fire was already reduced to smoldering embers.

Daphne's next step would be calling Lawrence to tell him the truth and ask him to conference with her, Nia, and Chris to discuss a full reveal plan. Well, if Lawrence didn't dump her on the spot. Which he might, but they were prepared for that. If he did, the next call would go to her editor, Alicia, with the same conference-call request.

They had plans and backup plans and contingency plans, and if the end result was that the publisher canceled her book and the reading public told her to go screw herself, then that was their choice. Daphne hoped it wouldn't come to that. She was voluntarily stepping from the shadows, telling her story and apologizing sincerely. That must count for something.

Daphne was about to set her phone aside when she remembered it'd been a while since she checked her spam folder. She wouldn't want to miss a message from Nia or Sakura because a word triggered a spam false-positive.

At a glance she saw nothing. Just the usual garbage. Oh, and a few messages from Robbie. Great.

She'd ask Chris for advice on dealing with Robbie. Maybe he could help . . .

Wait, he *had* helped. She'd forgotten their make-out session had ultimately been a ploy to make Robbie leave her alone. But what if he didn't take the hint? What if he got competitive? Worse, what if he felt like she'd led him on, and he retaliated?

She looked down at her spam folder, with its three messages from Robbie, and her shoulders slumped.

She opened the first, sent yesterday.

    Call me. Now.

It was a true mystery of the universe how guys like Robbie got laid. He certainly did. According to the neighborhood chatter, there was a regular stream of female visitors at his rented place, and they weren't there to walk his dog.

She opened the next one.

```
I know you're very busy with Chad, and I hate
to interrupt your Chad-screw-fest, but this
is important. Call me. NOW.
```

There was a brief second where she worried that there could be an actual issue. Her house caught on fire. Tika had run away from the neighbor. One problem with being a writer was she could see all the possibilities, most of them dire. But after rereading, no, he just sounded pissed off.

Pissed off enough to storm into the sunset, never to be heard from again? One could only hope.

Email three.

```
Fine. You don't want to call. Let's do it
your way.
```

She kept reading, and as she did, her stomach clenched. It kept clenching until—

Her heart stopped. Everything stopped.

Oh no.

Please, please, please, no.

She read the email again and there was no doubt what Robbie was saying. No doubt at all.

CHRIS

Chris wasn't going to hurry his sister off the phone after she'd finally broken down and admitted how bad things were and how "not okay" she was. Her ex was a leech who'd sucked Gemma emotionally dry, and he wasn't done yet.

Chris was fuming by the time they got off the phone. He rubbed his hands over his face. He needed to set his anger aside. Gemma could handle it, and all she needed was support, which he'd given. She was going out with their parents tonight, and she'd be fine and didn't need him seething on her behalf.

The adjoining door was cracked open. He rolled his shoulders, ran his hand through his hair, and found his equilibrium. Then he strolled through.

"Sibling-support call done," he said. "Now about that shower..."

He trailed off as he saw Daphne. She was on the bed, huddled at the headboard, knees drawn up, gaze down, her expression...

He ran forward and sat on the edge beside her, laying a hand on her arm. "D?"

She looked up, her eyes empty, as if she hadn't heard him come in.

"What's wrong?" he said.

"It's...Robbie."

Robbie? It took a moment for him to remember that was her asshole neighbor. The one they'd scared off with their make-out session.

"Did something happen to him?" he asked.

Daphne made a noise, almost like a derisive snort. Then she lifted her hand, her phone in it, thumbed to an email and passed it over.

The email was from Robbie. Chris read it.

```
Fine. You don't want to call. Let's do it your
way. I have this niece who runs a blog thing
online. She's weird, always holed up with a
book. I don't talk to her much. Then out of
the blue, she's texting me about some author.
She read this book, it was great, blah-blah,
```

and she was posting about it on her blog thing, and she looked up the author, who lives in the Yukon and OMG, her uncle lives in the Yukon. Do I know the author? Like I know everyone in the Yukon. I ignored her. Then she sent a photo, and it turns out I do know him. Saw him just last week, practically banging you against a tree.

Seems your Chad is some kind of author. Whatever.

But the kid doesn't let up. OMG, you've met Zane Remington? Where does he live? Here are some photos of his place. Do you recognize it?

Oh yeah, I recognize it. That's why Chad was at your house. He was pretending it was his. I knew the bastard was up to something. So I did a little digging and found out there is no "Zane Remington." It's what they call a pseudonym. Not only is he a fake, living in a fake house, but he's using a fake name.

That's when I remembered the BBQ last year, when Pam was going on about some short story she'd written and how she wanted to get it published and shit. Talked my ear off for ten minutes, with Ren right there, pleased as punch because his woman could string together a few sentences. Then you overheard and got talking to Pam. Ren asked if you wrote, and you said you did.

So I start thinking, and wondering, and I go online to see this book, and I find a free copy of it on some website. I start skimming through. It's about a girl, which has me wondering why a guy would write that, unless he's some kind of perv. Then, right in the first chapter, there's this part where the girl's dog falls through the ice, and it happens just like that time Tika fell through chasing a hare, only in the book they were running from a zombie.

Chad didn't write that book. You did. Maybe he hired you or whatever. Don't know. Don't care. I just know that you wrote it and now you're lying to people, and I talked to my niece, and she says that's a really bad thing. She says people who do that get cancelled. If this comes out, you're done, and not just your book. You.

I've only told my niece that I think I know who wrote the book and that it's a chick. She wants details. Begged me to give her names so she can be the one who outs you.

Little shit, huh? Goes from "OMG, this book is so good!" to "Let me be the one to ruin the writer!" in a heartbeat. Everyone wants their fifteen minutes of fame. But you'd know all about that, wouldn't you?

So here's the deal. I'll keep your secret...if you give me something in return. I want a one-year free rental of your house.

```
That's it. Reasonable, right? You have twenty-
four hours to decide.
    Now will you call me?
```

As Chris had read the email, his fingers had tightened around the phone. As he reached the end, the edges bit in, and it was everything he could do not to keep squeezing until it broke in his hand.

Daphne reached over and gently extricated her phone from his grip.

"It's not the end of the world," she said, her voice barely above a whisper. "I can give him the house for a year." She audibly swallowed. "It's temporary. I'll find another place. I have enough money to do that."

"No."

She looked up at him, her jaw setting. "Yes. I got into this mess, and if this is the price I pay to get out of this, so be it. I won't take chances."

"This is your house, Daphne. *Yours.*"

She shook her head. "One year is nothing."

"He's not really asking for a year rent free. That's like asking for ten grand when you know you could get a hundred. If you talked to whoever owns that place he's currently renting, I suspect you might get a story."

Daphne frowned.

Chris continued, "Remember the friend I took on as a partner? He knew tenancy law, and when things went south, he used it to full advantage. Once Robbie's in your house, he's not going anywhere. I can tell you what to demand in a rental agreement, but I have a feeling he won't sign it with those clauses."

Her shoulders slumped. "I *have* heard that his current landlord has been trying to evict him."

"Right. You'd eventually get him out, but it's going to be a fight, and I don't think you need to go that far." He tapped her phone. "He may know tenant rights, but he doesn't understand blackmail. He literally wrote out his demand and sent it from his own address. Let's see what Nia has to say about that."

He expected that would get a smile. A sudden beam of sunshine in the gloom. Instead, Daphne stayed quiet, and then said, "Does it matter?"

"Hmm?"

She looked up at him. "That's the thing about blackmail, isn't it? If an ex threatens to post your nudes online, you can have them charged with blackmail...while they put those pictures up anyway. If I threaten Robbie, he can just pass on my name to his niece. Hell, in *making* a blackmail charge, I need to admit what I did, and then it'll seem as if I only came forward because I was under threat of exposure." She pulled her knees in, one arm going around them. "I lost my chance. I could have gotten ahead of this, and I screwed up, and now it's going to come out and my career is over."

"No," he said firmly. "This isn't the end. It's a bump in the road. That's all. Our timeline still works. We just need to slow Robbie's roll. Make him think he's going to get what he wants. Show you're panicked. That's all he needs right now."

"To think I'm planning to agree."

"Yep. You're freaked out, partly because you aren't sure you can give him what he wants. There's Tika to consider, and with the lack of housing in Whitehorse, you don't know where you'll stay, and you can't leave the area because it's an off-grid house that needs some monitoring." He feigned taking a deep breath. "It's all so much, and you're going to make it work but..."

"I need more time," she said slowly, as if seeing that light through the gloom. "Act like I'm in a total panic, just got his message and oh my God, what am I going to do? Beg him to bear with me while I figure out the logistics. Buy myself time to get past the tour and tell the truth."

"Yep."

She glanced over. "Do I admit he's uncovered the truth? I don't want to— No, wait. I can say he's misunderstanding the situation, blah blah, but if his niece goes public, even with the wrong story, it'll ruin my career."

"Perfect. Don't admit anything in writing."

"Should I call instead? I'd really rather not. I can pull this off better in writing."

"Email him. Just don't admit to anything. Don't deny it, either. Stick to the 'misunderstanding' line, which is technically true, since he's misunderstanding why I'm playing Zane."

"So he can't pull that out later and accuse me of lying."

"Which he won't anyway, because once you come clean, Nia can inform him that he's threatened you with extortion, and if he goes public, he'll be charged. Which lets you come out of your own volition."

"What about his niece? She's a book blogger. After I come out, she can still claim I only did it because her uncle knew who I was."

"Again, if she tries that, it sets Robbie up for that extortion charge. Nia will warn him, and he'll keep her quiet. He's not exactly uncle of the year. He'll have no problem shutting her down."

Daphne took a deep breath. "Okay. This could work."

"It *will* work."

A slow nod. "It's what Robbie will expect. Panic but capitulation. I'm not considering refusing his demand. I'm just all a-flutter over the details. Give me forty-eight hours and I'll have a contract for him. No—don't mention a contract. I'm too flustered to think of that, which is to his advantage. Give me forty-eight hours, and I'll have a move-in date for him. Does that work?"

"Brilliantly. See? We really do make a good team."

He smiled at her, but instead of smiling back, her eyes filled with tears.

"I'm so sorry, Chris."

"About what?"

"Dragging you into this. I've made such a mess of it, and this isn't what you signed up for. I wish I'd never sent that query."

"I don't," he said softly.

She looked at him.

"If you hadn't sent it, I wouldn't be here," he said. "You would never have needed a Zane Remington."

A heartbeat. Then her eyes widened. "Oh! That was inconsiderate of me. You needed this job. I don't mean I wish *that* never happened. I just should have come out sooner. As soon as things got complicated, before you got dragged into—"

"—nothing," he said, meeting her gaze. "I got dragged into nothing, Daphne. And that's not what I meant at all. Screw the job. After I met you, that was fifty percent excuse anyway, and by the time the book came out, it was a hundred percent excuse. I didn't need the job anymore. I just wanted to be with you. That's what I was trying to say. If there was no Zane Remington, I wouldn't have had the chance to meet you. Maybe that's selfish, but I'm going to be completely selfish right now and admit that I would never, in a million years, want to give up the chance to spend time with you, to get to know you better . . . to fall in love with you."

Did you really just say that?

Yep, he did, and he wasn't taking it back, because it was the truth, and he was damned well going to acknowledge that, whatever the consequences.

Daphne stared at him. Just stared.

Reverse! Reverse! Laugh it off. Pretend she misheard. Do something!

Nope. If it wasn't something she wanted to hear, she could say she didn't think of him that way, and that would be that.

And by "that would be that" he meant that he'd never mention it again. Not that he'd tuck his hurt feelings under his arm and slink out of the friendship. *If you don't want me, I guess I'll just leave.* Or wave his hurt-feelings flag and storm out. *If I can't have you that way, I don't want you around at all.*

More silence as she stared at him.

Okay, he wasn't going to take the words back, but he could nudge them aside. Let her know it was okay if her answer was—

"I'm scared," she blurted. Then she rubbed her hands over her face. "I didn't mean to say that."

He tugged her hands down. "But it's how you feel, so it needed to be said. Just like I needed to say what I did. If what I said scared you, if it's moving too fast, then you can say that."

She shook her head. "It's not that. It's ... everything. I do want more but I'm ..."

"Scared. Of ...?"

"I'm not sure I'm at the right place in my life for this, Chris. If it was anyone else, I'd say no, but I feel as if this could be something, and that sends me spiraling into the future, with all kinds of complications that I shouldn't be worrying about yet."

"Like the fact we live over a thousand miles apart?"

"Yes, and I don't want to get into a situation where I'm giving up one dream for another. Nor do I expect you to give up your home for me. Then there's the writing. It's a new career, and it takes up so much of my time and attention."

"But it's your dream. Same as the house."

She nodded.

"And I'd never ask you to give up, either. I'm not saying I can see myself living in the Yukon full-time, but I am saying I would never expect you to walk away from what you've built there. Same as your career." He met her gaze. "I'd expect you to respect my home and my career, so I offer the same, and I'm not sure how that works out, but…"

He took her hands in his. "I'm not asking you to commit to anything. I just need you to be open to the idea that this is more than a fling." He quirked a smile. "Nothing can be certain. That'd be like writing a book and deciding it's going to be an instant bestseller. But you wrote it in hopes it would be the start of something real. A possible new direction for your life. Yes?"

She nodded again.

"That's all this is," he said. "Our first chapter. Pen to paper with the hope of finishing the story." He met her gaze. "Do you want to start a story with me, Daphne?"

She kissed him. He didn't see it coming. He was too focused on his tone and his expression, being absolutely certain she knew he meant it. Meant all of it.

Then she was kissing him, a deep and passionate kiss that answered all his questions.

The first page of a new story.

When the kiss broke, she put her lips to his ear. "I think you're amazing, Chris. I think if you walk out of my life, I'm never going to get over it."

He cupped his hands around her face and brought it back to his. He held it there, looking deep into her eyes, pausing as if to make some grand speech, and then saying, "Same."

She sputtered a laugh, and she looked so damned gorgeous that he was transfixed, words and thoughts drying up. Her mouth lowered to his, and he closed his eyes and inhaled the scent of her and—

—the hotel room phone rang. Daphne broke the kiss with a groan and dropped her head onto his shoulder.

"Why do phones exist?" she said. "To keep us apart forever?"

"I think so. In this case, though, I believe it's a sign that our dinner has arrived and we should hit Pause on this until after the signing. Which is probably for the best."

Her brows shot up. "I think we have very different definitions of 'best.' A concerning difference that could have a serious impact on our relationship."

"Mmm. That depends. My definition of 'best' is a night together, with all phones turned off, hours of no interruptions...rather than setting a timer for ten minutes before we need to get ready for the event."

"I don't know. Ten minutes doesn't sound so bad when it's ten minutes to finally get something you've been lusting after for weeks."

"Lusting after me? Or after..." He waved a hand down his body.

"Depends. The first time I met you, I lusted after..." She tilted her head. "Well, nothing, really."

"Because I stole your parking spot? I thought that was supposed to be sexy. I've read the articles, you know. They say that stealing a woman's parking spot is guaranteed to show her what a selfish prick you are, and she'll be unable to resist. Lies?"

"All lies. Sorry. However, once you got past that, things improved. Once you sent that photo of you half naked with the cub, they really improved."

"The lusting began?"

"Yep. Sending me brownie photos. Walking around my house topless. Swimming in my lake almost naked. Such a tease."

"Hey, I know my strengths."

"You do indeed, and I loved every second of seeing you flaunt them. You are one *hell* of a sexy man. But do you know where the sexiest part of you is?" She leaned down again, fingers under his chin and looked him in the eyes. "There."

He lifted his fingers to her hair and pulled her in for a kiss, their lips touching and—

—the hotel phone rang again.

"Huh," she said. "That must have stopped earlier."

"Didn't notice," he murmured. "If you really want those ten minutes, we could…"

She sighed. "No, you're right. We should wait."

"Now who's the tease?"

She bent for a quick kiss. "I've realized ten minutes will not be enough."

He smiled. "It will not."

"Okay, then. If you can go down and get dinner, I will write a damn email to Robbie. Get that out of the way. Will you check it over before I hit Send?"

"Absolutely."

"Then let's get through this event. How fast can you sign books?"

He grinned. "You're about to find out."

CHAPTER NINETEEN

DAPHNE

This was the first "real" signing, and Daphne had been so excited. Yet once she got there, it wasn't what she expected.

The problem was Chris. Oh, fine, Chris himself wasn't a problem. The opposite, actually, which was the problem. She'd come to see and hear readers, and the only person she could see and hear was Chris, standing at the podium, talking to those readers.

She could blame her vantage point. She was seated at the signing table, next to the podium, where she was facing Chris. But she *could* watch the audience if she turned her head. It was just so damned hard to do that when he was standing up there, bathed in light, his voice seeming to come from the speakers all around her.

Mine.

That's what her brain kept saying. Her brain and other body parts.

Mine, mine, mine.

There was no note of propriety in the words. It was the giggling chant of a gleeful inner girl, turning cartwheels with delight. He was hers.

Chris was talking about the book, and she was struggling hard to pay attention, but all she could hear was his words from earlier.

I'm going to be completely selfish right now and admit that I would never, in a million years, want to give up the chance to spend time with you, to get to know you better . . . to fall in love with you.

After Anthony, Daphne hadn't given up on love. She'd known there was someone out there for her, but it became that much harder to open up and take a chance. Holing up in the wilderness and taking a break from dating was a lot easier when your choices were Robbie and, well, Robbie.

Chris was worth taking that chance on, and now she could only stare at him and try *not* to think of a couple hours from now, when she'd have him all to herself.

For now, she'd share him with this audience, and when she could pull herself away from starry-eyed gaping, she could see just how wonderful he was with them. Articulate, charming, witty, even modest now that he'd thrown off the jerky parts of the Zane persona for good. Chris was being himself up there, and the audience loved it.

Would Daphne be able to measure up? Would readers be as captivated by her once the truth came out?

It wasn't just that she lacked that jawline, those biceps, that wavy dark blond hair. It was that she lacked the confidence to stand up there and talk about her book and presume anyone gave a damn. But she'd need to develop it, and this was how she'd do that.

She'd look out and see the barely teen girl clutching *Edge* in both hands. She'd see the college-aged one reading it, still on the first few chapters but too engrossed to even glance at Zane. She'd see the two women in their forties, whispering excitedly and just when she thought it was about Zane, one would crack open the book to show a part she'd bookmarked. She'd see the man standing at the back with two copies in his hand, for himself or loved ones, it didn't matter.

She could do this. She *would* do this.

Being in the spotlight would be hard, but this part would make up for it—getting out here and meeting readers and letting them know how much they mattered.

Following Sakura's advice, the event was structured as a very short talk followed by a longer Q&A period. At first, no one seemed to have questions, but once a few got up the nerve to ask—and weren't immediately incinerated for their burst of extroversion—more put their hands up and then more and more until Sakura noticed some of the audience getting restless and called for "one more question from someone who hasn't had a chance yet."

Chris answered that, and while the staff gave instructions for the signing line, he came over to sit beside Daphne.

He leaned in. "How'd I do?"

"Amazing, as always."

He grinned, his face lighting up, and he leaned closer, hand grasping her arm in a quick squeeze. "Now we see how fast I can sign?"

"I've got my timer."

Another grin and another arm squeeze, and Daphne noticed they'd caught the attention of some attendees, who whispered and pointed, and if any were disappointed to discover that Zane Remington had a girlfriend, they didn't show it.

CHRIS

The last person stepped up. It was a staff member. All the staff had waited until the end. Some obviously were just adding to their collection of signed books, but this one—a teenage girl—smiled shyly and pushed the book forward.

"It was great," she said. "Really."

"Ask him!" one of her colleagues shouted.

The girl rolled her eyes. "He's not going to tell me."

"She wants to know who Theo ends up with!" the colleague called.

"Ah. That is an excellent question. I believe Daphne here knows the answer." He glanced over. "Who does Theo end up with, D?"

"Whoever is the best choice for her as a person," Daphne said. "Whoever challenges her to grow and trust herself the most, and whoever supports and trusts *her* the most."

A few claps from the staff group.

"Well, there's your answer," Chris said. "Whoever challenges and supports Theo the most. Which means in the end, it'll be Theo and Mochi, together forever."

Laughter, and the young woman looked at Daphne. "That *is* a good answer, and it means it's going to be Atticus."

Daphne only smiled, and Chris reached under the table to squeeze her hand. It *was* a good answer. A really good answer. Also, he was totally rooting for Atticus. Did authors' boyfriends get to ask for series spoilers? He was going to find out.

The author's boyfriend. Daphne's boyfriend. He liked the sound of that. He also liked lover, partner, fiancé...

Whoa. Slow down there.

He smiled. He wouldn't rush it, but there was nothing wrong with knowing where he'd like to end up.

He signed the book and said a few words. While he'd joked about speed-signing, there was a limit to how fast he could go without making people feel like he had somewhere better to be. Which he did, but that was no insult to the readers. Right now, he couldn't imagine anything that would be fair competition to his late-evening plans.

As Sakura herded the staff away, Chris laid his hand on Daphne's thigh, hidden under the long tablecloth. Then he played with the hem of her skirt, letting his fingers slide along the inside of her thigh, keeping them low. Nothing too risqué but it still made her lips part.

"Was I fast enough?" he whispered.

"Very fast."

"And that's the last time you're going to say that tonight."

A stifled laugh. Then she leaned his way. "Is that a promise?"

"It's a guarantee. That's the only reason you haven't had a midnight knock on your door. I am an *expert* at self-control."

"Are you now?" She leaned closer, her own hand sliding up his thigh. "That sounds like a challenge."

"It is absolutely a—"

"Zane?" Sakura called. When he looked over, she waved. "Come for a staff photo."

He started to rise, and then sat quickly.

"Everything okay?" Daphne whispered.

He looked down.

She followed his gaze. "Ah. I see. Well, no. To properly see it, I'd need to reach over and unzip your—"

"Not helping," he said, through his teeth.

"Just hold a copy of the book over your crotch," she said.

"Distract them, please, while I recite a few formulas."

"Will you do it out loud?" she whispered. "Math is so sexy."

He shot her a glare. She reached across him and grabbed a book.

"Just a sec!" she called. "He doesn't want to forget to sign these."

There were a few books at his elbow that had been bought by people who hadn't been able to make it. Daphne pulled the small stack over.

"Actually, that's better," Sakura said. "Everyone get behind the table with Zane!"

He pulled in his chair so fast that Daphne snickered. As the staff came over, she tried to step aside but Sakura said "No, no, stay there," which Chris appreciated. Daphne *should* be in the photo. He gave her a book to hold, which would be even better—once the truth came out, the store would still have pictures of the actual author with the book.

"All right then," Sakura said after the photos were done. "Before we go, Zane, are you okay with signing store stock?"

Uh…

He cleared his throat. "Of course."

By now, he could stand, and he walked to the rack holding the remaining half dozen copies of *Edge*. In a few days, they'd be collectors' items with the original "Zane" signature. Just six books to sign and then—

Wheels squeaked. He looked up as one staff member appeared, pushing a trolley full of books, another behind her…with another trolley.

"All the regional chain stores sent their stock," Sakura said. "That's why we only hit indies this afternoon."

"I…see."

"A signed book is a sold book," Sakura chirped.

"*Now* how fast can you sign?" Daphne whispered.

"Call Guinness," he whispered back. "Because I'm about to set a world record."

CHRIS

The books were signed. All two hundred of them. Did they want to make sure he didn't have the use of his fingers tonight?

Apparently, he was going to have some time to recover, because the damned town car had left. Sakura had booked it for four hours, and when nine thirty hit, the driver calculated that he couldn't get them back to the hotel by ten and declared his shift done. That left Sakura scrambling for a replacement. Chris had protested that a taxi was fine, but they were in the suburbs, and getting a town car would be faster.

Sakura was spending the night with a local friend, and she'd tried to insist on staying behind, but Daphne had shooed her off.

A few staff members had offered to wait with them, too, but they'd said no, the store was closing and they weren't making anyone stay late.

"We'll be fine," Daphne had said. "I have Zane to protect me."

She'd been teasing. Did he still think it sounded kinda hot? Yes, he did.

Now they were tucked into a shadowy emergency exit as the staff exited, all of them looking over to say goodbye, which really put a damper on the possibilities of that shadowy spot.

Daphne took the time to massage his hand, which he had to admit felt good, her thumb rubbing his palm, her fingers massaging the base of his thumb.

Finally, there was the distant click of a door lock, and the manager waved and called a goodbye as she headed to her car.

"I do believe we're alone," Daphne whispered in his ear.

"Seems like it."

"Absolutely alone." She looked out at the now-empty lot. "Sakura's gone. The staff is gone. There are no security cameras, and the car isn't due to arrive for another twenty minutes. Whatever will we do?"

He pulled her to him in a deep kiss. She was into it for about one minute. Then she pulled back.

"Too public?" he said.

She laughed softly, her eyes glinting in the near dark. "Not at all. Is it too public for you?"

"Not at all."

"Too public if I...?" She fingered his belt buckle. "Unbuttoned this?"

He opened his mouth and had to settle for shaking his head.

"Any restrictions?" she said. "Things you'd rather I didn't do until we're in a more private spot?"

He looked around. As exposed as the spot felt, it really was hidden. No one was going to whip around the corner and get a show.

"This seems private enough to me."

"So no restrictions?"

"None."

She smiled. "Excellent. Then I think I'm going to test that *expert* self-control of yours."

"Go ahead."

She undid his belt and tugged it from the loops. Then she rolled it up and tucked it into her bag. As she leaned in to kiss him, her hands returned to his waistband, sliding along it before flicking open the button on his fly. Her fingers glided over his abdomen and down in a teasing exploration. A tug on his fly, slow and steady, until it was open.

He pulled her back into a kiss as she reached into his boxers. At first, she deftly avoided touching where he really wanted her to touch. Then her fingers tickled along the length of him, and he groaned, kissing her harder.

Her hand slowly closed around him, seeming to take forever before she had him tight in her grip. At the tingle of a cool breeze, he broke the kiss and looked down.

She'd pushed down his boxers. Her hand slid down him, leaving him exposed. He looked at the parking lot, and yes, it was empty, but he was still standing outside a bookstore with his cock out, rock hard, Daphne's hand sliding down to cup his balls.

"Too much?" she murmured.

He shook his head. While he could hear the roar of distant traffic, everything around them was completely silent and empty. He didn't need to worry about flashing himself to an innocent stranger, but he was still in a public place, the cool night air tickling his cock as Daphne's hand ran along it, and that was hotter than he could have imagined.

With her free hand, Daphne unbuttoned his shirt. Her tongue slid down behind each opened button, and when she made a move to bend her knee, she looked up at him. "Still okay?"

He tried to speak but could only nod. She lowered herself in front of him, and he leaned back against the wall, eyes half closing as her tongue slid along his cock.

He reached to put his hands on her head, not pushing or pulling or speeding her along, but toying with her hair as she toyed with him.

Her tongue slid along him again, and her lips teased—

Tires crunched on pavement.

Chris's eyelids flew open as a black car turned into the parking lot, and his first thought was: *It's fine. They can't see us.*

Except even if they were hidden, this car was here for them, the driver *looking* for them.

Daphne quickly stood, shielding him.

"Damn it," she muttered. "They're early. I had a timer set for five minutes before they were supposed to get here." She helped him zip up his trousers. Then she paused, a slow smile on her face. "The cars have a privacy screen, right?"

"They do."

"May I continue in the back seat?"

He grinned. "Absolutely."

DAPHNE

Every town car they'd taken had a barrier between the driver and the back seat. And now they got the one damned town car without it.

Daphne had tried to figure out a way around that. Going down on Chris was out of the question. But maybe putting a jacket over his lap and sliding her hand under it?

That would be so much easier if they'd brought a jacket. Or a sweater. Or anything.

"Well, this is inconvenient," she muttered as she glared at the lack of a divider.

Chris chuckled against her ear. "Probably for the best."

"There's that phrase again. Define 'best.'"

He nuzzled her ear, his fingers toying with the hem of her skirt. "I'd been about thirty seconds from proving that my expert self-control isn't all that expert. Which would *not* be for the best. Also, the trip back to our hotel is simultaneously too long and too short."

She arched a brow.

He continued, whispering at her ear, "Too long for me to get through it without coming, and too short for me to be ready again once we're out of this car. However…" He inched the skirt up her thighs. "While the length of the ride might be wrong, the length of this skirt is exactly right, along with the angle of the seat and the rear-view mirror." He lowered his voice. "I'm a math guy. I can calculate these things."

His fingers slid to the inside of her thigh.

"May I?" he said.

She could only nod mutely.

He took his time, just as she had in the parking lot. She now wished she'd moved a little faster, for his sake, but she'd make up for it soon enough.

As his fingers crept up, her mind went back to that parking lot, to Chris against the wall, his cock rock-hard under her fingers, under her lips, under her tongue.

When his own fingers reached their destination, Chris gave a soft chuckle, finding her as ready as he'd been.

"I was just thinking about you in that parking lot," she whispered.

"You liked that?"

"I did. I just wish I could have had more time."

His fingers slid into her as his mouth came to her ear. "What would you have done if you had more time?"

"Do you kids want something to eat?" the driver asked.

Daphne's legs clamped together so fast, Chris chuckled again. His fingers slid out as he leaned forward.

"Hmm?" he said.

"The lady who called the car said you might want to eat on the way home."

"Mmm, yeah, I could eat something," Chris said. "But I'll wait until I get back."

"You want to go through a drive-thru?"

"Nah." Chris's fingers tickled the inside of her leg. "I've got everything I need right here."

Daphne bit her cheek to keep from laughing.

He leaned to her ear. "How about you? Up for a little something to eat when we get back?"

"Oh, I wouldn't call it little."

He laughed against her ear. "Good. Then we can both enjoy—"

"So where you kids from?" the driver asked.

Chris looked from Daphne to the driver. She eased back in the car, removing his fingers from her thigh.

"Soon," she whispered. "Think of it as building an appetite."

He shook his head and then answered the driver's question.

DAPHNE

The driver eventually returned to driving, which allowed Chris to return his attention to Daphne. He also returned his fingers to her thighs, sliding them up under her skirt, slowly, as if expecting the driver to start chatting again. When the driver turned up the radio, Chris relaxed, and she did, too.

Chris's fingers reached the edge of her panties, and he leaned into her ear.

"These seem to be in my way," he said, plucking the lace of her panties.

Her breath caught, and she glanced at the driver, who was busy watching traffic as they entered the city. Also, the seat would clearly block his view even if he did glance back.

"I'm sure I can get past them if you'd rather not take them off," he whispered.

"Do it for me," she said.

His grin sparked. While she kept an eye on the driver, Chris slid her panties down, managing it far more gracefully than she would have. Then, panties balled in his fist, he tucked them into her bag.

Chris checked the driver again. The seat firmly blocked the man's view, but Daphne still inched a little Chris's way as his hand slid back under her skirt. His fingers grazed her inner thigh, but this time there was no tickling advance. They slid straight in, making her gasp.

"Better?" he said.

She could only nod. Then she realized her expression was probably not rearview mirror appropriate and quickly smoothed out her features. It wasn't easy. Chris took zero time finding the right spot, and he might have joked about being an expert at self-control, but he *was* an expert at this.

She pretended to look out the side window, like nothing was happening, like she wasn't in the back seat of a town car, panties off, Chris toying with her clit like a goddamn pro. And it was...

Hot.

Damn it was hot.

An exercise in self-control, indeed.

Her fingers dug into the leather seat, and she let out the smallest gasp, her breath coming fast. Then her legs snapped shut.

"Stop?" he said as he paused.

"No, just…" She swallowed. "Give me a sec." She snuck a look his way, trying to bring her temperature down a notch. "Anything I can do for you?"

"Yes, but it'd be tricky. And you might not want to."

"Tell me."

He whispered into her ear. "Take off your bra."

Heat singed through her. It started at her cheeks, but then it surged all the way down.

"Up to you," he whispered. "It's always up to you."

She was wearing a rare button-up blouse. A D-cup usually meant no button-ups, but this one fit her well enough not to strain. If she took off her bra… The blouse was teal blue, and no one could see through it but yes, it would be obvious she wasn't wearing a bra.

So what?

There wasn't a "no bra, no service" sign on the hotel door, and they'd be going straight up to her room.

She slid her hands up her back. The clasp let go with a snap of relief. Getting it off discreetly was, as Chris said, a bit tricky. But the blouse was loose, and she was determined, and soon it was in her hand and then in her bag.

"Nicely done, Houdini," Chris said.

"I was properly motivated."

He smiled. "Yeah, I bet that gets uncomfortable."

"Oh, not that." She leaned over and snuggled against him. "You told me to take it off, and I am in the mood to do as I'm told."

That grin sparked again. "Are you?"

"You know how some people like to be behind the wheel and some like to take the passenger seat? I like both. Switch it up."

"Then, as long as I'm driving…" His hands went back under her skirt. "Sit back and enjoy."

Daphne glanced forward, making absolutely sure the driver couldn't see anything. Then she relaxed.

Chris's fingers found their place, and he leaned toward her ear. "Do you know how hot you look right now?"

She closed her eyes and struggled to keep her expression neutral as he worked his magic. Her rock-hard nipples pressed against the fabric, and with his free hand, he pulled her blouse tight, as if getting a better look.

"You sure you want to go back to the hotel room?" he whispered. "I could take you out dancing. Show you off."

She groaned and parted her legs a little more.

"You like that?" he said with a low chuckle. "Take you dancing like this? No panties, no bra, looking so damned hot? I wouldn't be able to keep my hands off you. Get you into a dark corner, pull up your skirt and…"

He whispered the rest. She bit back a hard gasp as the first wave hit. He didn't stop. Not with his fingers and not with his words, spinning the most deliciously dirty fantasy as waves of orgasm rocked her. When they slowed, she snuggled into him and slid her hand down to his crotch, where he was so damned hard—

"Here we are!" the driver chirped.

Daphne flew back away from Chris, who only chuckled and reached past her for the curbside door. He helped her out and remembered her bag. He even carried it, which was so thoughtful and not at all because he needed it to hide the erection tenting his trousers.

Two seconds later, they were in an empty elevator.

"Cameras?" Chris said.

She looked around the ancient elevator. "I don't see any."

"Good."

He swung around and pinned her against the wall, shoving her skirt up as he wrapped her legs around—

The bell dinged, and he spun around, just as the doors opened. A guy got on and hit the button for the next floor. He looked over at Daphne, his gaze settling on her chest, where it was—yep—really obvious she wasn't wearing a bra.

Chris moved to block the guy's view. The elevator stopped again, and the guy got out. The moment the doors closed, Chris had her against the wall, hiking her skirt as he pressed into her.

She double-checked. Definitely no cameras? All right then. She pulled her skirt up around her bare hips so she could lock her legs around him better, and pressed into him. As he kissed her, his fingers went to her shirt buttons. A brief pause, making sure she was okay with it, and when she didn't react, he unbuttoned them and reached in to cup her breasts—

The elevator dinged, and she jumped.

"Our floor," Chris said.

He set her down, shielding her as the doors opened until he seemed confident no one was around. Then he squeezed her bare ass before letting her skirt fall and putting his hand around her waist.

"Coast is clear," he said as he leaned out of the elevator. "Up to you whether you want to button up. I'll just be unbuttoning it again the moment we're in our room."

She read the challenge there. The sexiest kind of challenge, where he was suggesting something just a little bit dirty, and giving her every opportunity to say no.

She left the shirt unbuttoned after he made sure the hall was indeed clear. Then he led her to his room, pressed her up against the wall, and kissed her again. Another challenge? All right then. She hiked her skirt and got her legs around him, the air-conditioning from the hall cool against her bare ass. He spread her shirt wide as his hands cupped her breasts. His fingers teased her nipples, making her gasp. A quick look up and down the hall, and she slid her hand between them, flicking open his button and then unzipping his fly and reaching in.

His one hand left her breast and he pulled back, wordlessly lifting the key card.

"Probably wise," she whispered against his ear. "Unless you want me riding you in the hallway."

His breath caught, and she grinned. She pulled his cock out of his boxers, her hand wrapped tight around him while she listened for anyone in the hall. Then she arched up and rubbed the tip of him against her, letting herself close around that tip. He gasped and fumbled to open the hotel room door so fast she had to laugh.

He swung them inside, and the door was still closing when he had her against the wall, skirt up. She reached and wrapped her hand around him.

"Do that again," he rasped.

"Yes sir." She pulled him into her, just a little and he let out a deep groan.

"Or maybe not," he said. "Or you'll see how bad my self-control is."

"Good." She leaned toward his ear. "Show me how little self-control you can have, Chris Stanton. *That's* what I really want to see."

He chuckled. "Good thing I brought a full box of protection."

"Only one box? Then it's a good thing I brought my own."

She put her arms around his neck and pulled her to him.

CHAPTER TWENTY

CHRIS

They'd forgotten to close the hotel room drapes. No idea how *that* could have happened. It wasn't like they'd been busy or anything.

Chris chuckled to himself as he stretched in bed. Busy was one way of putting it. Followed by exhausted.

The curtains had been closed enough that they hadn't been putting on a show, but they *were* cracked open and he roused from sleep as sunlight seeped in. He glanced at the clock. Another twenty minutes until the alarm went off. Good.

He stretched again, his leg rubbing Daphne's. They'd lost the sheets at some point, and he wasn't complaining about that. He folded his arm on the pillow, head propped on his bicep as he took in her naked form.

Oh, he'd looked plenty last night, but this was different. Last night they'd both been in motion. Lots of motion. A glimpse of her breasts, a blur of her thighs, all of it caught in separate snapshots. Now he got to feast his gaze on the whole of her, stretched out, the swell of her wide hips, the curve of her thighs, smooth and taut with muscle, and then her breasts, full and...

"Are you ogling me, Stanton?" Her voice came heavy with sleep, eyes still closed.

"Absolutely."

She shifted onto her back, and lifted her arms, folding them behind her head to give him a better view.

"Tell me the alarm didn't go off," she said.

"The alarm did not go off."

She opened one eye, long lashes parting.

"I'm serious," he said. "We have eighteen minutes left."

She groaned and stretched. "Not enough."

"You can sleep on the plane."

That one open eye turned his way. "I don't want sleep, and what I do want is best not done on planes."

"Are you sure? 'Cause those business-class restrooms are pretty big."

The other golden-brown eye opened as she poked his chest. "Don't tempt me. That would be wrong. Fun, but wrong. And if we end our tour getting barred from plane travel, we're in trouble."

"Nah. We'll rent an RV with a king-size bed. Have sex in every state and province as we cross the country back home."

"That is oddly tempting." She lifted her head. "But you know what's even more tempting? Finding out how much it would cost to change our flight today."

"Actually, that might be a good idea. I think I'm coming down with something." He fake-coughed. "I've shaken a lot of hands in three days. A few more hours in bed should fix it."

"A few more hours in bed would fix a lot of things."

He reached over, picked her up, and pulled her onto him.

"I *can* fake sick," he said. "And I would, if I didn't think you'd feel guilty later. But by my calculations, we don't *need* to get up for another forty-five minutes, if you're willing to grab breakfast at the airport."

"I love breakfast at the airport. Cold eggs and stale bagels are the *best.*" She leaned down, hair falling to tickle his face. "We can shave off even more time if we shower together."

"Mmm, not sure that would *save* time."

"Fair point. We should start with the shower then."

"Excellent plan." He scooped her up, and he was just about to lift her out of bed when someone knocked on the door.

Chris glanced over. "Did you preorder breakfast?"

"Kinda wish I'd thought of it, but no."

"Because that would require the hotel having a restaurant."

"True." She swung her leg over him and slid to stand beside the bed. He waved that he'd get the door and started looking for his clothing.

She continued, "Can we hope they decided to make up for the bullshit yesterday by ordering us a breakfast tray from somewhere?"

"Sadly, I doubt it. But on that note, we should have time to take the town car through a drive-thru. Better than airport food."

He was still hunting for clothing as the knock became a banging.

"Do you even *remember* where you took off your clothes?" Daphne said, looking around.

"Pretty sure I wasn't the one who took them off."

"Right. Not sure how I forgot that. Definitely memorable."

He smiled and grabbed his gym shorts from yesterday; as he pulled them on, he headed into the sitting room part of the suite. There was his shirt. He yanked it on and checked through the peephole.

Sakura stood there, raising her hand to knock again.

He checked his watch, which he wasn't wearing. It was only seven, right? Car pickup at eight thirty? Flight at eleven?

If there was a problem, Sakura would have texted or called.

Except they'd both turned off their phones last night, determined not to be interrupted again.

He opened the door. "Did you try calling? I'm sorry. We switched off—"

"Is Daphne in there with you?"

"Uh, yes…"

"Of course she is." The snap in Sakura's voice said they'd definitely missed urgent messages.

"Is there a problem with the flight?" he said.

"I need to talk to both of you. Put on some clothes."

He glanced down. He was decent—gym shorts and an unbuttoned shirt—but he wasn't going to argue.

"Just a sec."

He let the door go. Sakura caught it and stepped into the entranceway. He strode into the bedroom, where Daphne was dressing.

"What's up?" she whispered.

"I don't know. She must have messaged."

"I didn't get— Shit! Our phones!"

Daphne scrambled for her phone on the bedside table. "I should have turned it on before we went to sleep."

"It's seven in the morning," he said. "We turned them off after eleven. That isn't unreasonable."

He was grumbling. He knew that. But he didn't like anyone making Daphne feel guilty for disconnecting overnight.

"It's probably a last-minute interview," he whispered as he pulled clothing from his bag. "Morning radio or whatever. If so, I'll apologize, but they can't really expect that without notice."

Daphne stopped. Her phone must have switched on, and she was holding it up.

"Anything?" he asked.

"A voicemail and two texts about twenty minutes ago. The texts just say to call her."

Chris scowled. Twenty minutes ago? It wasn't as if she'd been calling for hours.

"Take your time," he said as he tugged on a T-shirt. "I've got this."

He slid from the bedroom. "Hey," he said, as nicely as possible. "Daphne's almost ready. So what's up?"

"I need to speak to both—" Sakura's phone chirped. She glanced down. Then she froze. Her finger moved to the Decline button, but at the last second swerved to hit Answer.

"Sakura Mori speaking," she said.

Pause.

"Hello, sir. Yes. I'm in their room right now. Can I call you back—" Pause. "I haven't had a chance to speak—" Pause. "Yes, I understand."

She hit Mute and lowered the phone.

Daphne walked in. "What's going on?"

"I have Russ Milner on the line." When Daphne's blank look didn't change, Sakura said, "The publisher."

"A representative from Daphne's publisher?" Chris asked.

"No," Daphne whispered. "*The* publisher, the person in charge of the imprint that published *Edge*."

Chris suspected Milner wasn't calling to congratulate Zane on a tour well done. Before he could ask, Sakura unmuted the phone.

"Sir?" she said. "You are now on speaker. I have Daphne and Chris in the room."

"Who?" a man's voice snapped.

Sakura looked Daphne in the eye. "The actual author and her boyfriend, who has been playing the role of Zane Remington."

Chris's jaw tensed. He wanted to grab Daphne's arm and storm out.

He couldn't imagine Sakura had turned them in without warning them. Unless something happened and that was her only chance of saving her job, and while he could be furious about that, he wouldn't blame her. But she could have taken two seconds to tell them what was happening before dropping that bomb.

He glanced at Daphne. She stared straight ahead, her face slack with shock. Chris took her hand and guided her to the sofa, and she didn't fight him. Sakura laid the phone on the coffee table and sat in the opposite chair.

"Daphne's agent should be part of this conversation," Chris said. "Has Lawrence Capano been contacted?"

"I attempted to do that and received voicemail."

That wasn't good enough. Even Chris knew Lawrence should be part of this conversation.

"I really think Lawrence needs—"

"He will be looped in later. As will the lawyers. For now, this is a preliminary attempt to resolve this issue. I presume you know what's happened?"

"I haven't had a chance to speak to them yet, Mr. Milner," Sakura said. "Let me do that now." She looked at Chris and Daphne. "Two hours ago, the publishing house received a message from a major social media influencer."

Chris inhaled sharply and laced his fingers in Daphne's.

Sakura continued, "This person claimed that Zane Remington is actually a woman masquerading under that name, who had conspired with her boyfriend to defraud the public."

"Defraud?" Chris sputtered. "It's a pen name. No one hid that. The product is the book, not me."

"So you did not write it," Milner said.

Chris froze.

"No," Daphne said, her voice eerily hollow. "I don't deny that I wrote the book and that I hired Chris to play Zane Remington. There was no conspiracy to defraud anyone. I made a mistake."

Chris opened his mouth, but she gave him a look and pushed on.

"We had plans to come clean to the publishing house after the last event. I have an email chain with my lawyer to prove that, if it helps—"

"It doesn't. This girl is threatening to reveal that our biggest book of the season is a fraud."

"The book isn't a fraud," Chris said. "It's a work of *fiction*."

"The author perpetrated a deception on everyone who worked on this book."

Daphne went still. Chris surged forward to argue, but her tightening grip asked him not to defend her.

"I'm sorry," Daphne said. "That was not my intention. The question now is what to do about it. My suggestion would be that I come forward immediately—"

"No."

"I know that will have ramifications for the last two signings, but I feel it's best for me to throw myself on this sword, take the blame, and make a genuine apology—"

"You will do nothing of the sort. Our lawyers are looking at this, and until a decision is made and discussed with your agent, you will continue on as normal. Is that clear?"

"Yes, sir," Daphne said, that hollow tone in her voice again.

"I'll be in touch," Milner said...and hung up.

Daphne looked at Sakura. "I am truly sorry. Whatever you need me to do, I'll do it."

Sakura scooped up her phone and started for the door. "What I need is for both of you to be on this morning's flight. You have everything you need. You can go straight to your hotel. The car will pick you up. I have work to do, and I'm taking a later flight."

"I really am sor—" Daphne began.

The door closed behind Sakura.

DAPHNE

The signing was in a few hours. They had yet to hear back from her agent, her editor, or anyone else at the publisher, and Daphne was...

She wasn't sure how she felt anymore. After Sakura left, she'd been a mess. A puddle of regret and guilt and, buried at the bottom, the tiniest spark of anger.

Milner had made her feel as if she'd committed the worst betrayal in the most brazen and thoughtless way. That wasn't what she'd intended, and she was eager to fix her mistake. But no one seemed to be listening, much less giving her any clues as to how this could affect her career.

Before catching their flight, she'd called Nia for advice. Then Daphne and Chris had spent that flight sketching plans for every possible outcome and contingency. And now they were in their hired car heading to the hotel. She used the middle seat belt so she could sit right against Chris, taking comfort in his arm around her shoulders.

Had there been a moment when she'd wondered whether she should set him free in case he got caught in the crossfire? Yes, but it had only been a flicker of animal panic before she realized that he was an adult. If he wanted out, he'd say so.

When the car pulled to the curb, she peered through the window and frowned, not seeing a hotel. Chris opened the door and helped her out, his hand around hers as he led her toward...

"A bakery?" she said.

"Claims to have the best brownies in town," he said. "We're about to test that. Along with samples from two other places claiming the same."

Her eyes teared up. She hadn't shed a single one since the news dropped. She'd been too numb, too frightened, too humiliated. Now, standing outside this bakery, Chris's hand in hers, the tears came.

He didn't miss a beat, just shielded her from any passersby and hugged her.

"It's going to be okay," he said. "Even if I have to print out copies of *Edge* myself and stand on a street corner in a Speedo to sell them."

She hiccupped a laugh. "You just might."

"Then I will. Me, on the corner, in a skimpy bathing suit with a tray of baked goods, for those who prefer cupcakes to beefcake. But I won't have to because the book will sell itself."

She nodded, and she was glancing at the bakery when her phone rang. Every muscle tensed, and she yanked out her phone.

The number on the screen wasn't in her contact list, but it was a New York area code.

She hesitated, and then answered carefully. "Daphne speaking."

"Daphne McFadden, author of *At the Edge of the World?*"

Her hand gripped the phone tighter. Not her publisher. Someone from the media? Had Robbie's niece gone ahead and leaked the story?

"It's Lawrence Capano," the man said. "Your agent."

She crumpled. Chris caught her, alarm on his face, but she shook her head and stepped away.

"I'm sorry," she said.

Lawrence exhaled. "I know. Your message said that at least a half dozen times. I'm sorry it's taken so long to call. I was out of cell range this morning, and after I got your message, I had to make some calls and check on a few things to prepare. Do you have a moment to talk?"

"Yes. Please."

CHRIS

They were back where they'd begun the day. In bed. And "in bed" in a good way, not huddled under the covers waiting for this hellish day to end.

The call with Lawrence had helped a lot. The agent wasn't thrilled, but he'd been more understanding than Daphne dared hope. Chris wasn't as surprised. Lawrence had always seemed like a decent guy, and Chris suspected he had pulled up that first query letter and done a bit of soul searching. What if it had been signed "Daphne McFadden"? Would he have set it aside as just another grown-up *Hunger Games* and *Divergent* fangirl writing young adult dystopian? Did putting "Zane Remington, MFA" make him see the letter in a different light? Make him open the manuscript and start reading?

Whatever the reason, Lawrence had put aside any anger or embarrassment at being misled and told Daphne that unless this made her change her mind about being his client, he was still onboard. He advised her to wait for Milner's call, which he had insisted on being looped in for, and then they'd see where they stood.

After that, Chris and Daphne had picked up brownies, checked into the hotel, and abandoned the treats in favor of another kind of comfort. Last night had been passion and hunger and abandon. This afternoon, it was pure lovemaking, sweet and slow and intimate beyond anything Chris had ever experienced, leaving him dazed and euphoric, like someone had slipped a little extra into those brownies they'd nibbled.

"We're going to be okay," he said, nuzzling her as they lay there, entwined. "You and me. You and your career."

She nodded and snuggled closer.

He continued, "Whatever happens, it doesn't change the fact that you're a writer. Even if you'd never been published, you'd still be a writer. But you *have* been published, and you will *stay* published, and you will continue to *get* published—one way or another—until you want to stop. This is just a bump in the—"

Chris's phone rang, and Daphne thumped to the pillow with a groan.

"Let me answer it quickly." He glanced at the screen. "It's Milner."

She lifted her head. "Why's he calling *you?*"

"I have no idea." He hit the Answer button and then Speaker. "Mr. Milner. It's Chris. You're on speaker with Daphne."

Silence. Then, "All right. If that's what you want."

Chris frowned, and Daphne shrugged.

"Is Lawrence on the line?" Chris asked.

"This isn't a police interrogation," Milner said. "You don't need representation. I wanted to speak to you in advance of the official call. I'd like to work this out if we can."

"I'd still ask..." He trailed off as he caught Daphne's look. While he did want Lawrence there, it could delay this call, which would delay her learning her fate with the publishing house.

"Fine," Chris said. "We'll loop him in later. But I'm going to step back now and ask you to speak to Daphne. It's her book. I really was only the face of it. I know that means I'll need to make a statement, and I'm prepared to do that. Otherwise, it's all about her."

"No one is blaming you for this," Milner said.

Chris squeezed the bridge of his nose. "I didn't say that, and I hope I didn't imply that. I knew what I was getting into, and I fully support Daphne."

"Good," Milner said, which eased the ball of tension growing behind Chris's eyes. "That's going to be a huge help here."

"I hope so," Chris said. "I want it to be clear that I support the book *and* Daphne."

"I am very happy to hear you say that. I believe you are going to be our silver bullet here, Chris. You're articulate, intelligent and—as the female members of my staff tell me—very photogenic."

His hackles rose. What did it matter if he was articulate, intelligent, and photogenic? Daphne was the author, and she was also all those things.

"Thank you," he said slowly. "While Daphne hasn't been taking center stage, I think you'll find she's equally articulate and—"

"But you have been the face of the book, and as such, you have done an excellent job. Like good cover art, if that's not insulting."

"It's not," Chris said. "Because that's an excellent analogy. What Daphne did was like picking a cover that may have attracted extra attention. That's marketing."

Daphne finally spoke up, saying, "It's not quite the same, and I understand that, but yes, Chris has been a great ambassador for the book."

"He has been," Milner said. "Which is why I would like to see him continue in that capacity."

"What?" Chris said.

Daphne said slowly, "Are you suggesting paying off this influencer and continuing to pretend Chris wrote the book? That won't work long-term. Suspicions have been raised."

"Which is why we—all of us—need to take control of the story."

Daphne visibly relaxed. "Thank you. Are you asking Chris to stay on as the face of Zane? Openly admit that the real author is a woman who would prefer to remain anonymous, but Chris will continue acting as Zane in public?"

"No," Milner said. "The problem you've created, Daphne, is that the person they think wrote the book—this intelligent, articulate, photogenic man—did not. That's going to be disappointing to readers in a way I don't think you understand."

"I don't understand it, either," Chris said. "And I think readers would find it insulting to imply that they care what Zane looks like."

"They *will* be disappointed. However, I think we've come up with a way to fix this mess, which is why I'm running it past you before we involve agents and lawyers. I believe that if handled correctly, we might even be able to turn this fiasco into a publicity win."

"That…would be good," Daphne said as Chris silently seethed.

"And, to be clear, I have spoken to one of our lawyers, and he has no concerns with my proposed solution."

"Good."

"Chris, we'd like Daphne to step out from the shadows as your coauthor."

"My…coauthor?" Chris said. "But I didn't write this book. *Any* of it."

"Handled correctly, that won't matter. For this first book, you won't discuss who did what. We'll say that's covered by an NDA. For future books, we'll have talking points, and we'll expect that Chris will legitimately play a role in the creation, whether it's brainstorming or editing."

Chris turned to gape incredulously at Daphne, but she was staring down, lost in her thoughts.

"That is my proposed solution," Milner said. "Think it over, talk to your agent, and then we'll have a conference call with everyone."

He hung up before Chris or Daphne could say a word.

DAPHNE

After hanging up, Daphne was too numb to move. When Milner had made that suggestion, something in her had crumpled.

She had never wanted to be the public face of *Edge*. She'd been terrified that her self-consciousness and introversion would hurt her book's chances of success. But when she'd decided she was stepping forward, she'd slowly made peace with the idea and found the confidence to say that she wouldn't be the world's worst spokesperson for her book. And now...

She knew what Milner really meant by "coauthor." Oh, the publishing house would want to keep up the pretense that Chris contributed, but all they really expected was that he'd play Zane. He'd do the interviews and the signings. His photo and autograph would go in the books.

Why was that such a problem for her? Wasn't it what they had already been doing?

Yes, and she hadn't realized how relieved she'd been about ending the charade until Milner suggested they not.

She wanted to be angry. She reached deep inside herself to find that, knowing it must be there. Anger, even rage. But it was smothered under the fear of having this new dream crushed by her own mistake.

"It could work," she said softly.

Chris was pacing along the end of the bed. "Hmm?" He pivoted to face her.

"His plan. It could work."

He stared at her. Then he said, "We are *not* doing that, D."

That crumpled bit inside her collapsed completely, and her voice didn't even sound like her own when she said, "I'm sorry. You're right, of course. I'd never ask you to make that kind of commitment—"

"It's not the commitment. It's the lie."

Her cheeks heated. "I wouldn't ask you to do that, either. If you did agree, we'd work something out so you could brainstorm or edit—and be paid for it, of course—and we'd be honest about the role you play."

Chris stopped pacing and sat beside her, his hand going to her knee.

"I'm not refusing because of the commitment or because of the mis-representation. I don't give a damn about that."

But he *was* refusing. That's the part she heard loud and clear, and the tops of her ears burned with humiliation. Milner was throwing her a lifeline. A chance to redeem herself and keep her career, and it relied on Chris, and he wanted no part of it.

Was this where she'd lose him? He'd said he was committed to sup-porting her writing, and yet, at the first sign of trouble, he wanted her to trample her new career underfoot.

We won't put up with this treatment. That'll show them.

He wanted to take an ethical stance, even if it cost Daphne her career. After all, he'd done something similar when he found out his partner was stealing from their clients.

But in that instance, Chris had done nothing wrong, and while he had taken a financial risk, his career was never in danger, and the tar-nish on his reputation was easily buffed away.

And now he found himself in another ethical quandary, where he could be accused of fraud because his new business partner—Daphne—had done something that could be seen as unethical.

Except the "unethical" thing wasn't stealing client money. It was using a male name because no one was paying any attention to her book and she wanted to see whether that made a difference. And it did, didn't it?

She hadn't stolen money to fund a drug habit. She'd played an unfair system to her advantage, and if she felt guilty about that, she also felt angry.

So *goddamn* angry.

Daphne walked to the window and looked out over the city.

Yes, she could be upset with the system, but she was overreacting by being upset with Chris before she'd given him a chance to prove she was wrong, that he wouldn't throw her under the bus.

She turned to face him. "Can we talk about this?"

"No."

That set her back, blinking. "What?"

His face hardened. "There's nothing to talk about, Daphne. I won't let them do this to you."

Won't let them do it to *her*? Or to *him*?

It's easy to say you support my career . . . until supporting it affects you.

Like Anthony, who'd stayed up with her all night as she sobbed in his arms after her mother's diagnosis. He'd vowed to be there for her through it all. Then came the day when the doctor admitted Mom's chemo wasn't working. The doctor wanted to speak to Daphne, and so she needed to reschedule her weekend getaway with Anthony.

Instead of hearing that her mother was dying, *truly* dying, he heard that he wasn't getting his weekend away. She'd come home and found a letter in her apartment, telling her that he needed someone who made time for him in her life, as if she'd canceled for a damned manicure.

Chris wasn't Anthony. She couldn't let that old pain and anger sweep her away. Chris would be reasonable. She just needed him to understand.

"I won't try convincing you to be my coauthor, Chris," she said. "That's obviously your choice. I just want to talk about options."

He shook his head. "There are no options here, D. You wrote the book. It will succeed without me. Don't let Milner hold this over your head. We'll go to the signing tonight and tell the truth."

"What? No. We need to talk to—"

"It's your career. You make the decisions."

She stared at him. He stood there, jaw firm, green eyes lit with righteous fury.

"*I* make the decisions?" she said, and the ice in her voice should have warned him off, but he only nodded, seeming relieved that she understood.

"I make the decisions," she repeated. "And do whatever you tell me."

He blinked, rocking back. Then he shook his head sharply. "No, that's not what I mean."

"But it's what you said, Chris. It's literally what you just said."

She snatched her wallet from the table and marched to the door.

"Hold on," he said behind her. "Let's—"

The door closed behind her, and she strode toward the stairs . . . and then broke into a run.

CHAPTER TWENTY-ONE

CHRIS

Math nerds had a reputation for being boring. As Chris had long ago figured out, sometimes "boring" really meant stable and dependable and responsible, all things he considered positive traits, even if, yes, they weren't very exciting.

Sometimes, though, being responsible got in the way of being the kind of boyfriend he wanted to be. The kind who raced after his distraught girlfriend and left his wallet, phone, and key card behind. He'd dashed to the door, of course. Then he'd thought *Key!* and turned to grab it, but it wasn't on the hall table, so he ran back into the bedroom, snatched it up, and took off.

By then, Daphne was long gone.

On the elevator, he ignored the responsible voice that said he was in his bare feet and didn't have his wallet or phone. Finding Daphne was more important. Show up in socks and shoes, and it would look like he didn't care enough to run after her.

He padded around the lobby. There was no sign of her. He surveyed the other guests, and picked the one most likely to have noticed Daphne—a middle-aged businessman waiting in the lobby while checking out the pretty desk clerk.

He asked and got a solid no, with a twist of the lips that said the guy wouldn't admit it even if he had seen Daphne.

Next Chris tried the desk clerk, who determined that this might not be information she should give out. He was breathless, shoeless, and asking about a woman who seemed to have fled his hotel room. The clerk was right not to give him anything, damn it.

He went back upstairs and called Daphne.

No answer.

He hesitated, and then tried Sakura. No answer, and he decided not to leave a message saying Daphne had gotten upset and fled. Daphne was too private a person for that.

He'd screwed up. He'd wanted to stand firmly at her side, furious with Milner and anyone else who threatened her career because she'd recognized the potential for industry-based sexism and worked a loophole. He'd meant that she shouldn't have to hide, and he wasn't letting anyone make her feel otherwise. What he'd *said* was something different.

Milner had called Chris articulate, intelligent, and photogenic. Chris had pointed out that Daphne was all those things, and Milner steamrolled right over him. The guy's attitude and suggestion proved that Daphne had been right sending out her book under a man's name.

Did Milner realize he was a dinosaur, clinging to his old preconceptions? Chris suspected that explained the off-the-record phone call. Milner might be packaging his prejudices as marketing—believing people really did care whether the author was the guy on the cover—but he knew enough not to present his coauthor idea in front of others. For every reader who was disappointed that the author wasn't the guy on the cover, someone else would be relieved that it was a woman writing Theo's story. They'd had that discussion at the book festival.

Milner wanted to scare Daphne into accepting his coauthor idea. If Daphne said it was what she wanted, Lawrence wouldn't argue. If the publishing company's lawyers didn't see an issue with the arrangement, then it saved them negotiating. Everyone would be happy. Except Daphne.

Now that Chris thought about it more, he realized Milner hadn't even made an overt threat. Did he say they'd stop publishing *Edge*? Did he threaten Daphne's future with the company? No. He preyed on a new author's inexperience to frighten her.

The answer then was clear. Fight back. Daphne couldn't see that because her mind was swirling with worry and dread. She was afraid to take this leap that he absolutely knew she *could* take.

That meant there was only one thing for him to do.

He picked up the hotel pen and writing pad and started a letter to Daphne.

DAPHNE

She'd spent the last hour swinging between the worry that she'd overreacted with Chris and the certainty that she had not. At first, she wanted to brand him a liar who'd said whatever she wanted to hear. That was her anger talking. Anger and old hurt over Anthony reignited by this new pain. She wouldn't let that infect Chris until she was damned sure he deserved it.

Daphne had been upset over Milner's call, and he'd handled it poorly. That wasn't cause to throw a new relationship on the trash heap.

Yes, she said she was ready to start a serious relationship with Chris, but was she really? Or would she flee at the first sign of trouble and take it as proof he wasn't the right guy?

She needed time to cool down and put her thoughts in order, and he needed time to realize he'd said entirely the wrong thing, and if he didn't mean it, then he could take it back. Then they would talk this out.

She went up to her hotel room and opened the door. "Chris?"

The blinds were drawn, the room still. Seeing the adjoining doorway open, she slipped over to it, calling softly, "Chris?"

No reply. She found her phone and started a text. As she did, she noticed a folded piece of paper on the coffee table, with her name written across it.

One second she was moving and breathing and thinking, and the next, everything stopped. When she forced herself to cross those few feet, it felt like moving through deep space, pitch-dark, dead silent, and ice-cold.

The last time she'd come home to a note on her table, it'd been Anthony's goodbye.

She shook herself. Now she really *was* overreacting. Chris had realized she didn't take her phone and left a note to say where he'd gone.

She deep-breathed until her heart rate returned to normal. Then she unfolded the letter.

> *D,*
>
> *I can't keep doing this. I need to step off the stage you put me on. You belong up there. You wrote Edge, and it's an amazing book. You need to take your place as its author, and that means I need to step aside.*
> *You can do this. I believe in you.*
>
> *Chris*

Daphne stared at the letter. Reread it. Tried to see where she could be misinterpreting, because he would not have abandoned her. Not now.

But she wasn't misreading. He was gone. He'd left her to fix this.

He wasn't just gone temporarily, either. There was no closing "Love" or even "Yours." No mention of calling or texting her. No mention of seeing her later.

He had been as sweet and supportive as he could be, but that only hid the real message.

I'm out of here.

Earlier she'd thought that if he wanted out, he'd say so.

Now he had.

Daphne's stomach clenched, and she ran for the bathroom. She didn't throw up, though. She clenched the sides of the sink and still tried to tell herself she'd misinterpreted the note. Chris would never have abandoned her like this. The note meant he was metaphorically stepping off the stage, but he hadn't *actually* left. He'd be here, beside her, supporting her when she revealed herself as the real Zane Remington.

Holding herself very still, she stiffly walked through the adjoining door. His things would be here. He would not leave. His bag—

—was gone.

Every trace of him was gone.

She ran to the bathroom and made it just in time.

CHRIS

Chris sat in his hotel room and looked at his phone. Still no call from Daphne. It'd been an hour, and the event was coming up fast, and he'd expected a call.

Was she angry with him? He'd taken that chance when he wrote the letter and switched hotels. He hoped she'd see this was for the best. If he was gone, the publisher couldn't blame Daphne for ignoring Milner's demand that she not come out as Zane. She'd need to step up at the signing and tell the truth. It'd be Chris's fault for putting her in that spot, and he was willing to take the blame.

He just... well, he'd hoped the blame wouldn't come from Daphne herself. He'd given her an excuse to step forward and the gentle push of support to do it.

Still, he shouldn't take her silence as a sign she was angry. Part of giving her that excuse meant it couldn't seem staged. She was being careful.

And maybe a little bit upset?

Shit.

His phone rang, and even when he saw it wasn't Daphne, he still exhaled in relief. Gemma. He could talk this through with his sister, who'd reassure him that he'd made the right choice.

"Another divorce meeting down," she said when he answered. "I'm trying not to think of what these are costing me. I promised I'd call, and I'm making good on that. I expect to be distracted. Give me exciting book tour news so I may live vicariously through you."

He told her about the signing the previous night. Then he gave her a detail-free summary of what happened afterward.

"Oh my God," Gemma said. "You actually scored with the hot novelist!"

"*Actually?* Wow."

"You can easily charm the pants off women you don't really care about. But when you like them? Awkward teenage Chris comes stumbling out."

"Thanks..."

"Did you tell her how you feel?"

"I did."

"And she feels the same?"

"Seems like it. She agreed to a test run of a committed relationship."

"You make that sound so romantic. Clearly you are not the romance writer in the family. Please feel free to come to me for tips."

"So you're writing again?"

Gemma made a noncommittal noise. "So what's next? Oh, the tour. Right. You have the penultimate signing tonight. Are you all ready?"

Chris sat cross-legged on the bed. "So about that..."

He told Gemma about the threat to expose Zane, paused to enjoy her profanity-laden outrage, and then told her about the calls from Milner, which escalated the outrage and the cursing to new levels. As a college English instructor, Gemma had a truly impressive vocabulary.

"This Milner guy is full of shit," she said. "Admittedly, I know next to nothing about publishing, but it's still a corporation. They won't tank a megaselling book. Or drop a megaselling author."

"Yep, it's all smoke and mirrors. One aging dinosaur roaring against his inevitable extinction."

"And Daphne knows that, right?"

Chris paused. Had he said that to her? He couldn't remember. He must have.

"So what's the plan?" Gemma said. "Please tell me she's going to stick it to the man, in the most spectacular way possible."

"I hope so."

A pause. Three seconds dragged by. "You are with her, right?" Gemma said.

"Not exactly." He told her about the letter.

"I'm sorry," she said when he finished. "Could you repeat that? You cannot possibly have said what you just seemed to say. You did not—not—abandon Daphne in a crisis."

A spark of anxiety ignited his worry, but he snuffed it out. "It wasn't like that," he said. "I gracefully bowed out and let her take center stage."

"By *letter*? Not by conversation and a mutually agreed-upon plan where you'd pretend to storm off and she'd be 'forced' to reveal herself, thereby avoiding any repercussions from sticking it to the man."

"I…" He took a deep breath to calm his racing heart. "Daphne's scared, understandably. But I know she can do it, so I gave her a nudge."

"She's an adult, Chris. Not a child who needs nudging."

He winced at Gemma's tone, which seemed to be getting sharper by the word. "I—"

"Also, you didn't nudge. You threw her off the damned deep end and told her to swim. You knew she was scared, and you *threw her in*."

The worry ignited again, only for him to stamp it out. Gemma was misinterpreting the situation.

Only she wasn't. Because that was exactly the right analogy.

Daphne was afraid of swimming. Would he throw her off the deep end? Absolutely not. Daphne was afraid of standing up in front of readers and admitting she had written the book they loved. And he hadn't *just* thrown her in. He'd thrown her in…then turned and walked away.

Sink or swim.

Holy shit.

"Where are you?" Gemma snapped.

"In a hotel. A, uh, few blocks from where we were staying."

"Does she know that? Tell me she doesn't think you came back to Vancouver. Tell me the note was clear that you were close by, and if she wanted to discuss this, she could."

"I…"

"Tell me you *at least* made it clear you weren't actually walking away. Leaving her for good."

"Of course. I…" He struggled to remember the letter. "I…I might have forgotten…Shit."

"For god's sake, Chris. How can such a smart guy be so—" She inhaled, cutting herself short. "Okay, that doesn't help."

"I thought I was being supportive," he said weakly. "I know she can do this, and I want her to take the credit she deserves. She wrote an amazing book."

"She did. And she chose not to come out as the author. That's why she hired you. It's not your place to decide when that ends, just like it's not the place of an asshole publisher or a bratty teen blogger. Supporting Daphne meant listening to her and helping her work it through. Did you try that?"

Daphne had tried that. She'd wanted to talk about it, and he'd refused and told her what to do.

"I screwed up, Gem," he said, his heart pounding. "I screwed up so bad."

"Yes, but not so badly that you can't fix it. When's the event?"

He checked his watch. "Just over an hour."

"Call her. Now. Work this out."

DAPHNE

The event was in one hour, and Daphne needed to pull herself together and decide how she was going to handle it. Pulling herself together meant she had to stop beating herself up for the mistake she'd made the previous night. For the mistake she'd been making for days now. Falling for Chris Stanton.

She thought she'd been careful, protecting her heart, but she'd let her emotions run roughshod over common sense. She'd told herself there was no place for love in her life right now . . . and then proceeded to fall in love anyway.

She'd blame Chris, whether he deserved that or not. He was too good-looking, too smart, too sweet, the whole damn package. Maybe it wasn't love after all. Maybe it was lust and ego. A guy like that wanted her? Swoon.

He wouldn't be the first person to claim he totally supported his partner's career and then decide she didn't know how to handle it. Just like Anthony wasn't the first person to say he valued his partner's close family ties and then get angry when those ties diverted her attention.

Was Chris gone for good? She had to presume so. Like her, he'd been swept away in the moment.

They'd enjoyed their time together. Had some really great sex. And then went their separate ways. Which was what she wanted from the start.

Someday she'd be ready to share her life with someone. For now, she had to focus on her career.

And that really *was* what she needed to focus on tonight. She'd heard briefly from Lawrence. She'd told him what Milner proposed, and he'd said to leave it with him. She'd wanted more, but asking for reassurances felt weak and needy.

Tell me there's another option. Tell me I won't lose my career over this.

Lawrence was working on it, and she had to let him do that while she concentrated on the event. She hadn't told Lawrence that Chris was gone. That wasn't an agent issue; it was a publicist one. She needed to speak to Sakura. But first, she had an event to prepare for.

Daphne climbed into the car and was relieved to find Sakura there. She'd realized she hadn't spoken to Sakura since that morning, and it was entirely possible she didn't have a publicist anymore, especially since she'd turned off her phone after calling Lawrence. She'd needed her head clear, and had been afraid Chris might call…and equally afraid he wouldn't. Better not to know.

Yes, the head-in-the-sand strategy wasn't very mature, but she had to protect herself right now.

Daphne closed the car door, and Sakura frowned over at her.

"Where's Chris?" Sakura asked.

"He's…not with me," Daphne said.

She tensed for Sakura to ask whether Chris was meeting them at the bookstore, but Sakura only gave a distracted nod.

"We need to talk anyway," Sakura said. "You and me. Without him."

"Sure."

"I want to know why you did it."

"Why I…?"

"Pretended to be a male author. Hired Chris. I might be able to guess, but I want to hear it in your words. From the top."

Daphne did just that. When she finished, Sakura stared out the side window for at least five minutes. Then she said, "Figures."

Daphne couldn't read her tone and said carefully, "It figures that…?"

"That you'd go from 'can't get an agent' to 'half-million-dollar deal' by putting a guy's name on your manuscript."

"It wasn't just that," Daphne said. "I tweaked the synopsis to emphasize the survival aspects and remove the hints of romance. Also, I said I—Zane—had an MFA, which I don't."

"How much of the *book* did you change?"

"None."

Sakura shook her head. "Figures."

"I can't say that a man's name made the difference," Daphne said.

"Of course not, because if you even suggested it, there'd be push-back. *Prove it*, they'd say. You can't prove it. Maybe your agent *would* have read it with your name on it. Maybe it *would* have sold just as well and been marketed the same. I can tell you it wouldn't have been marketed the same, but then *I'd* be asked to prove it, and I can't do that, either, because it's not like I have an email saying to treat you differently because you're a guy. I know it made a difference. It might—God help me—have subconsciously made a difference in how I pitched your book."

Sakura looked at her. "You didn't plan to pass yourself off as a man when you started writing the book. It was an act of desperation."

"Desperation and wine," Daphne said, forcing a wry smile.

"And you were afraid if you came out, you'd lose your shot at getting published."

Daphne nodded.

"So, like you said, you and your lawyer friend decided to hire a guy for a few photos, maybe an interview or two."

"It got out of hand," Daphne said.

"By which time, it felt too late to do anything. Which it was, to be honest. Give me the option of having you come out prepublication or posttour, and posttour would have definitely been my choice." She exhaled. "Okay, so where do we stand?"

Daphne told her about the second call from Milner. She wanted Sakura to be shocked, even angry, but the publicist only shook her head.

"I don't know how that guy still has a job," she muttered. "He had some massive hits twenty years ago, and now he just coasts. When Alicia wanted to buy *Edge*, he came in strong. Others said postapocalyptic young adult was dead, but he insisted *Edge* was different. By which he apparently meant that a man wrote it."

Again, Daphne wanted to ask what Milner could do to her career. But that wasn't Sakura's job, no more than Chris going AWOL was Lawrence's concern.

Which led to...

"Chris isn't meeting us there," Daphne said.

Sakura frowned at her.

Daphne gave an abridged version of the story, basically that they'd argued over the next move and Chris decided she needed to step forward as Zane. Then he left so she could do that.

She'd worded it carefully, letting none of her hurt seep in, casting Chris in the most neutral light.

"So you two agreed on this?" Sakura said.

Daphne hesitated, but as much as she wanted to protect Chris, she wasn't taking a hit for him. "We argued, I walked out, and he left a note."

Sakura stared at her. "What a *dick* move."

Maybe this should have felt like validation, but Daphne wanted someone to tell her it wasn't so bad, that maybe he'd even done the right thing. Except he hadn't, and she knew that.

"That is some patronizing bullshit right there," Sakura said. "People that good-looking always have a fatal flaw. Or fifty." She stopped. "You guys are over, right?"

"Seems so."

"Whew. Then I can insult him all I want. And now we'll put him aside and focus on you. His leaving puts you in a very awkward but also advantageous position."

"Not quite seeing the advantageous part," Daphne murmured.

"He disappeared before a signing. We can't get hold of him. Well, we don't want to, but let's go with 'can't' since no one will requisition our phone records. The show must go on. Therefore you must reveal yourself as the author and even Milner can't fault you for that."

Sakura tapped into her phone. "I'll prep a message right now. I'll say Chris took off, but we presumed he'd still make the event. Then, at the last minute, we realized he wasn't going to and you had to come out. I'll hit Send at the *actual* last moment, so it notifies everyone but doesn't give Milner a chance to stop you."

"Do I have to come out?" Daphne said, her voice quiet.

Sakura frowned over. "What else can you do?"

"Say Zane is sick? I have the bookmarks and such. I can talk about *Edge*, apologize, give out swag…Oh! And I have bookplates." Daphne rummaged through her bag and withdrew the box. "About a hundred bookplates that Chris signed before the tour for people who didn't have a book yet."

"But this is your chance," Sakura said. "This is the perfect excuse to—"

Sakura's phone buzzed. She glanced at it and swore. "Work. Let me take this. I won't lie and pretend Chris is with us, but let's hold off on the rest."

As Sakura took the call, Daphne sunk into her seat and into her thoughts.

CHRIS

Chris had discovered a flaw in his plan. Well, two flaws. First, it presumed Daphne would answer her phone. His calls had gone to voicemail, and his texts sat in Unread, meaning she probably had her phone off. That was fine. He knew where to find her. He just had to get to the bookstore.

That led to flaw 1.5, which presumed he could hail a taxi from downtown at rush hour. He eventually managed to snag a rideshare, but by the time it got him to the store, it was fifteen minutes to showtime.

Then came flaw number two: presuming he could sneak in undetected and talk to Daphne.

Waiting for his rideshare, he'd considered this and affected a disguise. He shaved off the beard shadow, left the glasses behind, and wore Chris clothes—jeans, sneakers, and a T-shirt. Yet the moment he stepped into the bookstore parking lot, two college-aged women did a double take. That did happen, so he told himself they weren't recognizing him as Zane…until he overheard them whispering about whether they could skip the line and ask him to sign their books now.

Chris slipped off in search of an alternate entrance. It was a big-box store, which meant he had a chance of finding one, but the only doors were into the café or the store, both up front. The side loading dock was firmly shut. He even tried knocking on it. Noticing a fire escape ladder, he considered climbing onto the roof and searching for a way in, but he wasn't James Bond, so that seemed unwise.

He was running out of time.

He had to speak to Daphne. Apologize, definitely, but right now, he needed to let her know he was there and give her the choice: Did she want to admit she wrote *Edge* or have him take over for another night? That was why he couldn't just stroll in as Zane. If she'd decided to come out, then he had to let her keep the excuse that she'd had to step up because he wasn't there.

Finally he gave up, pulled down the brim of his ballcap, put on his shades, and slid in through the café door. He made his way as fast as he could into the bookstore and then circled around the outer aisles, where he grabbed three books as customer camouflage.

From there he followed the rumble of voices. It didn't take long to find the crowd. It spilled from the event area into all the surrounding aisles. As he backed up into hiding, he overheard three teens passionately discussing the book, and his heart swelled.

This was what Daphne deserved. A packed store of ardent fans.

She deserved to be the one up there signing the books, the one answering their excited questions, the one basking in their passion for her story.

But she also deserved the choice of when—or even if—she did that.

That was when he saw Daphne, being led by someone from the store, and she looked absolutely terrified.

Yeah, because you abandoned her. You shoved her off the deep end, said "swim," and couldn't even stick around to make sure she didn't drown.

He was here now. If he could get her attention, they could delay the event start and give her the chance to choose.

He slipped around the bookshelves, only to find he couldn't get to her. Couldn't even *see* her.

He heard the store staff member making an introduction, and he eased through a few groups until he could see the podium.

Daphne stepped up, and Chris's heart plummeted. If she looked terrified before, she looked petrified now. She stood there, frozen, staring out at the crowd.

Go to her.

Rescue her.

"Hello," she said, her voice wavering. "I'm, uh, Daphne. I know I'm not the, uh, person you're here to see but, uh, Zane...Zane couldn't be with us tonight."

A rumble went through the crowd. Someone near him said "What the hell?"

"I'm so sorry," Daphne said. "He—he's unwell, and...And I know that's a disappointment but, uh..."

He couldn't do this. He could not stand here and watch Daphne drown in the pit he'd thrown her into. She wasn't ready to come out as Zane. She could only claim he was sick and face the mutiny alone.

Which he was absolutely not letting her do.

Chris yanked off his ballcap, popped the lenses from his sunglasses, and strode toward the podium to save her.

CHAPTER TWENTY—TWO

DAPHNE

As soon as Daphne heard there were nearly two hundred people at the event, she knew she couldn't tell them Zane was sick. She didn't have enough bookplates, but she also couldn't bring herself to disappoint that many people.

And if she lied, she'd need to hide behind the Zane curtain for much longer. How could she come forward later when hundreds of people knew she'd stood at a podium and told them the author wasn't there when the author had apparently been standing right in front of them?

She was furious with Chris for putting her in this position. Even if she'd decided to reveal herself tonight, she would have wanted him here to help her explain. At the very least, she'd have wanted him to help her work out a script and give her a chance to prepare and rehearse.

But the audience wasn't responsible for her decision to hire Chris, and they weren't responsible for his decision to abandon the role. They deserved the truth. Daphne just prayed she could give it.

She spent the pre-event time hiding in the bathroom. Sakura said she'd handle the staff and act as if Zane was running late. Daphne could plot her big reveal in peace...in the bathroom, hovering over a toilet and trying not to puke.

When it was time, Sakura came, and Daphne numbly followed her out. A staff member had been coached to make some vague introduction, after which Daphne would "say a few words."

Daphne wasn't sure how she made it to the podium. The next thing she knew, she was standing there, looking out at a sea of faces expectantly turned her way.

Expectantly awaiting Zane Remington and wondering why this woman was wasting their time.

She could do this.

She had to do this.

Her readers deserved the truth.

In the restroom, she'd quickly come up with a speech. Now she couldn't remember a word of it. She started a mumbled mess of apologies and explanations. It would have to do. Apologize for Zane not being here, pretend he was sick, and then tell them the truth.

"And I know that's a disappointment but, uh…" Deep breath. She could do this. "There's something I need to—"

Applause drowned her out, and for one wild second, she thought her brain was running behind her mouth, and she'd confessed and they were applauding her. Then she noticed everyone turning…as Chris waded through the crowd, waving a hand over his head.

"Here!" he called. "I'm here."

He strode up to the podium and grabbed the mic. Grabbed it right out from under her.

"Hello!" he called to the crowd. "I am so sorry for the delay. I was"—he held up a handful of books—"shopping. Can anyone walk through a bookstore without shopping? It's like walking past puppies without petting one."

A roar of whistles and cheers.

"Am I forgiven?" he said.

More cheers and claps, and Daphne stood there, her shock giving way to fury.

Chris had insisted she come out tonight, no matter what the publisher wanted. He'd walked away, forcing her to do it. She'd been about to tell the truth…and then he strolled in and stole the mic from under her nose.

He bowed her way. "Thank you, D. I am sorry to put you on the spot." His eyes met hers. "Sincerely sorry."

Her mouth opened, ready to tell him they needed to talk. Ready to grab that mic out of his hand if she had to. But he'd already turned away, and he was striding across the front, launching into his speech.

Daphne stood at the podium, desperately looking for a way to take this back, until a staff member sidled over and whispered, "You can step down now."

You can step down now.

Zane is here.

You are no longer required.

Daphne's cheeks burned, and she scrambled from the stage and fled into the stacks.

Daphne deserved an Oscar for her performance over the next hour. It helped that Sakura had found her, taken her outside, let her vent, and shared her fury at Chris's interference. But eventually, Daphne had to go back inside. Go inside and sit next to him and smile and play assistant, as if nothing had happened.

She was glad her act fooled the readers. Fooling Chris was another thing. On the one hand, she wanted him focused on the readers. On the other, though, she couldn't help hoping he at least noticed she was putting on a false face. Instead, when they were preparing the signing table, he squeezed her hand and said "I've got this" and smiled, and she wanted to scream.

He'd abandoned her during a crisis, insisting that she handle it herself, and just as she'd been doing exactly that, he swooped in and stopped her.

She remembered when he'd rescued her in the lake. She'd appreciated that because she'd actually been drowning. Tonight, she'd been floundering, but only because he damn well threw her in. She'd been keeping her head up, though. She hadn't needed rescuing. If he thought she did, he could have found some way to check in with her first.

All he had to do was arrive five minutes earlier and talk to her. If that wasn't possible, slip around the stacks, get to Sakura, and have the publicist pause the event while Chris and Daphne talked.

Daphne pushed that aside before her anger showed. Earlier, she'd been ready to come out because the readers deserved it. Now, they deserved her smiles and her kind words and the sense that absolutely nothing was wrong.

That was what she gave them: her undivided attention. If Chris noticed she wasn't glancing his way, wasn't refilling his water, wasn't replacing his worn-out Sharpies, he didn't give any indication. He just signed and chatted and occasionally squeezed her leg, as if to reassure her that he was there.

Nothing to worry about, little lady. The cavalry has arrived.

It was only when the line petered out that Chris finally seemed to realize something was amiss, leaning over to whisper, "Is everything okay?"

She could have laughed at that. Instead, she bit the inside of her cheek and said nothing, but he kept frowning at her, and the last few customers started frowning, too, realizing they didn't have his full attention.

"I'm fine," she murmured. "We'll talk later. Focus on the readers."

He did that, but when they wheeled in the stock cart, he turned to the manager and said, "I'm going to need a moment first." He made a show of flexing and stretching his hand. Then he jerked his chin, motioning for Daphne to follow.

She hesitated, her annoyance sparking at that casual gesture, presuming she'd follow, acting as if she actually was his assistant, pestering him when he was working.

"Is everything okay?" he whispered when they found a quiet corner.

She stared at him. Was he seriously asking her that? His gaze was slightly to the left. As if avoiding her gaze? Was that nervous sweat on his temple?

No, she was seeing what she wanted to see. It was warm in here, and he'd been working hard, hence the sweat. If he was looking away from her, it wasn't nerves—it was dismissal. Wanting to get on with this so he could get back to signing.

"D?" he said finally.

"No." She ground out the word. "Everything is not okay. I was trying to admit I was Zane, and you swooped in and took over."

"You were? It didn't look like that."

His brows knit in confusion, and her anger ignited.

"It didn't *look* like that?" she snapped. "Why? Because I was stumbling and stammering and making a fool of myself? Because I'm not as smooth as you?"

"No, you just seemed—"

"—like I'd been thrown to the sharks by someone I trusted?" She stepped toward him. "I seemed unprepared? Maybe because the guy who was supposed to have my back abandoned me? You left, Chris, and I didn't need you swooping in to save me, especially after you're the one who put me in that position. I was doing what you wanted—taking back what's mine—and I'm sorry if I was making a mess of it. Maybe that's just what I do. Make a mess of things."

"You—"

"But mess or not, I *was* doing it, and you stopped me without checking to see whether that was what I wanted."

At a throat clearing, they both spun to see a staff member hovering there, a copy of *Edge* clutched in his hands.

"I was working the line and didn't get a chance to ask you to sign this." The employee's gaze darted between them. "Is this a bad time?"

Daphne mustered everything in herself to find a gracious smile and said, "Not at all. Zane was just heading back to his table to sign stock. Come with me. I think I have a bookmark or two left."

She led the young man away and didn't look back.

CHRIS

All the books were signed. Finally he could talk to Daphne. She'd slipped off during the stock signing. Not that he blamed her. She'd been...kinda furious. And he didn't blame her for *that*, either.

Is everything okay?

Had he actually said that? Of course everything wasn't okay. He just hadn't known what else to say, and he'd been panicking. He'd planned how he'd explain and apologize after the signing, and he hadn't been ready.

He capped his marker, turned to Sakura, and found himself facing the publicist's retreating back. He said a quick thank-you to the remaining staff and strode after Sakura.

"So," he said. "Another signing done."

She turned and fixed him with a look that would freeze the sun.

"Er, um," he said, "about earlier..."

"Save it." She continued walking away and called back, "Save your taxi receipt, too. The publisher will comp it."

He hurried to catch up. "I took a rideshare, but it's fine. No need to reimburse me for my mistake."

"How noble. However, I meant the receipt for your taxi back to wherever you're staying tonight."

"Is Daphne around? We were talking and...I really need to speak to her."

"She left." Sakura veered into the staff area, which was thankfully empty.

Chris hurried after her. "She went back to the hotel?"

"No, she went to catch her train."

"Train?"

Sakura scooped up her purse. "A long string of metal cars, pulled by an engine. Otherwise known as a choo-choo."

"I mean why is Daphne..." The answer hit, and he sucked in breath. "Shit! We're not staying at the hotel tonight. We're catching the last train to Chicago."

And Daphne had gone on ahead, not wanting to share a car with him after his epic screwup. He took a quick breath to calm his rising panic. She hadn't abandoned him—apparently, that was *his* thing. She would be at the station, and they could talk on the train. He could explain everything.

He should have explained here, in the stacks, when she confronted him. She'd been right, with all of it, and while there were things he could explain—like that he'd planned to let her decide who'd take the stage—it would have sounded like excuses. She had a right to be furious with him and say her piece. Now he needed to explain and apologize. Mostly apologize.

He checked his watch. "What time does the train leave?"

"Ten thirty."

He blinked. It was already almost ten.

"I don't have my bag," he said.

"What a pity." Sakura looked up at him. "Maybe you'll actually go home and let Daphne handle this."

His jaw set. "I understand you're angry—"

"You abandoned her. Abandoned both of us, if I'm being blunt. If you'd seen how freaked out she was in the car—" Sakura headed for the door. "Never mind. You obviously don't care."

"Hey!" He ran in front of her. "I do care. That's why I came back."

"And saved the day?"

"I screwed up," he said.

"Royally."

"But I'm going to fix this."

She headed for a taxi. "Like you fixed it tonight?"

He pulled a face as she climbed into the cab. Then he started around to the other side . . . just as the taxi rolled forward.

"Hey!" he said. "I need a ride to the train station!"

"Then get it yourself," she called out the window. "Better hurry!"

The chance of getting a taxi in time was nil, but Chris lucked out and got a rideshare. He then promised the driver fifty bucks cash if she could get him to the train station in twenty minutes. She made it in twenty-four, but the train was still in the station, so he handed her the money and ran.

In the movies, running for a train was easy, especially if you were running to catch it before the love of your life left forever. The train was right there on the tracks, and you ran straight to it. In reality, especially in a big city, the process was somewhat more complicated. He had to race into the station and then out again, ignoring someone who shouted at him that he needed to show his ticket.

He made it to the platform just as the train jerked forward. He shouted "Wait!" aware even as the word left his mouth that it would do no good. The conductor wasn't conveniently leaning out an open window to overhear him.

Chris ran faster as he scanned for an open door he could swing through. Again, that was Hollywood, not modern trains that probably wouldn't budge until all the doors were secured.

He could still do this. The train was barely moving. He just had to get someone's attention.

No, he had to get *Daphne's* attention.

She'd be in first class, which was conveniently labeled on the side. It was the car right behind the engine.

Chris bore down and ran faster. Finally he spotted her dark head leaning against the window, as if exhausted. Because she *would* be exhausted. Because he'd screwed up.

No time for that now. He'd make it up to her, starting with this. Running to catch her train with nothing but the clothes on his back.

Lungs burning, he summoned one last burst of energy, ran full out, leapt at the side of the slow-moving train, and smacked Daphne's window.

She startled and turned…and he found himself looking into the face of a stranger, her eyes wide with surprise. Then she grinned and waved, as if a random guy had leapt at her window to say hi. Chris motioned frantically that he needed the train to stop. The woman kept smiling and waving…as the train picked up speed and pulled out of the station.

Chris reached the row of rental-car kiosks inside the station. All but one had shut down for the night, and that last one was closing.

"I need a car," Chris wheezed as he collapsed at the counter. "Rental. I need to rent a car."

"We're closed, son."

"Please. I have to catch that train."

That made the man pause, and Chris pushed on. "My girlfriend is on it. I was supposed to be—I have a ticket." He waved the electronic ticket on his phone. "But I didn't get here in time. We had a fight, and now she's leaving." Technically true. "It's all my fault." Definitely true.

The man eased back, eyeing Chris head to toe. "Caught you stepping out on her."

"What? No. I...She was having a problem—a big one—and I wanted to show her that I knew she could handle it on her own. So I left her to it. I meant it to be supportive."

"Yeah, that's not supportive, son." He met Chris's eyes. "Supportive is telling her she's got it, but that you're there in case she needs you."

Chris threw up his hands. "I know that now. Please. I need to catch that train. I ran after it, but that doesn't go the way it does in the movies."

The man's lips twitched. "No, I imagine it doesn't. Okay, let's get you set up. Outrunning a train isn't easy. I used to drive a truck around here, though. You pull up the route on your phone, and I'll see if I can show you a shorter one."

Chris's eyes prickled, and he had to resist the urge to hug the man. "Thank you."

CHAPTER TWENTY—THREE

DAPHNE

The train pulled into the station. Not her station, sadly. Normally, she loved train travel. So much more relaxing—and scenic—than air travel. But even if it hadn't been too dark to see anything, she'd have been too lost in her thoughts to notice if they'd been passing through the African savannah.

Chris hadn't called since the event. Hadn't even texted. Her phone was back on, and she had a string of messages, mostly from Lawrence and Nia, and one from Alicia. They all wanted to speak to her. Guilt had strummed through her at that, and she'd messaged them all to apologize and tell them to call whenever they could, whatever the hour.

She'd turned off her phone earlier to avoid Chris, and now she was checking her phone every five minutes, hoping he'd messaged. He'd left three voicemails and two texts before the event, but they were all variations on "Call me." Nothing more. Since the event? Since she confronted him after it? Silence.

If she wanted to hash this out, she shouldn't have left.

Sakura had told her the hired car was ready, and she should go, make sure she got to the train on time. Burning with embarrassment over confronting Chris—and having him just stand there—Daphne had leapt at the chance to flee. But she'd expected him to follow and talk it out, and when he didn't...

The rational part of her said she should be relieved. It was all over, and that was what she wanted, wasn't it?

But she wasn't always rational when it came to love, and even as her brain crossed its arms and sniffed "Good riddance," her heart hurt. It hurt so much. She'd wanted him to join her in the hired car. Or meet her at the station. Or at least call and say he'd meet her in Chicago. She wanted...

Damn it, she wanted an explanation, one she could accept. An excuse and an apology that opened the way to starting over.

Which proved she was a fool.

He'd come to her rescue, and she wasn't grateful. In fact, she was so ungrateful that she'd told him off for it. He was gone. Off to find someone who appreciated his—

"Is this seat taken?"

Her heart stopped as her head whipped up to see Chris, disheveled and panting, standing in the aisle and pointing at the seat beside her.

She froze then, certain she'd drifted off and was dreaming.

He crouched, voice lowering. "The car's almost empty, so I could take another seat if you'd prefer. I really would like to talk to you, though." He looked into her eyes. "I screwed up, D. Screwed up so bad. Can we talk? Please?"

Yep, she was definitely dreaming.

She woodenly moved her laptop bag off his assigned seat, and he slid into it, thumping back into the seat rest and then eyeing her unopened bottle of water.

"Any chance I could have a slug of that?" he said. "I don't think I've run that far since...well, since ever."

Wordlessly, she passed it over, her brain slowly processing that he might actually be there.

"How'd you...?" That's all she could get out.

"It's a bit of a story." He took a long drink and exhaled in relief.

"First, Sakura left me at the event, which yes, I deserved. I managed to get a rideshare. Bribed the driver to get me to the train station on time, which she did, if you consider 'on time' being 'as the train is leaving.' I ran to catch it. Banged on a window that I thought was you, but you're apparently on the other side. The train, shockingly, did not stop."

He glanced over, as if expecting a response, but her heart beat too fast to formulate one.

Chris continued, "Then I ran to rent a car, but the kiosks were all closed except one guy who was closing. I threw myself on his mercy, and he rented me a car along with tips for beating the train. Which—like stopping a train—is not as easy as you might think. I got here just as it was pulling in... and I may still have the rental keys in my pocket." He took them out and jangled them with a rueful smile. "But I made it."

He twisted to meet her eyes again. "When I left that letter, I thought I was doing the right thing, and I did the entirely wrong thing. I wanted to show my support. I wanted to prove that I believe in you, and I believe you should be Zane. I thought I was gracefully stepping aside to let you do that, when instead I was throwing you off the deep end. And, worse, doing it and then walking away."

When she didn't speak, he continued, "This afternoon I realized I'd messed up." He paused. "No, I'd like to say I realized it on my own, but I told Gemma, boneheadedly expecting she'd clap me on the back for doing the right thing."

Daphne had to bite back the smallest smile. "She didn't."

"She *blasted* me. I saw what I'd really done, so I called, but understandably you didn't want to hear from me, so I went to the event, only to find I couldn't sneak in and talk to you. I made it to the event area just as you began. I heard you say I was sick, so I rode to your rescue... when you didn't need rescuing."

"I really didn't, Chris," she said softly. "I know I looked like a stammering mess, but I was going to tell the truth. You should have gotten my attention so we could talk."

"I know." He slumped so dramatically that, in anyone else, it'd seem to be an act. But his expression was so sincere that she knew it was genuine.

He looked at her again. "I'm not good at this, D. I want to do the right thing, and I charge in without thinking it through. I veer between self-confident and self-conscious, sometimes in the same breath. I'm not this guy." He waved at himself. "And I think that makes it worse."

She frowned.

He pulled out his phone and flipped through photos, passing it over when he found one. "That's me at fifteen."

On the screen was a gawky teen. A real teenager, acne and all. She looked at Chris, and while she could see him in this skinny boy, it wasn't as if there'd obviously been a hot guy hiding behind the acne. He'd grown into his look as he aged. What she recognized most was the smile. And his eyes. Those were pure Chris.

She looked at that photo and knew, if he'd gone to her school, he'd have caught her eye. This would have been the boy she fell for, much more easily than she'd fallen for the gorgeous adult version.

He continued, "If I grew up looking like I do now, I'd have more self-assurance. I'd be better with women. Smoother. Less..." He threw up his hands. "Me."

"Or you'd be a complete asshole, confident that you could smile and charm your way out of anything." She passed back his phone. "But I do get what you're saying. You look like a guy who knows what he's doing when it comes to women. You also look like someone who..." She nibbled her lip. "Might bulldoze through my heart, trusting I'll let you get away with it."

He waggled his brows. "'Cause I'm hot?"

"You really are."

He reached for her hands. "But you *didn't* let me get away with it, and you shouldn't. I just hope you'll accept my apology. I made a mistake. Multiple mistakes. I see that now, and I regret it, and I'm here."

"Having run after a train to catch me?"

"I'm really hoping you have an extra toothbrush."

She leaned in, as if to kiss him, and when he moved toward her, she whispered, "You could have just called."

He stopped. Blinked. "What?"

"Called? Texted? Asked me to wait at the station? Asked me to hold up the train somehow?"

He stared. Then he closed his eyes, his head dropping forward. "Shit."

"Never thought of that?"

"No."

She laughed softly, put her hand under his chin, and lifted his mouth to hers.

CHRIS

Chris had never had a near-death experience, but he suspected it felt a bit like his last twelve hours. Or, at least, the period from when he told Gemma what he'd done until Daphne kissed him on the train. The part after that definitely felt like the aftermath of a brush with death, the shuddering relief and giddy elation where he'd wanted to talk nonstop and also *stop* talking and whisk Daphne off to the nearest bed. He'd managed to get in both. Yes, their train didn't have a bed, but it did have a decent-size first-class bathroom, and no eagle-eyed roaming staff. It wasn't quite the mile-high club, but damn, it'd been good.

Now it was morning, and they were in their hotel bed, and he was waiting for Daphne to wake. Waiting to be sure she didn't bolt upright, realize she'd made a terrible mistake, and kick him out.

When she first stretched one long leg, he held his breath, watching her eyelids flicker and then those golden-brown eyes peek out at him. She reached and ran her fingers down his chest.

"Good morning, gorgeous," she murmured.

He exhaled and pulled her into a kiss.

She curled up against him. "Mmm, I could get used to that."

"I'm hoping you will."

She hesitated and then eased back onto the pillow and peered up at him through half-lidded eyes. When she chewed her lip, his breathing slowed.

Shit. Had she changed her mind?

She lifted her gaze to his. "At the event, when I was up at the podium, I really was a mess, wasn't I?"

He released his held breath. "You were nervous. That's all."

She pushed up onto her elbows. "Last night, you said that people can misunderstand you because of how you look. For me, it's partly how I look—I'm tall and fit, which can be intimidating. I'm also decisive, which makes my shyness seem like standoffishness. I don't *seem* like someone who'd be terrified of doing interviews and meeting people."

He took her hand and kissed her knuckles. "But you are, which is why I shouldn't have thrown you to the sharks. However you decide to do this, I'll be there."

She nodded and then chewed her lip again. "I might have overreacted about you leaving the hotel."

"No, you didn't."

She wrapped her hand around his, pulling it to her. "If I did, then I want to explain." She took a deep breath and told him about her ex, a guy she'd been about to move in with when he—

"What?" Chris sat up abruptly. "He got pissy about you spending time with your *dying mother?*"

"He was trying to make his needs heard, and he expected me to reach out and apologize."

"I don't care *what* his reasoning was. I can screw up trying to do the right thing, but there's no 'right thing' in that."

She toyed with his fingers, her attention on them as she said softly, "He left me a letter. I'd been at appointments with Mom, and he'd been staying at my place, and I came home to that letter."

Chris's anger at this unnamed ex froze as he realized the connection. "Like I did," he murmured. "I wrote a letter and walked out while you were in crisis."

Her nose wrinkled, as if she didn't like his wording. It was true, though. She *had* been in crisis.

"I just wanted you to know," she said. "In case I did overreact."

She looked up at him. "I said I was scared of a relationship, and I still am. I rebuilt my life after he left and Mom died, and I made it just the way I want it. I moved to the Yukon. I designed my perfect home. I got a dog. I wrote. I sold a book and launched a career. I have a dream life, and instead of wanting to add the one missing piece— love—I'm terrified that piece will cost me the rest."

He opened his mouth, but she continued, "Last night, I realized that I didn't get those things by playing it safe. I took a risk moving to a remote location. Took a risk building an off-grid house there. Took a risk sending out my book, especially under a male name. So now"— she met his gaze—"I'm ready to take another risk for something else I want very much."

He pulled her to him in a deep kiss. Then he whispered, "I understand that you don't want to lose any of that. I have to confess, though, that being with me might cost you one part of it."

He swore he felt her heart stop as she looked up at him.

"Being in the Yukon," she murmured. "You can't see yourself there."

"No...Tika." He eased back. "I'm warning you now that I may try to win her away from you."

Daphne sputtered a laugh. "Like to see you try."

"Oh, it's on. Give me three months, and I will be her second-favorite human." He picked up his phone from the nightstand. "As for the Yukon question, while we aren't at the moving-in stage, I have devised a future plan." He opened his phone.

"Is that a spreadsheet?"

"Be happy it's not a PowerPoint presentation. Okay, so I know your life is in the Yukon. I love what I've seen of it, but my work—and family—is in Vancouver. Work from home is a possibility for both of us, though I need time in Vancouver for meetings, especially at tax time. If you're willing, I think we could swing dual residences. Summers in the Yukon. Winters—and tax season—in Vancouver."

"Vancouver winters—"

"They're rainy and cold, and you hate them. I remember that. So I've split the winter and fall between the two places. I *would* need to move. My apartment is tiny and not Tika-friendly. But the housing market is actually on the downswing right now, meaning I could afford the down payment on a condo in the suburbs as an investment. I'd rent it in the summer, while I'm up north."

He looked at her. "There are worse things than being lucky enough to have two residences, in two very different climates."

She pursed her lips. "I wouldn't mind living part-time in Vancouver. Nia's there. My grandparents are there. Most of my old friends are there. The issue was always Tika. I hate boarding her for long."

"You won't need to. She just needs to start racking up frequent flier points. Or we can drive. Make a road trip of it—"

Daphne's phone rang. She groaned, rolled to look at it, and then scrambled up and answered.

"Lawrence," she said, a little breathlessly. "Thank you. I'm sorry about yesterday. I had my phone off."

A response that sounded like Lawrence saying he didn't blame her.

"Chris is here with me," she said. "Presuming this is about Zane, may I put you on speaker?"

Chris caught enough to know Lawrence was saying it was her choice. She flipped the speaker on and set the phone between them.

"Chris is on the line now," she said. "We haven't heard from Mr. Milner, and I don't know whether that's good or bad. Sakura said the publishing company is handling the whistleblower, who agreed not to go public until tomorrow."

"Good," Lawrence said. "That gives you time to decide what you want to do. That's what I'm mostly calling about. Finding out what you want to do."

She glanced anxiously at Chris. "Okay."

"You can step out as Zane, or we can admit Zane is a woman *without* you stepping forward. In the latter case, the publisher would accept your decision to do only written interviews, with no in-person appearances or photos, but they'd prefer Chris stays on to play Zane for events and such."

Chris watched Daphne's face fall.

"They want me to keep Chris on," she said. "Admit the author is a woman, but let Chris keep playing Zane while I remain offstage. That's the price for keeping my contract."

"Price for...?" Lawrence laughed. "Daphne, your debut is a number one *New York Times* bestselling book. You got on there in your second week, and you're holding. The question isn't what price you'll pay for them keeping your contract. It's the price *they'll* pay to keep *you*."

"I...I don't understand. I lied about who I was."

"You openly used a pseudonym. Hiring someone to play you is irregular, but the publisher is mostly upset that they weren't in on the plan. What matters, though, is that you are making them money. A lot of money. They're already working on book two and making noises about offering on a third."

"So they'd like to keep me on, staying in the background, with Chris openly playing Zane."

"Not at all. I said that if you *want* to stay offstage, they'd rather you kept Chris. Having you come forward is the preferred option for all."

Daphne frowned at Chris. "Even Mr. Milner?"

A soft chuckle from Lawrence. "As of this morning, Mr. Milner is officially moving to a different imprint. Your new publisher is Alicia Koval."

"My editor?"

"Alicia will continue editing you, to her great delight. It's a well-earned promotion. She's been your biggest champion since she acquired *Edge*, and if anything, she's even more keen to work with you now. She's been instrumental in resolving this issue and, together with your publicist, they have plans for how to spin a reveal to your advantage. *If* you want to reveal yourself as Zane."

"I…"

She looked at Chris. He resisted any urge to cheer her on and whispered only, "I'm here either way. For whatever you need."

"Yes," she said to Lawrence. "I want to reveal myself as Zane."

CHAPTER TWENTY—FOUR

DAPHNE

While Daphne talked to Lawrence, Chris had slipped away and brought back the breakfast menu. She'd smiled and pointed out what she wanted. He went into the adjoining room to order, which made her forget what she was saying...probably because he was still naked and the view of him walking away was very fine.

After she finished the call, he came in, looking equally fine from that angle. "Thirty minutes to a fresh hot breakfast. Meanwhile, I made this."

She was so busy admiring his form that she didn't notice he was carrying coffees until he handed her one. She checked the time. Barely seven. Perfect. They didn't need to leave the bedroom anytime soon. If breakfast was a half hour away, that meant time to do more than ogle—

Her phone buzzed. Daphne hesitated before reluctantly glancing at the message.

"It's Sakura," she said. "She's wondering where we stand on...the interview? What—Shit!" Daphne nearly spilled her coffee as she sat straight up in bed. "That's why we were taking the train. You have a morning show at ten."

She checked the phone again for the next message. "Sakura says she can cancel. She'll say you're not accustomed to all the public speaking and you've lost your voice."

"Up to you," Chris said as he sat on the bed. "I can do this one last interview rather than cancel. I was thinking..." He cleared his throat. "Suggestion only. If you want to come out as Zane tonight, we'll do that. Either way we should skip the afternoon stock signings."

"Agreed. I don't want stores pissed off because they have two hundred copies with the wrong..." She trailed off. "Everyone who got their book signed before now has the wrong signature." Her heart pounded, and she felt herself starting to doom spiral. "They're going to be furious."

Chris reached out to hug her. "Not the *wrong* signature. A limited-edition alternate. We'll talk to Sakura, but I suspect we can spin even that to your benefit."

She nodded, taking deep breaths. Then she sent back a reply to Sakura.

"I owe Sakura a huge thank-you gift," she said to Chris. "I also need to write the most gushing recommendation to her superiors."

"I need to give her something, too. My stunt yesterday put her on the spot."

Daphne smiled. "Oh, I think she got her payment watching you stand there as she drove away." Her phone pinged. "She's replied. She might be late to the interview, but she'll take us to breakfast after." Daphne looked pointedly at the room-service menu. "Whoops."

"Guess we get a second breakfast."

She grinned and set her phone down. "Works for me." Another peek at her watch as she slid toward him. "We'll need to pop out and get you something to wear for the show, but we have twenty-five minutes to kill before our first breakfast arrives. Any idea how we'll fill it?"

Chris reached out to cup her bare breasts, and his very touch sent her pulse racing. His fingers grazed her nipples, still sore after last night. This only made them even more sensitive, and they jumped to attention at his touch.

He leaned in and whispered, "I may have an idea, but I'm not sure you'll go for it. It's a little...risqué."

"More risqué than sex in a train bathroom? Thirty *minutes* of sex in a train bathroom?"

"This possibly *is* more risqué. It can be a...delicate subject. Not everyone's idea of fun."

She grinned and met his gaze. "You have my attention."

"I propose we spend our twenty minutes..." He put his lips to her ear. "With some couple-based financial planning."

She smacked his bare chest hard enough to make him yelp.

"Is that a no?" he said, smirking.

"Depends on whether 'couple-based finances' is a euphemism for me paying you for sex. Which I totally could." She waggled her brows. "I *am* loaded these days."

He smiled. "Nah, I'll take my payment the old-fashioned way. In very expensive gifts."

"Scotch, right?" She reached for her phone. "Let me order you that case."

He caught her hand. "I was thinking baking supplies. My measuring cups are shit, and I've been eyeing this one set, but it's very expensive. Nearly thirty bucks."

"I believe I can afford that."

"Don't be so quick. I'll need two sets if you want me baking brownies for you in the Yukon, too."

She swung her leg over him to straddle his lap. "You know our twenty minutes is slipping by."

"That's my plan. I stall until we just get started, knowing breakfast will arrive at any second, and the door could open, someone walking in..."

She rolled her eyes. "The door is locked, Stanton. Locked and bolted."

"Of course. We don't *really* want someone walking in. We'll just pretend they could." He cupped her breasts again. "Or I could spend the next twenty minutes continuing to make up for yesterday. While last night's sex was great, I don't think it constituted a proper apology."

"And what *does* constitute a proper apology?"

He reached to set the alarm on his phone and then flipped her down beside him. "You're about to find out."

DAPHNE

Daphne took her usual assistant's seat at the signing table, in charge of the sticky notes and Sharpies. Chris was at the podium, and Daphne was trying very hard to keep her smiling assistant face on and not freak out, knowing what was to come.

Not that she knew *exactly* what was to come. They'd spent half the day discussing this—with Sakura, with Alicia, with Lawrence—sometimes individually, sometimes together via video chat. A lot of that discussion was about the higher-level issues, like how to handle previously signed stock, readers who wanted refunds, and so on. When it came to *how* to do the actual reveal, Daphne had worked herself into knots until Chris asked whether he could handle it.

While Daphne hated handing it over, she had to admit that was best for all. Her plan would be to throw herself on the mercy of the audience and beg forgiveness, and no one wanted her doing that. Not even Daphne, if she were being honest.

She *would* apologize. She *would* accept blame. But she was past the point of wanting to grovel. If people chose not to read *Edge* because she wasn't Zane Remington, that was their right. They were consumers. She supplied a product. It was on her to provide the best product she could, and she believed she had, and now the book had to stand or fall on its own merits, without viral videos of the author staring down grizzlies.

As for exactly how Chris was handling the reveal, she hadn't wanted details. The plan was Sakura-approved, and that was what mattered. He'd admit that he didn't write the book, and then she'd get up and explain.

Their event was at an independent bookstore, in an offsite auditorium. The crowd was nearly double the size of the previous night's. Well over three hundred people, the manager had told them, vibrating with delight. Each attendee had bought a book, and some bought two.

"I think we'll hit five hundred books sold for a single event," the manager had said. "That doesn't count all the signed stock we'll sell later."

The manager had suggested Chris come in early to sign stock, and normally, they'd have jumped at the chance to get back to their hotel faster. Tonight, though, Sakura had demurred, because they all knew that after Chris's announcement, the store might not want that signed stock.

They waited for the audience stragglers to find spots to stand—the seats were long filled.

At the podium, a staff member stepped forward to introduce Zane. Chris intercepted her with a few words, and she looked confused, but smiled and nodded and moved aside. He didn't want to be introduced as Zane. Not tonight.

"Good evening," Chris said. "Thank you all so much for being here. It's truly an honor to see so many people take time out to come tonight." He paused for a round of polite applause.

Chris continued, "Now, normally, I talk about the book and then answer questions. Tonight, I'm switching it up."

He lifted the podium and moved it aside, to a few whistles and laughs, as if this was part of the show—buff author carrying heavy objects.

Chris returned to center stage with a cordless mic. "Who here likes PowerPoint presentations?"

Silence. Then a strained laugh or two, from those who felt obligated to humor him.

"No one?" he said. "That's a shame. I love PowerPoints."

Daphne frowned. What *was* he doing?

Chris turned, walked to the back of the stage, and pulled up what looked like a screen. Then he reached behind the curtain and wheeled out a laptop.

A click of a button, and a slide was illuminated on the screen. It was a blank template with three words.

Chris's PowerPoint Demonstration

He hit the button. A photo filled the screen, one of Chris in a tuxedo. A few people whistled. Patches of laughter followed.

"This is me," Chris said. "Chris Stanton." He waited through the audience murmur, as the name surprised some people while others whispered to neighbors that Zane Remington was a pen name.

He continued, "I live in Vancouver."

Another click. A photo of Chris on a tiny balcony overlooking a busy street. He was shirtless and lifting a beer to whoever was taking the shot. Another whistle. More laughter, still sporadic and confused, as the audience tried to figure out where this was going.

You and me both, Daphne thought.

"This is where I work." A shot of Chris in an office, at a computer, surrounded by papers. "I'm a chartered accountant," he said.

That laughter again, even more awkward, now with a tinge of sympathy. This poor debut author was trying to be funny, but it really wasn't his forte. It was only his first tour, so they should cut him some slack. Hopefully the actual event would start soon.

"No, really," he said. "I'm an accountant. I have the math-geek creds to prove it."

A shot of teenage Chris holding a math award. In it, he looked like the guy in the photo he'd shown her the previous night, gawky and acne-riddled.

"Yep, that's me," he said. "High school was *not* the best years of my life. Weirdly, being a mathlete doesn't get you invited to a lot of parties."

"Math is sexy!" someone shouted from the audience.

"Thank you!" Chris said. "I agree. Nothing is sexier than a guy who can save you thousands on your taxes."

A few whoops from the audience.

"I can do that." He flipped to a photo of himself holding up a comic book and making a face at whoever was holding the camera. "I can also debate the strengths and weaknesses of all five Hawkman retcons."

Another couple of whoops.

"But you know what I can't do?"

He flipped to the viral shot of him facing down the grizzly. Cheers from the audience, along with a few gasps.

"You may have seen this video clip, in which I appear to be single-handedly scaring off a grizzly with the sheer force of my steely gaze. Now here's the full picture."

Another click, and the screen filled with a shot Daphne hadn't seen before. It must have been from the other camera. The angle was from slightly behind the bear, and while Chris was standing in front of it, Daphne was just behind his shoulder, talking, one hand on Tika's head.

"This is the real story," he said, "complete with my grizzly-encounter coach, Daphne"—he waved toward her, sitting out of the spotlight—"who is talking me through it, because I nearly walked right into that bear. *That* was why it walked away. Not my steely gaze, but the fact that Daphne was telling me how to react and standing right there with her dog, the three of us more than the bear cared to tackle."

"What's the dog's name?" someone called.

"Tika. That's Daphne's dog. Let's see her up closer." A click, and there's a photo of Daphne bent over, hugging Tika. "Gorgeous, huh?" A beat pause. "The dog's cute, too."

Obligatory laughter.

Chris continued, "Why was Daphne telling me how to handle the bear? Because this is where she lives."

A few quick shots of the Yukon.

"And this is how she lives."

A montage of shots that had to come from Nia. Daphne doing target practice with her bow. Daphne and Tika ice fishing. Daphne and Tika climbing a mountain. Daphne chopping wood.

"See this picture?" Chris said. The photo showed him with Tika on her property, with the house partly visible through the trees. "Not my dog. Not my house. Not my life. Remember this?" He flipped through the slides of him on his city balcony and in his office. "That's me."

Another slide. "This is Daphne." It was her with her laptop, deep in concentration as she typed. "And this." Daphne in elementary school, smiling as she held up a first-place award from a short-story contest. "And this." A shot of Daphne from last week, in her gym-library, with its floor-to-ceiling bookcases.

"Okay," he said. "Actually, that's something we have in common." The next slide was Chris with friends, the bookcase behind him equally huge and overstuffed. "We both love reading."

A louder whoop from the audience.

"But you know what I don't do?" He looked out at them. "I don't write. I admire the hell out of anyone who can, and I'm grateful for them, because I want those books, but the only thing I can write well is a balance sheet."

The room went completely silent. So silent that Daphne's ears hurt as her throat ached.

"I didn't write *At the Edge of the World*," Chris said, his voice softening. "It's not just that I don't write. I don't know the first thing about that kind of life, hunting, chopping wood, *surviving*. And I sure as hell don't know what it's like to be a teenage girl, with or without a zombie apocalypse."

He walked to the edge of the stage. "You know where this is going. You know which of us"—he gestured between himself and Daphne—"could have written this book. Which should have written this book. Which *did* write this book."

Silence, and in that silence, all Daphne could feel was the audience's disappointment. She didn't even dare look into their faces.

"Daphne's going to come up here," he said. "She's going to explain a few things, but I can tell you that she's going to do a crappy job of it because she doesn't want to make excuses—she wants to take full responsibility. She's going to apologize and reassure you that you can get your money back if you feel cheated. And you can. If you are disappointed to discover that I didn't write this book, the publisher will reimburse you and the bookstore will still keep their share."

He stepped forward and looked out. "But if you're unsure how you feel and you haven't read it, can I suggest you try it? If you still feel that the right person to write it isn't *this* woman"—he clicked to a shot of Daphne as a teenager on a camping trip with her mother and grandparents, grinning and holding a crossbow—"then I will provide an email address for you to write to, and I will personally refund your money."

Daphne looked over at him sharply. That personal refund had not been part of the plan. He studiously avoided her gaze, and her eyes filled with grateful tears for his support.

Chris turned off the presentation and then walked back toward the audience. "You're all wondering why. Why is it *my* picture on that book? Why am I the one up here pretending I wrote it? And you might be asking why anyone would do that. Like I said, you might not get the full answer from Daphne, but you'll get the short version from me."

He looked out and met their gazes. "I'm sure we have some writers here. What would you do to get your story into the world? Not to make tons of money off it—if you know the business, you know you're better buying a lottery ticket."

Soft laughter.

Chris continued, "What would you do to get your story out there? Would you let someone else pretend they wrote it? Would you put someone else's picture on your book cover? Would you sit at that table and smile and pretend to be the author's assistant? Which part is most important to you? Being up onstage talking about your book? Signing copies of your book? Or writing it and getting it out there in the world and maybe, if you're lucky, getting the chance to write another?"

He looked over at Daphne. "I might not be a writer, but I'm in love with one, and I've seen what she's gone through and the sacrifices she made and the guilt she feels. I've also seen just how damn much she loves what she does...and how much readers love it back."

Then he turned back to the audience. "Now, I'm going to go over and talk to Daphne. I'll stand in front of her, giving anyone who wants to leave the chance to do so discreetly. Then she's going to come up here and speak to you herself."

He did just that. He walked over to the table and blocked her view of the audience. Not that she'd have dared look. Not that she *could* look anyway. Her entire attention was on him.

"That was..." she began. Her words stuck in her throat.

"The worst PowerPoint presentation ever? Hey, I said I liked them. I didn't say I was good at them."

"No." She stood and leaned over to press her lips to his. "It was incredible. Thank you."

They talked for another minute. Then he said, "Are you ready?"

She swallowed and nodded.

Chris stepped aside. Without glancing at the audience, she walked to the podium. Then she looked. There was one empty seat to her left, quickly filled by someone who'd been standing. A few people were settling, as if they'd also taken empty seats, but when she looked at the crowd, she couldn't see any difference. Most people were still there. Still there and looking up at her and smiling. Someone clapped. Then another person joined in, and tears filled Daphne's eyes as she paused a moment to take it all in.

Then she stepped up to the podium and started to talk.

DAPHNE

Hello again, Chicago!" Chris said into the cordless mic. He paused and turned to Daphne, seated on a stool behind him. "It *is* Chicago, right?"

She held up a sheet of paper with the schedule.

"Whew, yes," he said. "Hello, Chicago!"

The applause echoed through the auditorium as he looked out at the packed auditorium. Five hundred seats, Sakura said, and it'd sold out two weeks ago.

It'd been a year since the night Chris first brought her onstage as the author of *Edge*. The following few weeks had been chaos, handled by Sakura, who'd earned herself a promotion with her incredible work.

Oh, there had been critical media—some very critical. Daphne was a charlatan. She'd done it for the publicity. She'd betrayed women writers everywhere by taking a male name. But Sakura had spun it into the right kind of story, with a feminist angle, and for every critical story there'd been two positive ones.

Her career had survived. Better than survived, if this sold-out theater was any indication.

As for her relationship with Chris, it was also thriving. As planned, they were dividing their time between Vancouver and the Yukon. He was settling into northern life, and Daphne had even bought a cottage down the lake for rental income plus extra room when his family visited. Even better? It was the cottage where Robbie used to live. The owner had finally evicted him and sold it, and Robbie had moved back to wherever he'd come from.

Chris had taken his business mostly virtual, and she was easing out of architecture, only finishing jobs she'd committed to pre-*Edge*. That was partly to focus on writing and partly to slow down and enjoy life. And these days she was absolutely enjoying life.

Onstage, Chris said, "You are the first stop on our eight-city tour." Then he turned to Daphne again. "Still eight?"

"Ten," she said. "They added two Canadian stops."

"Does that make it a North American tour?"

"It does."

Chris fist-pumped the air. "Next up, international!"

The audience whooped.

"Thank you for coming out tonight," he said. "We're so excited to be here, celebrating the launch of *At the End of Tomorrow*, the sequel to *At the Edge of the World*." He held up the hardcover. "My name is Zane Remington, and I wrote—"

He made a show of glancing at the book. "Wait, I didn't write this." He reached back to the table and picked up a copy of *Edge*. "Fine. I wrote…" He made a show of looking at the new cover, emblazoned with both "#1 *New York Times* bestseller" and the byline "Daphne McFadden."

"Huh, seems I didn't write this, either." He peered out. "Does anyone have a copy with Zane's name on it?"

A few hands rose in the audience, some waving old copies.

"You know those are collector's items now," he said. "You can get, oh, maybe fifty bucks for them on eBay."

"A hundred!" a voice called. "I have two. One for me, one for eBay."

The audience laughed. Chris flashed a thumbs-up.

Behind him, Daphne picked up her mic. "We can probably get you even more than a hundred. Just get Chris—whoops, *Zane*—to sign it."

Laughter, and then the young woman called, "Will you do that?"

"Absolutely," Chris said. "That's what I'm here for. To sign old books. To replace D's worn-out markers. To be sure she spells your name right. And to play photographer."

"What if we want you in the photo?" someone called.

He gave an exaggerated eye roll. "If you insist. But I have to keep on my shirt. I have been warned that under no circumstances may I remove my shirt. The best I can do is this." He rolled up his T-shirt sleeves to his shoulders and flexed to hoots and laughter.

"Now that I'm done clowning around, let me introduce the person you really came here to see." He held out a hand toward Daphne. "The actual author of these books. Daphne McFadden."

The audience roared their approval, and he bowed and stepped aside, ceding his place at center stage for good.

Chris was still massaging her hand when their town car dropped them off at the state campground. Not that her hand really hurt that much—she just liked the massage. As for the campground, they were doing what Chris had joked about last year—renting an RV for tour.

When they neared the RV, a dog started barking. Chris unlocked the door, and a gray-and-white ball of fur launched itself at him. With a laugh, Chris scooped up the puppy—Kai—and reached in to grab the leash and a light jacket.

Tika came out more solemnly. With a puppy in residence, she seemed determined to set herself apart as the calm, mature dog who did *not* chew anyone's slippers. She waited for Daphne's hug and leaned into it with a sigh that seemed to say, *Never leave me alone with him again*. Daphne hugged her tight and then snapped on her leash.

They headed out, each with a leash in one hand, their other hands clasped together as they walked down the empty path. The night was still, with a blanket of stars above, the chirp of frogs the only sound. When they reached the lake, they stood on the edge as the dogs snuffled at something, Tika grumbling at Kai when he got in her way.

Daphne stood there, feeling Chris's hand, warm and tight on hers, and looked out at the star-dappled water. She felt...happy. So damned happy.

"Hey, is that a bottle?" Chris said.

She turned to see an old glass pill container floating on the current. As it headed out, Chris yanked off his shoes and socks and handed her Kai's leash.

"You're chasing garbage?" she said.

"*Litter*. I'm a conservationist in training."

She shook her head.

He scooped up the bottle and then stopped. "Wait, there's a note in it." He waved it over his head. "A message in a bottle."

"Someone stuck trash into trash, Chris."

He stepped back onto the shore. "No, it looks like a note." He took Kai's leash and handed her the bottle. "You can do the honors."

Daphne sighed but reached in and fished out a tiny piece of folded paper. She opened and read it aloud. "*Turn around*." When she looked up, she was alone on the beach.

"Chris?" she said.

"You're bad at instructions, aren't you?"

She turned around...to see Chris down on one knee, holding an open box with a ring inside. A gold ring with a diamond.

Daphne couldn't speak. She just stood there, staring.

"Oh, right," he said. "I forgot something." He looked up at her, still on one knee. "Daphne McFadden, will you marry me?"

She could still only stare. He waggled the box.

"Yes," she said. "God, yes."

"Whew. That was getting awkward. Also, my jeans are *soaked*."

He stood, and she threw herself into his arms and hugged him. Chris put his hand under her chin, lifted her face. His lips came down to hers—

Kai whined and tugged on his leash.

Chris sighed, shoulders slumping. "We're never *not* going to be interrupted, are we."

"That's why we rented an RV with a bedroom door." She kissed him. "Now let's get you out of those wet jeans so we can celebrate properly."

"Uh, can I put this on you first?" he said, lifting the box.

"Oh, right." She lifted her hand so he could do the honors.

He slid the ring on and leaned in to whisper, "Thank you for letting me be your Zane, D."

Her eyes prickled with tears. There were things she regretted about how she'd handled the situation, but if she could go back in time, would she wish she'd never put the name Zane Remington on that manuscript?

She leaned in and pressed her lips to Chris's.

Never.

AUTHOR'S NOTE

The spark for this book came from a conversation with author friends. We were each reminiscing about the horror of that moment when, as newly published authors, we realized that our publisher expected us to go out in public and talk about our books, and even—gasp!—read from them. For most of us, there's a reason we're writers. We communicate best in writing, preferably done in an empty room where no one can hear us cursing and chuckling or see us grinning and grimacing as we hammer out our stories.

As a longtime novelist, I'm not quite as terrified and tongue-tied as I used to be. But during this stroll down memory lane, an author said that they wished they could have hired someone to play them in public. How much easier would those early days have been if we could have hired an actor? Found someone smooth and glib and witty, who would be a much better spokesperson for our books. And I thought, *That's a rom-com!*

When I'm seized by a new idea, I've learned to indulge my creativity by putting aside what I'm working on and running with it for a few days. I soon had the first few chapters of a rom-com about a woman who sells her book under a male name and then decides to hire a guy to play her pseudonym.

There was just one problem. Well, two problems. First, I had a full schedule. Second, I don't write rom-coms. I write fantasy and mystery and horror, usually with romance and humor in them, but the thought of writing a full-on romance—especially one that was supposed to be funny—terrified me. So I put the book aside.

Fast-forward a few years. I'm heading to hang out with a writer friend, and I watch *The Lost City* on the plane. The humor in it reminds me of that abandoned rom-com and how much fun I had with it. When I get to my destination, I open the file and discover that I still like it, and it still makes me smile.

I have some wiggle room in my schedule, so I take a few days to work on the rom-com. The writer friend I'm with reads it and encourages me to at least mention it to my agent. I do that, and my agent asks to read what I have. I brace myself, send it, and expect to gently be told it's best if I just have some creative fun with it. Instead, my agent promptly calls asking me to let her send it out on submission. It took some (okay, a lot of) convincing for me to agree. But I eventually did, and the result is *Finding Mr. Write*.

In the book, my protagonist, Daphne, jumps at the chance to have a professional play her in public. At that point in my own career, I'd have done the same. But now, looking back, if I'd really had that choice, would I have advised my new-author self to take it? No, I wouldn't. Yes, getting out in public and talking about my books is still nerve-wracking, but it brings with it one of the best parts of the job. As writers, we do our work alone in quiet rooms, trusting that there is someone out there who will want to read it. Going to events turns those hypothetical readers into real people whom I can meet and talk to and, when I go back to my quiet writing room, hold them as the examples of the audience waiting for me to finish the book. I wouldn't miss that part for anything.

ACKNOWLEDGMENTS

First, I want to thank my agent, Lucienne Diver. As I said in my author's note, this book wouldn't exist without her support, enthusiasm, and encouragement.

I also want to thank Melissa Marr, the writing friend also mentioned in that author's note, who read the early first chapters and encouraged me to keep going.

Thank you to Leah Hultenschmidt, my editor at Forever, for her spot-on editorial suggestions that made this a much better book.

And finally, thanks to two more writer friends who gave it a read. First, Arlene Mahood, who knew how nervous I was about writing a romance and made excellent suggestions for punching up some weak spots. Also, Christine Rees, who made a whole lotta great catches and suggestions. Thank you!

ABOUT THE AUTHOR

#1 *New York Times* bestselling author **Kelley Armstrong** believes experience is the best teacher, though she's been told this shouldn't apply to writing her murder scenes. To craft her books, she has studied aikido, archery, and fencing. She sucks at all of them. She has also crawled through very shallow cave systems and climbed half a mountain before chickening out. She is, however, an expert coffee drinker and a true connoisseur of chocolate-chip cookies.

Find out more, at:
  KelleyArmstrong.com
  Facebook.com/KelleyArmstrongAuthor
  X.com/KelleyArmstrong